LOVE ON THE SHELF

LOVE
ON THE
SHELF

SHEILA ROBERTS

MIRA

/IIMIRA™

Recycling programs for this product may not exist in your area.

ISBN-13: 978-0-7783-0582-8
ISBN-13: 978-0-7783-0742-6 (Hardcover Edition)

Love on the Shelf

All illustrations by Katie Smith.

MIRA
22 Adelaide St. West, 41st Floor
Toronto, Ontario M5H 4E3, Canada
MIRABooks.com

HarperCollins Publishers
Macken House, 39/40 Mayor Street Upper,
Dublin 1, D01 C9W8, Ireland
www.HarperCollins.com

Printed in U.S.A.

26 27 28 29 30 LBC 5 4 3 2 1

To the bookstores, with love

CHAPTER 1

"GOOD GRIEF, ALICE, you've got to stop hiding in books. Wake up and see what's going on around you."

Alice Willoughby frowned at her older sister. Scarlet had always been a little bossy. Which was hardly surprising, since bossing was what older sisters did, even when they were only two years older. But this was . . . bossy plus. Not nice.

"It's bad enough that beast king is turning men into lemmings with his stupid radio show and podcast, but now he's trying to take down your business. You should be going after him," Scarlet informed her.

"My business?" Alice repeated. "He's said stuff about the store?"

"He might as well have."

Scarlet was heated, Alice got that. Parker Black, radio personality and host of the popular radio talk show *Jock Talk*, had evolved into Parker Black, woman hater. He'd been using his platform to encourage men to quit being, as he put it, doormats. She'd heard some of their customers complaining about him. They were becoming upset as their boyfriends and husbands began following him for more than his sports commentary. He was the new champion of American males.

Scarlet's husband, Mark, was turning into a Parker Black lemming, going out with the guys after work whenever the spirit moved . . . or the spirits called, and spending what he referred to as *his* money, money he was goaded to spend because he worked hard and deserved it. All talk of starting a family had been put on hold because their love life was paused, and their marriage of three years was circling the drain.

"You've got to do something," Scarlet repeated as if Alice hadn't heard her when she first blew into the bookstore. "Now he's dissing romance novels."

"I didn't know anything about that," Alice said.

Scarlet did the eye roll of disgust she'd perfected by the time she was eleven. "Of course, you didn't, because you hide in here all day and talk about living happily ever after with dukes and dragon trainers."

Alice could feel embarrassment draping itself over her face like a red flag.

But she rallied. "It seems to me you've been showing up for a lot of those happily-ever-after conversations when your book club meets here."

"Those are historical and we're learning about history," Scarlet said, sounding like a total snob. She was a regular at the Back in Time book club, one of four that met at the store.

"You've been known to be seen hanging out with the Chili Peppers a few times, too," said Alice.

That group liked their books smutty and their heroes smexy. In addition to author signings, the book clubs kept Alice busy most nights. The Closed-Door Club preferred sweet romances and Darkness and Dragons was all about dark fantasy. Alice sat in on all the club meetings, selling them books and passing out home-baked treats.

She didn't read much of what the Chili Peppers read. When she wanted to escape it was usually into another time, where women wore beautiful gowns and lived on large estates. Where men fought duels, and words of love rolled off their tongues like poetry. But she also enjoyed a good contemporary story, especially if the hero was a millionaire. With a yacht. And a little getaway place in Italy. She was a closed-door girl, preferring love scenes that faded to black like a classic movie. Although she'd been known to give in to the temptation to peek through a keyhole or two . . . and wish. Like she did with every book she read. Sighs and yearnings. Happily-ever-afters.

Sighs and yearning, that summed up her love life. Actually, *nonexistent* summed it up much better.

"Okay, so I like spice," Scarlet said. "So, sue me. But we're not talking about that. We're talking about what this man is doing to you. To all of us."

"I don't know what you expect me to do. I'm trying to run a business," Alice protested. Even though she was only half owner, HEA Books took up all her time and energy. "Anyway, one angry man isn't going to affect the bookstore. Almost all our customers are women."

"Well, Parker Black is affecting men and they're affecting your customers. Like me! That's why you need to take this guy on, to fight on behalf of women," said Scarlet. "This man is a two-legged virus. He needs to be eradicated."

"Why don't *you* take him on?" Alice argued.

"Because I don't have the clout you do. You're the expert on romance."

On *books* about romance. There was a big difference.

"Mom should do it," said Alice. "She's the one with the real clout."

"You both should. Where is Mom?"

"She's home baking brownies for the Back in Time meeting tonight. Are you coming?"

Their mother, Nola Willoughby, was the other owner of HEA Books. *Dedicated to Happily-Ever-After for All* was their motto. And, like Alice, she was busy and perfectly happy focusing on the store as well as their weekly podcast, where they discussed the latest book releases and chatted with authors. That was their world. For Alice, the only things that intruded on it were Costco runs and occasionally getting dragged out for a girls' night with her sister or her loyal customers who had become friends. She was content to let the chaos and quarrels of the world roll on past her, and she saw no need to start a squabble with someone she'd never even met.

"Yes, I'm coming, but don't change the subject. Seriously, Alice, something has to be done about this man."

"What do you propose we do?" Alice countered.

Unlike her sister, who tended to be larger-than-life, Alice was small and quiet. She preferred her life pared down. She'd grown up living her best life in books and had dated very little in high school. Unlike Scarlet, the social queen, who, with her eye-catching red hair and striking green eyes, had been born to be a princess, Alice had been born to read about princesses. She was a shadow compared to her sister. Half the curves, half the hair glamour (brown hair wasn't as sexy as red, no matter what her mother said) and half the personality. If they were characters in a novel, Scarlet would be the one slaying dragons, and Alice would be her armor-bearer, probably struggling under the weight of carrying all that armor. Her eyes were brown, not green, and her freckles had always been an embarrassment. So, in a way, had her smarts. Nicknames like Show-off and Big Head had curbed her desire to be the first to raise her hand in class, and the timidity only got worse as she entered adolescence. She'd found it impossible to master the art of flirting and so had decided that book boyfriends beat the real thing.

Her one serious real boyfriend in college—well, she'd been serious—had gone to France on a summer study program and come back engaged to a French girl. Who probably knew how to toss her hair just so and understood exactly what to do with her tongue when she kissed someone. French girl, French kissing—of course, she knew. So, no happy ending for Alice there.

A couple of false starts after losing to the French kiss queen had proved to Alice that the best place to find love was on the shelf. You found the most romantic adventures between the covers, not under them.

It had been the best day of her life when, after she graduated from college, her mother had offered her the chance to continue working at the bookstore, no longer as an employee but as a partner.

A bookworm, happily embedded in a bookstore—that was who she was.

Scarlet threw up her hands. "I don't know what you should do. *Something.* It's bad enough he's gone after every woman in America who expects her man to grow up and act like a man. Now he's making fun of the books we read, and you sell! He's finding the worst writers and reading the cringiest passages of their novels as his happy little program wrap-up. What kind of sports show is that, anyway?"

Alice shrugged. "People have always dissed romance novels." Which really wasn't fair, considering how many other people loved to read them.

"He's not only dissing romance novels. He's saying they feed discontent and it's not fair for women to expect men to act like the men they make up."

"I don't think Lina's smexy books make her discontented," Alice mused. Lina Flores, who had started the Chili Peppers book club, loved her spicy reads. And her husband loved how they inspired her in the bedroom.

"You don't get it. Godzilla is at your door, ready to crush you, and you're baking brownies."

Scarlet was exaggerating. "Mom's baking brownies," Alice corrected her. Scarlet was not amused. "I don't think he's Godzilla," Alice continued. "I think he's a sleeping dog and we should let him lie."

"He's already lying about women," Scarlet grumbled. "But fine. Don't say I didn't warn you. I'm going to go home and shower. I'm a mess."

Yes, one hair was out of place. Even in jeans, Uggs and a parka, with the vibrant red hair Alice had always envied pulled up in a messy bun, Scarlet looked perfect.

"You don't look like a mess," Alice said.

"I'm a giant sweat ball. Barnes called in sick today and Lisa and I had to move a ton of furniture around all by ourselves. It was a pain in the butt."

"Couldn't you have called Mark to come after work to help?"

"The only thing I'm calling Mark right now is names," Scarlet said, the corners of her mouth dipping down. "Anyway, it wasn't anything we couldn't handle. So, who needs him?"

Alice searched for something positive to say that would take them away from the subject of Scarlet's misbehaving husband. "I bet the house looks great." When it came to staging houses, her sister was one of the best in Seattle and she had a client list of Realtors who kept her busy. When she wasn't doing that, she was working her side hustle, trying to become a social media influencer by sharing decorating tips. She was already in the process of turning the fixer-upper she and Mark had purchased a few months earlier into an HGTV-worthy project. Although lately Mark wasn't being much help.

Alice's flattery brought back a smile. "Yes, it does." The smile was short-lived. "Something's got to be done about this Parker Black. He's messing over people's lives right and left. And that's not just couples like Mark and me. It includes you and Mom and every other romance bookstore owner. You're right in his crosshairs."

"That's your sister the drama queen," their mother Nola said when she returned to the store and Alice told her of Scarlet's dire warnings about Parker Black. As always, Nola Willoughby looked perfectly put together, wearing her favorite leggings and a long, red sweater under her faux fur coat. She carried a large plate of brownies as well as some lavender sugar cookies.

Temptation on Fiesta Tableware. Alice told herself not to look. The curse of being short, there wasn't as much storage space for carbs.

"What does she expect us to do?" Nola asked.

"She didn't say exactly."

Nola shook her head. "I'm sorry Scarlet is having marriage troubles, but shutting up one grumpy man isn't going to help her. And we have our hands full making our own little corner of the world a better place."

"Scarlet talks like he's coming after us."

Nola set down the plate next to the plastic glasses and bottles of wine Alice had set out. "Well, when he does, we'll give him some cookies and a book to read."

"It is pretty mean what he's doing," Alice said, "picking on women and trashing what we like to read."

"Mean people are everywhere. If the man is so angry he's ranting against women on the radio, you almost have to feel sorry for him. Bitter people aren't born that way. But it's nothing to us. Don't worry about it."

Mom was right. Let the angry people stomp around their angry world. At HEA Books it was all love and kindness. The bookstore was a haven and a happy place, with walls painted an unashamed pastel pink and a small selection of necessary reading accessories such as handcrafted bookmarks, mugs with book-themed quotes and chocolates by local chocolatiers. Here in Romance Land, all was well.

Except in Scarlet's neighborhood. She showed up several minutes before the others were due to arrive and started working on Nola.

And wound up as irritated with her mother as she'd been with Alice. "This man is wrecking relationships right and left, including mine, and you're going to just stand by and let him? You know, this is why bad things happen in the world, because good people do nothing."

Nola had buried a husband, raised two girls single-handedly and started a business. When it came to daughterly scolding, she was Teflon. "We're not talking genocide or war or economic collapse," she said.

Scarlet had an instant comeback. "He could collapse *your* economy."

That made their mother laugh, deepening the creases at the corners of her eyes. The romance heroine, scoffing at the misguided tycoon who was trying to put her out of business. Nola looked the part, with her even features, chestnut-colored short curls and her statuesque figure.

Which Alice wished she'd inherited. Oh, well.

"Do you seriously think one disillusioned male is going to stop our customers from buying romance novels?" Nola posited. "He has nothing to do with us."

It did sound preposterous when she put it that way.

"Well, he has something to do with me," Scarlet shot back. She scowled and grabbed a cookie, just as Bettina Cross, the store's right-hand woman, arrived, bringing another plate of cookies.

Bettina was middle-aged and happily single, unworried about the gray hairs taking over her head. "I have the perfect life," she liked to say, "book boyfriends by the ton and total control of the TV remote." She was fiercely loyal to the Willoughby women and considered herself their personal guardian.

"Scarlet, I'm glad you came. You need something good in your life right now. Like us." Bettina pulled the plastic wrap off her plate. "Here, have a cookie."

"Thanks," Scarlet said and helped herself. "I'm glad *someone* understands what I'm going through," she added, shooting a look at her mother.

That was definitely Bettina. When it came to Scarlet's marriage, Nola was focused on offering unbiased advice, and lately she'd offered a generous motherly share of it. Bettina, on the other hand, was a big believer in bias when it came to people she cared about.

The next Back in Time book club member came into the store. She was followed by another and then another, and Scarlet's frustration got swept away on the stream of lighthearted chitchat. The ground was slushy from the Snowmageddon of a whole three inches that had fallen two days before. It had cleared grocery store shelves and kept Seattleites off the streets, but no book club member would let a little slush keep her from meeting with other book lovers.

Everyone soon settled in to discuss the World War II novel they'd read. And devour the last of the goodies.

"These are to die for," said the club's leader, Georgia Bishop, on her third brownie. "So was *Safe Harbor*," she added. "I had never heard anything about the Night of Broken Glass."

"I'm really happy Erich and Nissa survived to be together in the end," said another woman. "I do love a happy ending."

"They went through enough awful things getting there," said another woman.

"We all go through hard things. It's how we deal with them that counts," Nola said, casting a quick look in Scarlet's direction.

Scarlet said nothing.

"So, Alice, have you got a recommendation for us for our next read?" Georgia asked. "We depend on you, you know."

Alice loved being depended on. "I do," she said. She held up a book with a cover showing two women walking in the rain under an umbrella. The Eiffel Tower rose in the background. "This is a World War I novel, and the main characters are both strong women. I think you'll all find it inspiring."

"If you're recommending it, I know it will be good," said Georgia. "And it has a happy ending?"

"Absolutely," Alice assured her.

Her assurance was met with excited chatter, and everyone grabbed a book to purchase.

Including Scarlet. "This is the only place I'm going to find any romance," she grumbled, and her words fell heavily on Alice's heart. Her sister was beautiful. Why was she having so much trouble making her marriage beautiful?

"Then you'd better get busy looking in your own backyard," Nola advised.

"You just don't get it, Mom," Scarlet said in a huff.

"I get that marriage can be hard, but you can't be blaming other people for your problems," Nola said sternly, and they all knew she was referring to Parker Black.

Scarlet gave her mother her famous eye roll but still kissed both her and Alice on the cheek before leaving.

Once everyone had left, mother and daughter did a quick cleanup, then turned out the lights on their little kingdom.

They stepped outside and Alice locked the door behind them. The air felt icy and brittle. Like some sort of metaphor.

"They've only been married three years," Alice said. "Shouldn't they still be happy?"

"Three years is plenty of time to start seeing the flaws in what looked like a perfect picture," said Nola. "I don't think their differences are that big. Mark just needs to grow up and Scarlet needs to be less demanding."

"Scarlet less demanding. Good luck with that. I remember what it was like sharing a room with her," Alice said.

Nola chuckled. "Don't worry about your sister. She'll be fine."

"And what about us? Will we?" Could one man's ranting really trickle down to affect sales in their store? Surely not.

"Of course, we will." Nola put a kiss on her fingers and then transferred it to the glass door of the store, her usual closing ritual. "Love always wins in the end."

Later that night, in bed, her cat Mr. Darcy curled up next to her, Alice did an internet search for Parker Black. He was everywhere. She studied the pictures of him posing with various superstars from Seattle sports teams. With that cocky smile one would have thought he was a member of those teams. There was one of him throwing out the opening pitch at a Mariners game. Had it been a good throw? The picture didn't show that. There were also several head shots. He had a nice head topped with short-cut, thick black hair. Equally dark eyebrows sat over deep-set gray eyes. He sported a carefully trimmed dark beard that made her think of pirates under very nice lips, the kind of sensual lips that belonged on a romance hero. The kind of lips a woman would think—a lot—about kissing. One full body shot showed him in a suit.

A man in a suit. Sigh. In another he wore jeans and boots and a black T-shirt. His chest wasn't Incredible Hulk massive, but still nicely muscled. So were the biceps on those arms he had crossed over that nice chest. In all the pictures with sports heroes he was smiling, but the smile was missing in his solo shots. What had happened to make that man so angry and divisive?

"He's not a very nice man, Mr. Darcy," she said, stroking her cat's head.

Mr. Darcy purred in agreement.

"And it's mean to insult authors' hard work. But he'll get what's coming to him eventually."

Alice turned off her phone and set it on her nightstand to charge, then grabbed her book. She read a lot on her e-reader, but at night there was nothing she liked better than to go to bed holding a physical book. Mr. Darcy knew he was about to be ignored so made his way to the foot of the bed as Alice turned to page thirty-eight, where she'd left off.

There was her latest love, Sir Victor, in all his perfection, waiting for her (and Allegra the heroine) at a masked ball. Alice thrilled as the lightning (metaphorical, of course) flashed between the two characters. She watched the scene unfold as Sir Victor threaded his way through the throng and smiled down on the lucky woman of his dreams.

The things that smile promised made Allegra tremble. They got Alice a little shivery, too.

> "I was beginning to think you'd changed your mind about coming," he said to Allegra, his voice like a tiger's purr.
>
> "I almost did." Her own voice came out breathless, and she caught her breath as his hand reached out and circled her waist.

She was breathless but then she caught her breath—a little boo-boo the author's editor had missed. Was that something Parker Black would see and sneer at?

> He bent to whisper, his breath hot against her hair. "I'll make you glad you came."

If only there were men out there in real life like that. Even if there were, they'd pass Alice by. She wasn't the kind of woman men stopped to stare at. She wasn't good with . . . being seen.

She wanted to be though. Maybe eventually she'd figure out how to make that happen.

Meanwhile, so what if she didn't have a man in her life? That was why book boyfriends were invented.

She snuggled deeper under the covers and read on, living vicariously through every kiss and every perfect word on the next page. She finished the chapter just as the evil earl who wanted to ruin Sir Victor and take Allegra for himself found the couple out on the ballroom's balcony. Alice wanted to read more but she needed to put the book aside and go to sleep. She did set it aside, but she did so reluctantly.

Sir Victor would still be there, waiting for her the next night. And who knew, maybe if she was lucky that night she'd see him in her dreams.

She did see someone in her dreams, but it wasn't Sir Victor. Instead, it was Parker Black who came up to her at the masked ball. "I know you've been waiting for me," he whispered in her ear.

"All my life," she said, and he laughed.

And then she woke up.

What did that dream mean? Nothing, of course. She burrowed under the covers. Maybe it would be better if she didn't see anyone in her dreams.

CHAPTER 2

PARKER BLACK WAS tired of all the man bashing he was seeing everywhere. According to the latest social media post he'd read, all men were jerks and women were happier without them. The only thing a woman wanted was to come home from work to her cat and a glass of wine. Oh, and her book boyfriend.

"But where's your book boyfriend when you can't open that jar or when you need to lift something heavy?" he said after sharing the post with his listeners. "Seriously, guys, are we all cheaters and beaters? Are we all lazy, selfish, controlling and toxic? Would women really rather spend time with their cats than us? Come on, major gaslighting here," he finished in disgust.

That made the lines light up. It was his Let It Out segment, the last one of his morning talk show, *Jock Talk*, where Parker normally allowed callers to rant over whatever they didn't like about their favorite team. It seemed that lately his listeners would rather engage in complaining and commiserating about their woman troubles than talk about their frustration with their sports teams and coaches.

"My woman just spent five hundred bucks on a purse, but when I talk about getting a new truck, she throws a fit," complained his first caller, ready to join in the ranting.

"Bro, there's a big difference in price between a purse and a truck," Parker pointed out to be fair.

"Yeah, but I need the truck for work," said his caller.

"Well, that's different. What are you going to do about it?"

The angry voice became subdued. "I don't know, man."

"You don't know? What are you, a carpet? Don't let her walk all over you. You need the truck? Get the truck."

"Parker, you're forgetting one thing. Women are afraid of men," said the next caller.

"Is yours afraid of you?" Parker asked.

"Well, no. But this chick she follows—"

Parker cut him off. "Is poisoning her mind."

That statement would be all over social media by afternoon, along with suggestions of what all those angry women would do to him if they ever got the chance. The number of his haters was becoming almost as large as the number of his fans. But Parker was willing to risk their wrath. He had a message to get out.

"My wife is addicted to those romance novels, like the ones you've been reading from," said another caller. "It's kinda messing with, um, well, when we're . . ." The words trailed off.

"Performance anxiety?" Parker suggested, keeping it clean. "Hey, guys, listen to Coach Parker. There's nothing wrong with your game. Don't let your women smack-talk you. The men in those books they read aren't real. We can't all be billionaires or cowboys," he added with a sneer.

His show was a media men's club, but occasionally his screener allowed some estrogen to leak in just to keep things interesting. He took the next call.

"Grace, welcome to *Jock Talk*," Parker said. "What's on your mind?"

"My husband loves your sports talk, but this new spin you've put on your Let It Out segment is ridiculous," the woman said.

"Oh, yeah? Why?"

"Because you're doing more harm than good."

"Hey, I'm just here trying to stick up for the guys. Right, Barker?" he said to his producer, Jay Barker. Parker and Barker—they were a team.

"Right," Jay rang in, and Arne their board operator, a hefty guy who was big into fantasy football, smirked.

"No, you're not. You're angry," said Grace.

That hit a nerve. Parker ignored it.

"And you're stirring men up so that you'll get higher ratings."

"Like I need to do that," he scoffed. Okay, so maybe he was. Better ratings meant bigger influence. Plus, as Jay kept reminding him, they had to stay fresh if they wanted to keep the show alive. This particular segment was a win-win.

"You know what? I feel sorry for you, Parker," she said in a snooty tone of voice.

Oh, brother. "Don't feel sorry for me. Feel sorry for all the poor men out there who've twisted themselves into pretzels trying to be what women want. 'Open the door for us. Don't open the door for us. We can pay for our own meal. What? You're not paying for dinner, you cheap dirtbag?' Men, make no mistake, we all pay. On so many levels."

He had paid all right. First with Amber. He'd just put money down on a ring when he learned she'd cheated on him. She'd broken his heart into a thousand pieces. He'd found most of them and put them back together and been doing fine, living life, dating, doing love lite.

Until Luna, three years later. Once again, he'd fallen hard. And then gotten broken.

She'd been the final straw, living under the influence of her romance novels, expecting him to buy her expensive dinners, jewelry and even help her with her car payments when she got jammed up with money. Which, fool that he was, he did. But it didn't stop there. He had to be the perfect on-call lover, talk like a poet, always look like a cover model and, of course, be an alpha male except for when she wanted to walk all over him. Somehow, no matter what, he always succeeded in being not enough. Yep, they'd been the perfect couple for almost two years, Luna and Pretzel Man.

First Amber had broken his heart and then Luna had taken a baseball bat to his self-esteem and beaten the snot out of it. He'd finally realized he was drowning in toxic waters and had to swim for shore. He'd tried to pry himself loose as gently as possible, but she hadn't taken it well. She had issues.

And now so did he.

"You know why I love sports, Grace?" he asked his caller. "Because in its purest form it's all about fair play. I believe in fair play both on the field and off. If men and women all played by the rules, this world would be a better place."

"But you men make the rules," she argued.

"Not always," he insisted.

Luna had set the rules for them, and her rules allowed hitting below the belt. People always took sides when a couple broke up, and she made sure everyone they knew took hers. He was stingy, selfish and emotionally abusive. She was an innocent lamb. And she didn't want to talk about it.

Only all the time to everyone and anyone. That was a hurt of a whole other kind. She won the breakup battle and took the couples they'd been friends with as spoils.

But that wasn't enough. She went on to write a romance novel with a villain modeled on Parker. Same eyes, same beard, which Dirk Harrowood, evil sports promoter, liked to stroke when deep in thought. Dirk was a brute. He secretly hated athletes because he, himself, was a failed one—a jab to Parker's baseball career which was short-lived thanks to a blown-out shoulder. Dirk was Parker. And to make sure Parker knew it she'd dedicated the book to him. *For Parker. Thanks for the inspiration.* Seriously?

When she sent him the book (anonymously) he'd been offended, then half amused. What else could you do but laugh? But the half that wasn't amused was steamed.

He'd shared it with Jay, who had come up with the bright idea of reading an excerpt on air. A sports romance novel written by someone who knew zip about sports. It would get a laugh for sure.

"Revenge, man," Jay had said, egging him on.

Parker thought he was bigger than that. Until someone informed him that Luna was on a podcast, talking about her inspiration for Dirk Harrowood. Her ex-boyfriend, the narcissist, was a popular sports show host on a radio station in Seattle. A failed ballplayer and, sadly, a failed lover. There were so many narcissistic men out there. Ladies beware.

Talk about gaslighting. So why not make fun of a sports romance novel written by someone who knew nothing about the sport? *Hey, Kraken fans, can you spot the hockey mistakes in this scene?*

His reading not only got a laugh, it also got a demand for more of the same. They started including a romance read once a week in his Let It Out segment. After those so-called romance reads, "Coach Parker" dished out advice, often using Jay as his foil. Parker and Barker. Add in a chance for listeners to complain about their love lives and—boom!—rising ratings.

Before he quite knew what had happened Parker had become the champion of every male doormat in America. How did that make him a bad guy?

He ended the conversation with Grace but some of her words had stuck to the back of his mind like superglue. Did men make the rules? That hadn't been his experience or the experience of his callers. But still, he felt like a batter who'd just struck out. *Shake it off.*

It was hard to shake off superglue.

"Okay, guys, it's time for our morning read." Ha! Best way to dissolve superglue.

He grabbed the latest romance novel Jay had found for him to mock and began to read the highlighted section. "'Sir Victor was waiting for her. Tall and elegant, his strong body hidden beneath the long, scarlet cape.' Have you guys noticed how many of these dudes have perfect bodies? But you never see them anywhere working out." Parker continued with his reading. "'His eyes met hers from across the crowded room and lightning flashed between them. He threaded his way through the throng and smiled down on her. The things that smile promised made her tremble.' Anybody ever make a woman tremble? I don't think that's a good idea these days." Parker read on. "'"I was beginning to think you'd changed your mind about coming," he said to Allegra, his voice like a tiger's purr.' Oh, come on. Hey, Barker, when was the last time you purred?"

"Just last night when I got my pizza order," Barker cracked.

Parker rolled his tongue. "Yeah, man. I'm a tiger." This stuff was so ridiculous. "Okay, back to our story. '"I almost did." Her own voice came out breathless, and she caught her breath as his hand reached out and circled her waist.' She was breathless but then she caught her breath. Guess the woman wasn't as breathless as she thought she was." Parker lowered his voice dramatically for the last sentence. "'He bent to whisper, his breath hot against her hair. "I'll make you glad you came."'"

Parker and Jay looked at each other from opposite sides of the glass partition, and both started laughing.

"There's more, lots of *You complete me* type stuff, but we're out of time," Parker said. "Come on, women. How about going on a no romance novel diet and taking a bite out of the real world. With real men. Who aren't gonna let you cut off our . . . important parts," he finished. Keeping it clean for the FCC.

Anyway, his mom would expect him to watch his language. With his relationship fails dashing her hopes of wedding showers and grandkids, the poor woman didn't have many expectations left. He could at least meet that one.

"If any of you knows one good reason why anybody should waste time on these books, I'm all ears. Come on the show and enlighten me. At least explain to me why you people who write these books can't get your facts right when you toss sports in the mix. Sheesh.

"Okay, that's enough letting it out for today. It's New Year's Eve, and I'll be watching *Heart of Champions* with my men. For those of you who happen to have a good woman, have fun. For the rest of you, stay strong. I'll see you next year. And don't forget, there's still time to sign up to join me for spring training with the Mariners. Don't wait too long though, because the tickets for our special kick-off party are going fast. You snooze, you lose," he finished, then signed off with his usual, "Keep your head in the game."

"Good show," said Jay as Parker vacated the booth for the next radio personality, a popular politico. "You were fire."

Parker smiled. Yes, he was.

"Keep this up and we're golden," Jay continued.

He didn't need to add that Parker had to be golden. Their show's ratings the previous quarter had slipped some, and they needed to get them up if Parker and Jay wanted to keep their jobs at the station.

But Parker wasn't worried. He had the podcast with supplementary content to help broaden their reach. More importantly, he was carving a new niche for himself. Men needed someone on their team, someone to keep them in the game, and Parker was that someone.

"You still hanging with me and Arne tonight?" he asked Jay.

"May as well. Got nothing else going," he said and frowned.

"Hey, I'm sorry you guys split."

"I can't help what I do for a living," said Jay.

Or who you work for, thought Parker. But if who her man worked for was a bigger deal than her man, Jay was well rid of the woman. Parker almost said so. Almost. Why he didn't, he wasn't sure.

"Anyway, there are still some twelfth women out there who are into the Seahawks and don't read romance novels," Jay said. "And who wouldn't want this bod?" he joked.

At six-three, Jay, the former high school basketball star, was a giant stick of kindling. He wore a Mariners baseball cap to hide the fact that his hair was sneaking off his head. But he was funny and, unlike Parker, didn't have an ax to grind. He'd have no trouble finding another woman to help him run up his credit card bills. He was a magnet for that type. Some men never knew when to get out of the game.

Parker did. And he had. He tossed the book he'd been reading from in the garbage on his way out.

The station's receptionist, Peggy, caught him before he left. "Parker, Girl Scout cookies will be going on sale soon. Daisy's hoping you'll buy a box." Last time Peggy's granddaughter had won some kind of a patch.

"What's she shooting for this year?" Parker asked.

"She wants to go to a Build-A-Bear Workshop."

"Well, we better see about getting her there. Put me down for a couple of boxes of each kind," he said. He was a cookie snob—nothing compared to his mom's home-baked chocolate chip cookies—but he was a sucker for a good cause. And the cookies always came in handy when the guys came over to game or watch a movie.

"Thanks, Parker. You're not only helping Daisy, but you're also helping an organization that teaches girls to become self-reliant enough to make their dreams come true."

"I'm all for helping girls make their dreams come true," he told her.

"Maybe some of them will even grow up to write romance novels," she teased.

He laughed. "Maybe they'll write some good ones." But from what he'd seen he wasn't holding his breath. Of course, he knew what his mom would have to say about that attitude. Which was why they steered away from the topic of romance novels.

He texted her on the way to his car. Reservations at 11 for Tilikum tomorrow OK?

Of course, it would be. She loved the Tilikum Place Café as much as he did. They were both addicted to the restaurant's Dutch babies.

She texted back. Sure you'll be recovered from your night of debauchery??

Yep 😊

Any women coming to your place tonite?

Nope not into debauching women.

He could almost hear her frustrated mental response that he wasn't into being with women at all anymore. He wouldn't be able to find one even if he was looking. He'd turned into a love pariah.

Gonna b a good nite just the guys, he added.

He got the expected frowning emoji.

Pick U up 10:30, he texted and punctuated it with a heart.

He got three in return. They'd do their traditional New Year's Day breakfast and talk about her New Year's resolutions. He'd keep his about growing the show and getting a book deal to himself. Those wouldn't be resolutions she'd want to hear. Then they'd share recommendations for upcoming movies and books, of course, but not mention the one he'd written. Some topics were best avoided. They still wouldn't lack for conversation when it came to books. Mom read more than just romance novels. That was a given, considering who she was related to. All in all, it would be a good morning.

His mom was the best. Why weren't there more women like her out there?

CHAPTER 3

LATE NEW YEAR'S Eve day, Alice went two stores down to Flowers L'Amour to pick up an arrangement for the refreshment table for the bookstore's New Year's in New York party. Which had to do with the time zone rather than the city. Happily, the night was clear, and Seattleites were ready get out and ring in the New Year. The loyal customers of HEA Books were no exception.

Because Nola and Alice were regular customers, Brittany, who owned the shop, always gave them a deal. This time it was on a small wintery arrangement, consisting of three white roses, tucked in among fir and pine boughs and pinecones painted silver and gold. Perfect for a New Year's Eve party.

"It's beautiful as always," Alice told her. "You are a genius."

Brittany smiled. "Yes, I am. Have fun at your book party tonight."

"Thanks," Alice said. She didn't bother to invite Brittany. Reading wasn't her thing. That was hard for Alice to wrap her mind around, but no shade, no judgment.

She and her mother were setting food on their decorated

table when Scarlet arrived, dressed in jeans, boots and a shimmery silver top. By herself.

"Don't you think you should be celebrating with your husband?" Nola suggested.

Scarlet shrugged and set the champagne she'd brought on the drinks table. "Right now, there's nothing to celebrate."

Alice still had a hard time digesting the fact that her beautiful and talented sister had nothing to celebrate. What good was being beautiful if your love life was ugly?

"You two need to sit down and talk things out," Nola chided.

"It's not like when you and Dad were married," Scarlet informed her. "Men are different now."

"Darling, people haven't changed all that much," said Nola.

"Yes, they have," Scarlet insisted. "And I don't want to talk about Mark," she added.

Alice heard the wobble in her sister's voice. She looked at their mother. *What do we do?*

Nola shrugged. *We party.*

Right on cue, there came their first arrivals. Lina Flores, who ran the Chili Peppers book club, blew in with her husband, Eduardo. Lina was an influencer on social media book platforms with a growing following. She wore a scarlet party dress and boots, and Eduardo was equally dressed to impress in black slacks, a white shirt and a red necktie.

Bettina was next. Then came two of the members of the Darkness and Dragons book club, along with their husbands. Right behind them came Georgia Bishop with her husband carrying a plate of mini quiches.

A new Chili Pepper named Kara Bane blew in with a veggie tray. She turned to Scarlet and asked, "Where's the hubs? Six feet under?"

"Playing poker, smoking cigars and losing money," Scarlet said. "Money we can't afford to lose."

"What's that all about? I thought you guys were on a budget," said Lina.

"We were until his fool friends started giving him a bad time about it. Just because I'm the one taking care of the bills it was, 'Dude, who wears the pants in your family?'" Scarlet said. "Then all of a sudden Mark decided he needed to be able to buy whatever he . . . needed," she finished with air quotes.

"Don't tell me, let me guess. He's still listening to that jerk Parker Black on the radio," said Kara.

Parker Black again, thought Alice as she joined the circle. This man was like a ghost, haunting them.

"Parker Shades of Black," Lina said in disgust.

"He is. And lately, thanks to him, all I hear is that I don't need to be in charge of everything and Mark doesn't need a mother. I'm sure those guys are all listening to some rerun of a Parker Black podcast right now and beating their chests."

"I'm okay with some chest beating. If Eduardo wants to get all macho and push me up against the wall—after the kids are in bed, of course—I'm fine with that," Lina said and smiled at her husband, who was talking to another man who had just arrived with his wife.

"Eduardo is a sweetie," said Bettina.

The year before Eduardo had earned good guy points when he came in the store and bought books for his wife for Valentine's Day. He was short and compact and walked with a swagger, and Alice suspected that swagger had a lot to do with what happened between him and his wife in the bedroom.

"If anyone's going to get pushed against the wall in our house it's going to be Mark," said Scarlet, "but it's going to be his head pushed into the drywall. I'm still steamed about him buying that pricey sound system for his stupid truck. His money, he can spend it however he wants," she said, her tone of voice mocking. "Meanwhile, we have a budget that's broken and a fixer-upper that needs fixing. We were supposed to be saving to redo the bathroom this summer. At the rate Mark's spending we'll wind up with the toilet falling through the floorboards."

"Yikes!" exclaimed Georgia.

You could say that again. Christmas had not been holly jolly thanks to the big money fight between Scarlet and Mark, and things weren't looking good for the New Year, either. They should have been together on this holiday night.

"So, what are you going to do about this?" challenged Kara.

Scarlet's chin raised a notch. "I already did something. I cut up all Mark's credit cards."

This brought about a collective gasp.

"Oh my gosh, you didn't!" Georgia looked shocked. "If I cut up Bill's credit cards he'd have a heart attack."

Scarlet shrugged. "Oh, well, Mark's insured."

"Scarlet," Nola scolded from where she stood, filling a small plate with appetizers.

"Just kidding, Mom," Scarlet said with a flick of her hand.

"When did you do that?" Lina wanted to know.

"Day after Christmas. One a.m., to be exact."

"Good on ya," said Kara.

"He'll just get them replaced," Georgia predicted.

Scarlet's eyes turned to slits. "He'd better not."

"Don't you think that was a little . . . extreme?" Georgia suggested. It was the same thing Alice had said when she'd learned about it.

Scarlet gave Georgia the reply she'd given her sister. "Desperate times call for desperate measures."

"Men. Can't live with 'em, can't . . . live with 'em," joked Kara.

"I'm living with mine just fine," said Lina.

"Of course, you are. There's nothing that sweet man wouldn't do for you," said Bettina.

"And me for him. That's how we roll. Plus, good sex solves a lot of problems," she added with a wink. "Speaking of sex, who read *Stocking Stuffer*? I gave that book five jalapeños. That scene with the red velvet cake . . . oh, my." She lifted her long, black hair and fanned herself.

"I thought that scene was stupid," Kara said.

Lina never liked being disagreed with. She frowned at Kara. "You, girlie, are hard to please."

"That's what my ex used to say," Kara cracked.

The others laughed and moved on to analyze the heroine's character and behavior.

"Some heroines are too stupid to live," Kara said. "Any woman who lets a man get away with the stuff Noel let Ranger get away with doesn't deserve a happy ending." Kara was a trainer at LA Fitness and was ripped. She once joked that her husband didn't leave her, he fled. Alice believed it.

"I agree. I don't care how hot the love scenes were. Who wants to have sex with a jerk? After a while, it's not worth it," Scarlet said with an emphatic nod. "Which is why I'm about to kick Mark to the curb."

"Whoa, don't do anything hasty," cautioned Georgia. "All heroes are redeemable, even yours."

"Not as long as he and his useless work buddies are listening to that horse's rear Parker Black on the radio," said Scarlet.

"My brother just started listening to him," said one of the romantasy readers. "You wouldn't believe some of the stuff he had to say about Parker at Christmas. He actually told men not to buy romance novels for their women."

"But why?" asked Georgia.

"He said they build up false expectations," the woman replied. "That no man can compete with a book boyfriend."

"You've got that right," sneered Scarlet.

"I heard that he read a romance on his show today and totally dissed it," said yet another woman. "I guess he does that a lot."

This produced narrowed eyes and growls.

"I heard it all started with a hockey romance," Georgia said. "He tore the woman's novel to shreds."

"Poor woman," said Lina.

"Where did he get the book?" Kara wondered.

"Not from here, that's for sure," said Nola, who joined them and began refilling glasses with white wine and sparkling cider.

"Somebody's going to have to do something about him," said Georgia. "What he's doing is cruel."

"Put him in his place, the loser," added Kara.

"Did you hear he's issued a challenge?" said another woman. "He dared someone to come on his show and explain to him why anyone should read a romance novel. Somebody needs to take him up on that."

"We really do need a literary Joan of Arc," Bettina said. "Someone with influence, who can speak with authority and stop his romance bashing. Like you and Alice, Nola. The only thing necessary for the triumph of evil is for good women to do nothing," she added, conscripting a famous quote.

The others all looked to Nola, their romance Joan of Arc.

Nola wasn't one to get involved in social media squabbles or culture wars. They came and went. Parker Black was a coward who did his bullying from the safety of a soundproof booth. He needed to learn a thing or two—about romance and about manners—but to learn, a person had to be willing to be taught. This man obviously wasn't.

"A man convinced against his will is of the same opinion still," she quoted back.

"So don't convince him, expose him," Bettina argued. "Reading books written by women on air and publicly mocking them? Really? Who does things like that? It's crossing the line."

"He's bombing Romance Land," added Georgia.

"And he's getting away with it," said Scarlet. "But that's because he hasn't yet met his match," she added, looking at Nola.

"He issued the challenge. You're the most qualified to answer it," Bettina urged.

"Actually, you have to," said Scarlet. "I didn't tell you. I called the station this afternoon and left a message."

Oh, no. What had her daughter done? "What kind of message?" Nola asked.

"I just told them that I knew the perfect person to come on the show and debate Parker Black. If he wasn't too chicken. I gave them your name and the name of the bookstore."

"Yes!" Bettina cheered.

Nola frowned at her impetuous older daughter. "Scarlet, I wish you'd consulted me before you did that."

"What are you going to do if they call you?" asked Alice. She half hoped her mother would take him on. The others were right. Someone needed to.

"This man wants to declare war on romance, then, okay. We go to the mattresses," Bettina said in her best *Godfather* accent, speaking for Nola. "He has a lot to say but he's a man. He has half the word power we do. You can win a debate with him hands down, Nola."

"We are not going to the mattresses," Nola said.

"But you're our hero," protested Bettina. "You can't refuse the call."

"No one has called," Nola reminded her.

"But if they do?" pushed Scarlet.

Bettina raised a fist. "To the mattresses!"

"But not for love," added Lina. "If anyone can take him down, you can, Nola. And Alice, too," she added, which made Alice blanch.

Kara looked dubious. "Nola, you're so sweet you might end up going to the mattress and offering him a pillow."

Nola had to laugh at that. "I'm tougher than I look."

People often mistook her for a pushover because of her perennial smile, but that wasn't who she was or ever had been. She'd been on the debate team in college and had never been afraid to disagree with a pompous professor. As a mom she'd set a certain volleyball coach, who needed to give all the girls on the team a chance to play, straight, and as a businesswoman she'd battled the IRS. And won. One mouthy man wasn't going to bother her in the least.

"You don't know my mom. She about killed me growing up," Scarlet said, and everyone laughed.

Nola smiled at her. "And look how great you turned out."

It was true. Neither of her girls was perfect, but they were great. Although Nola was convinced that they'd have turned out that way no matter what she and Art had done. Her husband would have been so proud of them and all they were accomplishing.

But he'd have worried about Alice still not having found anyone to share her life with. He'd also have been upset to see how Scarlet's marriage was sliding south.

That relationship had started out like a Hallmark movie. It had been a meet-cute scripted by Cupid. They'd both attended a mutual friend's wedding. The bride had tossed her bouquet, and a tipsy Scarlet had dove for it and wound up falling into Mark's lap. She'd laughed, everyone had laughed, and Mark had grinned like he'd won the lottery. But in the pink haze of love they'd failed to consider the fact that they had some personality traits and goals that didn't match. At the moment neither of them seemed to want to meld those differences into a compromise that worked. They both needed to grow up.

So, it would appear, did this Parker Black.

Scarlet raised her glass. "Here's to Mom. Take him down," she said, and the others chimed in with their support.

"We'll see," Nola said, determined not to get pressured into anything. "Meanwhile, Alice has some fun planned for us," she said, and turned the evening over to her daughter.

She watched proudly as Alice interacted with their customers. Here in the bookstore, she was in her element—confident and happy. If only there was some way Nola could nudge her beyond the safety of their pink walls. Her daughter had the wings to fly. She just needed to realize it.

Alice's first activity involved the men, pulling them away from their clump at the refreshment table. Lina's husband Eduardo, along with the others, were good sports and competed for the title of Mr. Happily Ever, a competition that involved muscle flexing and submitting the most romantic phrase. His, *You are the reason my heart beats*, won hands down, and Alice was sighing right along with everyone else.

"Can we clone him?" she joked to Lina.

"Afraid not, he's one of a kind," Lina replied. Then she put an arm around Alice's shoulders. "Your one of a kind is out there somewhere." She cocked an eyebrow at Alice. "Are you wearing your red underwear like I told you?"

According to Lina, wearing red underwear on New Year's

Eve was a guarantee of good fortune when it came to love. Alice wasn't superstitious—not at all—but she had invested in a pair of red panties. Just to be festive.

She blushed and nodded.

"Good for you," Lina approved. "Everyone, are you all wearing red?" she asked the group, and they laughed. Most of the women (and Eduardo) answered in the affirmative.

Except Kara. "I'm wearing yellow. I want to make more money this year," she said.

"Money is good," Lina said. "But not without love," she added, smiling at her husband. "Eduardo proposed on New Year's Eve. Guess what color my thong was?"

"TMI," joked Bettina and one of the husbands actually blushed.

"I bet you're wearing red," Lina teased.

"At my age? I'm wearing green for good health," Bettina replied.

"That's good, too," said Nola, who had not divulged the color of her panties. "Okay, everyone, that's enough. You're making the men blush."

"Anyway, it's time for Book Bingo," said Alice. "Everyone grab a card and let's see who wins a book to enjoy on New Year's Day." There was a rush for the bingo cards.

"Oooh, I love this book," gushed their first winner. "Now I have a copy to send my cousin in Indiana."

It was a book Alice loved, too. She especially loved its hero, swoon-worthy Evan Hunt. He was all macho and strength when it came to protecting the woman he loved from danger, but he was too smart to try controlling her. Instead, he treated her with respect and devotion, drawing her to him with kindness and sweet words. He was the kind of man Alice had always dreamed of but never met.

There had to be someone out there who, underneath

his sexy, rough exterior had a tender heart. Someone who wanted a woman who was almost pretty and who made fabulous fudge. Someone who loved books as much as she did. Wherever he was, he was doing an excellent job of hiding.

The fun and games continued, ending with a toast at nine, midnight in New York.

"It's going to be a good year," Bettina predicted.

"It's still early. We should do something," Scarlet said to Alice as the partiers were saying their farewells. "Let's go watch the fireworks at the Space Needle."

Alice loved hanging out with her sister—streaming movies, wandering Pike Place Market on a Sunday, enjoying lunch at The Pink Door, or staying closer to home and going out for drinks and appetizers at Lady Jaye and downing a Wagyu chopped cheese sandwich. But it had been a long day, and keeping the party rolling until nine had drained her. The idea of getting jostled by a crowd of strangers didn't come close to sounding appealing.

"I'm pooped," she said. "How about coming over and watching that new K-drama?"

Scarlet frowned. "Not in the mood. Never mind," she said, giving Alice a hug. "You go home and hang out with your TV show and your book and recharge your battery. I'll see you next year." She gave Alice a sisterly kiss, then, after sharing one with their mom, left.

"I should have gone with her," Alice said as Scarlet followed the last of the partiers out the door.

"You should. You're too young to end the night so early," said Bettina, who was hauling plates with cookie crumbs off to the garbage.

"No, you should go home and relax. And don't worry about your sister. She will be fine on her own," Nola said. "And she'll pull out of this," she added, reading Alice's worried thoughts.

"I hope so," Alice said. "She and Mark seemed so happy at first."

"They can be happy again. They just have to work out the kinks. Every couple does."

"Every couple? Not you and Dad."

"Even Dad and me. Wonderful as he was, it took us a while to learn to pull together, especially when it came to parenting. Your father was the world's biggest soft touch."

"Is that why his favorite phrase was always, 'Ask your mother'?"

"You guessed it," Nola said with a grin. "Go on, get out of here. Bettina and I can finish up. Your book boyfriend is waiting."

Maybe someday Alice's real boyfriend would be waiting. Meanwhile, she'd have to settle for a perfect man someone else had created.

Once home, she changed into her favorite flannel pajama bottoms and old T-shirt and settled in with hot chocolate and her book. At midnight, she took out the wineglass she had sitting in the fridge with twelve grapes, a grape for each month of the coming year. Another Mexican tradition Lina had shared with her.

The explanations on how the magic of the grapes worked were mixed. When Alice researched the tradition, she found that some people turned eating them into a race. The first one to down all twelve would be very happy in the New Year. But Alice liked what Lina had shared. All Alice had to do was toast family and friends with the grapes, then eat them and expect they would bring her that many good wishes for the New Year as well.

She didn't have twelve wishes. She really only had three. She wanted her sister to be able to work things out with Mark and live the romance dream, she wanted the bookstore to keep doing well, as much for her mother as herself. The store was everything to Mom.

Lastly, she wished for a real man to come into her life, someone more substantial than the amorphous variety formed from words on the page. Happily-ever-after she wasn't so sure about. That felt like asking for too much, considering her love history. But happily for the year? That would be a good start.

Maybe she should also wish to become a little bolder. Maybe Scarlet was right, and she was hiding out in Romance Land, and she did need to . . . do something.

"I want to be a real-life romance heroine," she wished.

Well, that was vague. But it was the best she could do.

She lifted her glass and said, "To my family and friends, both in town and online, I wish you all a New Year filled with love."

With that she popped a grape in her mouth. It was a very juicy grape, and she wound up choking. She hoped that wasn't some sort of sign.

CHAPTER 4

SCARLET DIDN'T END up going to the Seattle Center to see the fireworks. She was more in the mood to declare war than to party. What happened at Christmas had really slid things sideways.

She'd seen the charge card bill earlier in December and had almost blown through the roof. They'd agreed to stick to a tighter budget until Mark had gotten his handyman side hustle going. Buying the house had been a stretch and they'd been feeling the pinch, so no out-of-control spending. And then he'd gone out of control.

He'd promised to get in extra hours at work to pay for his crime and she'd let him live another day. After that, they'd talked about not spending much for Christmas.

"Just Starbucks and chocolate, that's all I need," she'd told him. "We really have to cut back now," she'd added, and he'd frowned at the subtle dig. He could count himself lucky she'd gone from screaming to subtle.

By Christmas Eve things were almost back to normal, the dust finally settled after their big fight over his reckless spending. Peace on earth, goodwill toward her man.

She'd been thoughtful and gotten him gourmet beef jerky that had cost a small fortune to ship plus a bottle of his favorite tequila, using the money she had squirreled away in her underwear drawer.

"I guess this means I'm forgiven," he'd said, grinning over his haul.

"Maybe," she'd said back playfully.

Then she'd opened his present for her (wrapped by his mother, of course) and seen the dollar store candy box, topped with the Starbucks gift card for ten dollars. "Ten dollars, really?" His gift had felt like an insult, and she'd been ready to break the bottle of tequila over his head.

"Hey, you said not to spend much," he'd reminded her.

"Well, you managed that," she'd snapped. "You spent almost nothing."

"It's the thought that counts," he'd protested.

And there was the problem. His measly offering showed just how much he thought of his wife. And after spending so much on himself!

She'd fumed her way through Christmas Day, forcing a smile when they went to his parents' house for brunch, watching bitterly as his mother fussed over him and made sure that he got a second huge helping of breakfast casserole. No wonder men were a mess. Look at how their moms spoiled them. She'd ground her teeth when his brother asked him how the new sound system was working. By the time they'd arrived at her mom's place for Christmas dinner Frosty the Snowman would have been complaining about how cold it was in their car.

Mom and Alice had both been great, loading Scarlet up with books and more Starbucks. Their kindness shined a spotlight on her husband's selfish behavior and made her even angrier.

It was a quiet ride home. The Grinch had stolen Christmas. No, actually, he hadn't been needed. Mark had managed the heist all on his own.

That very night, unable to sleep, she'd gotten up and cut all his credit cards into puzzle pieces. *What's in your wallet, Mark? Hahahaha.*

Mark had not been laughing when he discovered what she'd done. "Real cute, Scarlet," he'd roared.

"Yeah, about as cute as you spending a wad on yourself when we'd already agreed we were going to tighten the budget. And right before Christmas!"

"We didn't agree. You decreed."

"Ooh, big word," she taunted. "Where'd you learn it?"

"From you!" He'd pointed a finger at her. "You don't get to tell me what to do. You're not my mom."

"If I had been you wouldn't have grown up to be such a selfish boy-man!" He'd always been happy-go-lucky, but he hadn't always been so selfish. Or maybe he had and she hadn't noticed?

She was noticing now. Yep, happy holidays.

Mark was still missing when she returned home from the party at the bookstore. Still out with the boys, probably telling them what a witch he'd married. Lucky for him she wasn't—she'd have turned him into a frog and then had frog legs for dinner.

Whew! Violent thoughts. That dark fantasy novel she'd started was bringing out the worst in her. She went to bed and picked it up, then thought maybe she should be reading something a little lighter, a little happier and kinder. A sports romance.

Nope. She cast aside the one she'd started a month ago featuring a football player and the new team owner. The last thing she wanted was to read about a football player who was a tough warrior when she was married to a spoiled baby whose football glory days had ended with high school graduation. She settled for a cozy murder mystery.

It was almost midnight when she heard Mark come in. She set aside the book, turned off the bedside lamp, and rolled onto her side, keeping her back turned to his side of the bed. She squeezed her eyes tightly shut when he entered the bedroom and listened as he shed his jeans and shirt, shoes and socks. Felt his side of the bed sink as he slid in next to her.

Once upon a time, she'd loved the feeling of security when the mattress surrendered to his big frame. She'd loved surrendering to it, too. Tonight, it was just irritating how the bed shuddered beneath him and jiggled her side.

"You're not asleep," he said.

"How do you know?" she snapped.

"Because I can feel the steam coming off you. Did the Peppers get you mad all over again? Oh, yeah, I forgot. You never stopped being mad."

She didn't roll around to face him.

"Come on, babe. Enough's enough. It's almost a new year. New beginnings?"

She did roll over at that. "What kind of new beginning are you going to make?"

"I don't know yet. What about you? You gonna make a resolution to quit ragging on me?"

"Ragging on you! You selfish boy-man."

He sighed deeply. "I said I was sorry."

"Not sorry enough to return that sound system."

"How could I? It was already installed. And if anyone should be sorry, it's you. You cut up my credit cards? Seriously?"

"You get an allowance."

"Yeah, like a kid."

"That's because you spend like a kid! We're supposed to be on a budget."

"*Your* budget. I work hard. I should be able to get something once in a while."

His once-in-a-whiles were costly. "We both get an allowance, Mark."

"Oh, boy, here comes another lecture. You're a saint and I'm a shit."

"Well, sometimes you are," she said hotly, and punched her pillow. And to think she'd wanted to have a child with this man. She'd not only hit the snooze alarm on her biological clock, she'd smashed it. So what if she had slipped past thirty? No way did she want to get pregnant with a little Mark Junior and have two children to deal with.

He punched his pillow, too, and rolled over. And that was that. They went to sleep back-to-back, not touching, to the sound of fireworks outside, ringing in the New Year.

A thick fog of resentment hung over their house the next morning as Mark came into the kitchen where Scarlet was making coffee.

"How much money did you lose?" she greeted him.

"Doesn't matter. I have an allowance, remember?" he replied, all belligerence.

"Is that all you spent?"

"I'll put in for overtime," he mumbled.

She threw up her hands. "Unbelievable. You don't spend New Year's Eve with me and then you go and blow more money. After what you already did!"

"Hey, you made it pretty clear you didn't want to hang out."

"You could have come with me to the party," she shot back, and he made a face.

To think only a year ago they'd danced the night away on New Year's Eve and then started the New Year off making love and making plans for all the things they wanted to accomplish. She'd accomplished a lot, making new contacts and growing her business. And she'd gained a ton of new followers on Instagram. He'd accomplished . . . nothing. She'd learned to make pavlova, his favorite dessert. He'd . . . gotten her last-minute flowers for her birthday, which she was sure he'd forgotten, and topped off the year by giving her dollar store candy for Christmas.

"Come on, Scarlet, don't do this, okay?"

"Do what?"

"Jump all over me. You've been doing it for months and I feel like a trampoline."

"I have not," she muttered.

"We need to move on," he said, and it quickly became plain that "moving on" meant all he wanted to do was go over to his parents' house, lay around and watch football.

"We need to spend the day together," Scarlet insisted.

"We're gonna," he said, not getting it.

"The two of us. Mark, we need to sort some things out."

"Oh, no. Here we go again. You're gonna get on my case."

"No, I'm not." Well, maybe a little. Okay, a lot.

"Look, it's a new year. Let's stop all this . . ." He shook his head. "Whatever this is and go have fun. Okay?"

"I don't want to have fun. I want to stay here with you." That hadn't come out right. She frowned.

He frowned back at her. "We've been going to my parents' on New Year's Day for the last two years. Everyone will be there."

"Everyone but us. We need to stay here." Why was he being so dense?

He rubbed his forehead. "Scarlet, you're making me nuts."

That hurt. "I didn't used to make you nuts."

"You didn't used to nag." He headed for the bathroom. "I'm getting a shower."

She was seated on a barstool at their kitchen counter, trying to console herself with caffeine when he came back out. He looked so nice in jeans and the brown sweater she'd gotten for him on sale the year before, his blond hair freshly dried, waiting for her fingers to run through it. Who cared how he looked?

"So, are you coming with?" he asked as he poured himself a mug of coffee.

She folded her arms across her chest. "No. And you need to stay here."

He downed a couple of slugs of coffee, frowned, set down the mug. "What I *need* is a break. I'm out of here."

"Yes, you are," she growled as he went for his coat and truck keys. She got on her phone as the door shut behind him and began searching for a locksmith who would be willing to come out on a holiday and change the lock on the door. Mark needed a wake-up call for the New Year and he was going to get it.

By the time he returned the locksmith had come (for a hefty fee) and gone, and Mark's clothes and sports card collection were in large plastic tubs sitting outside the door, right along with his football and baseball glove. She was curled up in her rescued vintage armchair that she'd re-upholstered, reading her book when she heard him trying to make his old key work in the new lock. A corner of her mouth lifted and she turned a page in her book as he banged on the door and hollered her name. She let his call go to voice mail, then smiled wider as she listened to his angry message.

"What's going on, Scarlet? Did you change the locks?" A moment of silence was followed by, "You did, didn't you? What do you think you're doing?"

Showing her husband the consequences of being selfish and childish, that was what she was doing.

Her smug smile dissolved when she listened to the second message. "Looks like Parker Black was right."

She called Mark. "What's that supposed to mean?"

"That you make us pay when we don't jump through your hoops. I do one thing you don't approve of and you kick me out."

'You did a whole bunch of things, Mark. And today was the final straw. I begged you to stay home so we could work all this out, but you chose your mom over me. So fine. You can just stay with her for a while."

"Yeah, well, fine with me. You're so perfect, you don't need me, anyway, so get a cat."

Get a cat? What was that supposed to mean?

He didn't bother to explain. Instead, he ended the call. The house had lost its cozy vibe and suddenly felt empty. And she felt sick. Then the tears spilled over. What now?

She looked mournfully down at her book. The plot was twisty, and it didn't look good for the hero and heroine, but she knew the writer would find a way to work things out for them.

If only she could find someone to write her and Mark back to what they had when they first got together.

CHAPTER 5

"MOM, YOU WON'T really debate Parker Black, will you?" Alice asked as they drove to the bookstore the day after New Year's.

"I'm not sure. I just might if someone from the show calls me. I always did love a good debate," Nola said.

"What happened to a man convinced against his will?" Alice argued, quoting Nola's saying from the New Year's Eve party. "You won't change his mind."

"No, but I might be able to change the minds of some listeners. And we can tell our customers we did our part."

"He doesn't sound like a very nice man," Alice said.

"That doesn't worry me." Nola had dealt with her share of difficult people in her lifetime. "You could help me if you like," she suggested.

Her daughter's complexion went from pale to ghost. "Me?" she squeaked.

"You're part owner."

"I'm not good at debating," Alice protested.

Unlike her older sister, who was always up for an argument, Alice avoided conflict. She liked her world compressed and safe. Growing up, her circle of friends had been small, and her best friends had been books. But she'd risen to the challenge of running a bookstore. She could easily help with this.

"I wouldn't expect you to, but I'd appreciate it if you did some research for me," Nola said.

"I could do that," Alice said, suddenly eager to help as long as it was from a safe distance.

"And you could sit by me and feed me facts, so we can work as a team. Like we do on our podcast."

"I can do that. But you'd be the one talking, right?" she added, looking for confirmation.

"Of course," Nola assured her. Her daughter was certainly smart enough to carry the day, but taking the lead would be entirely too stressful for her. "And you don't have to be involved at all if you'd rather not."

"We're partners. If Parker Black offers the challenge, I'm with you," Alice said. "But all we'll do is boost his ratings."

"And champion writers. Your father had a motto he lived by: *Never go looking for a fight but if one comes knocking you open the door and have your fist ready*. I didn't want to bother with this nonsense, but to read books by authors we know on the air and mock them, that's another animal. If Parker Black knocks on the door looking for a fight, let's give him what he wants."

"Maybe he won't call."

"A man like him? The chance to debate will be catnip," Nola said as Alice parked the car. "He won't be able to resist."

When it came right down to it, Nola couldn't resist the idea herself. It had been many years since her college debate team days, but she hadn't lost her edge, and the more she thought about it the more the idea of putting this young fool in his place appealed to her.

That settled, they got to work before the store opened,

culling books that had sat on the shelf too long and would have to be returned to the publisher for a refund. They tried to avoid doing that whenever possible, often wrapping up lonely books in brown paper with a note hinting at the plot and then offering them as a blind date with the book. But some dates never happened. And, sadly, if a book sat around longer than ninety days chances were it never would find a new home.

Bettina had arrived and they were all still sifting through books when the call from KWOW came. "This is Jay Barker," the caller introduced himself. "I produce Parker Black's *Jock Talk* on KWOW and I'm looking for Nola Willoughby."

"This is Nola," she said. Here it came, the invitation to go to the mattresses.

"We were given your name. I understand you own this romance bookstore."

"I do. We're in West Seattle."

Alice left her pile of books behind and came over to where Nola stood.

"I don't know if you're familiar with what Parker's been doing on his show lately."

"Misbehaving?" Nola said.

Jay Barker's chuckle was a little weak. "I guess you are."

"Word's gotten out," she said. "I believe your boy is looking for a fight."

"Boy?" mouthed Alice, who had come to stand next to her.

Nola winked. *Put your opponent on the offensive.*

"Not a fight, just a good debate," Jay Barker corrected her. "Would you be willing to come on his show as a guest? He's nationally syndicated. It would be good exposure for your bookstore."

"Or for my neck," said Nola. "But I'll accept your challenge."

That got Bettina's attention, and she joined them, a grin on her face.

"Great. I'll get back to you with details," Jay said, and that ended the call.

"It's a go," Nola said, stating the obvious.

"Yes!" crowed Bettina. "That man is in trouble now."

Alice was already having second thoughts. "What if this doesn't go well?"

"Why wouldn't it? The facts are in our favor. This will be like taking candy from a very big baby."

"It's a go," Jay said to Parker. "Harlan's gonna love this."

"Let's hope so," said Parker.

"Talk about a publicity gold mine falling right in our lap," Jay said, rubbing his hands together like a hungry glutton at a Thanksgiving feast.

Parker gave his beard a thoughtful stroke. "I wonder if my mom knows her."

You'd better hope she doesn't, came the thought.

"Huh," mused Harlan, their program director, when they met to fill him in.

They should have run the idea past him before getting the ball rolling, but Jay had been confident Harlan would be an easy sell. And he was.

"We'll talk it up and get twice the listeners we've been getting," Jay predicted.

Harlan was all over anything that would make his radio personalities look good and impress their station manager, Ben Stricklund, and, even better, Joe Morris, the GM. "You think you can pull this off?" he asked Parker.

"Or course I can," Parker said. "Slam dunk. Somebody needs to bring up the fact that women are writing sports novels . . . about sports they don't know anything about."

Harlan nodded slowly. "Yeah, the sports angle works. Okay. Go for it." Yep, easy sell.

"All right," Jay said. "I'll get it set up."

He didn't waste any time. By Monday afternoon all parties had agreed to a date and the debate was on. "We're set for Friday. Even Big Ben is smiling and little Harlan's pretending this was all his idea," Jay reported.

"As long as they're happy I'm happy," Parker said. And keeping both Harlan and Big Ben happy was what it had to be all about if Parker wanted to keep his show going.

"They will be as long as our ratings go up, and that will even impress Joe," said Jay, referring to the general manager. He grinned. "This is gonna be good. I am brilliant."

As if this had all been Jay's idea. It wouldn't be Jay having to be at the top of his game. That would be Parker.

But no worries. Parker may have had a short-lived baseball career, but he was no dumb jock. After blowing out his shoulder and losing a major league career he'd gone to school, majored in communications and aced every course. He thought fast and could talk fast. The debate would be a shutout. Total win.

Parker's literary agent, David Fox of Fox Literary, was like a Seahawks fan who'd just learned the Hawks were headed for the Super Bowl when Parker shared with him about the debate. "We've already got interest in the book. I can use this," he said.

"That's what I thought," Parker said. Yeah, this was going to be good.

For a second, he could see his mom frowning in disapproval. There'd been a lot of that since he'd written *Bye-Bye Babe*. Which was why it was best to avoid mentioning the debate.

"I hate to see you so bitter and angry," she'd said the day he'd called to crow about getting an agent. "And so publicly," she'd added. "You might live to regret seeing all your ranting winding up in print."

"I won't," he'd insisted. And his book wasn't a rant. It was . . . cultural commentary focused on breaking men free from unrealistic female expectations. Parker had pulled no punches when it came to damaging influences, and romance novels had been cited as one of the worst (which was why if his book did get published, Mom would not be getting a copy for Christmas). But he knew what he was talking about. Those novels had sure been a bad influence on Luna. And she'd elevated the genre from an unrealistic escape to a deadly weapon.

"And I'm not bitter. I'm wiser," he'd informed his mom. "Anyway, it's time someone clued men in to what women have become. Not you," he'd added quickly.

"Not most women," she'd argued.

What did Mom know? Well, having been a librarian for thirty years, she knew a lot. Just not about how things were between men and women anymore. She hadn't dated in years, and she lived in the same unrealistic world as this Nola Willoughby and her customers. Mom had no idea what it was like out there. Women had turned into psychic vampires.

Of course, she liked to argue that there were men who were just as bad prowling around, too. Parker's dad had been nothing more than a sperm donor. Not that she talked about him much.

"I still believe in the power of love," she liked to say. She also liked to add, "One of these days you'll discover that power, too."

"Don't count on it," he would answer.

This debate was going to be fun. But it would be best not to tell his mom about it.

CHAPTER 6

TUESDAYS WERE BOOK release day for publishers, which meant staying late on Mondays to stock the shelves. They were always happy days at HEA Books.

But this day no longer felt so happy for Alice. It had started out great, but ever since Mom had finalized details for the debate with Parker Black's producer she'd felt under a cloud. Even though they would be ready, the shadow of the big verbal battle hung over her.

She envied her mother's confidence. Nola wasn't concerned in the least. "Here are the Courtney Walsh books we ordered," she announced after she'd opened a small box.

"I love her," said Bettina.

So did their customers.

"And look. We also have Melissa Ferguson's latest release. Our closed-door girlies are going to be in seventh heaven," Bettina said.

In addition to tried-and-true authors, they also had a few novels by new and lesser-known writers. They never ordered more than three by a new author. Even though publishers reimbursed them for returned books, shipping costs still added up, so it paid to start out cautiously. If the books sold, then they would bring in more. They always did their best to help those books along, especially if they'd been written by local authors.

"This cover is so gorgeous," Bettina said, holding a book with a cover featuring a bouquet of some sort of pink flowers. The edges of the pages had been sprayed pink to match. "*From Me to You*. Nola, wasn't this one you read?"

"Yes, that's the one about the husband putting flowers on his wife's grave every week," Nola replied.

"That sounds cheery," Bettina mocked. Bettina was not a fan of romance novels that required an entire box of tissues.

"It's really sweet," said Nola. "Her ghost is watching over him and leads him to a grieving single mother with three young children."

"Sounds like the ghost has a sick sense of humor," said Bettina.

"He and his wife could never have children," Nola elaborated. "I loved the ARC, which is why I reached out and invited the author to come on the podcast."

"Who are you two featuring on tomorrow's podcast?" Bettina asked.

"We're going to do the closed-door duo review, so save out one of each for us for props before you build the display," Nola told her.

Alice loved doing their podcast. It was where she felt happy and at home. Confident. She just wished they didn't have to ruin the evening by mentioning the upcoming debate, which was right around the corner, leering at them. They only had a few days to get ready, and even though Alice knew they would be, she still didn't feel well prepared.

The next day, they left Bettina to close the store, and come six o'clock she and her mother sat at Nola's dining room table in front of Alice's laptop, reviewing books on the podcast. She was killing it with her reviews, judging from the comments.

We love you, Alice! . . . Keep the recommendations coming . . . So insightful.

"What do you think makes the heroine in *So Over You* so lovable?" Nola asked as they discussed the last book on their list for that evening.

"Besides the fact that she's into chocolate? I mean, who's not? I think it's because she's not afraid to be who she is because she likes who she is," Alice replied. Now, there was a true heroine.

"Do you want to elaborate?" Nola prompted.

Alice shrugged. "She's not perfect. She's not a size two or size ten, but she doesn't care. She goes ahead and goes to that Caribbean resort by herself and packs a bikini. And she doesn't try to change herself for a man because she already did that and wasn't true to herself."

"I think we need to be true to who we are," said Nola. "We also need to not be afraid to be ourselves. Anyone out there struggle with that?" she asked. "I think we women are often our own worst critics."

Her question brought a flood of comments.

"I hear you, Jenni82," Nola said after reading one woman's lament that she'd lost seventy pounds to make her boyfriend happy only to have him leave her because he thought her saggy skin was a turnoff.

"His saggy ego sounds like a turnoff to me," said Alice. "That's so . . . superficial."

"Everyone, be proud of yourself and who you are and what you're accomplishing," Nola said, and Alice knew it was meant for her.

She was proud of what she was accomplishing. She smiled back.

"And for sure read this book," she said. "We just got in copies today and we are happy to mail anywhere in the US."

"Now, one more thing before we sign off," said Nola. "I am going to be debating the infamous Parker Black this coming Friday. This man loves to slam the books we read on his sports show, and with my daughter's capable help, I'm going to educate him on the importance of romance novels. So be sure to tune in and root for us. Also, for our Seattle book girlies we will be opening HEA Books early and providing coffee and muffins for all of you who would like to come in and listen to the debate. We'll also be offering a ten percent Show Romance Some Love discount that day."

"We could use the support," put in Alice. Boy, could they.

"That's it for this time," Nola said. "We're always happy to have you join us as we . . ."

"Book Binge," they said together—a reminder of the name of their podcast.

"I wish we'd set the debate for next week," Alice said as she shut the laptop. "It would have given us more time to prepare."

"It will be fine," said Nola. "We've got our facts. We just have to sit down and organize our thoughts."

Her mother was right, of course. When it came to a battle of the minds, Nola Willoughby was born ready.

"And the morning coffee party will be good for business," Nola finished with a confident smile.

She was relishing this. Alice had a hard time wrapping her mind around that, but there it was. Better her mother than her.

Parker had found the HEA Books website—pink and flowers everywhere, of course—and poked around. *Dedicated to Happily-Ever-After for All*, he read at the top of the page. Gag.

He clicked on the About Us option and shook his head as he read their mission statement.

> We love our location in charming West Seattle, and our goal is to be a welcoming and inclusive place for all those readers who, like us, believe in the power of love. We are here to help our customers find the romance they're looking for.

Oh, brother. He moved on to the Meet Our Staff section.

There he found a picture of his debate opponent. She was slim and fit looking with reddish-brown hair. Not a hint of gray, which probably meant she dyed it. Dressed in a black top and sporting a scarf. Smiling happily. Maybe around his mom's age? He read her bio.

> Nola Willoughby graduated from the University of Washington with a liberal arts degree. She was an avid reader even at a young age, and her favorite place to shop has always been a bookstore. When she had the opportunity to open one, she happily grabbed it because she knows books bring people together. While Nola reads in all genres, her favorite is romance, and she loves being able to support all the wonderful writers and readers who make up the romance community. She always has two or three books going at a time and especially enjoys historical romance and romantic suspense.

Below her was a younger woman who looked to be around Parker's age. Light brown hair, brown eyes, kind of cute face with a hint of freckles across the nose. Unlike all the women he'd ever dated she didn't appear to be a fan of makeup. She was a canvas waiting for paint. He studied that face. The smile looked . . . timid, like someone had dragged her in front of the camera against her will. Shy little bookworm, probably.

Her name was Alice Willoughby. Probably the daughter of the owner. He read her bio. Yep.

> Alice Willoughby has her degree in literature from Seattle Pacific University. Like her mother, she has always loved books. She enjoyed working at HEA Books through high school and college, and it was a dream come true when her mother brought her on as a partner. Alice has a sixth sense when it comes to knowing just what her customers need to read and loves matching them up with the perfect romantic escape. She prefers historical romance but also enjoys contemporary and some romantasy.

Romantasy. What the heck was that? Who cared? HEA Books was the supplier that fed romance pablum to discontented women.

The third staff member, Bettina Cross (*Book boyfriends are the best*), had steel-gray hair and shoulders like a fullback, and her smile looked more like she was baring her teeth. This one could eat dragons for lunch. He was glad he wouldn't be debating her.

He finished off his beer and shut his laptop. And shoved away the question that kept trying to get into his mind. *What's Mom going to think about this?*

Nothing. She'd never know. She didn't listen to his show, and he didn't read her books, so no problem.

Anyway, nothing personal, Mom. His beef wasn't with her. It was with his ex and the women like her who were out to grind their high heels into a guy's gut.

The American male was an endangered species, and somebody had to stick up for him. It looked like that job had fallen to Parker. He was ready, willing and able.

CHAPTER 7

ALICE HIT SEND for their store special edition newsletter, announcing the day and time of their debate with Parker Black. Her mother was determined to get the word out to as many women as possible. To Alice the whole debate still seemed like an exercise in futility. It was a sports show, for heaven's sake. His listeners weren't their people, and they didn't want to be.

"A sports show that's making fun of romance novels," Bettina said in response to Alice's concerns when Alice emerged from the back room to announce that the newsletter had gone out. "Ask me how much sense that makes. The man needs help."

Something had pulled Parker Black off track, that was for sure. Alice had checked out one of his podcasts where he'd been ranting about the inaccuracies in a particular sports romance. Well, there was his excuse for dissing the genre, she supposed.

"If you're not into sports, don't pretend you are," he'd said. "And don't pretend you know something." Parker Black was definitely on the proverbial soapbox. And his callers had agreed. This was going to be a tough crowd.

"There won't be any women tuning in, and she'll be outnumbered and ganged up on," Alice argued. "I still think this is a waste of time. It'll be Mom against him and his fans."

"Not now with word getting out. Our book girlies will show up and your mom will have plenty of fans in her corner," Bettina said.

"It's not like we're going to be in a stadium where everyone has seats and can root for us," Alice pointed out.

"Yes, but they'll be in the store. Maybe people will even be able to call in."

"It's in his best interest to allow that. He thrives on controversy," said Nola, finally joining the conversation just as a customer came up with a book she'd selected to purchase.

"Are you doing something special I need to know about?" the woman asked.

"My daughter and I are going to be debating Parker Black on his sports show," Nola told her. "He's the one—"

The woman held up a hand. "No need to tell me," she said with a frown. "My husband and my son both listen to him. My husband listens for the sports talk and just thinks this weird kick the man is on is a passing thing, but my son is eating it all up faster than cupcakes. The other night he was talking about how women take advantage of men. This from the boy who doesn't have a steady girlfriend and still lives at home and gets his laundry done and all his meals cooked by me."

"How old is he?" asked Alice, picturing a boy maybe just out of high school.

"He's twenty-two. It's time he moved out."

"Maybe so," Nola said diplomatically.

"I'm not into sports, and I don't like that show, but I'll listen and comment," the woman promised. "When are you on?"

"This coming Friday," Alice told her, and her heart rate goosed up simply at the mention of it.

"We're having a party here that morning to listen to the show. Coffee and muffins at nine," Bettina added.

"Good for you. I'll be there to cheer for you. Some men need to be put in their place."

Parker Black certainly did, but Alice was glad she wouldn't be the one doing it. Her mother would handle all the heavy lifting. All she had to do was take care of the pre-debate research and be there for support.

Two more customers came in. One of them strolled over to the romantasy section. The other one, Julia Whitehorn, made the proverbial beeline for Alice, which meant that, at least for a short while, Alice wouldn't have time to obsess over the upcoming debate.

Julia's divorce had become final right before Thanksgiving and had hit her hard. Once a happy soccer mom, shuttling kids back and forth between their many extracurricular activities, she was now a despondent divorcée, still trying to come to grips with her husband's extracurricular activities, which had ended their marriage.

"We were at our high school reunion. There was the old girlfriend, newly divorced and needing a shoulder to cry on," Julia had confided in Alice.

Everyone confided in Alice. Sometimes she felt like she was working in a confessional instead of a bookstore.

"Next thing I know he's changed the password on his phone," Julia had continued. "And then he wants a divorce. I've lost all faith in love." And to prove it, she'd dropped out of both the Back in Time and the Closed-Door romance book clubs, not wanting to be around the other members. "It's too hard. They're all happy," she'd said.

Alice wasn't sure that was the case. She knew of a couple marriages that were struggling, including her own sister's.

She couldn't stand to see Julia so disheartened, so she'd

purchased a book for her and sent it to her as an early Christmas present. *You'll find someone better,* she'd written in the note she'd enclosed, and hoped she knew what she was talking about.

Really, she didn't know anything. She was no expert on love. But she was an expert on books and knew which ones would make a woman reach for the tissue box, which ones could make her laugh and which ones would leave her feeling encouraged. And which ones would manage to accomplish all three.

Julia had appreciated Alice's gesture and enjoyed the book. She'd come into the bookstore looking for more of the same, and Alice had introduced her to an author she was positive Julia would enjoy. "She writes second-chance romance, and she knows what she's talking about," Alice had said. "The writer's husband left her, but in the end, she had the last laugh. Another man came along who is simply amazing. He's her soulmate and they travel all over the world together. Her life now is ten times better than the one she'd had with her first husband."

Julia had indeed loved the book, especially the author's letter to the reader:

> You hear about other women getting hurt, being betrayed by the one they love and you think it can't happen to you. But then it does, and you start to think that it's not worth it to try again, that what you read in a romance novel is nothing more than fiction and that finding genuine true love can't happen to you. But it can. I'm living proof.

Alice had the entire letter memorized.

"She's had it happen to her. That means it could happen to you, too," Alice had assured Julia, and Julia returned and bought the author's other two novels.

Now here she was, back and hungry for more happiness and encouragement. "Who else can I read?" she asked Alice.

"I have just the author," Alice said, and led the way to the opposite wall in the store. "She used to live in Seattle. This is her debut novel. It's selling really well. The hero is to die for."

"Will I die with a smile on my face?" Julia quipped.

"Possibly," said Alice. She pulled the book off the shelf and handed it to Julia.

Julia looked at the cover with the two characters standing back-to-back. "Does it have a happy ending?"

"Oh, yes," Alice assured her. "The baddie in it is simply awful, and it's so satisfying to see him get what he deserves in the end."

"I'm all about the baddie getting what he deserves in the end," Julia said. "I'll take it."

"I hope you'll like it," said Alice as they walked back to the counter where her mother was ringing up a sale for the other customer who'd come in.

"Alice, I like everything you recommend," said Julia.

Nola had overheard. "She has a gift for knowing what people need."

"It's sure worked for me," said Julia.

It was nice to be so praised, nice that her mother thought she had a gift.

Nice. The word seemed to sum up her life. She was nice, her job was nice, her book besties online were nice, her little one-bedroom ADU behind her mother's house was nice, her cat was nice.

Vanilla ice cream was nice. But when paired with hot fudge sauce and whipped cream it was delicious. Was there a way she could make her life a little less vanilla and a little more yummy? Where was the hot fudge sauce?

Kara Bane stopped by the bookstore on her way home

from work. "Did you guys save me the sequel for *Hexing the Gods*?"

Vampires, witches and things that went bump (very loudly) in the night weren't Alice's thing, but she'd known Kara loved spicy tales with fiery, kick-ass heroines, and Alice had recommended the first book in the series to her. The second book had come out, and Kara was ready to devour it.

"Of course, we did," said Alice, and got it for her.

There's a heroine who's far from vanilla, she thought as she rang up the sale. The strength of the series' anchor character was truly inspiring. And the sexy vampire she was in love with was everything a man should be. Well, minus the bloodsucking part. Why was it that even the most evil character in those dark books turned noble when it came to winning his woman's love? Could love light a darkened heart? Could a man truly change for the woman he loved?

Parker Black came to mind.

Probably not.

"All right," Nola said as she and Alice settled on her couch after work with their hot chocolate and cheese and crackers to prep for the debate, Alice with her notes and iPad and Nola with her favorite yellow legal pad. "Let's pull together our talking points."

"I wish I knew what his were," Alice said.

"I'm sure it will be the usual: Romance is inferior, it's nothing but porn, it's not realistic. So, what do we want Parker Black and his band of bad boys to know about romance novels and the women who read them?" Nola prompted.

Alice gave a corner of her lower lip a gentle chew. "That they encourage love and sacrifice?"

She started to type but her mother's words stopped her.

"He'll just say something obnoxious, like men are expected to do all the sacrificing. We have to go beyond that."

"That they give women hope?"

"Okay. How can we elaborate on that?"

"Even if you're going through something bad, you read about people realizing they can overcome their differences and build a life together, and it makes you want to do that, too."

"Well said, daughter." Nola began writing on her legal tablet even as Alice tapped away on her iPad.

"Since we know where he'll be coming from, I think you need to point out that romance novels don't raise unrealistic expectations any more than men's adventure novels do for men," Nola said as she moved her pen across the page.

Wait a minute. "*You?* Mom."

Nola looked up. "What?"

"You said *you*. You're going to be the debater. I'm just backup." Being a good business partner and daughter.

"Of course," Nola assured her. "I misspoke. But remember, you're part of the team."

Yes, the invisible part. "I know."

Nola tapped her chin with her pen. "I wonder if we . . . *I* should really pin him down and ask him who hurt him? Who turned him into such a cynic?"

Alice smiled. "That would be interesting."

"And does he really believe that women can't tell the difference between fiction and reality?" Nola continued, writing furiously.

"Last I checked I hadn't been searching any dating app for a vampire," Alice said. She hadn't been on any dating app, period.

"Oh, that's cute," her mother approved with a smile. "We need to continue to drive home the fact that romance novels are a positive influence."

Alice consulted her notes. "There's evidence suggesting that romance novels can positively influence intimacy and satisfaction in relationships."

"Excellent. Doesn't every man want his wife inspired in the bedroom?" Nola posited as she wrote on her tablet.

Seeing her mother's smile, Alice suspected Nola was thinking of her own marriage. Her parents had enjoyed a close relationship, and she could still picture in her mind times that, as a child, she'd come upon them in the kitchen, sharing a kiss. The way her father had looked at her mother—oh, how she would love to have a man look at her like that.

They continued their brainstorming, and after an hour Nola pronounced them ready for the big debate.

Alice nodded in agreement. She felt like she was back at Disneyland, getting a second chance to go ahead and ride Space Mountain. But she didn't want to. She wasn't looking forward to this, even if her mother hadn't required her to enter the fray. She'd still be there on the battlefield, part of the whole uncomfortable exchange.

Her mother could read Alice's emotions like a large print book. She laid a hand on Alice's arm. "I appreciate your support. You're a smart woman, sweetie, and you've contributed some good points here. They'll come in handy when we face Parker Black."

"You," Alice corrected automatically. She was aware of her mother studying her, and she suddenly felt squirmy.

"Sometimes I wonder if it was such a good idea to bring you into the bookstore," Nola mused.

"What?" Good grief. Where had that come from? And why was her mother even saying such a thing? "I love the bookstore."

"I know you do, and I love having you with me. With the book clubs you've started and the birthday discount program, the special parties like New Year's in New York, you're a big part of why we've been so successful. But it's a constricted world. I worry that you don't get out enough."

"I get out," Alice insisted.

"Going out with your sister or with Lina and Georgia doesn't really count. You need to expand your borders."

"I'll go to the next Northwest Booksellers convention with you," Alice promised. She wasn't wild about the big crowds, but she'd go. "I'll join the gym."

Wait a minute. What was she saying? She hated gyms, with their boats you rowed nowhere and bicycles that never left the spot where they were anchored. And the women who always dressed to kill and looked like they could kill with those well-toned arms and legs. But she'd do whatever she needed to. Anything.

"I'm not trying to remake you, sweetie, but I would like to see you spread your wings and fly a tiny bit. Join a club that's not a book club, go to a concert, take dancing lessons."

And dance with strangers? Alice could feel the blood rushing from her face.

"I worry," said Nola.

"No need to," Alice assured her. "I'm happy here. I really am."

She'd found her tribe. Just like in college, when she'd finally gotten to take classes in her major and had found other people who loved talking about the Brontës and wishing Jane Austen had found her own real-life Mr. Darcy.

Nola nodded. "I hate to see you reading about love and talking about love but never experiencing it. I know you had your false starts."

Let's not talk about that.

"I do believe that somewhere out there is the perfect man for you, someone who will appreciate your gentle spirit and kind heart. Someone who might even bring out a little spunk in you."

Alice the spunkless frowned. "Make me like Scarlet."

"I don't expect you to be like your sister. One Scarlet in a family is enough," Nola said with a smile. "But I do want you to become all that you can be."

In the army. Wasn't that their recruiting slogan? Alice's frown dipped further south. "I will, Mom. Don't worry about me."

Nola smiled and let out a small resigned breath. "I know whatever your future holds it's going to hold something good because that's what you deserve. And I really do love having you here in the store with me," her mother concluded.

Good. That was settled.

"And I'll be very happy to have you by my side for this debate."

Where Alice would strive to prove to her mother and herself that even if she lived in a sheltered world, she could still be a woman of the world. Now that they had their talking points, she assured herself that she could feel more confident. And ready. To assist. This silly unease was totally unfounded. She would carry the flag in their verbal fight, and her mother would fire the shots.

Nola sneezed.

"Mom, are you getting sick?" Alice asked in a panic. She was ready, but not to take on Parker Black single-handedly.

"It's nothing. I'll be fine," Nola assured her.

"Take some cold meds and go to bed," Alice said. "And don't worry about coming in tomorrow. I've got it covered."

Nola released a tired sigh and nodded. "You know, I think I will go to bed. I'm a little tired."

"I'll make you chicken soup," Alice promised. Chicken soup fixed everything, right?

As soon as her mother went upstairs to bed, Alice raced back to her place. She took the last of a roasted chicken from her fridge, along with onion and celery, and some broth from the cupboard, and then got busy, cutting, cooking and stirring, all the while chanting, “Don’t be sick, don’t be sick.”

Nola didn’t look even remotely close to better when Alice delivered the soup the next morning.

“I think I will stay in bed today,” she said.

Nola Willoughby never stayed in bed. *No, no, noooo.*

Alice called later that day to see how her mother was doing.

“I think I’m feeling better,” Nola said, and barked out a cough. This was not good.

The chicken soup didn’t save the day. Come Friday morning Nola woke up with laryngitis. Hot tea with lemon and honey didn’t help. Cough drops didn’t help.

“Try a little more tea,” Alice urged.

“No more tea,” Nola whispered. “It’s only going to make me have to run to the bathroom. We need to postpone this. I’m calling the station.”

“If we back out now think of how it will look,” Alice protested. What to do though? Alice couldn’t take on Parker Black alone. “I’ll call Scarlet. She can come over and help me debate him.” Scarlet would be perfect. She had the looks, she had the fire, plus she hated Parker Black. “You can sit there, and she can do the talking. I’ll feed her the notes.”

“She’s working,” Nola pointed out in a whisper.

“I bet she can get away for a little while. She’ll love doing this.” Alice grabbed her mother’s phone, which was on the table, and called her sister.

“Hey, Mom,” Scarlet answered. “Good luck with the debate.”

“It’s not Mom. It’s Alice.”

“Oh. Why are you calling me on Mom’s phone? Where’s Mom?”

“She’s here, but she can’t talk. I need you to come help me.”

"Alice, I'm in the middle of staging a house here and it's got to be ready for the Realtor's preview by one. The furniture just arrived. I can't get away."

"You have to. Mom's got laryngitis and she can't debate."

"Well, you can still talk," said Scarlet, sounding maddeningly reasonable.

"But we were going to do this together."

"So have Mom sit next to you and smile and you talk."

"I can't," Alice protested. "Mom was going to be the main debater."

"For heaven's sake, you talk about books all the time."

"But not to him." This wasn't going to go well.

"Alice," Scarlet said firmly. "Put on your big girl panties and do what you have to do."

"Thanks a lot," Alice said in disgust.

"You've got this. You'll be fine."

No, she wouldn't.

"I'll be listening. Go slay this."

"She can't come," Nola guessed as Alice ended the call.

"No. She's deserting us in our hour of need." Having the nerve to work instead of dropping everything to come bail out her gutless sister. That left only one option. "I'll do it without her." Had she just said that?

"I don't want you to have to take him on by yourself," Nola whispered.

"Someone has to." *Nora Roberts, help us!*

"I don't care if it's last minute. We'll cancel." Nola reached for her phone.

Alice snatched it away. "No. We're on in an hour. We can't bow out like this."

"Laryngitis is a reasonable excuse for postponing," Nola said.

"But calling this late?" Now they only had forty minutes till showtime. "He'll think you're faking. It will look completely unprofessional. He'll make us look like losers. Plus, we've told all our customers you're going to be on the show. They'll all be listening. I can do it, Mom." They had their facts, their arguments. She could be bold. "I'll explain that you have laryngitis. You sit there and smile. And be my coach."

Nola sighed.

"Weren't you just saying I need to spread my wings and fly?"

"Well, yes."

But from her mother's expression Alice could tell she didn't have much confidence in Alice's wings.

Actually, neither did Alice. *You can do this. Be bold!*

Mom was right. They should have canceled.

CHAPTER 8

NOLA FILLED THE coffee mugs that they used for their podcasts and brought them to her dining room table. Alice's had a cute cartoon woman on it, sitting in front of a bookcase filled with books. The caption read, *Just a Girl Who Loves Books*. Nola's featured pastel book spines, listing various popular romance tropes. The mugs would serve as their debate talismans.

Alice knew she wouldn't so much as take a sip from hers. She already had adrenaline jitters.

They took their seats side by side. Nola was poised with her yellow legal tablet and a Sharpie so she could coach Alice. She gave Alice an encouraging nod and Alice took a deep breath, opened her laptop and clicked on the link she'd been sent.

You've got this, she told herself. Why couldn't she have been the one with laryngitis?

Nola was still in her favorite pajama bottoms, but from the waist up, the part that would show, she looked sophisticated in her favorite black sweater, paired with a black and white scarf she'd picked up on a trip to Paris with her best friend the year before. Small gold hoops—a tenth anniversary present from Alice's father—hung from her ears.

Alice felt like a cliché in her pastel pink blouse and wished she'd thought to put on earrings. She should have at least worn the heart-shaped gold locket that had been her grandmother's. But Parker Black would have probably made fun of that so maybe it was just as well she hadn't.

"You look lovely," Nola said.

And scared. She had to look as scared as she felt.

Nola patted her hand and whispered, "You'll do fine. I'm right here with you. I'll help." She held up her tablet with all her notes as a visual reminder.

It reminded Alice all right. The iPad! She'd left it back in her place, and it had the list of talking points and stats. Good heavens, she'd been so focused on her mom, her brain had short-circuited.

"I need my iPad." But she could access her notes on her phone. Quick! Where was her phone?

Left behind on her kitchen counter. What sane woman went off without her phone? She jumped up but her mother pulled her back down.

"Too late," whispered Nola.

Too late. Too late to run for her technology. Too late to run for the hills. Too late for her to develop laryngitis. She took a deep breath. She could do this even without the crutch of her technology. Every fact she'd gathered, every point she needed to make was embedded in her brain. Her mother was right there, with her copy of the notes. *Be bold, Alice!*

Next thing she knew, they were talking to Jay Barker, the show's producer.

"Two against one?" he joked.

"My mother has come down with laryngitis, so I'll be

doing the talking," Alice explained. "I'm the other owner of HEA Books."

"Two for the price of one. Great. All right, ladies, we'll bring you on right after this commercial break," he said, and Alice's pulse skyrocketed.

She'd be dead from a heart attack before they ever went on.

A crowd of HEA's loyal customers gathered in the store to listen to the big debate between Nola, Alice and the evil Parker Black. It was being simultaneously recorded and would also be available as a podcast on Spotify, YouTube, you name it. Nola and Alice were going to be everywhere, championing women and romance. Meanwhile, Lina had her laptop open and was on KWOW's website.

"I just hope Nola's feeling better," said Bettina, as Lina brought up Parker's show.

"Don't worry. They've got this," Lina said.

It felt like forever waiting to get brought on, but it was barely a blink. Next thing Alice knew there was Parker Black's face on the screen. And there, on the other side of the split screen, sat her mom and her, Nola smiling calmly and Alice staring wild-eyed like a woman in a B movie who'd just seen the creepy monster. Next would come the scream. She gulped it down.

On the other side Parker looked casual and cool in a brown T-shirt under an open button-down shirt with the sleeves rolled up, a model ready for his *GQ* shoot. He was handsome in pictures, but on the screen where that face could come to life, he was a breath-stealer. Or maybe Alice simply was having trouble breathing because she was terrified.

"Hey, dudes, no jocks with us today but we do have two coaches. Nola and Alice Willoughby own HEA Books in West Seattle, and they are love coaches, keeping women supplied in those romance novels we've been talking about lately. Welcome, ladies," he said, and his smile was puckish. "It's good to have you here."

Said the big, bad wolf. Alice gulped again.

"Thank you," Nola whispered, and gave Alice a gentle nudge.

"We're glad to be here," she said. What was she supposed to say after that? Something. It was playing hide-and-seek at the back of her brain. Her mother gave her shin a little nudge under the table. "To set the record straight," Alice added.

That was what she was supposed to say, right? She sneaked a look at her mother, who gave her a smile and a small nod.

"Ah, is that what you're going to do?" he mocked.

"Well, yes," said Alice. "I'm afraid romance novels don't get the credit they deserve."

"Oh, I've been giving them a lot of credit," he said with a smirk. Even a smirk looked good on this man. He had such a beautiful outside. It was a shame his heart matched his name.

Nola gave Alice another gentle prod with her foot.

Alice cleared her throat.

"Nothing to say, Nola?" he taunted.

"I'm afraid Nola has come down with laryngitis," Alice said. As if he didn't already know. His producer would have told him.

"Ah, so you're her mouthpiece," he said, making Nola frown.

"I'm the other owner of HEA Books, and I have a degree in literature," Alice said, determined to show her creds.

Parker wasn't impressed. "I'm sure you're already aware of what I think of those books you sell in your store. But hey, give me one good reason why I should change my mind," he challenged.

Someone needed to wipe that smirk off Parker Black's face. With a nice big piece of sandpaper.

Nola was writing furiously on her legal pad. She held it so Alice could see. *Talking Points.*

Oh, yes. Those. *Come on brain, work!* "For starters, romance novels are the highest earning genre of fiction," Alice said.

"Written by women for women," he said, unimpressed.

"And more women read than men. It doesn't say much for men, does it?" Alice shot back. That hadn't even been a talking point, but it had been sharp. Surprisingly, delightfully sharp. Yay her. She *could* be bold. She shared a little smirk of her own.

"Maybe men don't have as much time on their hands."

"Yes, playing video games can be very time-consuming," said Alice, and his eyes narrowed.

Had that just come out of her mouth? It was something Scarlet might have said. Or a character in a book. Maybe a character in a book had said it? Well, now Alice had said it.

She could see her mother's proud smile out of the corner of her eye and something inside Alice swelled. Confidence. It was as if a kick-ass heroine had stepped out of the pages of a book and entered her brain. *You've got this, Alice!*

"Cute," he said with a frown. "And a typical woman put-down," he added.

Put-downs probably weren't allowed in debates. And it hadn't been very nice. Alice lost her smirk.

"Half the women who write this stuff don't even do their research, especially when they're writing about sports," he continued. "Someone gave me a book where the hero was a hockey player. The author obviously wasn't and didn't know anyone who was. Or else she had no idea how to do research. She got a ton of stuff wrong. But then, it's not about being accurate, is it? Your readers don't care. It's just about getting that rush when the couple gets it on."

Eek! What to say to that?

Nola had started a fresh page and was scribbling frantically, and Alice was scrabbling around in her brain, trying to find the proper response while her confidence tried to slip away.

She read her mother's words. "Most authors we know research meticulously. And at least we write our own novels, which is more than some big-name male authors do."

"You write fantasy. No man can live up to the heroes you women make up."

"They can try," Alice argued. "If they did, we'd all be better for it," she added. "And really, take a look at some of the popular men's adventure novels," she continued. "The hero is an ex-marine or navy SEAL and never has an ounce of fat on him."

"Like in your books," Parker interrupted.

She forced herself to continue. "He knows every fighting move possible, and there's no gun he can't fire. No matter how sweaty he is or how long he's been wearing the same clothes every woman he meets falls in love with him the minute she meets him. That sounds like fantasy to me."

"Hey, we know that's fantasy."

"It's fun fantasy, and you enjoy it. We know fiction when we see it, too," said Alice. "But romance novels give us hope. They set the standard and remind us not to settle for less."

"Compared to the men in those books every man is less," Parker snapped. "Looks like we've got some calls coming in. Jeff from Little Rock. How are you, man?"

"Frustrated," said Jeff from Little Rock. "My woman expects me to know every move in the bedroom that her book boyfriends do—everything she wants, everything she likes, everything she thinks she might like. I never get it right."

RELATIONSHIPS, Nola wrote in large letters.

Relationships, relationships. "Relationships are important," Alice said, and then stalled out.

"Yeah? So how do those books you sell in your store do

anything to help relationships?" Parker argued. "You heard Jeff just now."

Nola was searching through her papers.

"Umm," said Alice.

Nola found the one she was looking for and jiggled it.

It was what Alice had found when she was looking for facts to share. Why hadn't she been able to bring that to the front of her brain?

"There's evidence suggesting that romance novels can positively influence intimacy and satisfaction in relationships," she read. She sounded stilted, like the voice on her app that gave her driving directions.

"They can wreck them, too," Parker argued, those gray eyes of his flashing. Those same eyes were probably enough to melt a heart when they weren't. "We can't please you women. Maybe instead of ranting about all our faults and burying your noses in books you should take a closer look at your men and see what's good about them. These books aren't helping people in the real world. Heck, you women aren't even in the real world with the rest of us. If all a woman wants to do is sit and read how is that good for a relationship? If she expects her man to spend money on her like he's a billionaire from a book so she can feel special, how is that good for a relationship? If she expects him to talk like a romance hero, even if he's not good with words, how is that good for a relationship?"

"Come on, Alice, say something!" Lina yelled at the computer, and Bettina groaned.

"I can't listen," said Georgia Bishop as she grabbed another muffin from the refreshment table.

"Poor Alice. She was doing so well, and now he's slashing her," said Bettina. "This is awful. I knew they shouldn't have done this."

* * *

Parker Black's words were coming out rapid-fire, pelting Alice. Her mother was rattling papers. Her head was going to explode.

"Well, what do you say to that?" he demanded.

Something. Nothing.

Alice put her fingers to her aching temples. "I can't think." She was about to add, "Give me a minute," but he didn't. No way was Parker going to even give her a second.

The bumper music was starting, signaling an end to the segment. "Time for a commercial break, dudes," he said. "And Alice, since you're having trouble focusing we won't hold you over. Go take some time to *think* about what I said. Nola, I hope you get your voice back, although there's nothing you could say to change my mind. But hey, thanks for joining us."

"Wait, we're not done," Alice protested. It did no good. She'd been muted.

And then it was over, and Alice had failed in her mission. She stared at the computer screen where, only a moment before, she'd seen Parker Black's smirky pirate face and wanted to crawl inside a rom-com and hide.

Jay the producer came back on. "Thanks for joining us, ladies."

"You cut me off," Alice said.

"Sorry. We were up against a hard break," Jay said. "Appreciate you coming on."

So Parker could trounce them.

"Leave," Nola whispered.

Alice got out of there before Parker's producer could rub any salt in the wound. "That was awful," she said miserably as she shut her laptop. She should have been the one who couldn't talk.

"You did fine," Nola whispered, and patted her arm.

"Until I didn't. Mom, I froze. He was coming at me so fast. You were right. We should have canceled. I should never have done this." Even if she'd had her iPad, she'd have blown it.

"You were the voice of reason, not him," Nola insisted. "You made some good points, and you got in some good digs."

"No one's going to remember that. They're only going to remember him verbally pummeling me. I thought women are supposed to speak three thousand more words a day than men. Where did mine go?"

She'd been doing so well, up there on a performance high wire. Somewhere along the way she'd looked down and lost it.

"We made our point, that's all that matters," Nola whispered. "And now I need to go back to bed."

"I wish I could go to bed," Alice said. And pull the covers over her head. Hide there for about a millennium. But she needed to get to the bookstore and help Bettina.

Actually, the bookstore was the best place for her. The books were her comfort, and the bookstore was her fort. She needed to retreat behind the safety of its walls.

A win! Yes. Not as easy a win as Parker had anticipated. Alice Willoughby was smart and gutsy to come on the show. He hated to admit it, but she'd scored some points. Just not enough. Game, set, match to Parker.

Still, he was finding it hard to savor his win, thanks to the image of Alice Willoughby looking all shocked and flustered that had burned its way into his mind.

It was a debate, he reminded himself. *You either win or you lose.* That was how debates worked. That was how sports worked. That was how life worked. There was no reason to feel like . . . a jerk? No, not a jerk. He refused to feel like a jerk. No one had forced those women to come on the show.

The commercial break ended, and he pulled his thoughts

back in line. "Okay, that's enough of that. Let's talk sports, dudes, which is why we're really here," Parker said into his mike. "Who thinks this could be the year for our Mariners? Last year was their best offense ever and they came so close to winning the World Series. Think they can make it happen this season?"

There came his first caller for the new segment, Brian from nearby Tacoma. "I think they got as much chance of getting into the playoffs as I do of getting my woman to go to a game with me. I do all kinds of stuff she wants to do."

Oh, boy, here they went back into rant mode. Parker was sick of ranting and sick of talking about women. He had shifted gears, hoping to get back to something he understood. And he wanted to scrub the image of Alice Willoughby from his brain.

"Well, Brian, all I can tell you is don't give up," Parker said, and lost Brian from Tacoma. "I think our Mariners have got a chance. Who's going to meet me at spring training this year and check out the team? Remember, those tickets for our big bash are almost gone."

A few more calls trickled in, and Parker carried the rest of the load until the end of the program. He kept the Let It Out segment short and sweet, reading from another sports romance where the author praised a football player for his big heart, calling him a modern-day gladiator.

"We all know what happened to the gladiators, right? They were just there to fight and die and give the crowd a show of blood. Is that what our Seahawks are, guys? Hey, wish we had time to take your calls, but the clock is ticking. Gotta go. See you all tomorrow. Meanwhile, keep your head in the game."

And that wrapped up another show. And he should have felt much better than he did. Downright triumphant in fact.

"Great show!" Jay enthused, resettling his ball cap on his head. "You hit it out of the park on the debate, man. You crushed it."

No, he'd crushed Alice Willoughby, and he didn't want to

think about it anymore because he felt like a bully. And he didn't want to feel like a bully. *She got some pretty good digs in, too*, he reminded himself. It didn't help.

"Yeah, well, that's over and done," he said.

"Hey, maybe they'll want a rematch."

Parker frowned at Jay. "No. No rematches. At some point we need to phase out the romance novel reading. It's getting stale."

"Are you kidding? It's a great angle and it's bringing in the listeners. Anyway, I thought you were on a mission."

"I am."

"And men need a place to vent. You're their fearless leader right now, their shrink."

Parker frowned. "Yeah, right."

"Serious, man. This is working, so, let's ride this horse until it drops."

Parker sighed inwardly but nodded. "Okay, I'll stick with it for a while longer." He just hoped the horse wouldn't fall on him.

Alice arrived at the bookstore to find her loyal supporters waiting to console and encourage her. And, of course, everyone was buying books. Pity purchases. Ten percent off wasn't that big of a discount.

"Thank you all, for your support," she said, smiling at them. "I just wish I could have done a better job defending romance."

"You did fine," Lina said.

"Yes, you did," Georgia Bishop agreed, and gave Alice a chocolate muffin.

She took it and thanked Georgia, but she didn't eat it. After the mess she'd made of the debate she'd lost her appetite, even for chocolate. She took it to the back room where she dumped it in the garbage and then shed her coat.

"That Parker Black is a bully," said Bettina when Alice returned to help ring up sales.

"Well, it *was* a debate," said Georgia.

"I thought I could take him on, but I couldn't," Alice said. She and her mother had been nothing more but a couple of female Don Quixotes, tilting at windmills.

"He'll get what's coming to him at some point," Bettina predicted.

"You should get revenge," said Lina, warming up to the idea of the man getting what was coming to him. "Send him some of Georgia's cookies with Ex-Lax in them instead of chocolate chips."

"And get sued," Bettina said, sounding as horrified as Alice felt.

"Time wounds all heels," Georgia said. "You just wait. I bet an opportunity to get even will arise."

"I won't take it," Alice said. She wasn't about to indulge in petty revenge. Although the idea of Parker Black getting his just deserts did appeal.

"Well, you did your part," said Georgia. "You got your message out, and we all love you. And mark my words, you'll get more customers after this."

"Georgia's right. Parker Black will eventually get what's coming to him," said Bettina.

Maybe he would, but Alice was going to ignore the further adventures of Parker Black. She was going to forget she ever saw him.

Yes, she was.

Those eyes. They were . . .

Never mind about his eyes. Or any other part of him. She was wiping him off her internal hard drive.

And later that night she'd have a hot date with her book boyfriend. Fictional men were the best.

CHAPTER 9

JAY AND ARNE had been busy all afternoon, and Jay was chortling when he stopped by Parker's Alki Beach condo later that day. "You are gonna love this," he said as he settled on Parker's leather couch with his phone.

Parker handed him a beer. "Okay, enough with the big mystery. What's up?"

"We made a meme from today's slaughter. Put it on our socials and people are already all over it," Jay said, and turned his phone so Parker could see.

Parker had made his point. He'd figured that was enough. This was just plain mean-spirited. He stared in shock at the image of Alice Willoughby, with her fingers to her temples, her face screwed up, hovering over a picture of T-Mobile Park, where the Mariners played. "I can't think."

On another post she danced over a picture of Parker and the caption beneath said,

KWOW fans! Parker Black killed it today.

"Take it down," Parker commanded.

Jay's brows pulled together. "What?"

"You heard me."

"Are you nuts? Why?"

"'Cause it makes me look like a shit."

"If you're a shit, you're a shit. Wear the brown proudly," Jay cracked.

"Look, we won today. There's no need to gloat, so pull that down," Parker ordered him.

Jay shrugged. "I can, but people are already picking it up. The chick's out there now and you can't stop it."

Parker groaned.

"I don't know what your problem is," said Jay. "You won the debate. You're the king of the hill. You're out there defending the bros and you're getting new followers on social and have new subscribers to your YouTube channel. You should be doing victory laps. Everybody loves you, man."

Parker looked again at the pained expression on the face of the Alice Willoughby meme. *Not everybody.*

As Alice approached the bookstore Saturday morning, she saw her mother and Bettina through the window. They were at the register, huddled together, looking at something. She opened the door and the little bell over it gave a playful jingle. At the sound both women jumped apart. What on earth was going on?

"What were you two looking at?" asked Alice.

"Nothing," Bettina said quickly and stuck her phone in her sweater pocket.

What was on Bettina's phone? They obviously weren't going to tell her, and that couldn't be good. And what was her mother doing there when she should have been home recovering and finishing off the chicken soup Alice had made her?

"I thought you were going to stay in bed another day," Alice chided.

"My voice is coming back. I feel better," Nola said.

"I could have driven you in," Alice pointed out. She lived on the same property. It was silly to take two cars.

"I needed to run an errand on the way in. I didn't want to bother you."

"It's never any bother, Mom," Alice said. "You still don't look good," she added, taking in the dark circles under her mother's eyes. Mom had applied concealer, but it was doing a poor job of hiding evidence that she hadn't slept well.

"How did you sleep?" Alice asked, although she knew she wouldn't get an honest answer.

"I slept fine."

Definitely no honest answer. Had her mother been obsessing over how poorly the debate with Parker Black had ended? It wouldn't surprise Alice to hear that. She'd had trouble nodding off herself. It was hard not to keep going over everything she'd said and thinking of everything she *should* have said.

"Even though I failed you?"

Nola gave her a disapproving frown. "You did not fail me. You were a warrior princess, and I was proud of you."

"Till I went brain-dead," Alice muttered.

"That beast trampled you," said Bettina. "He's awful. The romance community needs to rise up in arms. Especially after . . . well, they just need to."

Why hadn't Bettina finished her sentence? "Is there something you're not telling me?" Alice asked.

"Of course not," Bettina said. "I think it's time for my coffee break," she added, and scurried off to the back room.

They hadn't even opened yet. It was too early for a coffee break. "Something is going on and you're not telling me," Alice accused her mother.

"Yes, and that something is us getting back to business," Nola said firmly. She unlocked the door and turned the sign to Open.

"Mom, what were you and Bettina looking at?" Alice demanded.

"Nothing," said Nola. Their first customer entered. She smiled at the woman and said, "Welcome to HEA Books." And that ended Alice's questioning.

The woman smiled back. "Thanks. I heard about your debate. I wanted to come in and support you all."

"We appreciate that," Nola told her. "See?" she said to Alice as the woman moved away to browse a selection of book-related merchandise. "Good things often grow out of bad. And, speaking of good things, have you decided what you're going to wear to the gala next week?"

Alice was always nervous before the gala affair. It was a crush of writers and booksellers, important people in the book community. She felt like an imposter when she attended, but still she wouldn't miss it for anything. Hollywood had its Academy Awards ceremony, but it couldn't compare to the Washington Book Association gala, and Alice was looking forward to seeing some of the authors she and her mother had interviewed on their podcast.

"I'm not sure," she said.

"I think you need a new dress," her mother suggested. "Why don't you leave early, take the business charge card and your sister, and have some fun."

"Clothes aren't a legitimate deduction," Alice protested.

"Then take my charge card. This is on me," Nola said.

No matter what Alice bought she never liked what she saw in the mirror. Clothes seemed to wear her instead of the other way around. But maybe Scarlet could help her pick something fabulous.

It was sweet of her mother, but she certainly wouldn't leave early if they were busy. "Thanks, Mom. Let's see how the day goes," she said.

She ditched her coat and scarf and gloves and stuck her bagged tuna sandwich in the mini fridge, then went back out into the heart of the store, ready to greet their customers. Yesterday had been a disaster but yesterday was gone. Their supporters had treated her wounds and now this was a new day, and she was where she was meant to be. She'd spend it with what she loved most—books and the people who appreciated them.

Books. They marched along the shelves on three walls and cuddled together on all those rolling shelves. Some showed off in window displays. To the outsider they were just bound pages. To the readers who loved them they were individual treasure chests filled with adventure, love, hope, romance and witty banter. They were the ticket to exotic locales and ballrooms lit by a thousand candles, and they beckoned the tired, the sad and the imaginative, eager to build images from words on a page. They held the perfect fix for every lonely heart and they inspired readers in happy marriages. Books didn't discriminate. They welcomed one and all. They entertained the extrovert and understood the introvert. Books had the unique ability to be all things to all people.

Someone like Parker Black, who probably only read *Sports Illustrated*—for the pictures—couldn't possibly understand the importance of what was to be found at HEA Books. He was a Philistine. A primitive. Debating him had been foolish. It had been throwing pearls before swine. Alice may have lost that debate, but Parker Black had lost something important, long before they faced off: the ability to care. He was cut from stone and if he wasn't so unlikable she'd have felt sorry for him.

Her mother was right. They'd done their part. Now it was time to move on. The gala would be the perfect way to do that. It would be packed with local authors, such as Garth Stein and Robert Dugoni, and would host a veritable constellation of favorite romance and women's fiction writers ranging from Kristin Hannah to Debbie Macomber. Alice always wound up in fangirl mode, gushing over her favorite authors. Some often had an advanced reader copy of an upcoming book to share, and Alice collected those like trophies.

She definitely needed to find something fabulous to wear.

Her sister must have sensed them talking about her earlier because after lunch she showed up at the store. She wasn't there to talk about shopping though.

"Have you seen this?" she demanded, turning her phone so Alice could see.

Eep! What was this?

"Don't show her," cried Bettina.

Too late. Alice had seen. There she was, hovering on some comic's TikTok post, with a picture of a pile of Amazon boxes on a front porch. The caption read,

My Wife When I Ask What She Spent All That Money On.

Alice, the stand-in for the wife, had her fingers to her temples and looked like she had gas. She was dancing above the boxes, saying, "I can't think."

"Was this what you were showing Mom?" she demanded of Bettina.

Nola chose that moment to come from the back of the store, wearing her red winter coat and hat. "I'm going home early and see if I can kick the last of this bug," she said as she pulled on her gloves. "You girls are in charge." She looked at the expressions on their faces—Scarlet's angry, Bettina's frustrated and Alice's . . . She had to look as horrified and sick as she felt.

"Who showed her?" Nola demanded.

"Who do you think?" Bettina replied and scowled at Scarlet.

"You have got to get even with this piece of garbage," Scarlet said.

"We're not getting even. We're moving on," Nola said firmly. "Close up early," she said to Bettina. "Scarlet, you're to help your sister with shopping. Help her find something gorgeous to wear to the gala. I assume you have the time since you're obviously not at work or meeting your husband somewhere to make up," she added, her frown showing what she thought of that.

"He's still staying at his mother's, and he can stay forever for all I care," Scarlet said, and raised her chin.

Nola's lips pressed together and she marched for the door. "I need to go back to bed," she said. "Alice, this will all blow over so don't you dare give that man another thought," she commanded, and left.

"Go ahead and shop for your new dress. I can hold down the fort here until closing," Bettina said to Alice. "You need something fun to do to take your mind off . . ." She halted and cleared her throat. "You need something fun to do."

"Shopping?" The only other word dearer to Scarlet's heart was *chocolate*. "I'm on it. We need to find you something sexy to wear and turn you into Cinderella."

"That won't be hard," Bettina said. "You've got a great canvas to work with. So go on, get out of here. We're not that busy."

"Oh, brother," muttered Alice, but she got her coat and followed her sister out the door. "Cinderella" was her favorite fairy tale.

Besides, if she stayed in the bookstore, she was bound to encounter customers who'd seen the meme and wanted to console her. She didn't want to talk about the meme. It was already all she could think about.

Scarlet insisted on driving, so they dropped off Alice's car at her place. As soon as she was in Scarlet's Alice found herself wishing she'd driven separately. There she sat, a captive audience while Scarlet ranted about the evil Parker Black.

"Can we please talk about something else?" Alice begged as they crossed the West Seattle Bridge, heading for downtown.

"Good idea," said Scarlet. "But you need to know, I haven't forgotten what he's done to you. He will pay." Scarlet the avenging angel. "Meanwhile, we'll focus on making you fabulous for the gala. We're bound to find something at Nordstrom Rack."

"I was thinking more like Ross Dress for Less," said Alice, who was opting to pay for her dress herself.

"Let's aim a little higher," said Scarlet.

Since she was at the wheel Alice didn't have much say in the matter.

There were bargains to be had at the store, and Scarlet insisted Alice try on both a slinky black dress with a scooped neckline and a lack of back, which Alice was sure would leave her freezing to death, as well as a red number with a fitted bodice and a full fifties-style skirt. That one had netting of some sort over the satiny material and was sprinkled with red sequins. Alice couldn't help wondering how she'd look in the sophisticated black dress, and she had fallen in lust with the red one. She knew she wouldn't be able to pull off wearing either though.

"These aren't going to work," she predicted as Scarlet led her to a changing room.

"You don't know that," Scarlet said.

Yes, she did.

She tried on the black dress first. Gosh, she didn't look half bad in it. From the neck down. But with her pale skin and lack of makeup it was hard to think of herself as anything other than Wednesday Addams.

Scarlet, who'd insisted on being in the room with her, turned her this way and that. "Perfect fit," she says. "My gosh, it proves you have boobs after all."

It was a little low-cut. Alice tugged at the neckline and Scarlet swatted her hand away.

"Stop that," she commanded.

"I feel exposed," Alice said.

"Exposed is nude beaches and costume malfunctions. You're barely showing any cleavage. This is sexy, not slutty. Although at this point in life." Alice looked at her, horrified, and she said, "Never mind. Try on the red dress."

The red dress was so not Alice, but she wanted it to be. It called to her, saying, "Party, party. Find Prince Charming and have fun."

"Oh, yes, this is you," Scarlet approved.

Alice did love the dress. She felt pretty in it. But was it too sexy for her? Could she pull off a dress like this?

"Gosh, I don't know," she said. "Is it too much?"

"Too much what? Too much fun? Get it."

Alice studied her reflection and bit down on her lower lip.

"You really need to get in touch with your inner heroine, the one who puts on her party dress and goes to the ball and has the prince falling at her feet," said Scarlet.

Alice half laughed. "You know there won't be any princes at the gala. It will all be married men and their wives or divorced men and their girlfriends. There are no single male writers in Seattle who aren't gay."

"You might meet someone who's just moved here," Scarlet suggested. "Anyway, even if you don't, wouldn't it be fun to meet some of your favorite romance writers looking like you belong in one of their novels? You're a story waiting to happen. I'll come over early, and we'll do your hair and makeup. You won't even recognize yourself."

Not recognizing herself, that sounded like a nice change. One night as a red dress kind of woman, one night getting to see how Cinderella felt as she walked into the ballroom. Alice studied her reflection, gnawing on a corner of her lower lip. The dress fit beautifully. Like the black one, it had a scooped neckline, but the scoop didn't scoop up quite as much flesh. Just enough to show the world she had breasts.

The red sequins winked at her. The dress whispered, "You look sexy, girlfriend."

She nodded, decision made. "I'm going to get it." If she was going to be a story she might as well make it a good one.

"Yes!" Scarlet approved. "Okay, next you need shoes."

The first shoes Alice tried on had heels so high she was sure she'd get a nosebleed, and she wobbled in them. "I'll break an ankle," she predicted.

"No flats," Scarlet said firmly. "Your legs will look like sticks."

"I don't want to feel like I'm walking on stilts," Alice said, just as firmly.

"Okay, maybe a kitten heel," Scarlet said.

They finally found a pair that Alice liked and Scarlet approved—black heels with a little black bow on top. The heel was still higher than Alice would have chosen but she thought she could manage to walk in them. She looked down at her feet and smiled. Yes, she was getting these shoes.

"You are going to be so cute," Scarlet said, beaming.

"I'm going to feel cute, anyway," said Alice.

They completed her outfit with a silver shrug Alice could wear if she got cold. "Only if you're absolutely freezing to death," Scarlet instructed. "Otherwise no covering up and hiding."

Scarlet wound up getting a pair of silver heels, then dragged Alice back to where they'd left behind the black dress and bought it in her size. It was a Scarlet kind of dress, and with her red hair she would look stunning. Alice wouldn't have to even try to hide at the gala. She'd be invisible in her sister's shadow. But that was okay. She understood her place in the world. It would be enough for her to enjoy her new dress and pretend she belonged in the spotlight.

"It's too bad Mark isn't going to get to see you in that dress," she said as they left the store.

"He doesn't deserve to," Scarlet said with a frown. "And I'll have more fun without him."

What was the point of having a man if you had more fun without him? "Don't you miss him, even a little?" Alice ventured.

Scarlet shrugged. "Yeah, I do. I hate going places all by myself. And waking up alone feels weird."

"But you miss *him*, right?" Alice prompted.

"I miss . . . some version of him, of what we were. But . . ." Scarlet shook her head. "It's hard to put into words. We were so happy at first. I guess I hadn't spotted his flaws yet."

"We all have flaws," Alice pointed out.

Some people might have seen Scarlet's larger-than-life type A personality and lack of patience as a flaw. Maybe poor Mark had gotten worn out trying to keep up. Maybe he wanted a break from all the planning and pushing and just wanted to be happy together.

"Flaws I can live with," Scarlet insisted. "But downright rebellion—nuh-uh."

Said Queen Scarlet. *Off with his head.*

Well, at least no one would ever walk all over Scarlet. Too

bad Alice hadn't kept in touch with her inner Scarlet when she'd debated Parker Black.

Put it out of your mind, she advised herself. Parker was history. He had no place in her world, and she'd never see him again. She didn't need to keep letting him live rent free in her head.

But it seemed like he tried to keep breaking in.

Nola wasn't out for petty revenge, but she also was not going to take turning her daughter into a laughingstock lying down. The next day, feeling stronger and ready for battle, she put in a call to Parker Black's producer, timing her call for right after the show ended so she would be sure to catch him in.

"You back for a second round?" he taunted.

"No, I'm back to inform you that if you don't take down that meme of my daughter you will be hearing from my lawyer," Nola said tersely.

"You and your daughter have a podcast, right? That makes you both public figures. She's fair game."

Nola's blood pressure shot for the moon. "I guess we'll have to go to court to settle that."

"Hey now, there's no reason to get adversarial," he said, backpedaling. "We've taken it down. But if it's been copied and has gone viral there's nothing we can do about that. Sorry," he added.

"I'll just bet you are," said Nola. "I think we might still have to sue you."

"If you feel you need to, but I'd hate to see you waste your money. KWOW has some pretty impressive lawyers."

She bet it did. She didn't acknowledge that though. "You'd better hope this thing dies down in a hurry," she said, and ended the call just as Alice walked into their back office.

"Who were you talking to?" Alice wanted to know.

Nola had been encouraging her daughter to ignore what was being done to her and move on. *Well, do what I say, not what I do.* When it came to their children being hurt, mothers didn't move on.

"I was talking with Parker Black's producer, threatening to sue."

"Mom, we can't afford the kind of legal muscle it would take to go up against the station," Alice protested.

"I'll come up with the money."

"How? You just got the house paid off last year."

"There is such a thing as a loan."

"And there is such a thing as letting go," said Alice. "Yes, my face is out there, but the good news is, nobody knows who I am."

Nola let out a frustrated breath. "We probably don't have much of a case since he claims they've taken down the meme."

"Then eventually it will fade away," Alice said and hoped she was right. She moved to where Nola sat at her desk, crowded with paperwork, and hugged her. "Please don't feel bad. I'm the one who made the mess. I'm the one who insisted on going through with the debate, not you. And for a while there I was really kicking it. I felt like . . . Wonder Woman. Felt like I was really something."

"You were and you are," said Nola.

"Pride goes before a fall," Alice said, turning fatalistic. "Maybe there's a lesson in there somewhere that I'm supposed to learn. But thanks for being fierce on my behalf. You're the best."

Nola just shook her head sadly. "I should never have accepted that invitation to debate. My hubris did this to you."

"No, Parker Black and his henchmen did this to me."

Alice hoped she was right when she'd predicted that the nasty meme would fade away. But even if it didn't, she was determined to let go of her angst. To never again see or talk about Parker Black. He would be banned from all further conversations, especially on their podcast. Men like him fed on that angst and she was going to starve him to death.

Except as they were interviewing a local author about her new rom-com, there he came, Trojan-horsing his way into their podcast.

"You both do so much for romance," said Desire Jones, their guest author. "And I just want to take a minute to thank you for championing our books."

"We're happy to," said Nola. "It's why we're here."

"And Alice didn't deserve to be bullied the way that Parker Black did when you went on his show."

Alice could feel the sizzle on her cheeks. Yes, she liked doing her podcast looking like an overripe strawberry. *He is a bully, and next time I see him I'm going to hit him over the head with a hardbound copy of* The Kiss Quotient.

Don't say that!

Alice cleared her throat, preparing for a less violent response, but nothing came to mind.

"He's misguided," said Nola. "But we all know how important romance novels are, don't we?"

"I certainly do," said Desire enthusiastically.

"And didn't you write this book when you were on bed rest with your second baby?" Alice asked her, returning to their scripted questions.

Desire beamed. "I did. I kept imagining myself in Rome and wondering what it would be like to see the Trevi Fountain in real life. Then I got to thinking, what would happen if someone accidentally fell in the fountain? And the story just took off from there."

"That is a funny scene," Alice said. "I love how the hero just happens to be there, filming a show about stupid things tourists do. Have you ever done anything embarrassing as a tourist?"

Other than a family trip to Disneyland when she and Scarlet were kids and a trip to Victoria, Canada, to celebrate her graduation from college, Alice hadn't ever been a tourist. How she'd love to see that famous fountain in Rome. Maybe someday she'd get to go there, and not simply in her imagination.

"Not yet, but I'm sure I will," Desire answered with a laugh.

"I love how you kept that enemies to lovers trope fresh," Nola was saying. "Is that a favorite trope of yours?"

"Oh, yes. There's nothing like a battle of the minds and the wills to make sparks fly."

There came Parker Black again, settling in and putting his feet up on Alice's hippocampus. *Would you please get out!*

"And I do love to see a misbehaving hero get a good humbling," Desire finished.

Wouldn't that be nice? It was too bad things didn't work out in real life the way they did in fiction. Seeing Parker Black on his knees, begging for forgiveness—publicly, of course—would be so satisfying. Maybe so would turning that into a meme. Let him repeat over and over again, "I have the blackest heart. I deserve your hate."

"It's been lovely to talk with you," Nola said. "For our local readers, we have plenty of signed copies of *Love in the Ruins* on hand, and we do ship anywhere in the US. I know all of you who enjoy a good rom-com are going to love this one."

And then it was time to say goodbye and sign off.

"Thanks again for having me," Desire said after they'd ended the podcast and it was only the three of them. "Your store is so wonderful, and I really do love how you both champion writers. You need to know we're behind you all the way. And some of my friends and I have been talking about a We Love Alice campaign."

It wouldn't get rid of that awful meme, but Alice was touched by her kindness. "Thank you," she said.

"We do love you guys, and we all love HEA. We have to stick together and be there for each other," Desire said, impassioned.

"Yes, we do. And we love supporting authors like you. Be sure to let us know when your next book comes out. I know you're going to be a star," Nola told her.

"Thanks to bookstores like yours," said Desire.

"I hope what Desire said helps," Nola said to Alice after they'd left the virtual studio. "I felt like we lost you there for a while."

"I was fine until she mentioned Parker Black," said Alice. "I truly think I hate that man. He's evil."

"He's certainly no choirboy," said Nola. She laid a hand on Alice's arm. "I'm sorry you took the brunt of his meanness. If I could go back in time, I'd postpone that debate."

"It's not the debate. It's what he did afterward," Alice said. "Putting up that meme was uncalled-for. And just plain cruel."

And really, it didn't help telling herself nobody knew who she was. Somebody was bound to recognize her at some point. She was never one to seek the spotlight and it was horribly ironic that she'd been thrust into one in such an ugly way. The thought made it hard to keep back the tears.

"The meme wouldn't have happened if I'd protected you." Her mother's eyes were glistening with tears of her own. "That awful man! I'm so sorry, darling."

"Mom, please remember, none of this is on you. I wanted to debate him." Wanted to be bold, step in and save the day. Stupid her. She could have lived with getting trounced. That was what happened in debates. Someone won and someone lost. But the humiliation that had followed. "How could someone be so cruel?" she wondered.

"I don't know," said Nola, "but I can tell you one thing. You are now a true heroine."

Alice's brows pulled together. "Because I've been made a fool of?"

"Because you don't deserve to be made a fool of, because you're better than what happened to you. 'She's tolerable, but not handsome enough to tempt me,'" Nola quoted. "Poor Elizabeth Bennet. How many generations have read that slam in *Pride and Prejudice*? In the end Mr. Darcy redeemed himself, but he'll never totally be able to live down his boorish behavior."

"Well, it's too bad Mr. Black and I aren't fictional people. Then he would get what's coming to him," Alice said, and brushed away an errant tear.

"Who's to say he won't? And trust me, his boorish behavior is being noted all around the country."

So was Alice's frazzled moment. Being a heroine was very, very overrated.

CHAPTER 10

THE LOYAL SUPPORTERS of HEA Books were up in arms over the Alice meme and the expressions of outrage continued.

"Unbelievable," said Lina when she and a new Chili Pepper recruit, Tracy Paulson, dropped by the store. "That man is the spawn of Satan."

"The station should drop his show. We should all write letters," put in Tracy, her eyes flashing.

Alice was sick of talking about the debate and Parker Black. Every time she'd gotten her emotions settled down and her thoughts under control someone came along with condolences or suggestions of what should or shouldn't be done about the man and gave her a fresh spin in the cosmic blender.

"We just got in a new book I think you two will like," she said, changing the subject.

Her ploy worked and they were diverted from the topic of Parker Black.

The same ploy worked when Kara Bane came in, ready to karate chop the evildoer. But not before Kara advised Alice to sue the creep for defamation of character. "Or something," she added. "Like breathing."

"It doesn't matter," Alice lied. If she said it often enough, eventually it wouldn't. "By the way, we just got in a book by a new author I think you're going to love."

Kara's eyes lit up like Times Square. "Yeah?"

And with that the subject of the meme was forgotten.

Scarlet, however, was undistractable. She bought Alice dinner after work to help her forget her troubles. Then proceeded to dwell on them.

"That meme is still everywhere," she reported. "We need to think of some way to make sure Parker Black gets what's coming to him. He's ruining both our lives."

"My life is not ruined," Alice insisted. "It's just . . . temporarily sucky."

She could almost see an image of Parker Black's pirate face floating on the surface of her drink, laughing at her.

"He should be publicly shamed," Scarlet continued. "It's too bad nobody puts people in the stocks anymore."

Alice enjoyed the image that evoked—Parker Black in stocks in the middle of Westlake Center, with all their HEA Books customers throwing rotten tomatoes at him. She smiled.

Scarlet nodded thoughtfully. "Yeah, I like that. We'll think of a way to humiliate him."

"There is no way. The man has no shame."

Alice shoved aside her half-consumed lettuce boat. Food wasn't helping. Even chocolate wouldn't make her feel better. She was just going to have to suck it up and weather this emotional storm. Stay off the internet and stay in her books, where she knew, in the end, everything would turn out exactly as it should.

"I don't want to talk about it anymore," she said. "I refuse to give him any more headspace." *Out, damned spot, as Lady Macbeth would say.*

Except Lady Macbeth's spot was guilt induced, so bad comparison. Alice had done nothing to deserve what Parker Black had done to her. Which, of course, was why it hurt so much.

"Anyway, remember what Grandma Willoughby always said. Every dog has his day," Scarlet continued. "Yours is coming."

"Arf," said Alice, making Scarlet grin.

"You know another good one," Scarlet continued, on a roll. "Be careful who you kick on your way up. You'll see them again on your way down."

"I don't care if I ever see Parker Black again," Alice said. "I'm going to pretend this never happened and move on."

"Good idea," Scarlet approved. "But here's one more saying . . ."

"I don't get mad, I get even," Alice said with her. "It's not worth my time. I have better things to do."

"I don't," said Scarlet. "The creep has humiliated my sister and ruined my man. I will be happy to be your avenging angel."

And she would. "Thank you for always being there for me."

"Forever and a day," said Scarlet. She pushed Alice's plate back to her. "Now, eat your lettuce boat."

Alice grinned and took another bite of her food. It didn't taste as bad as it had moments ago.

They switched to talking about the upcoming literary gala. "Fingers crossed you meet some mysterious new man," Scarlet said.

Alice laughed at that. "Not holding my breath. But I do hope I'll see Marie Bostwick."

"She's worth twenty mysterious men," said Scarlet. "You go ahead and keep Marie. I'll look for a mysterious man."

"I'm sorry you and Mark are still fighting," Alice said. "He should be coming with you."

Scarlet shrugged. "He should be doing a lot of things, but oh, well." She downed the last of her drink. "Let's go, sis. I've got important things to do."

"Like what?"

Scarlet smiled. "You'll see."

She did see when Scarlet texted her a picture the next day of what looked like a man's old sneaker. Next to it sat a 3x5 card with *Be careful who you kick on the way up. You'll see them on your way down* printed on it. *Be sure to wave at Alice and all the women you've messed with*, Scarlet had written underneath.

This is getting mailed to Parker Black today, Scarlet texted and followed it with a string of laughing emoticons.

Alice giggled.

You made my day, she texted back. Where did you get the shoe?

> One of Mark's I found under the bed. Overlooked it when I was packing up his crap. I'd been after him for months to toss those shoes. Too bad he's not home to rescue them.

Poor Mark. But the shoe was pretty beat-up.

Gotta love the irony, Scarlet continued. She was obviously loving it.

Wipe all that down and wear gloves so you don't leave fingerprints, Alice cautioned.

Already did, texted Scarlet. Even when handling the card. By the time I'm done messing with him he'll be a meme—a dude on his knees, holding his shoe and crying and begging for forgiveness.

It would never happen, Parker Black would never change his bad attitude or his equally bad ways, but it was a lovely fantasy.

If Alice was inclined to dwell on it. She wasn't. She had plenty of perfect fictional men to dream about. Book boyfriends were the best.

Parker dropped the old shoe on Jay's desk. "Hey, what the heck?" Jay protested.

"Just a little present from another fan. Thought I'd share." Parker flipped the card onto the desk.

Jay picked it up. His lips turned down as he read it. "Cute."

"Yeah, that's what I thought. I need a break."

"*You* need a break? Harlan just chewed my ass off about that meme."

"Good. Did you take it down like I said?"

"Yeah," said Jay, resentment in his voice. "I wasn't going to, but her mom called and threatened to sue. Then Harlan found out about it and got nervous. You're right. Chicks rule the world these days and we're all whipped."

Parker heaved a sigh. "I'm gonna become a monk."

Jay guffawed. "Yeah, I can see that happening."

"Or at least move to a desert island."

Except he already felt like he was on one. His love life wasn't even in the toilet. It had been flushed. He kept telling himself he liked the peace and quiet in his condo, enjoyed being able to eat what he wanted when he wanted, to sit around in his underwear and read a book, to lounge on his deck and watch the waves kiss the beach at Alki. Play his video games, watch movies. Half the men in America wished they were him. So why did being him feel so hollow?

"I should go on air and apologize," Parker said.

Jay gaped at him. "Have you lost your mind?"

Only my peace of mind. "Hey, I can say I still stand by everything I said, but the meme wasn't my idea and I'm sorry."

"Oh, yeah, throw me under the bus," Jay said with a scowl.

"You deserve to get flattened."

"You'll look like you've got no balls, man. You're a sports talk host, a jock. Are you wanting to commit career suicide? Let me look around. Maybe I got a sword you can fall on."

Parker glared at him. Jay's stunt had put both their butts in a sling. But Jay was probably right. To apologize would make Parker look weak. Except he hadn't been the one to put that meme up. He didn't mind stirring the pot. It didn't bother him that women were pissed at him for having opinions. He was just telling things the way he saw them. But that meme had been a low blow, and he hadn't been the one to throw it.

"You know I'm right," Jay said.

No, he wasn't.

"Okay, maybe the meme was a misstep," Jay admitted, "but guys are still into ranting about their woman troubles, and we need the ratings, so don't wimp out on me. Check with Stu. He's found another book for you to read from tomorrow."

There would be something else happening tomorrow before that.

The next day Parker went off script. "Hey, guys, you might have seen a meme going around featuring the woman I debated last week. I need to set the record straight. I didn't put that out there."

He could see Arne's eyes turning into golf balls and Jay looked ready to throttle him. Too bad.

He hurried on before Arne could mess with the board and silence him. "I don't hit below the belt, and whoever did this is something I can't say on the radio, but I bet you can guess what it is. Anyway, that's not to say we don't stand up for ourselves. We don't wimp out. Get in touch with your inner running back and toughen up, men. But play fair."

"Real cute," Jay said after the show had ended.

Parker shrugged. "I didn't name names. Just trying to clear mine."

"As if all the women who hate you now won't."

"I don't care about all the women," Parker said. "Just the one you screwed over."

Jay squeezed out a laugh. "Oh, that's rich, considering how you bloodied her."

"In a debate. Big difference, dude, and you know it."

Jay's face was taking on a reddish tinge, so Parker let up on him. Jay wasn't a bad guy. He'd gotten carried away with the whole battle of the sexes thing. And maybe that was partly Parker's fault.

"Hey, listen," Parker said. "Some of this is on me. I know we want the ratings, but we don't have to turn into the shit twins here. Let's back off a little. Maybe we can lighten up on the rants, turn it more fun. Things Mom always cooked that I hate, honey-do's I don't want to do, ridiculous things my woman wants me to do with her, stuff like that."

Jay half shrugged, not totally on board. Well, Jay wasn't the one who'd been sent a stinkin' shoe.

"Come on over Sunday and watch the game and we can brainstorm," Parker suggested.

Jay nodded. No smile. He'd get over it.

"Meanwhile, go see the new *M:I* flick. You'll feel better," said Parker.

"Maybe."

"Don't pout or I'll drag you to that fancy dinner I'm going to with my mom on Saturday." Not his favorite thing to do, but it was a big deal to his mother, so he went with her every year.

"The book people? No thanks. And stay away from the romance writers. They'll be gunning for you."

True. Fortunately, there would be other writers present at his mom's table, including his uncle, who wrote men's adventure fiction. He always liked hanging with Uncle Jerome. It was a literacy fundraiser, so the cause was a good one, and, considering the venue, the food was bound to be great, so the evening wouldn't be a total wash. He wasn't wild about wearing a tux—most men he knew weren't. Was that a chick-driven thing? Might make for interesting conversation on a future show. Anyway, he could handle it for one evening.

And if the romance writer army was out in full force, hunting for his head, he'd have to handle that as well. He'd meant every word he'd said in that debate. He stood by his position, and no woman toting a book with a couple of cartoon characters on the cover was going to change his mind.

Alice did feel a little like Cinderella as she and her mother and sister entered The Ruins, a unique event venue in Seattle's lower Queen Anne neighborhood. One of mystique, it was the perfect setting for writers and literary giants to gather, featuring all manner of sensory surprises, including an antique life-sized animatronic elephant built in 1931 for the Paris World Exhibition.

"Wow," said Scarlet as they moved into the ballroom. "This is the kind of place where anything could happen. Do you feel it?"

Alice did, indeed. With its huge hand-painted mural and stage where a string quartet was playing, the ballroom looked like a movie set. Here was a scene fit for a romance heroine. In a new red dress with winking red sequins. She almost laughed at her whimsy. But a girl could dream.

Tables were set up with place cards and a hostess dressed like a fairy-tale princess escorted them to theirs. Kay and George Oswald, a couple who owned a new bookstore in nearby Port Orchard, and Pam Laurel, a beloved author who had run the Northwest Romance Readers Conference for years, were already seated and happy to welcome them.

"Great to see you again," said George, standing to greet them.

"Hello, darling," said his wife, and hugged Nola.

"Your dress is fabulous," Pam said to Alice. "You look lovely."

A compliment to herself as well as her dress. Alice beamed. "Thank you," she said.

"You all know Alice. And this is my daughter, Scarlet," Nola said. "She's my plus-one."

"Scarlet, such a great name. I bet you have a trail of men following you everywhere you go, just like Scarlett O'Hara," said George the flatterer.

"Only a husband, but he's not trailing me at the moment," said Scarlet. "So, if you know any Rhett Butlers . . ."

"Oh, I think there might be one or two lurking around here," said George, and his gaze turned to the group seated three tables over.

Smiling, Scarlet looked that way.

So did Alice. Oh, no. Really?

CHAPTER 11

ALICE HAD TO be hallucinating. She blinked. No, there he still was, looking deceptively like a romance hero in that tuxedo, seated at a table with . . . she blinked again. Genevive Eden, a favorite local romance writer. Did he have any idea who he was dining with?

She took in the rest of his dining companions. The man on the other side of Genevive Alice knew was Jerome Riddle, her brother, who was a successful writer of high-quality men's adventure novels. His character, Jason Stone, solved mysteries and kicked butt. He was always chivalrous and respectful of the women who fell in love with him on his many adventures, and ready to protect them with his dying breath. He never died, but sadly, they always did, which left him forced to carry on nobly alone. Heartbroken, of course. Jerome had never been able to make it to any of his sister's book signings, but he'd always sent flowers.

Maybe Parker Black should read some of Jerome Riddle's books. He could learn a few things from that fictional character. He should also read all six of Genevive's. She knew how to write a perfect man. Her heroes were strong and capable of protecting their women, yet they also respected those women's strengths. And they were always kind and understanding. Parker Black didn't know the meaning of the word *respect*. He certainly wasn't kind. And he understood . . . nothing. About anything.

Scarlet grabbed Alice's arm as everyone took their seats at the table. "There's Parker Black," she hissed. "You should go over and let him have it."

Or, better yet, hide under the table. "I don't want to go anywhere near him," Alice hissed back.

"And look who he's sitting next to," Scarlet continued. "Isn't that . . .?"

"Genevive Eden," Alice confirmed.

"Is that woman out of her mind?"

He hadn't seen them, but Genevive had. She waved in their direction, then left her table, coming straight for theirs.

Scarlet pulled Nola into their conversation. "Mom, you need to tell Genevive who she's sitting next to."

Nola's eyes narrowed, but she calmly said, "I'm sure she'll find out. He couldn't be at a better table. Genevive will set him straight."

"He's lucky he's not sitting at our table," said Scarlet. "I'd set him straight."

"Lucky for us all," Nola said. "Boorish as he is, we're not going to sink to his level and create a scene."

"Nice of you to jump in and defend Alice," Scarlet accused, making Alice squirm.

It hadn't been their mother's fault that Alice had insisted she could handle debating Parker Black.

"Complaints have been lodged, and threats made," Nola said, unrattled by her daughter's judgmental attitude, and left it at that.

"She threatened to sue the station," Alice shared.

"Really? Wow, Mom, that's impressive."

"It's not happening," Alice said. "Unless you want to go into debt and pay the lawyer's fees."

Scarlet frowned but shut up.

"Anyway, I'm past that," Alice told her sister. And herself.

"It's not right," Scarlet said, heated. "That man deserves to be publicly humiliated like Alice was."

"This is not the time. Put on your lady face," Mom said to her as Genevive approached their table.

Scarlet left her scowl firmly in place. Nola stood to greet the author, positioning herself in front of Scarlet like a human wall. "Genevive, lovely to see you. Your dress is gorgeous."

Everything about Genevive Eden was gorgeous, from her foxy lady silver hair, done in a chignon, to her perfectly sculpted body, which testified to her dedication to the gym. She'd accented her metallic satin gown with diamond studs in her ears and a necklace with a single diamond pendant hanging from it. She looked like a snow queen.

"You look great, too, as always," said Genevive. "And, Alice, it's lovely to see you, too. You look adorable in that dress."

Nola stepped aside, revealing her other daughter. "I don't think you've met my oldest daughter, Scarlet," she said, and her motherly smile threatened a life with no more home-baked cookies if Scarlet didn't behave.

"I love your books," Scarlet said. And then, despite the threat, added, "I don't know if you're aware of it, but you're seated next to a man who hates what you write."

Genevive sighed. "Sadly, I am. But I have hope that he's not a lost cause."

"Good luck with that," Scarlet muttered, and Nola again stepped in front of her, blocking her from view.

"We're looking forward to having you at the store to celebrate your new book," she said to Genevive. "I know we'll have our usual good turnout."

"I so appreciate the support," Genevive said. "I'll have a door prize as always. Now, I'd better get back to my table. See you soon."

They hugged and Genevive left. Nola sat down and gave her oldest daughter a disapproving frown. "Honestly, Scarlet."

Scarlet gave her a big-eyed shrug. "What?"

Nola shook her head and turned her attention to Pam Laurel.

"Look at him over there," Scarlet said to Alice in disgust.

Alice was trying not to.

"King of the world. Somebody needs to dethrone him."

"Well, it won't be me," Alice said.

Scarlet sat, thoughtfully observing their archenemy. Genevive had returned to the table and was saying something to him. Giving him a pat on the arm. She continued to rest her hand on his arm. He was saying something to her, leaning in toward her.

"Ha!" Scarlet crowed and pulled out her cell phone.

Alice watched with curiosity and creeping unease as Scarlet moved her fingers on the screen, zooming in for a close-up. She took the shot then turned the phone so Alice could see. There was Parker Black, looking chummy with a woman old enough to be his mother.

"One picture is worth a thousand words. What does this picture say to you?" Scarlet asked.

"That he likes older women?"

"That, too. But also that he's a hypocrite. Cuddling up to a well-known romance writer. I think this needs to go on every possible social media platform. Woman hater has secret hots for romance writer." Scarlet's grin was Machiavellian.

Alice grinned, too. "Almost as good as a meme," she said. "But we'd better not. We carry Genevive's books. Who knows what kind of fallout that could produce?"

"Good fallout," Scarlet predicted. "Anyway, who's going to tell her it's us who did it."

"*You* who did it," Alice corrected.

"Okay, me. It's not going to affect her book sales. She'll just look like a successful cougar. He, on the other hand, will look like the hypocrite he is."

"I don't know." Maybe Alice was scarred for life after her disastrous debate and was scared of everything. Or maybe she was psychic. Or maybe she needed a drink.

She wasn't a big drinker, but with Parker Black in view and her sister plotting revenge . . . there had to be something that would settle her nerves without burning up her throat.

"I'm going to the bar," she announced.

"Oooh, I hear they do vintage drinks. Get me a sidecar," said Scarlet.

That sounded intriguing. "What's in a sidecar?"

"Brandy, orange liquor and lemon. It's tasty."

Tasty. Alice was at an event in a fantastical venue. Why not be adventurous and try something she normally wouldn't? She nodded and made her way to the adjoining room that housed the bar.

Sidecars. She took a sip of one after the bartender set them down. Wow. Potent. But Scarlet was right. It was good.

She took the drinks and turned around to return to their table and turned right into a broad male chest. The sidecar jumped off the track and spilled onto the man's tux, putting a look of surprise on his beautiful pirate face.

Alice's heart jumped off the track right along with the drink. If it had been anyone else, she'd have been quick to apologize, but watching it soak into the fabric, "I'm sorry" got stuck in her throat and she could only stand there feeling her cheeks heat.

He brushed at it and started to smile, maybe to graciously shrug off an apology. She knew the moment he recognized her because the smile tightened into a hard line.

"Rather petty revenge, isn't it?" he said.

Very petty compared to what Scarlet was proposing.

"I didn't do that on purpose," she insisted, and then couldn't help adding, "Unlike what you've done to me."

"I didn't do anything to you," he said, his eyebrows snapping together.

"Other than make me a laughingstock after you'd already won our debate. It wasn't very nice."

His expression lost its anger. "Oh. You're talking about that meme, aren't you? That was my producer, not me."

But he'd gone along with it. "I'm sorry about your tux," she said stiffly. "I'll pay for the dry cleaning."

"No need." He took the empty glass from her hand. "Let me buy you another drink to replace this one."

Oh yes, that was what she needed, Parker Black buying her a drink, thinking that would absolve him for turning her into the latest joke on the internet.

"No, thank you," she said, her voice frosty. "What are you doing here?" she demanded.

He raised an eyebrow. "Supporting a good cause, just like you. I *am* literate. Just like you. Only I have better taste in books." The man couldn't help himself. Rudeness just poured out of him.

She raised her chin to the proper haughty angle any self-respecting Jane Austen heroine would affect and said, "Send the cleaning bill to HEA Books. *Some* of us actually have manners."

Ha! That showed him. Elizabeth Bennet would have been proud.

"I do have manners. Let me prove it and buy you a drink."

"No, thank you," she said. As if buying her a drink would make up for what he'd done? "By the way, in case you don't know it, you're fraternizing with the enemy. Rather hypocritical, isn't it?"

He frowned. "No. That's different."

"Of course, it is. Double standards always are," she said, then left her nemesis standing there with a frown on his face. Her dress swished as she walked, and she hoped those red sequins were winking, "Goodbye, good riddance," at him.

"Only one drink?" asked Scarlet as Alice slipped back into her seat. "I thought you were having one."

"I was till I spilled it on Parker Black."

Scarlet's eyes got big, then so did her smile. "Seriously?"

Alice nodded. "Seriously. Accidentally."

"Accidentally on purpose? I wish I'd been there to see that," said Scarlet, looking to where their archenemy was slipping into his seat. "Look at him over there, pouting. I love it. And just wait until the whole world sees him sucking up to a romance writer old enough to be his mother." She chortled. "Parker Black, you have no idea what kind of snake pit you've stepped into."

Alice loved the idea of Parker Black getting a taste of his own nasty medicine, but she couldn't shake the premonition that he wouldn't be the only one who got bitten in the snake pit. "This could backfire," she said. "I don't think you should post that picture anywhere."

"I don't see how it could. Don't worry, this is going to be the perfect payback," Scarlet predicted. Her smile was smug. "I swear, I should be in a book. I'm brilliant."

"Parker, what happened to your tuxedo?" his mother asked, looking at the stain on his shirt and jacket lapel.

"Close encounter at the bar. No big deal," he said. Just big enough to sour his mood.

He sat there and fumed. Alice Willoughby had a gift for making a man feel like a jerk. First the mess after the debate and now this latest exchange. She'd dumped her drink on him and yet here he was feeling like the weasel king.

It was those big Alice in Blunderland eyes of hers. She was like a heroine in one of the romance novels he'd been reading from, all innocent and perfect. She'd barely come up to his chin, but she'd managed to make him feel small, like one of the idiot heroes in those books. And to think his own mother wrote that stuff. Ugh.

He forced his eyes to look away from her. That glittery red dress drew them back like a magnet. With the neckline low enough to make a man wish it would go lower, and the skirt that swirled around her legs, she'd looked like she'd escaped from some classic movie. It was a take-her-out-and-take-me-off kind of dress.

Well, he had no intention of doing either.

Darn it all, why hadn't she believed him when he said he wasn't responsible for that meme!

He tried to focus on the conversation at the table, then wished he hadn't. The couple seated with them wrote mysteries as a team and were acquaintances of his Uncle Jerome. Unlike Uncle Jerome, the guy was a wimp, and his bulldozer wife kept running over every sentence he tried to finish.

"No, Edward," she corrected before he could complete his story. "We didn't meet them in Edinburgh. It was in London. We'd just done a reel featuring the Agatha Christie memorial," she said to everyone.

The man's face reddened. "That's right. I forgot."

"He forgets a lot," said the wife. She offered no gentle smile to accompany her words, no wifely pat on the shoulder. "But that's why you've got me, right?"

He nodded and managed a weak smile. "That's right."

Poor guy.

Waiters were appearing with wine. Parker reached for his glass as soon as it was filled, all the while wishing he hadn't finished off his drink. He could have used it. It was going to be a long night.

Somehow, he got through dinner. The food was excellent, but he didn't enjoy it any more than he enjoyed the speaker who came after. She droned on too long and too boringly about how reading as a child had helped her survive mean-girl bullying and then turned her into the literary genius she'd become.

"Her last book tanked and here she is doing the keynote," muttered their pain-in-the-butt dining companion as the woman finished to polite applause.

"Genre fiction never gets the respect it deserves," grumbled her husband.

"Yeah, we cry all the way to the bank," joked Uncle Jerome. "Right, sis?"

"Right," said Mom. She'd been doing well writing romances, well enough that she'd quit her day job.

She'd worked for years as a librarian—not the biggest salary in the world for a single mom, but she'd made it work. Uncle Jerome had been her backup, helping at Christmas, he and his wife taking them along on many of their vacations. Somewhere along the way she'd started a side hustle, helping him with research for his books, and that had led to her deciding to try her hand at writing. Mom had done okay for herself, and Parker was glad for her success.

He just wished she'd decided to write mysteries. Or science fiction. Anything but romance novels.

Luna had been one of her biggest fans. She'd even asked Mom for writing advice, which she'd been happy to give . . . before everything with Parker had gone sideways. Then she'd thanked Mom for her help by doing her best to humiliate her son. Mom had refused to give her a cover quote.

Thank God every writer wasn't a Luna. His mother and uncle were both class acts, and so were many of the other writers Parker had met through Uncle Jerome.

A well-known writer took over to hand out an award to an up-and-coming newbie, and Parker surreptitiously checked the time on his phone. Even though these literary events were always for a good cause, he wasn't a big fan of them. As with any profession's gathering, attendees came together to brag or bitch, depending on what was happening with their careers. Admiration and envy always swirled around this kind of affair, leaving some smiles genuine and some fake. Books were the key to happiness and would save the world. Just ask any writer.

Or they'd be a great way to take a shot at the guy who'd broken up with you.

Or they could be the way to boost ratings, if you made fun of them.

Suddenly, Parker found himself feeling small again. He was pulling the plug on his romance novel ranting. Enough was enough. Men had heard that particular message loud and clear and now it was time to move on. He could find plenty in the world of sports to rant about on his show. He didn't need the pink hearts.

"Oh, yeah?" Jay argued when Parker was back at the station come Monday, getting set to go on. "I guess you haven't seen the latest."

They'd both watched the game together on Sunday. What could have happened since then? "What are you talking about?"

Jay pulled his phone from his back pocket. Parker's unease grew as Jay punched the screen. He turned it to Parker. "Arne sent it to me last night."

There on some woman's feed was a shared post of Parker and his mom, him listening like a good son, her with her hand on his arm. "What the . . . ?"

"That's you, having an affair with a woman old enough to be your mother."

"That is my mother and you know it," Parker snapped.

"Yep, but all those women out there who hate you don't." Jay turned the phone back so he could read. "'Parker Black is a hypocrite,'" he quoted. "'He makes fun of romance novels but here he is out with Genevive Eden, who writes them.' And yeah, there are a lot of comments on you being a gigolo and a boy toy to boot."

"That's sick," Parker said in disgust.

"No, that's revenge. It's everywhere. And guess what people are choosing for music to go with the post."

"I don't want to know."

Jay ignored him. "'Love Is in the Air.' How's that for special? I'll give you three guesses who's behind this, but you'll probably only need one."

"Alice Willoughby," Parker said in disgust.

"It gets better," said Jay, and showed him a post by a radio personality from another station who was out for his ratings. *Woman-hater sports radio personality is a secret romance reader. Way to score points, Parker.*

Parker ground his teeth.

"You're gonna have a lot of calls to deal with today," Jay warned as he put his phone back in his pocket. "This is not the time to back off. In fact, you'd better double down. You've lost credibility."

Jay was right.

"What's the deal, man?" demanded one caller. "I mean, if you're into older women, hey, no judgment. But is she a romance writer like I'm hearing? You gone over to the pink side?"

"That's my mom. The real writer was cut out of the picture. I was there with her and my uncle, Jerome Riddle, who writes the Jason Stone books," Parker explained.

The real writer? Okay, that had been a poor choice of words.

"I guess Mom is a safe date. Or maybe you couldn't get a date," teased Jay, making sure he was on air.

Haha. Producers should be not seen and not heard.

"Yeah, well, we know you can't get one," Parker said. "Anyway, guys, not to worry. Your man is still blue through and through, watching out for you all. And, hey, speaking of watching, let's talk about yesterday's game."

Nobody wanted to talk about yesterday's game. Everybody wanted to either diss or tease him. Mostly, they wanted to rant.

"You're a fake," one man accused. "Go on, admit it. You're just as whipped as the rest of us."

Parker could see Jay frowning on the other side of the glass.

"Can't happen," he shot back. "Since I'm not with anyone."

Calls dwindled after that, and Parker wound up doing a long monologue about the latest Seattle Kraken team news.

"You got to do something to get your creds back before Harlan hears about this or we're both going to get flushed down the toilet," Jay said after the show.

"Me? It was your idea to read from those stupid books." Like the ones his mom wrote. *Please, God, don't let anyone Mom knows have been listening today.*

"Hey, you were all over it. And you're the personality."

Who had thought it was a good idea at the time and who

was now a hypocrite and a gigolo. Score one for Alice Willoughby. *Looks like you got your revenge, lady.*

"You're right," Parker admitted.

"You can't take this lying down," Jay said.

"What am I supposed to do?"

"I don't know. Think of something to give the ratings a boost."

Think of something. No problem.

CHAPTER 12

PARKER HAD GOTTEN out of the studio pronto, before Harlan could get wind of what had happened. He was at his condo, working up the questions he wanted to ask his morning guest—a former major league ballplayer turned celebrity author—when his laptop pinged to announce an incoming email. Harlan? Jay? Whoever it was, they'd have to wait. Parker ignored it and finished what he was working on.

"Always complete the task at hand," his Uncle Jerome used to tell him growing up. "Otherwise, you never get any traction." It had proved to be good advice, and Parker had gotten a lot of traction in his day job by following it. He'd also managed to write a book in a year and find an agent. Not bad for a thirty-one-year-old guy who'd had to reinvent himself at twenty-three.

The average career span for pro baseball players was a little over five years, although some made it clear to their forties. Parker hadn't even gotten in the five years, had barely gotten started. He'd just been called up from the Tacoma Rainiers, sampled that sweet taste of the majors before it all ended and he'd had to pivot. He considered himself lucky that he'd been able to parlay his half second of fame as a pro into a job he enjoyed. But it had been staying focused and working hard that had enabled him to keep it.

The questions ready for the next morning, he turned to his email. It was from David Fox of Fox Literary. Three question marks sat in the subject line, and he frowned as he opened it.

What's going on Parker? Seeing some disturbing things about you on the social platforms.

He typed out his reply.

Fake news. Someone took a pic of me and my mom at a fundraiser.

His phone rang about ten minutes after he sent the email. He wasn't surprised to see that it was David.

"Parker, you're going to need to do some damage control," he said. "We're trying to make a deal here, and this isn't on brand."

Getting called a closet romance lover hardly lined up with his image as a savvy misogynist who was showing men how to avoid relationship minefields. "Don't worry, I'm on it," Parker assured him.

Except he wasn't. He couldn't exactly gallop all over the internet and demand people take down that picture. Was he supposed to comment on every observation and joke every book babe on TikTok and Instagram was posting?

He was willing to bet that Alice Willoughby was laughing her head off over this. *How does it feel, Parker? Hehehehe.*

Jay was next to call. "Guess where I've been."

From his tone of voice, Parker knew it was nowhere good. "Okay, I'll bite. Where?"

"In Harlan's office, getting my ass chewed off. He'd have chewed yours, too, if you hadn't left the station before he caught you. Expect an email. Old pencil neck is ready to let the Kraken use us as hockey pucks."

"Who showed him the picture?"

"How should I know? But he saw it, and he thinks you look like a fool and a hypocrite and he's blaming me for not keeping you in line."

Parker tried to rub away the ache sneaking across his forehead. "This is getting out of hand. We need to go back to nothing but sports."

"He wants us to get proactive. Go on the offensive."

"Good old Harlan, using sports terms when the only team that turd in a tie was ever on was the chess team." Except there was a lot of mental strength and strategy involved in chess. Maybe Parker needed to start thinking like a grand master.

He checked his email again. Yep, there was one from Harlan, informing Parker that he expected to see him and Jay in his office the next morning right after Parker's show.

Parker frowned. That would be fun.

"Did you read the email?" Jay prompted.

"Yeah, just now."

"We need a Hail Mary, and we need it fast," said Jay.

"Come on over," Parker said with a sigh. "We'll think of something."

"I'll bring the beer."

Fun times.

But the fun times weren't ending. The next person he heard from was his mother.

"How lovely to learn that I'm in an incestuous relationship with my son," she drawled after he'd said a tentative hello.

"Mom, I'm sorry about that. It was petty revenge," he said.

"So much for your sweet little book lady," he couldn't help adding. "I'm laying odds she's the one who set this fire."

"Might I point out who brought the kindling?" said Mom. "Honestly, Parker. When you insist on stirring the pot you're going to get splashed. And I don't appreciate getting splashed right along with you. Oh, and it's nice to know I'm not a real writer."

His face had ignited with her first words, but with this last jab his entire head was on fire. His mom hadn't let him have it like this since he was in the ninth grade. And he deserved it.

"I didn't mean it like that," he said. How did she know what he'd said on the show?

"Oh, but you did. I heard you."

He tried to turn the conversation. "Since when do you listen to my show?"

"Since I heard you were dating your mother. No, actually before that. One of my friends had told me about your debate and I listened to that as well. Honestly, Parker. This nonsense needs to stop. It's unworthy of you."

"I know," he said. "I'm not going to read any more books."

"Maybe you *should* read some. On your own time instead of on air."

Not one of yours. Please don't suggest that. The last thing he wanted was to read a sex scene written by his mother. "You're kidding, right?"

"No, I'm not. All you've really done is read some cherry-picked excerpts from mediocre novels, starting with the one that horrible Luna wrote. You've certainly never read one of mine."

She sounded offended. "Mom, come on. You know how creepy that would be, reading sex scenes your mother wrote?"

"They're not sex scenes, they're love scenes, and they're mild. Tasteful."

Reading tasteful love scenes his mom wrote. He'd rather be beaten with a baseball bat.

"Why can't you write books like Uncle Jerome?" he complained. "Why do you have to write that—" *don't say drivel!* "—stuff?"

"Because I like writing about positive things. I like to write about love. I think it should be celebrated."

"Love," he scoffed.

"Parker, it's all around you. Look how happy Uncle Jerome was with your aunt. They were great for twenty-two years until the cancer took her."

"Yeah, there was a happy ending. You had a real happy one, too. The sperm donor who took off when I was a baby and never came back."

"Love didn't work out for me in the end, but it gave me you. Reading romance novels was comforting and allowed me to hope. I still believe that people can experience deep emotions and be good to each other."

"Yeah, the way Alice Willoughby's been to me," he said.

"How about the way you were to her?"

"If you're talking about the debate that wasn't me. Barker set that up."

"Maybe I need to put you two in a book," she said in disgust.

"Real funny," he said sourly.

"Look, you boys have strayed far from being professional. This isn't what your show is supposed to be about."

"It's all about ratings." That again. The words left behind an unpleasant taste in his mouth, and he had to remind himself that he was trying to help men.

"And how are your ratings doing now?" she taunted. "I listened to today's show. Remember? I heard few enough conversations about sports, few conversations, period. And a lot of monologues—you, filling in empty spaces? Where were your listeners?"

Shouldn't she have been writing?

"Look, Mom. Everything's under control," Parker lied. "I'm done reading the books on air and no more debates. And I'm sorry about the picture. But maybe you need to talk to this Alice Willoughby about that, tell *her* to show a little love."

"Mmm-hmm, like you've been showing," said his mother, and his face got hotter. "And you don't know that she's the one who posted that picture. It would be very out of character for her. Anyone could have taken it."

"Anyone on Team Alice," he grumbled.

"These days it's a large team."

He was about to respond, "So's Team Parker," but he'd lost players, so he swallowed that comeback.

"I've gotta go, Mom. I'm up to my ears here." In deep kimchi.

"All right," she said. "I hope you can find your way out of this mess. And maybe even, at some point, find someone who will prove to you that not all women are manipulative and mean-spirited."

"Well, my mom isn't," he said. Why couldn't more women be like her?

"The one you're dating? If you're not careful, she's going to break up with you," she joked, then ended the call after telling him she loved him.

Yeah, when it came to love, his mom got it right. She was always kind, always encouraging, never griped or tried to guilt him into helping her when she needed it. Not that she had to. He was always there when she needed him, whether it was for an oil change on her car or to unclog a plugged sink. She was there for him, too. And she never got on his case.

Until just then. But that had been short-lived. He knew

she wanted the best for him, and if she could find him someone like her he'd give love one last try. But his mom was obviously a rare kind of woman.

Despite that, love hadn't exactly worked for her. If it was so great how come she hadn't found someone? Why hadn't she been looking? Ha! He should ask her that.

She'd probably make some lame excuse like she'd been busy raising him.

Maybe she thought she still was.

He got on Amazon and ordered a big box of Godiva for her. It was the least he could do for the woman he was "dating."

Jenny Riddle, aka Genevive Eden, had finished writing her pages for the day. Time to reward herself. She made a cup of herbal tea and settled on her couch with her brother's latest novel.

It was hard to concentrate though, after the latest conversation she'd had with her son. She had her own suspicions about who might have been responsible for that picture of them together but deemed it best to keep them to herself.

Poor Parker. He was in a mess now. Sadly, it was a mess of his own making. Still, she understood his hurt, and his anger over being maligned by his ex.

Jenny had been angry, herself, and had let Luna have it when she had the nerve to send her editor to Jenny, seeking an author endorsement of her awful novel. As if Jenny would ever help someone who had hurt her son so badly, turning friends against him. Jenny had heard her on a podcast and been horrified at everything the creature said.

Still, Parker should never have allowed his hurt to turn into bitterness. It had taken root and turned him into a shock-jock wannabe. Before that he'd been great as a radio personality, talking about sports with his growing fan base, interviewing pro athletes. He'd even had his Uncle Jerome on the show more than once to talk about his pre-cop glory days as a fullback for the Kansas City Chiefs and to make Super Bowl predictions. She'd always listened when they were on together and, while she didn't understand much of what was said, she'd enjoyed their lighthearted teasing and snarky banter.

But Parker had wandered over to the dark side, and that grieved her. What was it going to take to bring him back into the light?

"That will teach the man," said Bettina when Scarlet stopped by after her latest staging job to show off the many sites where Parker was being condemned. "More effective than a lawsuit."

Alice had to agree, but, much as she liked seeing Parker get what was coming to him, she felt . . . it was hard to put into words what she felt. She should have been doing the Snoopy dance. Instead, something heavy sat in her stomach. Was dishing out this kind of tit for tat how a true heroine behaved? Posting that picture had been a bad idea.

It turned out her mother agreed, and Nola was not happy. "It was foolish and immature. And you've made Genevive look bad," she said, frowning at Scarlet.

"She doesn't know who did it," Scarlet protested.

"Who else was at that dinner and had a reason to? These things have a way of getting out. You'd better hope that if this does, Genevive has a sense of humor."

"Somebody needed to even the score for Alice," Scarlet insisted, her cheeks flushed.

"And you call playing some ridiculous prank that embarrasses an author whose books we carry evening the score?" Nola snapped.

At this, Bettina drifted to the back room to hide. Alice wanted to join her, but she felt like she needed to stay and defend her sister even if the revenge photo had been a bad idea.

"She was just trying to help," Alice said.

"It wasn't at all helpful. Honestly, Scarlet, this was so irresponsible. I'm very disappointed in you."

"So, what else is new?" Scarlet retorted, matching her mother's frown. "You've been disappointed in me since December. As if everything going on with Mark is my fault."

"Not everything, but you're contributing to the problem," Nola said.

If you asked Alice, their mother was right, but Scarlet would never admit it. Scarlet had always forged her own path in life, rarely stopping to ask directions, even if she was headed for a cliff.

That wasn't Alice. She preferred safe sidewalks.

The heated discussion would have continued if Georgia Bishop hadn't walked in. Alice was relieved to see her.

"Have you seen what's happening on social media?" Scarlet greeted Georgia, obviously looking for an ally.

Georgia shook her head and came over to where the women stood, and Scarlet showed her a post with the infamous picture.

"Oh, wow! Is that . . . ?" Georgia began.

"Yep," Scarlet confirmed. "It's Genevive Eden. With Parker Black cuddling up to her."

Nola was frowning. "She'll be here next week to talk about her new book. Hopefully. I don't know how I'll face her."

"Maybe she'll bring her sugar baby with her," Scarlet cracked.

Nola pointed a finger at her. "That is quite enough. We won't be making fun of Genevive for being with a younger man."

"Good on her, says I," put in Georgia. "Except why would she pick a snake like Parker Black?"

"I don't think she knows about this side of him. Someone needs to tell her," said Scarlet.

"*Someone* has done enough," Nola said in her mom voice, and Scarlet scowled.

But Alice was relieved. This didn't need to get escalated any further.

"At least maybe now he'll go back to talking about sports and we can talk about books," Nola finished.

One could hope. This would all blow over and they could pretend the ugliness and embarrassment had never happened.

Alice produced the novel she'd been saving for Georgia and passed it to her to inspect. "This is such a fascinating read. I know you're going to love it."

Georgia looked at the cover and beamed. "A heroine who has some curves. I like it already."

"She's a baker," Alice said.

"Ooh, are there recipes in the book?"

Alice nodded. "There's one for a strawberry-rhubarb custard pie and one for peanut butter brownies."

"Be still my heart," Georgia said. "I can make those brownies for Genevive Eden's book party if you want."

"We would love that," said Nola.

"Brownies and Genevive, that's going to be a great evening," Georgia predicted.

"I still think someone should tell her about Parker," Scarlet insisted.

"*Someone* will do nothing of the sort," said Nola.

Scarlet shrugged, refusing to be chastised.

In the end though, Alice knew Scarlet would drop her vendetta. Genevive Eden would find out the truth about Parker Black soon enough, but it wouldn't be the Willoughby women who burst her bubble.

CHAPTER 13

JAY WASN'T SMILING when he finally arrived at Parker's condo. Later than expected.

"What took you so long?" Parker demanded.

"I was talking with Cynthia. I forgot we were supposed to go out," Jay said as he laid a six-pack of IPA on Parker's kitchen counter.

"I bet that went well when you canceled."

"I didn't cancel. I postponed. I'm taking her out to eat after I'm done with you. So, start thinking fast," Jay said.

Parker shook his head.

"What?" Jay demanded.

"The hoop jumping is beginning. You're going to owe her big-time on V-Day."

Jay frowned. "It shouldn't be called Valentine's Day. It should be called Empty Your Pockets Day."

Parker laughed. "Now you sound like me. But you're right. She'll expect you to spend money, count on it," he said, remembering the many demands Luna had put on him—a weekend getaway, flowers, candy. And, of course, dinner out on The Day.

And where was the ring? Boy, had the teary pout been pulled out over that romantic fail. Her eyes had been teary, but his had been opened. He would never be enough. After that was when he'd begun to disentangle himself. And then wound up in a big tangle of drama.

Jay was lucky to be seeing the writing on the wall early. "This one's not a keeper, trust me," Parker said.

Was there a woman out there somewhere who was? Someone who didn't come loaded with expectations and make demands? Someone who wanted to be friends as well as lovers? Who just wanted to be romantic on Valentine's Day?

Romantic. He couldn't believe he'd just used that word. Cringe. Anyway, he already knew the answer. That kind of woman was extinct.

"She's just been brainwashed," said Jay. "You're right. Women these days . . . we can't win."

"Which is why we're done talking about this stuff," Parker said. "We need to bring our focus back on sports, return to our original format."

Would that help get him a book deal? Probably more than if he was all over the internet *dating* a romance writer. Except his book had been focused on the kind of thing they were talking about on the show.

"Is that gonna keep your listeners tuning in? We get more calls when you're doing your Let It Out segment than any other time," Jay reminded him. "Unless you've got a guest on."

"We'll get more guests then. Bring back sports trivia day. We're a sports program, and that's what we're gonna talk about. And not women's sports," Parker added.

"Yeah? You gonna tell that to Harlan?" Jay challenged.

"You bet your butt I am," Parker said.

Jay shook his head and grabbed a beer. "Houston, we got a problem."

The two men sat in silence, Jay sipping his beer, Parker drumming his fingers on the arm of his chair.

"Okay, I've got it," Jay said at last with a satisfied grin, and Parker braced himself.

"This latest—" Harlan shook his head "—mess, it's not good. Ben's not happy."

Unlike Harlan, Benjamin Stricklund was a jock, and he liked Parker. He'd even thought Parker's poking fun at sports romances was a good idea when the lines were lighting up every morning.

"It's making you look . . ." The head shaking continued. Harlan was a bobblehead who didn't know the right way to bobble.

"What?" Parker demanded, going on the offensive.

"Not good. I met with both Ben and Joe."

The station manager and the general manager. Yep, not good.

"They both think this latest development makes you look like a fool, and that makes the station look bad. And that's bad," Harlan finished, in case Parker hadn't gotten the message.

He had. He gripped the arm of his chair and tried to look calm.

"So, what are you going to do to fix this?" Harlan wanted to know.

"I'm going back to strictly sports," said Parker. "More guests. We've got Jerome Riddle lined up for tomorrow."

"And we did sports trivia this morning. We had a lot of calls," put in Jay.

Several of them had been guys calling in to taunt Parker about his mother. He decided it was best not to mention that.

He didn't need to. "I heard the show," Harlan said. "Thanks to that picture with the romance writer your listeners are getting disillusioned, and you need to fix that before they go somewhere else. You need to shore up your image, show them you haven't changed, that you're still a man's man and not a wimp."

This coming from the king of the wimps. "I am," Parker said. "A man's man," he added, just to clarify.

"You need to cement that image. If you lose your fans, you lose your ratings."

For a small, skinny guy, Harlan sure was good at intimidation. Parker frowned.

"And Jay, as his producer, you know this affects you, too," Harlan continued.

Jay frowned. "I know, Harlan. We all want Parker's show and the station to do well. And we're on it," he added, then proceeded to share the idea Parker had vetoed during their brainstorming session.

"Man-on-the-street interview, huh?" Harlan said and gave his pen a thoughtful tap on his desk blotter.

"It'll be good," said Jay. "It'll bring out his fans. We'll make it . . . lighthearted. Fun."

"Fun for who?" Parker grumbled.

"I really don't like the man-on-the-street idea," Parker said as they moved down the hall. "I told you I didn't want to do it and you did it anyway. Thanks for that."

"Hey, I'm trying to get some points on the board for our team. You gotta do something to save face. Listeners are eating up this man v woman stuff. Guys will love it, trust me."

Parker grunted. He didn't trust anyone, not even himself. "You threw me a curveball in there and I didn't appreciate it."

"I'm trying to save our butts, man," Jay said.

"You're putting them in a sling," Parker accused.

But it wasn't fair to blame Jay entirely for this latest development. Parker had been more than willing to fire the opening salvo in a battle of the sexes. And he'd been so sure of himself he'd even written a book.

So why was he balking at this? He still believed everything he'd written in that book, everything he'd said on air.

Didn't he?

Of course, he did. Someone needed to encourage men to stand up for themselves, to quit jumping through all those hoops women made them jump through. And did he want to look like a fool? Of course, he didn't. The thought of that nasty picture roaming the internet decided him. The meme of Alice seemed to have died but the romance community was sure keeping him front and center as a villain on social media. So why not hit back? It would make Harlan happy. Maybe it would make him happy, too.

"Okay, set it up," he said. "We'll take a poll, see how many men out there think that women need to back off on dissing them."

Anyway, he needed to come full circle and end where he started if he was going to squash those lingering jabs and snarky comments about him being a closet romance reader and a hypocrite.

"I'll get it set up," Jay promised.

Jay would set it up, Parker would make his appearance, put in a good word for all the maligned men in the US, and that would be that. Then they'd move on, back to the world of sports where the rules never changed and the players knew exactly where they stood and what was expected of them.

Parker slept well that night, and he was happy the next morning to welcome his Uncle Jerome to the show to talk about current issues in the NFL.

"Safety is a challenge," Uncle Jerome admitted as they discussed one of the major ones, "although more measures are being taken to ensure players' safety."

"Not sure that message is getting through though," said Parker. "Youth participation is starting to fall off."

"I can't blame parents for being concerned, although not every player ends up with CTE from brain injury. The odds are a lot worse for boxers."

"I know you came out of your time with the Kansas City Chiefs okay," said Parker.

"Got enough brain cells left to write," said Uncle Jerome. "I do like the fact that Pop Warner and the NFL are offering flag football leagues for kids. They still get the game strategy and the exercise. And I believe sports in general are good. You learn discipline and teamwork. And, I have to say, football was good to me."

"After that you were a cop, so you know both worlds pretty well," said Parker.

"That's what I'm comfortable writing about. Write what you know, they say. Makes research easier."

"We talked about your latest book, *Touchdown*, when it first came out. That was on the bestseller list for weeks. It centers around a messed-up football player with CTE. Were you kind of on a crusade to raise awareness more when you wrote it?" Parker asked, giving his uncle a lead-in to talk about his book again.

"I don't know if I'd go that far," said his uncle. "Sometimes you just want to tell a good story. Although, I've got to admit, this is something I've been following for a while."

"How important do you think it is to get your facts right when you're writing a book?" Parker asked. That question hadn't been on his list, but he couldn't help asking.

"Well, nobody gets everything perfect, but I think it's important to try."

"You know, we've read some pretty bad books on the show lately, and some of the worst researched seem to be the ones that are supposed to be about sports but are really just about hooking up."

Uncle Jerome's eyes narrowed, a sure sign that he wasn't happy with his nephew's surprise attack. Parker certainly hadn't planned it. He just couldn't seem to help himself.

So much for strictly sports on the show from now on.

"Like I said, we all try to get it right," Uncle Jerome continued. "Every athlete, whether amateur or pro, works hard to be consistent, but we're not robots. Sometimes you miss the mark, miss the shot, your timing is off. It happens to writers, too. Every athlete tries to give his or her best to the team and every writer tries to give his or her best story to the reader." The firm set of his jaw told Parker that was all he was going to get.

"Well, you give the reader your best in *Touchdown*. It's a great book, guys, so get out there and buy a copy. Chicks aren't the only ones who know how to read, right?" One last dig. "Okay, let's open up the lines. What's on your mind?"

Their callers had a lot on their mind. The first one wasn't happy about the rising cost of attending games. "I'm a twelfth man, but I won't be going to many Seahawks games this fall. The budget won't take it. We've got three kids."

Here was another poor schlub who needed a pep talk from Coach Parker, a guy who'd wound up at the bottom of the family ladder and was afraid to reach up a rung and grab on to one measly game ticket. To heck with strictly sports. Parker had to say it. "Maybe it's time to fix the budget," he began.

Uncle Jerome jumped in before Parker could elaborate. "But first you have to make sure you've got enough to cover what you need before you go after what you want. Prices probably won't ever come down. They haven't come down on much of anything. Save up for the game you most want to see and watch the rest on your TV. That's what I do."

That wrapped up the conversation, and Parker moved on to the next caller.

"Maybe prices would come down if the players weren't so greedy," he said. "I read somewhere that the average football player makes three mil a year."

"The average player has a short-lived career and takes a lot of health risks," Uncle Jerome was quick to say. "That salary looks like a lot of money because it's compressed, but the average working man will earn between 2.7 and 3 million in his lifetime, and most won't be forced out of their jobs due to injuries."

"I'm not gonna begrudge any pro player his salary. They all sacrifice a lot to get where they are," said Parker, earning points from his uncle. "And let me tell you, when we're first starting out we don't make squat. I sure didn't. Wouldn't trade my time on the diamond for a billion bucks though, even if it was short-lived."

More callers wanted to talk about sports salaries, and Uncle Jerome's book. The lines were staying lit, which had Jay smiling on the other side of the glass. Yeah, Parker was finally back in control. He smiled, too.

"Hey, Jerome, I've read all your books," said Dave from Bellingham. "I wanna know what you like to read. You into romance novels like Parker?" he asked, snitching Parker's smile.

Parker had told his screener to weed out the jerk wads but they still found a way to sneak past. "Not into romance novels," he said, his words clipped.

Uncle Jerome just chuckled. "I've got a family member who writes them. She's pretty good and I've read all of hers. We know how Parker feels, but I've gotta say, if you want a playbook for how to make your woman happy, read a couple."

Parker frowned at him. "So, there you go, Dave. If you find one worth reading let us know. Looks like we're out of time, guys. Get out there and buy a Jerome Riddle novel and keep your head in the game."

"Very sneaky, trying to drag me into your battle of the sexes," Uncle Jerome said after they were off the air. "But I'm a lover, not a fighter. Unlike you, I like my drama in a book or on-screen, not in real life."

"I didn't ask for that drama," Parker insisted.

"In your own weird and wild way, you did. And with that book you're peddling you've got more coming. But watch out, Parker. This is a game you might lose."

"I don't lose, Unk, you know that," Parker joked.

His uncle clapped him on the back. "Not against men, but women are a different matter. And, when it comes right down to it, you don't always want to win. You'll find that out someday."

"Oh, come on, don't tell me Aunt Ramona had you under her thumb," Parker teased.

"You bet she did, and I loved it." Jerome's smile turned sad. "She was the bright star of my life. I miss that woman every day, miss being under her cute, little thumb."

Jay came up to say goodbye. "Great interview, Mr. Riddle. Thanks for helping my man boost his ratings."

"Anything for Parker," said Uncle Jerome as he and Jay shook hands. "You two try and stay out of trouble."

"Where's the fun in that?" Jay cracked. "And talk about fun," he said after Uncle Jermone had disappeared. "We're ready to go with your man-on-the-street interviews and we're gonna do them right in front of that bookstore with all the romance novels."

Parker frowned. "Come on, man, really?"

The last thing he wanted to do was camp out in front of Nola and Alice Willoughby's bookstore, and the last person he wanted to see was Alice Willoughby, with those innocent eyes and that unsettling ability to make him feel like slug slime. Even when he didn't deserve to, especially after what Team Alice had done to him.

"Perfect backdrop. It'll be great."

It'll be great. The station would probably put that on their tombstones.

There would be no changing the game plan. Jay had already gotten Harlan's stamp of approval, along with the caution to get out there and get Parker's fans back. Parker thought he'd done a pretty good job of that on his last two interviews, and, other than his momentary lapse with his uncle, he'd kept the topic focused on sports, the foundation on which he'd built his show. He was back to batting a thousand. He didn't need this stupid man-on-the-street stuff. But he was stuck with it.

"Okay," he said. "But we do it after the store closes. I'm not going to mess with their business."

As if his sweeping generalizations already hadn't? He pushed away the uncomfortable thought with the reminder that a man was entitled to his beliefs. Especially when those beliefs were right.

Anyway, that was a week away. Meanwhile, he was going to keep his focus on sports where it belonged—far from the land of pink and all the frustration and misery that came with the landscape.

The night before the man-on-the-street appearance he drifted off to sleep only to see Alice Willoughby waiting for him. She was dressed like a Parisian Apache dancer and was leaning in the doorway of her bookstore. It turned out, he was dressed for the part also, in some goofy getup from the fifties, complete with black-and-white striped shirt and red scarf.

She looked him up and down and a corner of her upper lip

lifted. "If you think I'm going to dance to your tune, you're not thinking straight. Go through with this and you'll be sorry."

He jerked awake and found his heart was pounding. What was that about?

Nothing, he told himself. No different than pregame jitters. He remembered one such dream where he'd been trying to run the bases barefoot with his pants down around his ankles. He'd hit a home run the next day, bringing in the winning score.

The morning show went well. It ended with Jay and Parker doing one of their Parker and Barker routines with Parker asking Jay what he was going to be doing that night.

"Nothing much now that I'm single again," Jay said. He hadn't been excited about saying that line and the frown on his face was real. His relationship with Cynthia had been short-lived.

"Hey, my man, it'll be okay. Trust Coach Parker. He'll be okay, right guys? You'll have a chance to tell him in person because tonight we are in West Seattle in front of HEA Books from seven to eight, where we'll be doing man-on-the-street interviews. We want to know, how many of you think that women need to back off on dissing men?"

"And are those books your woman's reading helping your relationship or hurting it?" put in Jay. "Come on out and tell us what you think about the whole world turning pink. Go blue."

"Okay, guys, that's it for today. See you out there tonight. Meanwhile, keep your head in the game," Parker finished, signing off. "We weren't going to mention books," he reminded Jay as soon as they were off the air.

"You're right in front of the bookstore. You gotta," Jay argued. "This is gonna be good," he predicted.

You control the narrative, Parker told himself. *It'll be fine.* And at least the store would be closed.

Anyway, something had to be in the background. They'd stick to the topic Parker had settled on and everything would be fine.

By six forty-five he and Jay were ready to hit the street, bundled in their parkas and gloves and hats, with their videographer Butch along and Arne on hand to make sure all went well with the audio interface.

Game on.

Except the store was still lit up inside. They should have been closed. What the heck?

CHAPTER 14

"DID YOU CHECK to see if they had something going on tonight?" Parker asked Jay.

"No. What does it matter?"

"We're going to disrupt their business," Parker said, irritated. And they were going to disrupt his equilibrium.

"We're just on the sidewalk, man. We're not even blocking the door," Jay pointed out.

Still, Parker didn't like it. "We need to move."

"Too late. Here comes your first man. Hello there," Jay greeted the man coming their way, cell phone in hand. He wore jeans and a parka and boots—perfect footwear for slushy weather. And his whole outfit cried, "Testosterone!"

He looked up from his phone and gave Jay and Parker and their crew a suspicious once-over.

"Game on," Jay said to Parker.

Okay, Jay was right. Game on. They'd do their interviews and then get out of there.

"I'm Parker Black from KWOW's *Jock Talk*. We're conducting some man-on-the-street interviews. Got a minute?" Parker asked him.

"Sure," the guy said with a smile.

"What's your name?" Parker asked.

"Drew."

"Drew. Great name. Don't worry. We won't use it. I'm gonna ask you a question and all you got to do is be honest. You got a girlfriend?"

Drew took a step back. "That's the question?"

"No. Just wondering. I don't."

Drew frowned. "Yeah, same here."

"So, you'll be able to give an unbiased answer when I ask if you think women need to back off dissing men so much? I mean, you've seen all the stuff online, right?"

Drew's frown dipped lower. "Yeah, I have."

"Well, we just want your honest opinion about that," Parker said.

Drew looked confused. "Not about sports?"

"You think what women are saying about men these days is sportsmanlike?" Parker asked. "All you gotta do is let us know."

And so, the interview began. Parker smiled for the camera. "Here we are, checkin' in with the man on the street to see what the average guy thinks about the way things are with women these days." He turned to Drew and pointed the mike at him. "If this was a game, who do you think would have the most points on the scoreboard, men or women?"

The guy half laughed and spoke into the mike. "Women."

"Do you think there's a lot of us guys in trouble with women these days?"

Parker's question wiped the genial smile from the guy's face. "Uh, yeah."

"See, ladies? I'm not the only one," Parker said, and smiled. It was a good line. And safe. No dissing certain books or a certain store that sold them.

He finished his questions, then thanked the man.

"When's this gonna air?" Drew asked after they finished.

"Probably day after tomorrow. It'll be on my podcast."

"Cool," Drew said with a nod.

"Thanks for stopping, man," said Parker.

Drew gave him another nod and continued on his way.

Okay, no harm, no foul. Nobody had come out from the store and asked them to leave.

"Do you think women today are team players?" Parker asked their next man on the street.

"Uh, I don't know," said the guy.

Parker was willing to bet the man had a wedding ring on underneath those thick winter gloves. "You married?"

"Yeah." He looked almost embarrassed to admit it.

"Got a good one?"

"Yeah."

"Is she a team player?" Parker asked.

"You bet." This guy was no fool.

"You got any advice to us single guys who've been burned?" Parker asked.

The man shrugged. "Pick a good one?"

"And good luck with that," Parker said, smiling for the camera.

Another man came rushing up. "Parker Black, oh, yeah. I've been wanting to meet you."

"You one of my men?" Parker asked. Of course, he was. With his Seahawks jacket and his eager smile, this guy had crazed fan written all over him.

"Oh, yeah," he said.

Parker pointed to the jacket. "A twelfth man?"

That produced a "You bet."

"Pretty awesome our boys are headed for the Super Bowl this year," Parker said, showing they were just a couple of buddies, shooting the bull.

The guy nodded and grinned, gave two thumbs-up. "Go Hawks!"

"All the way," said Parker. "Hey, you up for a man-on-the-street interview?"

"That's why I'm here," the guy said, bouncing on his feet. "Lay it on me."

"So, if life was a championship game, who'd be winning, men or women?" Parker asked.

"The women." Then, before Parker could go on to his next question, the dude continued. "And I'm with you on those romance novels. My ex was always reading them and always giving me a hard time about how I wasn't romantic enough."

Parker was aware of two women in the background moving toward the bookstore and giving him and his crew the stink-eye. He hadn't planned on talking about romance novels but their judgmental looks were like a red cape to a bull. He relapsed.

"Have you ever read one of those books?" he asked.

"No," replied his interviewee, offended.

"Looks like there's something going on in the bookstore tonight. You could go on in and see for yourself." What was going on in there? Parker hadn't had a chance to check it out.

The guy let out a snort and made the sign of the cross like he was warding off a vampire. "No thanks, man. No woman's gonna make me her carpet."

"Stand strong," said Parker, and his new best friend gave another two thumbs-up.

Parker was pulling the mike away to end the conversation, but the guy grabbed it and talked into it, looking at the camera. "Any woman out there who likes beer and pizza and isn't gonna rag on me to help do the dishes, look for me, John the man. I'm on Facebook and I won't scam you."

That would get cut out. "Well, thanks, John," Parker said, reclaiming his mike.

"Love you, man," said John, and gave Parker a hearty bro hug.

"Bromance," teased Jay as John made his way on down the street, maybe in search of pizza and beer. And probably a woman who liked to do dishes.

A couple approached. The woman was hot, a Latina with a beautiful face and raven-black hair under a pink knit cap. She could have been a model. Maybe she was. Her husband wasn't as good-looking, a little shorter than her but fit. She had her arm threaded through his and he was smiling like a guy who'd won the lottery.

She had been smiling, but at the sight of Parker, her eyes narrowed to slits and her mouth compressed into a thin line. Uh-oh.

"I know who you are," the woman greeted him. She might as well have added, "The Dark Lord of Seattle."

It was a challenge. Parker had to accept. "Well, then, maybe you two have a word to say about how things are going between men and women these days," he said, and pointed the mike at her husband.

She grabbed it and redirected it at herself. "They're going great between us because my man is a hero. He's hardworking and loving and a great father," she said, her voice intense. "And he's great in bed," she added.

"So, a real player," Parker teased.

"A real man, who knows how to respect women. Which is more than I can say for you and your show," the woman snapped. "You know, we all love this bookstore, and we love Alice and what you did to her was positively evil."

That would be edited out. "I didn't make that meme," Parker said.

"Right," she sneered. "First you attack her on your show and then that. Come on, Eduardo," she said, tugging on her husband's arm. "We don't need to be talking to this idiota."

Parker couldn't resist, goading, "So I guess you go wherever your wife drags you, including chick bookstores?"

He met Parker's sneer with a smirk. "If it makes her happy it makes me happy. And let me tell you, she reads those hot books and then tries everything out on me, so no complaints."

Parker scowled as the woman led her husband away. *Yeah, sure, do whatever she wants. There'll come a time when nothing you do will be enough.*

Two older women were right behind them and had heard part of the conversation. They did an about-face and started walking the other direction. Great. Parker was driving away business from the store. Time to draw the line.

"We're done here," he said.

"You wish," said Jay, pointing to yet another man hurrying their way.

Lina was sharing about her verbal exchange with the evil Parker Black when Bettina reported to Nola that two of the women planning to attend Genevive's book signing had seen Parker and were going home. "He's scaring people away."

Jen Johnson, who ran the Closed-Door book club, was standing nearby and overheard. "Someone needs to put him in a romance novel," she said. "He's like a real-life Mr. Grumpy."

"Yes, but no Miss Sunshine would ever come near him," said her friend who'd come with her. "I'm glad we got here before he set up camp out there. He unnerves me."

Alice had been busy setting out food and greeting people so hadn't seen what was taking place outside. She looked out the store window and sure enough, there was Parker Black with his crew, his microphone stuck in some old man's face while the man threw his arms around and raved. Parker Black, the black plague, back in their lives again, on the very doorstep of their romance fortress.

"I'll deal with him," said Nola just as the store phone rang again.

"Nola, it's for you," called Bettina.

More readers reporting that Parker Black was scaring them away? Alice looked to where her mother stood, talking on the phone and frowning. Their guest author Genevive Eden was at the front of the store, visiting with a reader, blissfully unaware that Parker Black was out there, sabotaging her signing. Someone needed to chase him off. Where was Scarlet? She'd be the perfect one to do it.

Alice pulled out her phone and called her sister. "Where are you?"

"Running late. I'm on my way."

Which probably meant she wasn't even out the door yet.

"We could use you right now," said Alice.

"Why? What's going on?"

Alice told her and heard a growl in response.

"Mark had better not be down there talking to that creep," Scarlet said.

"I haven't seen him," said Alice. But she hadn't been looking. She hoped she wouldn't see him even if he turned up.

"If he's there when I get there I'll slap him."

Alice wasn't sure if Scarlet was referring to her husband or Parker Black. Maybe it was for the best Scarlet hadn't arrived yet.

"And why is he there when Genevive is?" Scarlet wanted to know. "Oh, wait, she must have dumped him. Now he's out getting even."

Georgia Bishop walked in. "That awful man is doing a man-on-the-street interview right in front of the store," she reported as her husband drifted over to join Eduardo at the punch bowl. "He as much as told Bill he's a wimp for coming with me tonight."

"Bill is a brave man," Lina assured her. "He tried to intimidate Eduardo, too, but Eduardo doesn't intimidate. Unless it's me doing the intimidating," she added.

"Alice, you really should do something," Georgia said.

Her mother was still on the phone. "No, the streets aren't bad, just a little slush on the edges. But if you're nervous, don't risk it. We can have Genevive sign a book for you and you can pick it up later. What? Oh, yes, we have her other books, too."

How long was that conversation going to go on? Was her mother going to read half of Genevive's book to the person?

Another woman walked in. "Who are those men?" she asked. Obviously, she was the only woman in Seattle who didn't know about Parker Black's vendetta against romance readers. "Someone needs to shoo them away."

"I'll take care of it," said Alice.

The last thing she wanted was to confront Parker Black. She was not good at confrontation. She'd learned that from their debate. But she'd survived their encounter at the gala.

Get in touch with your inner heroine, she told herself. *This is not that hard. All you have to do is go ask him to leave.* As if he'd leave simply because she demanded it. This man was a brick wall who wouldn't be pushed.

But someone had to try, and as part owner of the store that someone had to be her. She took a deep breath and moved toward the door. Slowly. Hoping her mother would get off the phone.

She did. But it rang again. "HEA Books, where we help you find your happily-ever-after," Nola answered.

Everyone deserved a happily-ever-after, especially women who'd been bullied and made fun of. And those women had to stand up for themselves. Crouching and cowering only encouraged bullying, right? Alice took in another breath and marched out the door.

He turned when she tapped him on the shoulder and the smile on his face fell away.

"What are you doing here?" she demanded, forcing herself to sound fierce. "As you can see, we're having an event tonight, and you're intimidating our customers. Honestly, considering who the guest author is, you should be ashamed of yourself."

He looked confused. "Who is it?"

"Parker!" called a male voice Alice knew well. Oh, no. Mark.

Mark hesitated for a moment at the sight of Alice, then closed the gap between him and Parker. "Hey, Alice," he said stiffly, giving her a nod. "Man, I love your show," he gushed to Parker, then stole a guilty look at Alice.

"Mark, this is a bad idea," she hissed. "Scarlet will be here any minute."

Mark shrugged. "So? I've got a right to be here. It's a public sidewalk. I heard you were doing man-on-the-street interviews," he said to Parker.

"You two know each other?" Parker asked.

"She's my sister-in-law," Mark said, and Alice noticed his face was taking on a reddish tinge that probably had nothing to do with the nippy night air.

"Does your wife know you're here, dude?" Parker asked.

"I can be anywhere I want," Mark said, and jutted out his chin. He turned to Parker. "Parker, thanks to you, I have seen the light."

He'd be seeing stars if Scarlet found him there. "Mark, you really need to leave. So do you," she said to Parker.

"Don't listen to her," said Mark. "Stand your ground, bro. It's a free sidewalk."

An older woman bundled in stylish boots and a coat with a faux fur collar had been coming down the street. At the sight of Parker and the men, and hearing Mark ranting, "Women don't rule the world even if they think they do!" her steps slowed.

Oh, no. Parker Black and his goons weren't going to scare away any more customers if Alice had anything to say about it. She would personally escort this woman into the store.

"Are you here to meet Genevive Eden?" she called.

"Genevive Eden?" Parker repeated.

He sounded like a man about to go into shock. If he did, he'd have to look for someone else to give him CPR.

CHAPTER 15

PARKER HAD TO have misheard. He turned and looked behind him, carefully taking in what he'd been ignoring—the display of books behind the window, many by different authors, and . . . right there, staring him in the face was his mother. On a poster, announcing her appearance in the bookstore that very night.

Crap.

Alice had heard the panic in his voice and seized on it. "You didn't know? I thought she'd have told you."

"What's going on?" the older woman asked, looking warily at Parker and his crew and the enthusiastic Mark who refused to leave.

"Just someone doing a man-on-the-street interview," Alice said. "Don't worry. He'll be gone soon. Come on into the store. We have some wonderful treats for you. And, of course, Genevive Eden."

"You're welcome to come join us," Alice said sweetly to Parker as she shepherded the woman past him. Her smile wasn't as sweet. She was enjoying his moment of discomfort.

"That's okay. We're done here," he said. "Nice talking to you, Mark."

"Hey, we barely started," protested his loyal fan.

"Well, now we're finished," said Parker.

Strength in numbers. Enjoying her victory, Alice walked the older woman past the testosterone barrier and into the store.

Take that, Parker Black, you big, bad wolf blowhard. Nobody's afraid of you.

Genevive came up to her. "Is Parker still out there?" she asked.

Oh, no. Who had told her?

The entire bookstore was buzzing. She could have overheard anyone talking.

"I'm very sorry. I think he's leaving," Alice said.

Genevive's eyes turned to slits. "Maybe not. It's about time he learned his lesson."

Nola joined them. "I'm so sorry," she said to Genevive. "I'm afraid your friend has a vendetta against us, but I'm not sure why he's stirring up trouble for you."

"I'm the one who should be apologizing for Parker's behavior, and he's not my friend. He's my son," Genevive said.

"Your son?" Nola repeated faintly.

"Your son?" Alice echoed. Were her ears working? Was she hallucinating?

"I hope you won't hold it against me," Genevive said as she pulled her cell phone from her purse and selected a number. A moment later she was saying, "Jerome. Are you almost here?" She paused, nodded. "Good. I need you to deal with Parker. He's in front of the store, making mischief."

Jermone Riddle, Genevive's famous brother, was coming. To deal with her son, Parker Black. This had to be a dream.

Alice cast about in her mind, trying to remember what she might have eaten for dinner to bring it on.

"This is so embarrassing. I should have told you when that picture of us first surfaced, given you a chance to cancel," Genevive said to them. "I'm sure this is some sort of sick payback for whoever put it up."

"Oh, dear. You're not the only one who's embarrassed. I was hoping I wouldn't have to fess up," Nola said and then proceeded to tell her what Scarlet had done.

Genevive just shook her head. "Our children," she said with a shrug. "I'm afraid Parker's had a bit of a chip on his shoulder thanks to his ex-girlfriend. Actually, two exes. Both times it was serious and both times he got hurt, but the last one, she was a horror. Now he sees himself as a man on a mission."

"Well, that does explain his behavior," said Nola.

"Character motivation, right?" Genevive quipped, but her smile wasn't a happy one. "Still, there's no excuse for this. I'm so sorry about the ruckus he's making. He didn't know this event was happening tonight or he would have steered clear, believe me. He may not love what I do for a living, but he would never purposely sabotage one of my events. I'm sure the station put him up to it. Anyway, my brother will be here in just a few minutes, and he'll take care of Parker. You can count on it. And I will have a few things to say to him later."

Alice noted the steely look in the woman's eyes and almost felt sorry for Parker Black.

No, not really. She moved to the plate glass window where she could get a ringside seat. Thank God Mark was gone. That was something. In his place stood a human tank who towered over Parker. He had deep-set eyes under a wide forehead, and a brick for a jaw. His narrowed eyes matched the straight line of his mouth.

Jerome Riddle had arrived. This should be good.

CHAPTER 16

THE SITUATION HAD gone from bad to worse. No, catastrophic to hopeless. Parker felt like he was ten years old again, about to get in big trouble with his uncle.

"Jerome Riddle, good to see you again," Jay said, ready to butter up Uncle Jerome like a giant spud.

"Not good to see you, Barker. What do you clowns think you're doing here?"

"Just conducting some man-on-the-street interviews," said Jay. "The station wants 'em."

"Right in front of the store where my sister's doing a book signing?"

A group of women arrived, staring curiously at the men before going into the store. Thank God they didn't hang around for the smackdown that was coming.

Jay lifted both shoulders. "We didn't know."

"Now you do, so pack it in."

"Fine with me, I'm freezing my ass off," Arne said, and followed Butch off down the sidewalk.

"You, too, Barker. Get out of here," said Jerome.

"No problem," said Jay, holding up both hands in surrender. Then, he turned and followed them. Another rat deserting the sinking ship.

"Hey, I didn't know until just a minute ago that Mom was having a signing here," Parker said as the others made their escape.

Jerome pointed to the poster in the window. "Now you do. And now you're coming in with me."

"What? Are you kidding?" Parker protested.

"No, I'm not. It's the least you can do."

"Oh, come on, Unk." Parker sounded like he was whining. Was he?

His uncle put a hand on his shoulder and steered him to the door. To an outsider it looked like a friendly gesture. Parker knew better.

He also knew better than to make a scene and protest. He may have been a grown man, but Uncle Jerome was still his uncle, his father figure and his hero. He'd take what he had coming to him. Like a man, as Uncle Jerome would say. Deep down, he knew he needed to. It hadn't been his intention to ruin his mom's night. Yet there he'd been, like a clueless fool, doing exactly that. He owed her.

But this? He felt like a lost soldier stumbling into the enemy's camp. He wasn't far off and that was proved by the wave of whispers and glares that greeted him. If tarring and feathering was still a thing, they'd be getting ready to smear him with tar.

"We're here, Genevive," his uncle called. "You can start."

Which, of course, made sure that anyone who hadn't yet seen Parker did now. He was greeted with more dirty looks from the women. A couple of guys standing by the punch bowl looked a little sorry for him. Or maybe that was wishful thinking.

If there had been seats available in the front row, Uncle

Jerome would have marched Parker all the way up there. Luckily for Parker, the room was packed and there was only room in the back. They settled in, heads turned back toward his mom, and he let out his breath. He was a blip on the radar and they were over him. Maybe he would survive this.

Until he realized Alice Willoughby was still looking at him, assessing him with a frown. He deserved it and it left him smarting. He wanted to stand up and shout, "I didn't know there was a party going on." No one would believe him. She certainly wouldn't.

He lifted a hand in greeting. *I come in peace.* She blushed and turned away.

Meanwhile, her mother was busy introducing his. "I know our guest needs no introduction, and you've all been anticipating both her new book and her visit, so I'll turn the evening over to *New York Times* bestselling author Genevive Eden."

The women applauded enthusiastically, and Mom smiled at them all. It was a proud moment, seeing her cheered like a visiting celebrity. Which, obviously, she was. If anyone deserved to be cheered it was Genevive Eden, aka Jenny Riddle, hardworking single mom who'd raised him without so much as a penny of child support. He'd never seen her cry (except at his college graduation), never heard her complain. And she'd spent her spare time turning herself into a writing sensation. Even though he didn't like the genre she'd chosen to write in he had to admire her accomplishment.

Everyone was laughing at something she'd just said. Was it about him? He reined in his wandering thoughts.

"Seriously, I try not to base any of my characters on real people. They're always a composite of people I know or a product of my imagination." She pointed to one of many women who had their hands raised. "And what's your name?"

"Cindy," said the woman. "And I love your books."

"Thank you," Mom murmured graciously.

"I'm wondering why you chose to let Brad off the hook. I don't think he deserved a second chance."

"Maybe I should have let him die instead of getting him to the hospital in time," said Mom. "But I thought he deserved a second chance. I think we all do," she added, looking to where Parker sat.

She smiled as she said it. Another one of his mom's good qualities. She couldn't hold a grudge against anyone, including him. Obviously—she couldn't even hold a grudge for a pretend person.

Another woman wanted to ring in. "I loved that Troy came to the rescue when Jen had lost all hope. And that scene when he came to the funeral wrecked me."

Good grief. These women were talking about his mother's made-up people as if they were real.

The next woman's question made him sink down in his seat. "What do you think of Parker Black dissing romance novels?"

Mom's smile was teasing. "I think he's sadly ignorant."

It was suddenly way too hot in the bookstore. He slumped down further.

"I hope someday he'll come to see the value of novels that offer hope. Maybe if he finds his own happily-ever-after in real life it will open his eyes."

"I doubt it," muttered someone, a latecomer with red hair who'd slipped in and was seated on the other side of Uncle Jerome.

She glared at Parker like he was her archenemy. Who the devil was that? She looked vaguely familiar, but he couldn't figure out why.

"I love giving my main characters a chance to live a good life together. Like with all of us, that takes some effort, but when I can help those characters work through their problems and shift their attitude it's as if I've put that encouragement out there in the universe, and I like to think that readers will take hope and work to make their own relationships better."

"We've been accused of not being able to tell the difference between a book boyfriend and a real man. Do you think that's true?" asked the Latina woman who'd lit into Parker outside the bookstore.

"I think most of us can tell the difference," his mother replied calmly. "I also think it's unfair to make those of us who enjoy a wonderful romantic tale feel like less. Romance is so much bigger than the pigeonhole its detractors keep putting it in. Romance is atmosphere and swashbuckling, adventure and sacrifice. It's beautiful settings and moonlight and sunrise. It's nobility and kindness. And think of how many classics we still read that are romances. Think of how much the world of literature would have lost if Jane Austen and the Brontës hadn't written their stories. And who doesn't love the tale of Cyrano de Bergerac? Not exactly a happy ending but talk about a noble hero. Yes, we all need love in our lives. It's what keeps us going."

She ended her speech and the room burst into applause. Mom had gotten the final word again.

She answered a few more questions and then read an excerpt from her book. It wasn't a sex scene, thank God, and it was . . . good. Well, why was he surprised? His mom was a smart woman.

"'Of course, she hoped things would change. What else could she do? Hope was all she had,'" Mom finished. More applause.

Nola Willoughby stepped up next to the podium where Mom had been standing. She carried a large wicker gift basket wrapped in cellophane and tied with a huge pink ribbon. He caught sight of a package of coffee and a mug under there and what looked like a box of candy, as well as some kind of scarf.

"It's time to see who won this lovely gift basket Genevive has brought for us tonight," she said.

Here came Alice, bearing a large bowl filled with raffle tickets. Her baggy black pants worn over what looked like somebody's lost army boots and the long, gray sweater did an excellent job of hiding her curves. Parker preferred the red dress.

She held out the bowl and Nola drew out a ticket and called out a name. The woman gave a happy screech and hustled up to claim her prize and gush over Mom. It made him think of old game shows he'd seen as a kid where people went wild over the prizes they won . . . which were a lot bigger than a gift basket.

"I know Genevive will be happy to sign your books, so let's go ahead and form a line," said Nola Willoughby. "Help yourself to the goodies. And, by the way, a big thank-you to Georgia Bishop for contributing those fabulous peanut butter brownies."

That was it. There was a stampede to where Parker's mom had settled at a small table piled high with books.

"I hope you learned something tonight," the redhead from their row hissed at Parker, then moved away to join Alice, who was gathering more books for his mom to sign.

Uncle Jerome chuckled. "Did you?"

"I learned to check with Mom next time she's making an appearance somewhere and then be far away." Uncle Jerome didn't smile, so Parker got serious. "I learned that my mom's a pretty good writer. And everyone loves her."

"You shouldn't be surprised by that," said his uncle.

"I'm not," Parker admitted. "What's not to love? Okay, I'm out of here. See you later."

His uncle grabbed his arm. "Not so fast, nephew. You're not done yet. You need to buy one of your mom's books."

"What? No."

"What? Yes. Buy a book and get it signed."

"Now?" He was in an estrogen hornets' nest. No way was he getting in that line in front of his mother's table.

"Yes, now. You owe her big-time."

His uncle was right. He did. He heaved out a sigh and nodded.

The woman at the cash register looked surprised to see Parker with his mother's book in hand, but she pressed her lips together—probably biting back some choice words—and took his charge card.

"Enjoy the book," she said, handing it back to him. Her tone of voice added, "Choke on it."

"Thanks," he said, and moved to the end of the line.

Women who'd already gotten their books signed passed him with a glare. Or a sniff, as if he was part skunk. "Hey, I'm here for the party," he said.

"You tried to ruin it," one woman accused. "You should be ashamed of yourself."

He was.

"Well, what have we here?" Mom teased when he handed her the book to sign.

"Just a new fan. You were good."

"You weren't." She said it with a smile, but it still stung.

"I didn't know you were going to be here tonight. Really."

"You didn't need to be here even if I wasn't." She scrawled something in the book and handed it back to him. "I'm glad you came in from the cold."

Like a spy? He shook his head and smiled. "Thanks, Mo . . . Genevive."

"You're welcome, Parker. I hope you'll enjoy the book."

He said nothing to that, just took it and got out of there as fast as he could, making sure to avoid even looking Alice's direction as he went. He didn't take in a decent breath until he was back outside. That had been torture. Once in his car, he opened the book to see what his mother had written.

Love always wins, Mom.

How was it she always got the last word? He laughed and tossed the book on the passenger seat. "So you say, Mom." Much as he loved his mother, that was where it would stay.

"What was the Lord of Darkness doing here?" Scarlet whispered as she joined Alice, who was helping Bettina ring up sales. "I can't believe he'd sabotage his woman's book signing."

"He's not her boyfriend," Alice said. "He's not even her friend. He's her son."

"Her son!"

Alice looked around nervously. "Keep it down, will you?" They'd had enough drama for the night.

"I can't believe it," Scarlet said. "What kind of son would diss his mother and what she writes?"

"A bad one. That's probably why she doesn't go around making it public that they're related. Speaking of bad kids, you better not go too near Genevive, since she knows you're the one who posted the picture," Alice said.

"I wasn't going to get a book anyway. I just came to support you and Mom. Which is more than Parker Black did for his mother," Scarlet added in disgust.

Nola was busy opening books for Genevive to sign when the mountain of a man who had hauled Parker Black into their midst approached. Jerome Riddle, whose novels graced the end caps of every Barnes & Noble across the country, whose latest releases could be found at every airport. She'd seen him at a convention or two and then at the gala she'd gone to earlier with the girls, but never had the opportunity to talk with him. This was the first time he'd been able to attend one of Genevive's book signings. It wasn't the first time Nola had felt her pulse quicken at the sight of that massive male body and heart-stopper smile.

"My brother's usually off speaking at a conference or on tour when I'm signing so this is a first," Genevive said, smiling at him.

"I'm glad you could come," Nola said to him, and opened another book to the correct page for Genevive to sign. "I enjoyed your latest novel."

"Did you now?"

"I've enjoyed all your books. I'd hoped to talk with you at the gala but didn't get a chance. I'm a big fan."

"I don't usually find fans in a romance bookstore," he teased.

"Just because I own a romance bookstore it doesn't mean I don't read other genres," Nola said.

"Same here," he said. "I've read all of my sister's books."

Nola smiled at him. "You are a good brother."

"He is," put in Genevive.

"I try. How about you ladies let me take you both out for something to eat when you're done here," Jerome offered.

"I'm wiped out," said Genevive. She smiled at Nola. "But I hope Nola will take you up on your offer."

"It's a little late for me," Nola began.

"Let me at least buy you a drink. To make up for my nephew's behavior earlier."

As if anything could make up for that. Still, drinks with Jerome Riddle of the massive body and equally big brain. Any woman would jump at the chance.

It had been years since Nola had jumped at any chance. She was out of practice making small talk with men. Except surely she'd find plenty to talk about with this one. Book lovers never ran out of things to talk about.

"All right. Drinks," she said. Maybe she could convince him to rein in his out-of-control nephew.

Although her oldest daughter wasn't behaving much better. Scarlet was going to be mortified once she learned how Parker and Genevive were related. And she deserved to be. Maybe this would teach her not to be so impetuous.

Forty minutes later Nola and Jerome were ensconced on a couch at the cozy Beveridge Place Pub, wine for her and a lager for him, talking about books.

Then it got personal. "So how is it that a lovely woman who owns a romance bookstore doesn't have a man in tow?" he asked.

"He died. It was the worst day of my life."

"I'm sorry, Nola, and I get it. The day my wife died I felt like my life ended."

"What did she die of?" Nola asked.

"Cancer. The damned disease." He downed a hearty gulp of his drink. "But here I am, still breathing. And out with a beautiful woman, so it would appear I'm living after all," he added, and smiled at her.

"And writing."

"Yeah, that, too."

"And being there for your sister."

"I try. She's the best. She raised Parker single-handedly."

Nola had been wearing a smile for him until he mentioned his notorious nephew. She took it off.

Jerome saw. "I'm sorry about that stunt tonight. I know he's been putting down romance novels on his show, but that's just one segment. His ex did a number on him."

And he's been busy doing numbers on other people ever since. "That *stunt* tonight was in poor taste."

"It was for publicity for the show, but he shouldn't have been doing it right in front of your store."

"It scared away some of my customers," Nola said. "Are you aware that your nephew made a meme out of my daughter Alice that went viral and humiliated her?"

His brow furrowed. "I didn't hear about that."

"It was hurtful. And what he did tonight was an embarrassment to his mother. I think he owes her an apology. He owes my daughter one as well."

Jerome nodded. "You're right. I'll work on making sure he makes one."

"Thank you." Not that an apology could turn back time, but maybe it would help ease the sting that remained on Alice's psyche. And it was the least he could do for his mother after misbehaving. If Nola had a son like Parker Black she'd disown him. It was hard to see him as the same man who'd escorted Genevive to the gala. She must have bribed him to attend.

"Meanwhile, maybe we can go to lunch," Jerome suggested.

"Maybe you can get that apology out of your nephew first," said Nola. She reached for her coat and purse. "I enjoyed talking with you. Thanks for the drink. And the conversation."

"Thank you for spending time with me."

He rose and helped her on with her coat, a small gesture of chivalry that was as common as dinosaurs. It had been too long since she'd stood so close to that much testosterone. It felt good.

Maybe they would wind up having lunch together, going beyond lunch and having fun. Developing a relationship. Mutual attraction had sown a seed, but what Jerome Riddle did next would either water it or starve it.

CHAPTER 17

THE MAN-ON-THE-STREET INTERVIEWS had done the trick. Parker was, once again, beloved by his fans. They called in to his morning show not only to talk about the Seahawks' and the Mariners' upcoming season and spring training but also to comment on his street interviews, which were already getting a great response. Lots of thumbs-up.

But he was ready to take a break from keeping his listeners as pissed as he was. He'd written a book, he'd ranted. Now he needed to keep to his resolve to just talk sports. There'd be a time and a place to be Coach Parker and encourage men to stand up for themselves once he had a book to promote. But that time and place was no longer at KWOW.

Somewhere at the back of his mind a psychic mouse set loose by his time trapped in the bookstore was nibbling at his convictions, asking if there *should* be a time and place. Of course, there should, but it was never going to be anywhere near that bookstore ever again.

Seeing Alice Willoughby once more had been unsettling. The whole experience had been unsettling. She may have gotten flustered during their debate, but she hadn't been flustered in front of her store. She'd been a warrior princess, defending her castle. Defending his mom!

And he'd been the black knight. Ugh.

He didn't want to be anyone's black knight. He especially didn't want to be Alice Willoughby's. If they weren't at war he'd have wanted to hang out with her, get to know her. Count the freckles on her face. See her in that red dress again.

Oh, no. He shook off the dangerous thoughts. He wanted nothing to do with Alice Willoughby. She had the potential to tip his world upside down and no way was he letting that happen. He'd barely gotten it right side up.

"Harlan's happy. We need to keep him that way," Jay said before Parker went on the air.

"Harlan will be happy as long as our ratings don't slip."

"Stuff like what we just did is how we keep them from slipping," Jay argued.

"This is how we get stale," Parker argued back. "It's time to move on. I mean it this time."

"We can talk more about that later but stick with the plan for today and give the guys with woman troubles some Coach Parker," Jay advised. "You can't ditch the Let It Out segment, especially after how well the man-on-the-street interviews are doing."

Parker did his usual Let It Out segment, but kept it sports focused, polling his listeners on what they thought about Seattle's hockey team losing their last game. "It's just one game. They've got a lot of season left still. Let's keep supporting our Kraken. There are still some tickets left for their game this weekend." Jay had begun to look antsy, waiting for Parker to switch to the topic of women. Okay, fine. He could do that. "Speaking of the weekend, Barker, my man, how's yours shaping up? Got big plans?"

Jay regarded him suspiciously. "Don't know yet."

"Still haven't found a replacement for Miss Not Perfect?" Parker jabbed.

Shining the spotlight on his nonexistent love life hadn't been part of Jay's game plan. Well, too bad. Let him take a kick in the shins for a change. Parker taunted him with a grin.

Jay was not smiling. "Not yet," he said, putting himself on air also.

"Who's got some advice for my man Jay?" Parker asked. "Should he go back to his girlfriend and start jumping through hoops again or should he stay strong?"

That lit up the lines, which would make Harlan and Ben happy. Sticking to the plan. Parker smirked.

"You gonna make a habit of turning me into your punching bag?" Jay demanded after the show.

"Hey, just sticking with the plan like you wanted. Thanks for taking one for the team," Parker said. "And we made everybody happy."

"Not me," Jay grumbled.

"You need to sweat a little, too," Parker informed him. It had been a good show, and it was shaping up to be a good day.

He'd left the station and was getting into his car when his uncle called. "I need you to do one more thing."

Parker had already done enough entering that bookstore. Talk about going into enemy territory. "For Mom?" If so, the answer would have to be yes. He owed her big-time.

"No, for me. And maybe for yourself, too."

"What?" Parker asked suspiciously. Whatever his uncle was about to say next, Parker suspected he wouldn't like it.

"I want you to apologize to Alice Willoughby."

"For what? For her making people think I'm dating my own mother?"

"I don't know about that," said Uncle Jerome. "But I do know from her mom that you created a meme which made her look ridiculous."

"I didn't do that. That was all Jay," Parker said, irritated. Good old Jay, feeding the publicity fire and burning his friend in the process. "And I already told her that."

"Yeah, but your prints were all over that stunt. And you need to apologize for your shitty behavior outside the bookstore."

"How was I supposed to know they were having a party there with Mom?" Parker protested.

"By doing your research. Or making Jay do his."

"We stopped the interviews, and I bought a book." And went into the enemy camp and risked death by a million glares.

"Would you have done that if I hadn't showed up?"

He'd at least stopped the interviews. Or been trying to when his uncle had showed up.

"I did my time. Give me one good reason I should do this," he said.

"I like the store owner. I want to take her out and she won't go unless you grovel to her girl. Come on, Parks, you've been creating enough trouble. A simple *sorry I was a jerk* will do it. You'll feel better, she'll feel better, her mom will feel better."

"And you'll feel better," Parker added cynically.

"Yeah, I will."

Okay, Parker could manage an *I'm sorry* for Alice Willoughby. Because, in a way, he was. It was one thing to stand up for men. It was another to do it while stomping directly on someone's business. He should never have allowed Jay to lead him into that mess and this was the price he was paying for it.

"All right, I'll do it," he said.

It would be a short apology though, just for camping out

in front of the store and scaring away the customers. Not that he'd scared very many. Most of them had marched right past him or let him have it. He supposed the women of HEA Books would be more than happy to light into him again when he showed up.

Maybe he'd luck out and Alice wouldn't be there.

Right. Of course, she'd be there. It was her kingdom.

Man up, he told himself. *You can do this*.

But he sure didn't want to.

"I've got to kick these post-menopause blues," Roxy Jones, a member of the Back in Time book club, announced to Nola and Alice as Nola rang up her latest purchase. "What I really need is something to inspire me in the bedroom. The thrill has chilled. Nothing too racy," she added. "Just something to warm me up. Julia said you might be able to help me, Alice."

Alice had unpacked a new release she was sure would be perfect. It was a second-chance romance, and she'd read the ARC for it. It was happy and fun, and the love scenes were emotional rather than graphic. Maybe they would inspire Roxy.

"I think I've got something," she said, and hurried to fetch it from the shelf.

"Alice has a gift. She'll find exactly what you need," she heard her mother say.

Yes, when it came to pulling love off the shelf, Alice was a pro. If only she knew how to find it in real life.

She'd just handed over the book to her mother to ring up when the little bell over the door jingled. She looked up with a smile, expecting to see another of their regulars. Instead, her smile melted away as her face heated at the sight of Parker Black. The last of the slush had left the sidewalk and he wore stylish shoes under his jeans and a jacket over a bluish-gray sweater that went beautifully with his gray eyes and dark hair.

She felt frumpy in her baggy slacks and flats and her bulky cream-colored cable-knit sweater. She wished she'd worn makeup. No, she wished she was in the back room so she wouldn't have to face Parker Black.

Yet again. There he stood, jangling her nerves by his very presence. Why, oh, why, did the man have to be so sexy?

Julia looked the invader up and down in disgust, then said a warm farewell to Nola and Alice before sailing past him and out the door. Bettina came in right behind him, bringing the sandwiches from Husky Deli that Nola had sent her out for.

She kept silent, although Alice was sure she had all manner of things she wanted to say to him. Instead, she settled for glaring at him, then made her way to the back room to deposit their lunch.

"Mr. Black," Nola greeted him, polite and frosty. "What brings you to our store? I'm afraid if you're looking for books to read on your radio program we can't help you."

"I came to apologize," he said, making Alice gape in surprise. "I'm sorry I disrupted your signing."

"Your mother's signing," Nola corrected him.

His cheeks took on a ruddy flush and he nodded. "My mother's signing. It was my producer's idea to conduct our man-on-the-street interviews in front of your store. I didn't think you'd be open, and I sure didn't know my mom was going to be there."

Blame shifting, how ignoble, thought Alice.

"You might want to apologize to my daughter, too," said Nola, deepening the flush on his cheeks.

He stepped further into the store, a man venturing into the tiger's cage.

"I'll leave you two to talk," Nola said, and started for the back room.

Alice wanted to plead, “Don’t leave me,” but that would have sounded cowardly. Instead, she tried to mask her cowardice. “You can stay, Mom.”

“I think you two have some issues to discuss,” Nola said, and kept moving.

Fine. Alice could do this. She took in a breath, forced herself to look Parker in the eye. And waited.

“I was a jerk last night,” he said. “Outside the store.”

You’re probably a jerk all the time. She kept the words inside her mouth.

“And I was a jerk to cut you off in our debate. But honest, I really wasn’t the one who made that meme. You can’t hold that against me. My producer Jay and my sound engineer got together and did it. Jay thought it would keep things stirred up.”

“It was . . .” Mortifying. Hurtful. Simply remembering how horrified she’d been when she saw that image, saw herself turned into a joke, made her want to cry. She shook her head and blinked hard, determined not to embarrass herself by crying in front of this bully. But the tears were there, near the surface. She lowered her gaze so he couldn’t see.

He hesitated. “Look, I know some things have gone sideways, but I was never out to make an enemy of you, Alice.”

“I guess coming over and saying a few words proves that?” They weren’t even heartfelt, she was sure of it.

“Let me take you to lunch.”

She looked up in surprise. Lunch with Parker Black, like they were . . . friends.

That was ridiculous. “We have lunch,” she said, motioning to the back room. Thank heaven. He was a human Venus flytrap, not to be trusted, not to be gone near.

And yet, what if all the rotten things hadn’t happened between them? What if they’d met at that fancy dinner before their debate, before she became a laughingstock. Before Scarlet got her revenge and he crashed the book signing? What if none of that had ever happened?

"Dinner then," he persisted.

Dinner? That was worse than lunch. It was too . . . intimate.

Being intimate with Parker Black. Her heart gave a little skip, and her nerve endings started dancing like a racehorse ready to run. Her body was all in. But then her body also considered it a good idea to overdose on Oreos.

"Don't you think you owe me?" His voice was softer, teasing. It goosed up her heart rate.

"Owe you?"

"You did some internet damage, too," he said. "You've got half the women in the country thinking I'm dating my mother."

"That was my sister. She did it on my behalf, for revenge." He frowned and Alice hurried on. "She didn't know Genevive was your mother. None of us knew."

"These days I'm her dirty little secret."

That was understandable. "Why do you hate women so much?" Alice blurted.

"Have dinner with me and I'll tell you. And by the way, I don't hate all women. Just the ones who are out to take down men."

"Nobody here is out to take down men," she said.

"No, here you just want to whip us into shape."

"Do you need whipping?" she asked. Okay, that hadn't come out right. She could feel her cheeks sizzling.

He gave her half a laugh. "I don't know. Maybe."

"Well, then I hope you find someone willing to take on the challenge."

It was the perfect parting shot, and for a second, she felt as if she'd channeled one of her fictional heroines. But that was all the channeling she was capable of. She turned to scurry to the back room.

"Alice, just because I think differently than you do it doesn't make me a bad person," he called after her.

She looked over her shoulder. "No, it doesn't. But the way you act does."

She almost added, "Thanks for stopping by," then caught herself. She wasn't thankful he'd stopped by, and she didn't believe his apology was sincere.

Her words left him momentarily speechless. There was a Parker Black phenomenon. She took advantage of it and speed walked to the safety of the back room.

"Did you accept his apology?" her mother wanted to know when Alice plopped down at their little catch-all table, which was currently piled high with ARCs and author swag. She and Bettina had started on their sandwiches, managing to squeeze them in at the edge of the table along with cups of coffee.

"He didn't mean it."

"Of course, he didn't," Bettina said. "I hope you're going to ban that creep from the store."

"I doubt he'll be back," Nola said. "He's done what he needed to and now we're checked off the list."

"Needed to do?" prompted Bettina.

Nola waved away her question. "Never mind." She picked up an ARC from one of their favorite local authors. "Which one of you would like to read this one?"

And that ended the conversation about Parker Black. Which was fine with Alice.

Parker fumed his way out of the bookstore. Once more a woman had put him in his place. Only this time he had it coming.

He'd seen the tears in Alice's eyes at the mention of the

meme. She hadn't deserved what had happened to her. No wonder she didn't want to go anywhere near Parker. He was poison.

But Alice's camp had done a good job of smearing him, too. And really, what did he have to feel bad about? He'd won a debate. He'd done a man-on-the-street interview, all part of the job.

He'd made Alice Willoughby cry. What had he turned into?

He texted his uncle, letting him know the appropriate apologies had been made. Unk could go chase after Alice's mom with Parker's blessing. At least someone would be happy.

He went home, watched ESPN for an hour and finished up on his show prep for the following morning. Then he went to bed, closed the door on all thoughts of Alice Willoughby.

But she returned to haunt his dreams. It would have been nice if she'd been all dressed up in that hot red dress, but she wore a black judge's robe and was seated high above him on the bench with a gavel in her hand. The end was heart-shaped.

"You're a jerk," she informed him.

"I am not," he insisted. "I'm a wounded hero. Please, show leniency."

He woke up. Wounded hero? What was he now, a character in a book? He shook off the dream, punched his pillow and went back to sleep.

And there she was again. This time in nurse's scrubs. And there he was, in a hospital bed.

"You're dying inside. You need CPR," she informed him.

She was going to kiss him. Yes! He held out his arms to welcome her as she approached the bed.

But instead of letting him embrace her, she began pushing on his chest and counting.

He woke up with a start and sat up. Aaaack!

Okay, that was it. He was not going back to bed.

It was almost time to get ready for work anyway. Work would be a welcome distraction, and he would not allow thoughts of Alice Willoughby to follow him into the sound booth.

He was glad to be in the studio, his home turf. It was going to be a good day. Fresh start, new game, and he was feeling good . . . until he and Jay finished going over show notes and Jay sprang his newest brainchild on Parker. *Oh, no. No, no, no.*

CHAPTER 18

PARKER BLINKED AS he stared at the computer screen featuring the poll Jay had created.

Should Men Boycott Cupid? Who's With Me?

"Whoa, what's this?" he demanded, staring at the heading.

"It's a done deal, that's what it is," said Jay. "Look at how many men have already taken it."

"Nice of you to run this by me," Parker said with a frown. "We're supposed to be a team. How come this is looking more like the Barker show than the Parker show?"

"Because Parker needs help," Jay said, returning his frown.

"I told you I want to get back to doing strictly sports from now on."

"This isn't the show. It's a publicity for the show."

"Uh-uh. Not doing it. No way."

"You already got the ball rolling with the man-on-the-street interviews. You can't stop it."

"Oh, yes, I can," Parker insisted.

"Ratings," said Jay.

Ratings or not, the idea of it made Parker feel like a weasel. "Not doing it. Take it down."

"You need to think about this," Jay said.

"I have," said Parker, and headed for the sound booth.

He kept the conversation strictly to sports during his show and ditched anyone Jay tried to get his screener to sneak in who wanted to gripe about women.

Except the last caller, who supposedly wanted to talk about team spirit. Mark from Seattle. It sounded like the same Mark who had cornered Parker outside the bookstore. No, couldn't be. There had to be hundreds of Marks in Seattle.

"Mark, does that mean you're joining us for spring training with the Mariners?" Parker asked after bringing him on.

"I am. I'm taking the money out of savings, and I don't care what the wife says. I'm coming to your Saturday night bash, too. And I'm volunteering to head up the Cupid Strike for Valentine's Day."

A big chunk of something leaden formed in Parker's chest. It was the same rabid fan from the bookstore. Husband of the dreaded Scarlet, brother-in-law to Alice. Trouble in the making.

"Uh, dude. That's just a poll on the website."

"Not anymore. It's happening. We got a page on Facebook. Cupid Strike with—"

Not Parker Black. No way. Parker hit the *shut him up* button. "Guys, boycotting V-Day is not a good game plan."

Now here was Jay, butting in. "Sure it is. Sometimes you have to go on the offensive."

Parker always had a comeback for remarks like Jay's. Why couldn't he find one now?

"Think of all the money you'll save," Jay continued.

"But you gotta pay to play," Parker said, his brain finally coming to life. That was all he had time for. The bumper music was starting. "Looks like our time is up. See you all tomorrow. Meanwhile, keep your head in the game."

"You're lucky I don't knock yours off," he said to Jay as soon as they were off the air. "You're kicking the wrong hornets' nest and we're both going to get stung."

"I'm trying to save our jobs," Jay protested.

"The best way to save them is to stay out of the pink zone."

"It's all good. We're just having a little fun on the side and boosting ratings."

"It's a bad idea and I'm not having fun," Parker snarled.

"Well, lighten up."

Jay's phone dinged with a text. He read it and frowned. "Harlan's office."

Parker pointed a finger at him. "Now you've done it. You've gone too far."

Sure enough. Harlan wasn't happy. "Enough is enough. You two should have run this boycott idea past me before you made it public."

It was the perfect moment for Parker to say that he'd had nothing to do with this latest harebrained scheme, but, mad as he was at Jay, he couldn't throw him under the bus. How many times did this make that he'd pulled his producer off Danger Street?

He didn't have a chance to get in a word anyway. "Poking fun at books, letting men whine about their women, offering fake advice, that was okay, but this kind of thing is bound to make some of our sponsors nervous," Harlan continued. "In case you forgot, yours isn't the only talk show on this station, and we don't just sell advertising to Dick's Sporting Goods."

"But Parker's your morning show, and we bring in the listeners," Jay argued. "Well, lately. And this is what's been bringing them in."

"I'm fine going back to sports," Parker said firmly. "We've

got the Super Bowl on Sunday. Plenty to talk about. I'll get my uncle in again."

"Good idea," Harlan approved.

"It's not gonna have the same spark," Jay argued.

"The Super Bowl? Are you kidding me?" Parker said, irritated.

"Spark is one thing, losing sponsors is another. And, Parker, you've skated close to the edge a couple of times. At the rate you're going you're going to cross the line and say something that will get us all in trouble."

"Hey, I haven't insulted women's intelligence, just their taste in books," Parker said, defending himself. "And there's nothing wrong with telling guys to grow a pair. But don't worry. I'm not on board with a strike. I know it's a bad idea."

"Parker is every man's hero right now. We need to ride that wave," Jay argued.

"And drown," Parker said. "Not doing it, and you should be glad I'm not, Harlan."

"Then what are we gonna do for Valentine's Day?" Jay protested.

"You two think of something," Harlan said. "I've got a call to make."

"Probably to his wife to tell her he was a good boy and told us to take down the poll," Jay grumbled once they were out of the office.

"That's fine by me."

"Now that you've messed up my plans, what are we gonna do for a show on V-Day?"

"Play some classic Parker. I'm taking PTO that day," Parker said.

There. That would take care of that.

Except it didn't. The poll didn't come down because, according to Jay, Harlan never specifically ordered them to take it down, and the Facebook page blew up. Mark Warner, Parker's Number One Fan, had the ball and was running with it. The Cupid strike was on.

"This is grounds for divorce," Scarlet said when she came over to Nola's to have dinner with her mom and sister. She turned her phone so they could see.

There it was, the Cupid's Day Strike with Parker Black Facebook Group. There was a collage of hearts, flowers and boxes of candy, all inside red warning circles. And there was a picture of Parker, looking masculine and sophisticated. The man every other man wanted to be. At least her husband.

"That man," Scarlet continued. "I still can't believe he's Genevive Eden's son. No wonder she's kept their relationship hidden."

"Let's not go there," Nola said. They'd already discussed Parker Black's relationship with his mother, and the role Scarlet had played in the bookstore's embarrassment, and it hadn't been a pleasant discussion.

"This is a new low even for him," Alice said.

"And now he's got Mark running the Facebook page." Scarlet refilled her glass from one of the bottles of sparkling cider she'd brought.

"Mark!" echoed Nola.

"He and some guy named Jay are the page administrators."

"Well, no one's paying Mark, you can be sure of it," said Nola.

"Can they do that on Facebook?" Alice wondered.

"Yes. Trust me, I checked," Scarlet said. "As long as there's no hate speech."

"It looks hateful to me," said Nola.

"The wording is careful. 'Tell Cupid what you think. Pass

on the flowers and candy this year. Save on your restaurant bills. Take PTO. Join the picket line and join the fun. DM for the location. Beer at Otter on the Rocks after.' And look, he added smiley faces."

"Ugh," said Nola, and reached for her glass.

"We should boycott Otter on the Rocks," Scarlet said.

"No, we don't want to punish any business," Nola told her firmly, and frowned at her. "Besides, they probably aren't sponsoring it."

"This is sick and wrong," Scarlet grumbled.

"This is partly on you, Scarlet. Just like you did with Parker, you escalated the problem between you and Mark and now you've created a monster."

Her mother's words stung. But she deserved them. "I should never have posted that picture and I'm sorry," she said, her voice teary. "I didn't stop to think about how it would affect the store. But Mark is another matter entirely," she couldn't help adding.

"He's hurt and he's being petty and immature," Nola said. "Both of you are."

"Gee, thanks, Mom." Scarlet turned to Alice. "Do you think I'm being petty?"

"Well, maybe he shouldn't have spent all that money," Alice said.

"There have been shouldn't-haves on both sides of the coin," said Nola, stepping in. "For heaven's sake, Scarlet, marriage requires teamwork. When was the last time you two talked about working as a team?"

"All the time," Scarlet insisted. "Until he started listening to that piece of pond scum on the radio."

Mark hadn't always been on board with all her ideas, but thanks to her they had a house.

What if they split? What would happen to the house? She couldn't afford to keep it on her salary alone. And she'd wanted to start thinking about having a baby. Bad idea. She was already married to a baby. A big, stupid one.

"Anyway, I don't know if I want to be a team with him anymore. He's obviously not a team player." Angry as she was, it hurt to say those words. Where had the man she'd fallen in love with gone?

"I don't think you've had the proper definition of teamwork in marriage," Nola said.

"He hasn't been very nice," Alice said. At least someone understood.

"Neither has your sister. Cutting up the credit cards? Changing the locks on the door?" Their mother looked disgusted. "I tried to keep quiet at first."

She had? That was news to Scarlet.

"But you need to hear this, Scarlet. You've been controlling and so you shouldn't be surprised that Mark reacted the way he did. Yes, he behaved like a little boy, but your behavior hasn't been any better, especially lately. You've been an emotional bully. So why should you be surprised that he's trying to find some way to reassert himself?"

Scarlet had endured her share of motherly lectures growing up, but never as an adult. So far Mom had gotten on her twice, and the year had barely begun.

"What am I supposed to do, go grovel?" she demanded, tears filling her eyes. Mark was the one blowing up their marriage, not her.

"Just stop and think. Ask yourself where you might have gone wrong instead of continually pointing the finger at Mark. You two fell hard and fast and you didn't take the time you needed to really know each other and to make sure you were on the same page when it came to building a life together. It would be good to take the time now."

"While he's on strike," scoffed Scarlet.

"Where there's a strike there's a negotiation. Turn the heat down on your temper and start thinking like a negotiator," Nola advised.

Scarlet frowned at her empty dessert plate.

"And ask yourself, do you want to be right or do you want to be happy?"

"Why can't I be both?" Scarlet argued.

"Because no one is always right. Even you. Even me," Nola added, her voice gentling. "I want to see you happy."

"So do I," said Alice. "I like Mark."

"You don't have to be married to him," Scarlet muttered.

"Neither do you," said Nola. "I guess you're going to have to ask yourself how much you love the man and how much that love is worth fighting for."

"You still love him," Alice insisted. Alice read too many of the books she sold.

Come to think of it, maybe so did Scarlet. But there were lessons to be learned in those books. Did she love Mark enough to try and figure out how to negotiate a better marriage and a life together? She wasn't sure.

One thing she was sure about. This strike was stupid. "Never mind Mark and me. What are we going to do about the strike?"

"What can we do?" Alice asked.

"We can take the high road. Let's make our next podcast about how to show our men we love them," Nola suggested. "Right before Valentine's Day. The timing will be perfect."

"Meanwhile, they'll be busy thinking how they can ruin the day," Scarlet muttered.

"I'm willing to bet that the ones out there on strike will be either single or separated. No married man in his right mind will want to get involved in this," Nola predicted. "And quit worrying about the strike, Scarlet. You have your hands full worrying about yourself."

"It's gonna be epic," Mark predicted as the guys lounged around in his friend Steve's man cave, loading up on more chips and dip during Super Bowl halftime.

It was just the men, no twelfth women present, and the disappointing eats reflected that. He and Scarlet had hosted a Super Bowl party the year before. She'd made a ton of food, everything from those little sausages in barbecue sauce to seven-layer dip. It had been fun.

He veered away from the memory.

"I think you're nuts," Steve said as he dumped more chips on his paper plate.

"In other words, Krystal won't let him," teased James, another of their pals.

"Hey, I don't want to end up with the locks on the house changed," Steve said.

Mark scowled. "You're whipped."

"But I'm still getting some," retorted Steve.

"Well, I'm joining," said Nate, and grabbed another beer from the mini fridge.

"You can afford to join. You don't have anyone," Steve said.

Nate hadn't had anyone for a couple of years. He'd gained some pounds and lost some hair and was currently looking for someone online using a ten-year-old photo of himself. So far, none of his meetups had progressed beyond coffee.

"Don't get me wrong. I think it's a great idea," said James. "I'll still be paying for Valentine's Day come Mother's Day."

"That's my point," said Mark. "We shouldn't have to bribe our women to love us. They should love us for who we are."

"I guess you're not enough," teased Steve.

"Real funny," Mark said sourly.

Except it wasn't. He was getting tired of hanging out in his folks' basement, even though his mom was making his favorite food for dinner and baking him molasses cookies.

His dad had told him he needed to talk with Scarlet and make things right. "Sometimes, a man has to admit when he's wrong," Dad had said when Mark first showed up. Then he'd said, "You're out of your mind, son," when Mark announced that he was helping organize Parker Black's strike. "And in front of her sister's bookstore? Bad location," he'd added with a shake of his head. "Go, make things right with Scarlet. Get your life back."

Dad just wanted to be able to set the Ping-Pong table up again, so he was biased.

"We got a lot of guys on board with this. We're up to a hundred members on the Facebook page," he said.

"A hundred losers," said Steve.

"This is gonna make the news," Mark predicted.

"Then you'll be a hundred famous losers," Steve jabbed.

"It's about time somebody took a stand," said Nate.

Steve didn't agree. "I know you're trying to make a point to Scarlet but this ain't the hill to die on."

Steve was wrong. This strike was going to be great.

And Scarlet was getting nothing for Valentine's Day.

His dad's words floated back into Mark's mind. *Sometimes a man has to admit when he's wrong.*

Yeah, but Mark wasn't wrong.

CHAPTER 19

NOLA AND ALICE did their pre–Valentine's Day podcast, starting with reviews on the Valentine-themed books they had in the store. That fell to Alice, and she had three novels to review. "That one was my favorite," she said after she'd talked about the last novel. "I love a good enemies-to-lovers story."

A vision of Parker Black popped into her mind. If ever a man qualified as an enemy, it was him. But there would be no moving from enemies to lovers for them. Even if he ever changed his wicked ways—which he wouldn't—he still wouldn't pair up with her. He'd pick someone who looked like a supermodel. After all, like called to like.

They moved on to how readers could celebrate love with the men in their lives.

"Very handy that Valentine's Day is falling on a Saturday this year, which gives you lots of time to celebrate," said Nola. "So, Alice, what suggestions do we have for our readers?"

Alice picked up the list they'd complied. "This is a fun one. How about a Valentine treasure hunt? Pick several stores for your man to visit and pre-purchase a little gift for him at each. Those can be anything from socks to his favorite candy. Golf balls from the pro shop, Ping-Pong balls or tennis balls from the sporting goods store. Bring the clerks in on it and have them save your presents for the next day. Then write out some clues and number them. You can go with him and make it feel like a car rally."

"Then, after he's found all his treasures, take him to a nice restaurant," put in Nola. "But don't stay for dessert. You will be dessert."

"And make sure you have something fancy laid out on the bed, so he knows what's coming," said Alice. "You can also do a variation of this and send him on a hunt to find you that will end up at the restaurant where you've made reservations and are there waiting."

"If your Valentine isn't into games, you can still make the day fun for him by texting him messages," Nola said.

"You mean sexting?" Alice asked. As if she'd ever sexted anyone in her entire life.

"I'd suggest PG rated flirting. Make sure no one else sees his phone," Nola cautioned.

"Those candy bouquets are fun, too," Alice said, moving down their list. "Get one delivered to his office."

"Or have it waiting when he walks in the door," Nola added. "That way he won't have to share it with the other men, who will all be jealous."

The comments were coming in.

Love this! . . . You two are so clever . . . Alice, are you going to be doing any of these?

As if Alice had a man in her life. She'd never said one way or another, but some of their fans simply assumed she did. All those recommendations. She felt like a fraud.

"I'm going to be pulling out a romantic movie," she said, going for an indirect answer. "There are so many good ones, like *To All the Boys I've Loved Before*. Then there are the classics like *Pride & Prejudice*. And *Sabrina*. I love the remake. Although all of those movies are probably best to watch with your friends on Galentine's Day."

A new comment came in. From Scarlet. Right there for everyone to see.

There's going to be a strike on Valentine's Day. Men are going to refuse to buy their women anything and they'll be picketing right in front of your bookstore.

Alice read the comment. Blinked. Read it again. In front of the store? She looked to her mother. *What should we do?*

"Well, now, this is news to us," Nola said.

Scarlet messaged.

It was just announced on Facebook. Come tell Cupid he's out of business. Beer o'clock after. Everyone make sure your man isn't going to be there. If he is he doesn't deserve anything for V-Day.

Lina was watching and was quick to comment.

If your man isn't picketing, be sure to reward him real well.

"I'm sure all of your men know better, book girlies," said Nola.

A reader named Marina posted a comment.

I'm worried my boyfriend is going to strike. What should I do?

Both Alice and Nola sat in silence for a moment. How to answer that?

Nola was the first to speak. "You celebrate love and happiness anyway. You know what the song says, you can buy your own flowers."

It was the perfect answer. Maybe Alice would buy herself some flowers.

"Oh, and don't forget February 15, chocolate at fifty percent off day. If your man doesn't come through with a box of candy, plan to pick up a bargain," Nola said.

Yes, bargain chocolate. Even if a woman didn't have true love, she could at least have chocolate.

"And now, we are out of time," said Nola. "We hope you'll all have a wonderful Valentine's Day. And if you're looking for fun reads, come on by the store. Alice will help you find the perfect book."

Yes, Alice was good at that. If only she knew how to find the perfect man.

Scarlet called their mother as soon as Nola and Alice signed off. Nola sat listening patiently, then said, "And what do you expect me to do?"

Alice couldn't hear, but she didn't have to in order to know her sister was on a rant.

"I told you that you needed to fix things with Mark. You still do. The strike is obviously going to happen no matter what, but you can still find a way to induce him to not participate. And no, I don't have any suggestions. I wish I did. Just take some time to think about what you want the rest of your life to look like, darling. Maybe you and your sister can brainstorm," Nola added.

Right. Alice was such an expert on love. "I don't know what she should do."

Nola listened some more, then finally said, "You know I

want the best for you. I love you." And that ended the conversation. She turned to Alice. "I want the best for both of you. Sometimes I wish I had a magic lamp."

"Maybe you do. You made my dreams come true," Alice said.

"Yes, you have an ideal job. I just wish you had an ideal life," her mother said.

"I do," Alice insisted. "I'm perfectly happy."

"Well, happy anyway, but I think you're still a ways from perfect."

"What are we going to do about the strike?" Alice asked, switching to the most pressing matter.

"Nothing. There's nothing we can do."

"But right in front of the store. Saturdays are busy days for us," Alice said.

"We'll be fine," said Nola. "Don't worry."

"I've got good news," said David Fox, Parker's literary agent. "We've got a bidding war going on your book."

Parker's writing debut, the playbook to help men stand up for themselves and stop getting manipulated by women. He still believed that message. He was living proof that women weren't the only ones who suffered in a relationship, that sometimes the shoe landed on the other foot. He should have been excited, Super Bowl win excited. Instead, he was ambivalent. No one ever won a game being ambivalent.

Except this wasn't a game. It was a mess, and he was the one who made it. He wished he'd never issued that challenge on his show, wished he'd never done that debate. Wished he'd never met Alice Willoughby.

No, that wasn't accurate. He wished he'd never met Alice Willoughby under the circumstances they'd met. Too late now.

The final thought put him in a sour mood for the rest of the day.

Alice couldn't shake her uneasy feeling come Valentine's Day. "I feel like someone put a target on us," she said as she and her mother and Bettina watched while men began to gather in front of their store like buzzards.

She took in the protests on the picket signs. *Cupid is a scam . . . She can pay this year . . . Romance Kills Wallets.* "We're cooked."

"Those fools are the ones who're cooked. They aren't going to be getting any love tonight," Bettina predicted.

"I suspect they already weren't," said Nola. "We are looking at a collection of angry divorced men and single men who can't keep a girlfriend. And the sad thing is, it's not that hard to keep a woman if you're good to her."

Alice caught sight of the hefty man with the blond hair wearing jeans and an old letterman jacket. *No more pink handcuffs*, read his sign. Oh, no.

She touched her mother's arm and pointed.

"Oh, Mark," Nola said, her voice filled with disappointment.

Et tu, Mark? If Scarlet saw this, it was all over for him and Rest in Peace would be stamped on the divorce papers.

"Pretty clever sign. Is he smart enough to do that on his own?" Bettina asked.

"Yes," said Nola. "He hasn't been smart about anything else though. But then neither has Scarlet."

Two more men had joined the picket line. Alice recognized one as Parker's producer. She looked up and down the street. Where was Parker, the evil mastermind? There was no sign of him.

The men were starting to march along the sidewalk and chant. It came through the plate glass window, muffled.

Alice cracked the door to hear better and the wave of sound came at her. "We're cool and chicks don't rule." It was mixed with laughter. This was all a big joke to these men. She shut the door in disgust.

"Don't they understand what this is going to do to businesses in the city who depend on this day to make money? I mean, these men all must have jobs," Alice said.

"But they're probably not business owners. In fact, probably some of them are union men. They're familiar with the concept of a strike," Nola said.

"Strikes are for higher wages, better working conditions. This isn't accomplishing anything," Alice said in disgust.

"Other than making a statement to their women," said Bettina.

"Ex-women," Nola corrected her as more buzzards arrived.

"Don't they need a permit?" Alice asked.

"As long as they're not obstructing traffic, I don't think they do," said Nola.

"Well, they're obstructing traffic to the stores on our block," Bettina said, scowling.

Oh, no, here came the crew from KOMO TV. This would be on the evening news.

Parker was in hiding. He'd meant what he said to Jay. No way was he going to join the strike. He let Jay's call go to voice mail.

One minute later, Jay called again. And again, Parker ignored it.

On the fourth call he picked up and demanded, "What?"

"You need to get down here ASAP," Jay said. "Olivia Carson from KOMO just showed up."

"Well, if she's wanting to talk to me, she's out of luck 'cause I'm home sick."

"You are not."

"Yeah? Prove it."

'You're gonna be even sicker come Monday if you don't show up, you big chicken. These guys are all expecting to see their hero and they're gonna be out for blood if you let them down."

"Are you forgetting what Harlan said?" Parker demanded. "We're supposed to be cooling it. You shouldn't even be there."

"Hey, I didn't organize it."

"You're condoning it. You're there."

"Well, somebody has to be. Shit, here she comes," Jay muttered.

"Don't talk to her. Get out of there before you end up with your face on the evening news," Parker said, and pushed End.

Then he went to his bathroom medicine cabinet to get aspirin. He tried not to look at the man in the mirror as he opened it, the man who was responsible for taking business from Alice Willoughby's store, the hypocrite who'd come in only a few days earlier to apologize for being a jerk.

Except what was happening hadn't been his idea. That wouldn't stop her and her posse of romantics from blaming him though.

Look on the bright side, he told himself. It would help stir up the bidding frenzy on his book.

Maybe he should go over there.

Put his head in the noose? Bad idea. Oh, yeah. Great idea. Except thanks to his producer's shenanigans, it already was. Darn that Jay.

The numbers had swelled and now one of the local TV stations was out front interviewing the men. And here was

Scarlet, calling their mother to see if her husband was there among the malcontents.

"Yes, he is," said Nola. "And don't come down here, guns blazing. I don't need you escalating things and getting on the news in the process. We're working on a strategy now. Stay tuned."

"We are?" Alice said when she'd ended the call.

A sly smile took over Nola's face. "Yes, we are. Let's rally the troops."

"And tell them what? Cross the picket line?" Bettina asked.

"In a way. Here's what we post," Nola said, and shared her plan.

Alice had to laugh. Her mother's two-pronged strategy was brilliant.

"Bettina, call our book club members and get them going. And I'm going to call Scarlet back. She needs to do this, too."

Heaping burning coals of kindness on the heads of the guilty. Oh, yes.

Nola slipped out the door to have a little chat with the news reporter, suggesting she return in an hour and see what was happening with the strike.

"I hope this works," Alice said. And she hoped Parker Black the hypocrite would be watching the news later.

The store phone rang. Alice picked it up and barely had time to speak before Brittany lit into her. "Your stupid debate with that Parker Black is the cause of this," she accused. "This is my busiest day, and do you know how many orders I've had for floral arrangements? A whole six. I'm in here twiddling my thumbs while all those men are outside partying and picketing."

"I'm sorry," Alice said. "Don't blame me though. Blame Parker Black. And we're working on damage control right now, so hang in there."

"You owe me chocolate," Brittany snapped, and ended the call.

No, Parker Black owed her chocolate.

Alice went back to work, posting everywhere while Bettina spread the word among their customers.

> Remember the song. If your man is on strike today buy your own flowers. Order flowers from Flowers L'Amour and then come on over to HEA Books and receive a free surprise.

They had a lot of advanced reader copies kicking around. This would be a great way to find homes for them.

But, "What if we run out?" Bettina asked.

"Then we'll give away some of the books that haven't been moving," said Nola.

"That could get costly," Alice protested.

"Maybe, but we'll consider it part of our advertising budget," Nola said. "It will bring people into the store, and you know how often people come in for one thing and then buy something else."

"Just like when I go to the grocery store," said Bettina.

"Good for business plus it's a donation to a good cause," Nola added.

"Let's hope it works," said Alice, and got busy collecting books to give away.

The strike was going great. Guys had brought thermoses of coffee and were smoking cigars and talking sports and cars. A few were still chanting, but most were just hanging out. It was a party. And Mark had been the main man behind it and had been more than happy to let the reporter from the news station know. He was feeling darned good about himself.

Until a pretty face connected to a great body showed up wearing a short jacket and black leggings that clung to her legs and that great butt. She wore the red lipstick that drove him wild and she was carrying some kind of plastic container. She wasn't glaring at him. In fact, she was smiling.

But it was kind of an evil smile. What was Scarlet up to?

He caught sight of another woman walking a few feet behind her carrying a big old platter of cookies. Cookies? What was going on here?

Scarlet walked right up to him and opened the container to reveal a batch of her chocolate-chip-oatmeal-everything cookies. Freshly baked. The aroma drifted out and kissed his nose. Cookies? Were they poisoned?

"What are you doing here?" he asked.

She shrugged. "Giving Cupid a hand. Don't worry, they're not poisoned," she added. His wife was a mind reader.

"Okay, what's the catch? Why are you being nice all of a sudden?"

"Because somebody has to be," she said with a little shrug. "Come on, have one. You need your strength."

"If you think this means I'm gonna forget you locked me out and buy you something for Valentine's Day you're wrong," he said, keeping his voice gruff.

"I was mad." She jiggled the container, prompting him. "Come on, you know you can't resist my cookies."

Well, he was hungry. He took a cookie and bit into it. Oh, man, it was good. Nobody baked cookies like Scarlet.

"How are things over at your parents'?" she asked.

Pride insisted he lie. "They're good."

"Yeah, your mom is a good cook." Scarlet dipped her gloved hand into the container and took out a cookie. "I do love these cookies," she said and took a bite.

There was a small dab of chocolate at the corner of her mouth. He wanted to lick it off. Instead, he looked away.

And saw another couple of women had arrived. Now three women were spread out among the guys, all offering them cookies.

"What is this?" he demanded.

She lost the smile, which in a way was a good thing because it was making him nervous. "It's about love, Mark. And being nice to each other. Happy Valentine's Day," she said, and moved off toward another guy.

"Hey wait! Where are you going with those?" he demanded.

"Just sharing the love," she said, and sidled up to a tall guy with a long beard.

The dude had to be fifty, and Mark could tell he didn't work out. Scarlet did Pilates and Zumba. She wasn't into men who were out of shape. Except look how she was smiling up at him. It was a nicer smile than she'd had for Mark. He said something and she laughed and held out the container of cookies. He bit into one and gave it a thumbs-up. She patted his arm, said something. He nodded, shrugged, shouldered his sign and sauntered off. She turned, gave Mark a little wave and moved on to another guy. This one was younger, and he was looking at Scarlet like *she* was a cookie. He helped himself to one and she cocked her head, took off her knitted cap and shook out that long, red hair. She was flirting with the guy. Flirting! And she didn't move on after he'd eaten his cookie. She stayed there, talking with him.

A new emotion swelled in Mark's chest, and it wasn't self-pity or anger. Who was that dude and why was he talking with Mark's wife? Mark strode over to where they stood and got there just in time to hear the guy say, "Wish my girlfriend was as nice as you."

"Nice as my *wife*?" Mark demanded, stepping between them.

"We're not together right now," said Scarlet. "Have another cookie."

"Don't mind if I do," said the guy. He reached around Mark, took one and gloated.

"Would you like another one, Mark?" she asked politely, tipping the container toward him. "Since you're here. Oh, look, here comes Lina. I bet she made her marranitos."

Mark grabbed a cookie and frowned at Scarlet.

"If my woman was like this I wouldn't be out here," the guy said.

"Well, we all make mistakes," Scarlet said lightly. "Maybe you being here is one," she continued. "There's a flower shop right over there. It's not too late to make the day great."

He nodded.

"Don't cave," Mark urged him.

"Yes, sex is overrated, isn't it?" Scarlet said.

That did it. "Thanks for the cookie," the guy said and started walking away.

"You're trying to ruin my strike," Mark accused.

"Am I? Maybe I'm just trying to show you how wrong it is. How wrong we've been. Want one more cookie? I need to get them gone so I can go buy flowers."

"You're buying flowers for yourself."

"Why not? If we buy flowers, we also get a free book from HEA. Cookies anyone?" she called to the two men nearest them.

"Cookies? Yeah," said one of them.

"Gotta go," Scarlet said, and skipped away to flirt some more.

Real cute. Real funny. Mark watched the deserter walk to the flower shop. Two women were already walking in ahead of him. The strike wasn't bothering them. He looked around to where his fellow strikers stood, talking with women. More women had shown up, all bringing treats. One woman was handing out fudge. This was not going according to plan.

And, oh, great. Here came the reporter from the KOMO News again. Mark scuttled away to the far end of what was left of the picket line. This was turning out to be a very bad idea.

Lina and Georgia walked into the store, each carrying a small vase of red roses. "The troops are scattering," Lina announced.

Nola smiled. "Mission accomplished. We've got a whole pile of books. Come pick one."

"That is such a generous offer. Are you sure you don't want us to pay you?" Georgia offered.

"No. Consider this our Valentine gift to you," Nola said.

A gift to the readers and it made the store look good. Plus, some of those writers whose books and advanced reader copies were being given away would maybe find new readers. Alice's mother was brilliant.

Alice looked out the window and saw the number of strikers was dwindling. The few remaining were visiting with HEA Books customers and eating cookies. Kara Bane was talking to a skinny nerdish man in his thirties. It was easy to tell from her expression that she wasn't exactly heaping words of kindness on him. If he wasn't careful, she'd probably roundhouse him. The poor man nodded and fled. Cookies were probably a better idea.

There was no longer any sign of Mark in the crowd, but here came Scarlet. "That was fun," she announced, and held up her empty container.

"Did Mark leave?"

"In a huff," Scarlet said, and giggled.

"Did you let him have it?" Bettina wanted to know.

"Yes, but subtly. You'd have been proud of me, Mom," she said to Nola.

"I'm always proud of you," Nola said. It was a motherly lie. Scarlet had spent too many years making their mother nuts to believe it, but Alice saw that it brought out her smile anyway.

The little bell over the door jingled and in walked Olivia Carson, followed by her cameraman. "What have you women managed? The men are scattering like cockroaches."

"Good analogy," cracked Bettina.

"Would you like to explain what just happened?" Olivia asked.

"We were showing a little love," Nola said. "Sometimes you need to set an example."

"You bribed them to stop with cookies," said Olivia.

"We offered an incentive."

Olivia laughed. "Let's get this recorded for the evening news." She signaled to her cameraman to start filming. "We are still at the scene of what started out as a Valentine's Day strike by a large group of Seattle men. But the strike has lost its steam. A lot of the men are headed for the flower shop, and it looks like the reason why can be found here in HEA Books, West Seattle's romance bookstore. I'm here with Nola Willoughby, the owner."

"One of the owners," Nola corrected her. "My daughter Alice is my partner."

"Your partner in crime?" quipped Olivia, and Alice backed around a bookshelf to make sure she didn't get pulled on camera.

"No crimes here. Just spreading the love," Nola said.

"So, tell us what happened?" Olivia prompted.

Alice watched with pride as her mother cleverly shared their strategy—all with grace and good humor. No accusations, no shade.

Although those men should have all felt guilty. Alice hoped that Parker Black would feel guilty, too, when he watched the news later.

I didn't do it, Parker texted his irritated uncle after the story of the Valentine strike aired on the evening news. This happened without me and you can tell that to Nola Willoughby.

"I didn't do it," he said when his mother called, wondering what on earth he'd been thinking. "This was Jay's bright idea, and then one of my listeners took the ball and ran with it."

"Right over the cliff, it would appear," said his mother. "What are you going to do now?"

"Move to an island in the Caribbean."

"Be sure to take a good book to read," she teased.

"Funny, Mom."

"Sorry," she said. But she wasn't.

"Have I mentioned that I'm thinking about becoming a monk?"

"Somehow, I don't see that," she said. "Look, I know you've been . . . upset about what's happened with your last two relationships," she began.

"I've been upset, as you put it, about what's been going on around me, by what I've seen on social media. You know that. I'm not the only one this stuff is happening to."

"I know, and I know you felt the need to write that book. It's your career and your life. You have to make these decisions for yourself." Translation: *I'm thinking of disowning you.*

"I'm glad you see it that way," he said. "I'm just trying to bring about change, balance the scales."

"But is this the way to do that? I wish you'd keep in mind that not all women are manipulative, any more than all men are selfish and abusers. I know you'd love to sell your book."

He was on the verge of doing just that.

"And the money will be tempting," she added before he could share an update.

"It's not just the money," he insisted. Well, okay, it was partly the money. It would be a nice chunk of change for his Roth IRA. And yes, he'd more than once envisioned sending a copy to Luna with the inscription, *Thanks for the inspiration.*

"But remember, once something is in print you can't call it back. What do you want to be known for, my son? What do you want following you down the road?"

"It's just a book, Mom," he said as much to himself as her.

"It's never just a book," his mother said. "Every author has a message. I want you to be sure this is the message you want to be known for."

Maybe it would be best not to share about what was happening with the book. The timing wasn't right. "This already is what I'm known for."

"All right. If that's what you want," she said, and she didn't sound all that happy about it.

A vision of Alice Willoughby holding the book and frowning swam into view. He pushed it away. Warrior princess Alice Willoughby with her big eyes and freckles needed to stay out of his thoughts.

"It is what it is," he said. And that was how it had to be.

CHAPTER 20

PARKER AND JAY were back in Harlan's office again. Two bad kids once more off to see the principal.

"What is wrong with you guys?" Harlan demanded, his face red with anger. "Didn't we just discuss laying off on the woman bullying?" He whacked his desktop with his pencil. "Now you're in the news again. With the fizzled strike you look like a fool, Parker, and the station looks foolish as well. Again. You'd better pray we don't lose accounts over this."

"I wasn't even there," Parker protested.

It was almost true. He had been there, just long enough to see the whole thing crumbling, then he'd scrammed. He'd been right to not want anything to do with it.

"We can't help it if some other guy ran with the strike idea," Jay added, conveniently neglecting to share that he had been involved.

"One of Parker's fans, right?" Harlan argued.

"I'm not responsible for what my fans do," Parker said.

"They did it in your name, and now you're responsible for fixing this. What are you going to do?"

Resign. Run away. "How should I know?" Parker replied with a scowl.

"It needs to be interesting, and it needs to be lighthearted, all in good fun," Harlan said. "And it can't be damaging to local businesses. If I thought it would help, I'd make you go around and buy out every florist shop in town."

"Hey, there's an idea," said Jay.

Parker glared at him. "You gonna split the bill with me?"

Jay's mouth slammed shut.

Parker rubbed the back of his neck where the muscles were corded and cramping. Harlan was right. They needed to do something. His show that morning had been a disaster, with men calling in to brag and businesses calling in to demand where he got off trying to ruin them. One flower shop owner had called in, suggesting that Seattle businesses boycott the station so Parker could see how it felt. He hadn't needed two guesses to know what flower shop that was. The one right down the street from the bookstore would have taken a hit.

"Well?" Harlan demanded, beating his pencil on his desk.

Jay looked at Parker as if he could pull a rabbit out of a baseball cap.

He threw up his hands. "I don't know."

"It needs to be something where you pay for your crime, so to speak," Harlan said.

"Me? Why me?" The strike had been Jay's idea. Just like the meme. Maybe it was time for a new producer.

Jay, of course, was on board. "We can make it like Harlan said, something all in good fun."

"Like the strike? Yeah, that was a good idea," Parker sneered.

"How about this? You spend a week working in that romance bookstore and one of the women does your show," suggested Jay. "A trading places gimmick. People love stuff like that."

"Do my show!" That was it. Jay had lost his mind completely.

"Yeah." Jay smiled, warming to the idea. "Teach Parker a lesson."

"I don't need a lesson," Parker snapped.

"Hmm." Harlan's pencil turned less violent as he considered the idea. "That could work."

"Why don't you just shoot me now and be done with it?" Parker grumbled. No one was listening.

"Put one of the bookstore ladies behind the mike and let her learn about sports," Harlan suggested. "The young, cute one. Listeners will love calling in to teach her. And she can dole out love advice instead of you."

"I'll lose listeners." And what about his podcast? Was Alice going to be the new face of that? Parker crossed his arms over his chest and glared at Harlan. "Not doing it."

"You are if you want to keep your job," Harlan informed him.

He'd have liked nothing better than to tell Harlan what to do with his job. Except, he didn't have a book contract yet, and he wasn't ready to run off to the Caribbean and live in a shack, especially with spring training and all the perks that were coming with it about to happen.

Spring training! "We can't do this now. In case you forgot, I've got Mariners spring training to cover. When am I supposed to fit in hanging out in a bookstore?"

"Before you go," said Harlan.

"No time. I'm scheduled to be there next week."

"Spring training goes clear into March, right?" said Harlan.

Here was proof that Harlan was not qualified to be program director. "So, I'm supposed to get there late, behind every other sportscaster in the country? That'll look good," Parker scoffed. Harlan was about as clued in as a rock.

"You already don't look good," Harlan said.

"Arrangements have been made, you know that. I'm supposed to fly out Thursday. I've got opening day interviews, plus we've got a party for the fans."

"Put in your time Monday through Friday and we'll get you out on Friday afternoon," Jay said. "You'll be there in time for the party on Saturday night and be ready to do the show first thing the next week. Alice can take your place Monday through Thursday. Then you two can do a wrap-up Friday morning before you leave."

Alice. Why did it have to be Alice? They'd tortured her enough.

"She won't go along with this," Parker said. "Not after the debate going sour."

"She will because she's going to get a warm welcome here," said Harlan.

"Not from my fans. They'll eat her alive." He'd already humiliated her enough.

"Yeah, the way they ate all those cookies when you tools sponsored that strike," Harlan said.

"We do need to incentivize her," said Jay.

"I'll run it by Joe, but I'm sure we can offer the store a couple of spots."

"Great idea," said Jay. "Who turns down free advertising?"

"I'll get back to you, then you can make the call and set it up," Harlan told Jay. "And act like a good sport," he ordered Parker.

"Why don't you just put me in a dunk tank in Westlake Center?" Parker grumbled.

"Hey, that could be fun," said Jay, and Parker swore.

"At least we still got jobs," Jay said once they were out of Harlan's office.

Parker glared at him. "Yeah, well, one of us doesn't deserve his."

"Come on, I'm in your corner, and you should be glad. With what happened with the strike Joe's been ready to can everyone from Harlan on down. We need to make this work."

"It won't happen," Parker predicted.

"I hope you're wrong," said Jay. "If it doesn't, we will be unemployed."

And Parker would be living as a monk in the Caribbean.

Nola and Jerome met for lunch at The Pink Door in Seattle's Pike Place Market. She suspected he'd invited her to the Italian American restaurant because of its elegant feminine décor. Its chandeliers and mauve tablecloths offered a charming touch. It was a date disguised as a brainstorming session. The purported goal: to help Parker see the light.

"You can see he needs to," Jerome finished after sharing his nephew's love misadventures, including how he'd gotten burned in a book by his vengeful ex.

"Yes, but he has a mom. He had you and your wife as an example of a good relationship, also, correct?"

Jermone nodded. "My wife was the best. And my sister's amazing, as you know. Our generation's off the hook. It's just the women his age he claims are the problem."

"Oh, brother," Nola said in disgust.

"It doesn't take much to bias people," Jerome pointed out. "Everyone loves to jump to conclusions. And I suspect in Parker's case that jumping's been reinforced by getting more listeners. It's cemented his conviction that he's right. But that's enough of him. Let's talk about you. What made you decide to open a romance bookstore?"

"I've always loved to read, especially romance novels, and

I've worked in bookstores, so I knew I wanted to open one. I saw a growing demand for the genre, so it seemed the logical thing to do. After all, who doesn't like a good love story?"

"On the page and in real life," he said, and smiled at her.

Their food had just arrived when the call came in from Parker's producer. "Mr. Barker," she said, her words frosted, and Jerome's eyebrows raised questioningly. "To what do I owe the honor of a call from you?"

"I want to negotiate a truce," he said.

"That's interesting considering you and your crew tried to ruin my business on Saturday," she said.

"I'm afraid one of Parker's fans got carried away."

And she knew exactly what fan that was. "But he wasn't the one who came up with the idea, was he?"

"The station has found a way to make it up to you and your daughter and make Parker pay for his sins."

This should prove interesting. "I'm listening."

"We're proposing that Parker spend a week working in your bookstore," said Jay Barker. "He can get to know your readers and have his views on romance novels proved wrong. Parker needs to see that romance novels can be an inspiration, for men as well as women."

Now, there was quite the sound bite. Nola wondered who had come up with it.

"That sounds interesting. Tell me more," she said.

"Actually, we'd like him and your daughter Alice to trade places."

"Alice!" *Oh, no. No way.*

"She'd be the logical one, since she was the one who debated him. He can learn about books, and she can host his show and learn about sports. Of course, we will give you ad spots on the afternoon show that week in exchange as well as a spot in the morning show when she hosts."

"In exchange for my daughter getting verbally abused by Parker's callers. I am not sending her into that lion's den. You can have me if you like but not her."

"Yeah, but, like I said, your daughter's the one who debated him. She's the one who confronted him in front of your store, too," Jay continued. "They're rivals. And trust me, the one who'll get abused is Parker. It'll be great publicity for both the station and your bookstore. A chance for Alice to undo some of the damage Parker's done."

"I'll think about it," Nola lied, and ended the call.

"What was that all about?" Jerome asked as she reached for a piece of bread.

"The station would like Alice and Parker to trade jobs for a week. She'd host his show, and he'd work in the store."

"What do you think of that idea?" he asked.

"Your nephew could learn a thing or two about women," Nola said. "He seems to have a habit of mashing us all into one ugly lump."

"Could be eye-opening," said Jerome.

Nola would have loved to see Parker Black get the humbling he deserved, but she had no desire to feed her daughter to the wolves. "I think he should come work in the store, but I'm not letting Alice go on his show. She's done nothing to deserve getting turned into a target."

He nodded thoughtfully. "I agree."

"So that's the deal. We get him and they can take me if they want, but they don't get Alice."

Jerome swallowed a mouthful of linguine. "It makes sense that they'd want Alice. She and Parker are similar in age."

"I won't do that to her," Nola said. Alice had taken enough hits thanks to Parker Black.

"What if Alice didn't get sent in alone? What if she had someone with her, a human shield?"

"Like?"

"Me. I've been a guest on the show more than once. I could go on as co-host, put anyone who tried to bully her in his place. Does she know anything about sports?"

"No. She's not the sporty type."

"Perfect. Callers can explain the mysteries of first, second, third and fourth downs to her. She might just convert some of them to book lovers, too. And help them with their woman problems. She'd definitely be a better help than Parker. Could be kind of cute."

Or it could be a complete disaster.

"Give her the chance to say yes or no. Either way, I like the idea of my nephew having to spend some time with women who have their act together. Considering the women he's wasted time on in the past, it will be a great education. God knows he needs it if he's ever going to be able to move on with his life. You'd actually be doing a good deed. If you can put up with educating him."

The idea of educating the recalcitrant Parker Black put a smile on Nola's face. "I would enjoy having Parker help out in the store, but I don't like the idea of sending Alice to the station, even with you beside her," Nola said.

"But she might. At least give her the option of deciding for herself."

"I don't know. She's so . . . shy."

"She wasn't too shy to debate my nephew," he pointed out.

Or face off in front of the bookstore. But still.

"Sometimes it's not a bad thing to nudge people outside their comfort zones."

"I know she needs to spread her wings," Nola said.

"Then why not give her the chance? Let her decide for herself?"

Because Alice wasn't ready to fly that high. What Jay

Barker was proposing called for the wings of an eagle. Alice was a dove.

"It wouldn't be right to put her on the spot. He'll have to take me. And I'm not sure I want to do this. It's nothing but . . ."

"Another publicity stunt," Jerome supplied. "If you play it right, it could be fun, and good publicity for your store as well. And my offer still stands no matter which one of you wants to get in the game."

The idea of sitting side by side with the Jerome for a week did sound appealing. Nola's husband had been a football fan. Not a fanatic, but she'd watched enough games with him, gone to enough Super Bowl parties to know a few things. She could probably hold her own. And the idea of getting free advertising for the store was appealing.

And Alice could hold down the fort at the store.

With the enemy inside the gates? No.

Nola shook her head. "This is a bad idea. I'm calling him back to tell him it's a no."

He nodded and sat silent while she called the station and left a message for Jay Barker, politely telling him to take a hike. "You're probably right to turn him down," Jerome said when she'd finished.

"I know I am," she said. "We've engaged in enough foolishness."

"How was your lunch?" Alice asked Nola when she returned to the bookstore two hours later.

"It was nice," said Nola.

"And you had a good time with Jerome?" Alice asked.

"Yes, I did."

"So, he's nothing like his nephew then," Alice persisted. Her mother's smile wasn't very big. If she'd had a nice lunch with a nice man, why was she being so lukewarm?

"He certainly isn't."

The store phone rang, and Bettina answered. "Alice, it's for you. It's a man."

"A man," Nola repeated. "I'll take it," she said and grabbed the phone. "Who's speaking?" she demanded. Then, "You already have my answer. Goodbye."

"Mom, who was that?" Alice asked as she put down the phone.

"It doesn't matter," said Nola.

Okay, something strange was going on here. "But he asked for me," Alice persisted. "Who was it?"

Her mother looked like she'd eaten a rotten nut. "It was Parker Black's producer."

"Him!" Bettina said in disgust.

"Why did he want to talk to me?" Alice asked.

"He's just being a pest," said Nola.

"Mom. I'm your partner. I have a right to know," Alice said. "You've been acting funny ever since you came back from lunch. What's going on?" Still, her mother hesitated. "I can call the station and find out," Alice said.

"They're just trying to pull another publicity stunt," Nola said in disgust. "And we're done playing their silly games and boosting their ratings."

"What is it?" Why was Alice having such a hard time pulling the details out of her mother? It had to involve her somehow.

"He wants to put Parker to work here in the bookstore for a week."

"To learn his lesson?" As if he ever could.

"Supposedly."

Working side by side with Parker Black, spending every day fighting off that unwanted attraction she felt for him. Could Alice do it? Probably, since he would be determined to be insulting and irritating.

"What are they offering us in return?" Alice asked.

"Free advertising on the station's afternoon show," Nola replied. Reluctantly.

"Advertising's not cheap," Bettina said.

It sure wasn't. Still . . . "I don't know if I could stand being around him every day for a week," Alice mused.

"Too bad. I'd love to have that boy in here to boss around," Bettina said.

"It would be in exchange for you hosting his show," Nola said.

"Ah, so that's the catch," Bettina said, nodding. "Trading places."

"I don't know anything about sports," Alice said.

"Which is why I said no. I told him it was me or nothing. Jay Barker was trying to get around that just now."

Free advertising for the store. Could she do it? "How long is this supposed to last?"

"A week," said Nola. "I won't have you doing it," she said firmly.

"I think she can handle it," Bettina said. "Can't you, Alice?"

Alice could feel her heart rate picking up. She'd already had to debate Parker on his show and look where that had gotten her. His fans would eat her alive.

"His listeners don't like women," Nola said to Bettina. "Remember the strike."

"Look what happened in the end with the strike," Bettina reminded her. "I bet his listeners aren't all woman haters."

"Like Parker," said Alice.

"Maybe *you* can read from some romance novels," Bettina said with a grin.

"Oh, no," Alice said. His listeners would really flay her alive if she did that.

"Not every sports romance gets stuff wrong," said Bettina.

"I'd still like to know what book sent him over the edge in the first place."

"According to his uncle it was one written by his ex," said Nola. "Remember that hockey novel ARC we received? By a Luna something or other? I think we wound up giving it to Lina to check out."

Alice thought a moment. "I vaguely remember the cover. What was the title? Oh, *Cold Hands*. Lina thought it was only okay, so we didn't order in more than a couple of copies. I think we wound up giving those away as part of our Valentine freebie offer."

"She made Parker the villain in it, then dedicated the book to him to rub salt in the wound. I guess she's been bashing him in interviews ever since," said Nola.

"How is it we didn't know that?" Alice said, shocked.

"Because we don't have time to listen to every podcast or interview every author who contacts the store. And we can't read every book that comes through," Nola replied. "Anyway, it's no excuse for his immature behavior."

"Agreed," Alice said, remembering their encounters.

Except their last one had been different. Maybe his apology really had been sincere. Even if it hadn't been, she liked the idea of him doing penance in the bookstore. She also liked envisioning herself as brave enough to go on the show.

"I want to do it," she said.

"Alice, that is not a good idea."

"I can do it, Mom," Alice insisted. "Remember how you told me you wanted me to get out there and do more?"

"Yes, but not this," said Nola. "It's a terrible idea and I won't see you hurt again."

Alice thought of everything she'd managed to do in the last few weeks. She'd debated Parker Black on air and survived.

Gotten bruised by public humiliation, but she was still standing. And she'd managed to help subvert his ridiculous strike.

"I want to," she insisted. Characters trading places was one of her favorite romance tropes. She would be a fish out of water, but she would be a beta fish. "I'm calling his producer," she said with a firm nod. "Game on."

CHAPTER 21

"CONGRATULATIONS, PARKER. YOU now have a two-book deal," David Fox said, and named the amount of Parker's advance.

It was more than Parker had hoped for. A two-book deal that came with a hefty advance. Who wouldn't want that?

"Thanks, David. This is great," he said.

"They're excited to have you," said David. "I'll be sending a deal memo tomorrow, so check it over."

"Will do," Parker said. He had a book deal. Life was looking good.

He called his uncle to share the news. Not Mom. That would probably be more a case of breaking the news because he knew she wasn't going to be happy. He'd tell her eventually, but not yet.

"Congrats. Looks like you'll be the next hot thing," said Uncle Jerome. "The battle of the sexes lives on."

"They're giving me a two-book contract," Parker said.

"And a hefty advance?" guessed his uncle.

"Probably not as much as you get but it's a sweet deal."

"Any idea what your next book's going to be about?"

"No clue."

"Title it *Everything I Know About Women*, then leave all the pages blank. It'll be a great follow-up for this one. You can call it a memoir."

"Funny," said Parker.

"I thought so. Glad they're giving you a decent advance. Make sure you spend some of it on your mom."

"Of course." Hard as she worked, his mom deserved some special treatment. Maybe a cruise. "You know what's really great about this? I can do whatever I want. No more jumping through hoops at the station."

His contract was up for renewal come August. He could go anywhere after that. Maybe he would. His podcast was doing great. He'd have money. KWOW needed him more than he needed them.

He frowned. They sure weren't acting like it.

"You better keep playing nice at your job for a while," cautioned his uncle. "You won't get that advance in one lump sum. They'll dole it out to you."

Parker almost heard his balloon of euphoria pop. His mom got royalties, but she'd never shared about her advances. All he knew was that she was doing okay. And that his uncle was doing great. He did have it at the back of his mind that he'd be rolling in a big lump sum like a happy pig in mud.

"This book could be a runaway hit, and you could be fine, but don't do anything impetuous," his uncle continued.

"Like?" Parker prompted.

"Like don't quit your day job. I know everyone's into streaming and podcasts, but radio still has a powerful reach. And it's paid you well."

"Right now, I'm the one paying," Parker said.

"Every job has its downside. Even writing. I know you've got talent, Parks. You just need to give yourself time to figure out how to harness it to something lasting, and the last thing you need while you're doing that is to jump off the financial cliff."

This wasn't the conversation Parker had expected. He didn't know whether to be encouraged or frustrated. Not a good way to begin the day.

It got worse when he arrived at the station.

"It's a go," Jay told him. "We've got Alice. We can't get her until Tuesday, but we'll meet with her on Monday to help her prep for the show. The bookstore is closed that day and we'll meet her and her mom there at two. Arne will be along to film a reel. We'll put it up that evening as a tease."

All those stupid stunts, and now here came the worst of all, right on the heels of getting a book deal. He wished he could quit right then and there. Wished he had more money in savings. Wished he didn't have a big, fat car payment. Wished he was getting that large lump sum he'd been fantasizing about. Wishing wouldn't help. For the time being, he was stuck.

"This is gonna get you off Harlan's shit list. It's a good thing," Jay told him.

No, it wasn't. "I just got a deal for my book."

"Hey, awesome. Way to go, bro."

"Except this isn't exactly going to lay the groundwork for promoting it. It's a nightmare with dynamite attached."

"Nothing we can do. It's a done deal. Anyway, it's only a few days."

A few days that would feel like a million. Parker wasn't sure what circle of hell he was entering but he wished he knew where the exit signs were.

He called his uncle again and filled him in on the latest complication in his life. "What would you do if you were me?"

"Wear shin guards."

Real helpful. "Thanks," he grumbled and ended the call. He'd find a way to spin this. He had to.

Jenny Riddle was reading over the latest pages she'd written on her new novel when her brother stopped by her house to let her know about her son's upcoming adventure in Romance Land.

"I hope they don't push a bookshelf over on him," Jenny said.

"He's tough. He can take it," Jermone assured her.

"He's only tough on the outside."

"He'll find a way to make it work. Parker has a gift for always landing on his feet," said Jerome.

Not always. He'd landed on his heart more than once. The last breakup had hurt his pride as well. Parker wasn't one to let go of insults easily.

In a way, Jenny couldn't blame him. The horrible Luna had manipulated and used him when they were together and then had humiliated him after he broke things off. She gave women a bad name, and as a romance writer she was a fraud because she didn't really understand the meaning of love. No romance heroine would be as selfish and vindictive as she was.

But then Parker hadn't exactly been giving men a good name lately. He certainly hadn't been making one for himself with his silly jibes at women. Maybe the bookstore was exactly where he needed to be. Her shock-jock son ringing up sales on romance novels. She had to laugh.

And she did.

The Chili Peppers were seated in a circle, busy discussing their latest read, when a new arrival settled on a chair behind Scarlet. She felt his presence before she saw him. Her nose picked up on the fact that he'd loaded up on her favorite cologne.

She looked over her shoulder and Mark gave her a tentative smile and a little wave. "What are you doing here?" she whispered.

"I came to see you," he whispered back. "And say I'm sorry."

"You have a lot to be sorry for," she informed him, and turned her attention back to the discussion at hand. *So do I. Say it!* She clamped her lips shut. Yes, she'd handled some things wrong, but he'd started it.

Still, here he was. And her heart was beginning to beat fast.

"I love a good second-chance romance," Lina was saying. She looked to where Scarlet and Mark sat. "Love when two people come to their senses and realize they were meant to be together. In books and in real life." She pointed at Mark. "Looks like we got a guest. Weren't you one of the strikers?"

Scarlet turned in time to see his face flushing red. "The strike's over," he said.

Lina's smile was mocking. "It sure is. Are you here to join our book club?"

The red got darker. "No, I'm here to talk to my wife."

"Second-chance romance," cracked Georgia Bishop. She moved to the refreshment table and put a shortbread cookie on a plate. "If you're going to be here you may as well eat," she said, handing it to Mark.

He murmured his thanks, not quite looking at her.

"So, what did you all think about the love scene at the end?" Lina asked.

"I think it was perfect," said Kara Bane. "If my man had known how to talk to me like that maybe we'd still be together."

"Men could learn a lot from these books," Lina said, and looked pointedly at Mark.

Yes, they could, thought Scarlet. But *some* men weren't teachable.

Still, here was Mark, sitting right behind her.

The discussion continued as the group analyzed how the characters had mismanaged their relationship.

"The problem was that Jackson didn't want to admit he was wrong," said Georgia.

"Big surprise. What man does?" sneered Kara.

"I want to," Mark whispered in Scarlet's ear.

Suddenly, she had no desire to stick around for any more of the meeting.

"I gotta go," she announced.

She gathered her coat and purse and headed for the door, Mark right behind her. She was aware of both her mother and sister, standing by the cash register, watching, probably both hoping for a happy ending for her.

She wanted a happy ending, too. Could they create one?

The minute they were outside, he grabbed her by the arms, pulled her to him and kissed her. "I can't stand it any longer," he said against her lips. "I miss you, baby. Please, give me another chance."

She was melting faster than a snowflake in the sunshine from that kiss, until she remembered how badly he'd behaved. How justified she'd been in how she'd behaved.

She pulled away. "Why should I? Give me one good reason, Mark."

"Because I don't want to lose you."

She shook her head. "Not good enough."

He frowned. "I was wrong, okay?"

Now they were getting somewhere. But she needed to hear more. She waited.

"I watched you at the strike, being nice to all those guys and I realized . . ." He stopped talking, clawed a hand through his hair. "I could lose you forever. There are a lot of men out there who'd love to have you, and thinking about it makes me nuts."

Very romantic. But selfish.

"You know, Mark. You're still talking about you. And what you want. Where's the us in that?"

"I want us to be together."

"With you doing whatever you want and then using some stupid radio sports jock to justify it? We're supposed to be a team," she pressed. "You haven't been much of a team player lately."

His focus shifted from her face to his feet. "I know. I was feeling . . ." His words trailed off.

"Feeling what?"

"Whipped. Like I had no say in anything."

His words shocked her. "Of course, you had a say."

"No. I just sort of went along, and then I got pissed because I did. But that's on me, not on you. Look, Scarlet, I want to start over."

"Just like that?" she challenged. "You come home and we pretend you were never a jerk." That wouldn't work. They'd end up right back where they were.

He shook his head. "Not like that. We go out, have some fun. Talk stuff over. Remember why we got together in the first place and figure out how to stay together."

She cocked her head, studied him. "A date."

He shrugged. "Why not? How about Saturday? Let's go to the market. I'll take you out for coffee."

"At Starbucks?" The original Starbucks was right across the street from the Pike Place Market.

"Starbucks," he agreed. "What do you say? Can we start over?"

Starting over, starting the fire between them again. Maybe

even building a stronger foundation for their relationship. Second-chance romance.

She nodded. "Saturday."

He grinned, wrapped an arm around her. "Come on. I'll walk you to your car."

Once there, he stood and waited while she got in her car. He didn't try to kiss her again, and she found herself wishing he had.

"I'll pick you up at ten," he said.

She nodded, shut the door and drove off. And called the bookstore to report in.

"Mark is taking me out on Saturday," she told her mother.

"Now, that is good news," said Nola.

"We'll see," Scarlet said.

"Remember, it takes two," said Nola.

It had taken two to fall in love but as far as Scarlet was concerned it had only taken one to wreck them.

Still, she couldn't help feeling excited as she dressed for their day at the market. The famous Seattle rain had stayed away, but the day was gray, and she knew the air would be cold. She made sure to add a knitted scarf and beret to her coat and gloves. Paired with her dark green sweater and long pants she was ready to look good whether inside or outdoors.

Mark arrived to pick her up wearing jeans and a turtleneck and the vintage-style wool blend blazer she'd bought him for Christmas two years earlier. They hadn't bought their house yet and there'd been no talk of cutting back on the spending. He'd bought her a ring with her birthstone—an emerald. It had been a fun Christmas. Unlike the one they'd just waded through.

"You look great," he said.

"So do you," she said. Mark was a big man, loaded with

muscles. He'd set her hormones jumping the first time she'd seen him.

They were jumping right then, creating sparks, and she told them to settle down as she climbed into his truck.

The market was busy with locals coming in search of fish, handcrafted items and dried flower arrangements. Tulips had already begun to make their appearance and come spring there would be bouquets of all kinds of flowers for sale.

Mark purchased her a coffee drink from Starbucks, then they strolled the market. She bought him some jerky and he bought her a dried floral arrangement featuring lavender and daisies. Then they settled in at Beecher's Handmade Cheese and ate grilled cheese sandwiches. And talked.

"I still don't really understand where it started, where we went wrong," Scarlet said.

He shrugged. "Not sure I do, either. I just felt . . . jammed into a corner. The house, you pushing me to get my side business going."

"But we both wanted the house," she protested.

"You wanted the house. I wanted you to be happy."

"You don't like our house?" she asked, horrified.

"It's gonna be a money pit, Scarlet. I said that, more than once."

But she'd known he had the skills to fix it up.

He hurried on before she could say anything. "But you're right. It's a good investment. I guess I wasn't ready to make the leap is all."

"Then why didn't you say something?" she demanded.

"How do you stop a tornado?"

She suspected he hadn't just offered a compliment. Suddenly, her grilled cheese sandwich wasn't tasting so good.

"Look, you're high energy and exciting, and that's what attracted me to you in the first place. But it's exhausting. And

I started feeling like I can't keep up, like everything I do is wrong. Like I married a mom instead of a wife."

"When you act like a child, what do you expect?" Scarlet said in her own defense. "Honestly, someone has to have some goals."

"Okay, okay. I know. I acted like a kid and not a man. I was wrong. That was my bad."

"It sure was," she said.

"And I'm sorry. But can we just slow down a little? I want to enjoy our life and there's no time. You have every minute planned, every penny pre-spent. You have *me* planned." He studied the cola in his glass. "Sometimes I feel like I'm not enough."

She'd made him feel like that. "But you are," she assured him. "You have so much potential."

He shoved away the glass and stared at her. "Scarlet, I'm not a project."

She blinked. Her eyes were the only thing working. Her brain and her mouth seemed to be out of commission.

"Everything was great when we first got together. I thought you loved me the way I was," he said.

"I did. I do," she corrected herself. But it was too late. She saw the hurt in his eyes.

He soldiered on. "Look, this is on me. I should have spoken up."

"About what?"

"About everything. Buying the house, building my side business. Coming up with money to do all the work on the house that we need to do. Sometimes it all felt like so much. And then you were already talking about when we should get pregnant. I felt like I was in my mom's pressure cooker."

She'd put that much pressure on him? "Mark, why didn't you say something?"

"I tried. Remember? I said maybe we should wait a while

to buy a house, but you kept telling me what a bargain it was, even though it was really more house than we can afford. But hey, I had the side business, and you had plans. I didn't want to disappoint you. In the end I did. And I disappointed myself. And I guess I was pissed at both of us, so I let some guy on the radio talk me into standing up for myself." He shook his head. "I don't know. It seemed like a good idea at the time."

He'd resented her that much. She blinked again, this time to hold back tears.

"Look, I was a shit. I'm sorry, and I'm selling the sound system."

"But it's already in the truck," she protested.

"I can take it out. One of the poker guys wants to buy it. Not for what I paid for it but oh well."

"Your sound system," she repeated.

"I don't need it. What I need is to be a man you can be proud of. A man I can live with, too. It's just going to take me a while. Okay?"

She reached across the table and took his hand. "Mark, I'm sorry I'm a tornado."

He half smiled at that. "You are a force of nature, babe. But you're *my* force of nature. I want us to work things out. Really talk about things from now on. No more playing games. No more locking me out."

That had been the worst game play of all. "No more locking you out," she said. Mark hadn't been the only one acting like a child. Then she added, "I have an extra key."

He smiled. "Yeah?"

"Maybe we should go back to the house and get it."

"Maybe we should," he agreed. "Second-chance romance?"

She smiled. "You were paying attention."

"Well, I'm starting to," he said. "Come on, babe, let's go home and start over."

CHAPTER 22

IT FELT LIKE an invading army when Parker Black and his team walked into the store on Monday past packages and boxes of books that still had to be put out for the next day. Nola was on hand to watch over the proceedings and Alice was glad she was. Her heart was thumping wildly and she felt like it was going to bang its way out of her chest any second.

She was aware of how put together Parker looked in his jeans and button-down shirt and how frumpy she looked in her pants and sweater. And the mascara and lip gloss weren't enough to make her feel sexy. Nothing was enough for that.

She didn't know what to say to him. Welcome? Glad you're here? She had no idea, so she said nothing.

He didn't look much more comfortable than her. He was stiff-shouldered and unsmiling.

His partner in crime was the first to speak. "It's good to see you ladies," he said. He held out a hand to Nola.

She didn't take it, and he shrugged and let it drop to his side.

"Again," she said. "The last time we saw you, you were here in front of our store, trying to scare away our customers."

He cleared his throat. "Yeah, well, water under the bridge, right?"

Neither woman responded to that. Instead, Nola turned to Parker. "Mr. Black, we are looking forward to having you in our store."

"I just bet you are," he said.

Alice realized the third man with them was holding a fancy video camera. "Are we going to be filmed?" She hadn't thought her heart could beat any faster. It could.

"I know all our followers want to see you both in action," Jay said. "And promotion is part of the deal. Parker, move over next to her. Let's roll it."

"Sorry," Parker said, then went into instant smile mode. "So, Alice Willoughby, representing HEA Books, how do you feel about trading places with me this week and hosting a sports show?" he asked.

"Probably about as excited as you feel about working in my store and talking about romance novels," she replied.

Had she been too honest? Should she have said something more diplomatic, like, "I'm looking forward to visiting your station"? Now, in addition to a heart on overdrive, her face was turning into a stove burner set on high.

Parker came up with a laugh that sounded fake. "There you have it, guys. I'm going to be undercover in a romance bookstore. Maybe I'll be able to teach these ladies a thing or two about sports."

Yep, here came the insults.

"Maybe they can teach you a thing or two about love," she said, her smile just as fake, and suddenly Parker's face looked a little overheated, too.

"So, there you have it. Guys, Alice will be in my seat tomorrow, with my uncle, Jerome Riddle, on hand to help her along. Try and teach her a few things while I'm away."

Then he had the nerve to hold out a fist to bump. What could she do but make contact? Her heart started jumping hurdles.

"Let's have a clean fight," he said.

What was that supposed to mean?

"That's boxing language, by the way," he explained. "No hitting below the belt, right?"

He was smiling for the camera. She forced herself to keep her smile, too, as if she was perfectly at home doing this. "Right," she said, and gave two thumbs-up.

"There's the million-dollar shot," Jay approved after the cameraman lowered his weapon. He beamed on the two of them like a proud papa. "That was great, you two. This is good stuff."

Good stuff. Good for whom?

"Okay, Butch, we're done. Thanks." The third man nodded and left, then Jay turned back to Alice and Parker. "Now, let's talk a little about how the program's gonna go tomorrow."

"You can use our back room. I have coffee ready," Nola said, and led the way.

Alice fell in step with her, and she whispered, "You were perfect, darling, but it's not too late to back out. You can stay here in the store, and I can insist on going on the show."

Going on the show and talking to people she couldn't see or being around Parker Black and never having him out of her line of sight. Which one would wear off every speck of her deodorant?

"I'm fine with doing the show," she said and tried to believe it.

Her mother nodded, resigned. "Okay. You will have Jerome Riddle with you."

That would be good. He'd be chivalrous and helpful. Which was more than she could say for Parker Black.

"If you want out at any time let me know and I'll step in," Nola said.

Alice appreciated the assurance. She also wondered if her mother doubted her capabilities. Was Mom worried she would fold up like a fruit roll and get eaten alive by Parker Black's fans? If so, Mom wasn't the only one.

But Alice was determined to show both her mother and herself that she was up to the challenge. "I can do this," she whispered.

"Okay." Nola smiled at her but it didn't hide the worry in her eyes.

Alice, Parker and Jay settled around the little table, Nola providing mugs of coffee and hovering like a guardian angel.

Official papers were signed, and then Jay began to walk Alice through the process of being a host on a radio program. There were ads to read, buttons to push. She'd have to talk about the Mariners and spring training and remind fans that Parker would still be going, as soon as he'd hit a home run at the bookstore.

Home run at the bookstore. Haha. Parker was pleased with how he was managing to spin this, as if he was in total control, as if it had all been his idea. He sneaked a look at Alice. She appeared to be calm and confident. He wasn't sure if she really was or if she was putting on her game face. Either way, he admired her. And he liked looking at that cute face.

He wished he didn't though. It was a waste of eye time. He and Alice would always be in different camps, looking at each other from across a vast divide.

"Spring training starts next week so you'll be talking about that," Jay said to Alice.

Jay should have been the one working in the bookstore. He was the one who'd done all the behind-the-scenes damage.

And Parker was doing cleanup. Three days of misery followed by a Jack and Jill wrap-up on Friday before he could catch a plane to Arizona. He was going to miss the first exhibition game. He was supposed to have flown out on Thursday and been set up to broadcast from sunny Arizona on Friday, opening day. Instead, he was going to be stuck in Seattle, doing time in this pink prison. And then stuck sitting in close proximity to Alice on Friday morning, trying to focus on their callers and not her curves. He wasn't sure which was going to be harder to endure.

You got this, he told himself.

"The Mariners will be doing spring training at the Peoria Sports Complex in Peoria, Arizona, and sharing the space with the San Diego Padres," Jay explained to Alice.

"The Padres," she repeated as if trying to commit the name to memory.

Parker admired her determination to succeed. She'd been thrown into this just like he had. But she was determined to get through it.

Jay handed her a printout. "Here's some info on the Mariners and the Padres—about their key players, the coaches. Read up on it so you'll be able to discuss it with Jerome tomorrow."

She nodded. "I can do that."

"Parker will meet with you after you two are both done with your jobs to talk about how it went and go over the program for the next day."

She nodded again but didn't look at Parker. The big, bad romance hater. Okay, so he championed men. Did that make him the devil incarnate? No, but everything he'd said and done sure did.

"You might find you enjoy doing this," he said, making an effort to be nice.

"I'm willing to try," she said.

This time she did look at him. No smile.

She probably wouldn't, not until he was laid out like a fallen buck and she was sitting triumphantly on top of him.

"We'll have you both together for the show Friday morning, Alice, and you two can talk about how it felt to trade places," Jay said.

Parker already knew how it was going to feel, and he wasn't looking forward to it.

"Okay, that does it for us," Jay said. "And don't worry, Alice. You'll be great." He turned to Nola. "Have you got any instructions for Parker?"

Nola Willoughby smiled, politeness wrapped in a sheet of ice. "Your job here will be easy. You just have to help ring up sales. I'll teach you how to work the cash register tomorrow. It's not hard."

Hard would be facing a hostile tribe of women, but he could do it.

"I'm ready for it," he said. As much to himself as her.

"We're good to go then," said Nola.

And Parker was ready to go. He and Jay said goodbye and left. He felt like he'd been released from prison.

"That was tense, man," said Jay. "Mama bear doesn't like us."

"Can you blame her? You should have to be in there right along with me."

"I know. Thanks for taking one for the team," said Jay.

"As if I had a choice," Parker grumbled.

"It'll all be over soon."

Which would be fine with Parker. And at least he wouldn't have to spend his time in the bookstore working alongside Alice with those big eyes. And the freckles. What was it about freckles, anyway? They made a woman look so girl next door.

If he'd grown up living next door to Alice, would they

have been friends? Would she have come to his high school baseball games? Would she have understood what a big deal it was to have seen his dream of a career in the big leagues vanish with the rude awakening of a ruined shoulder? Did any of the women in those books she read ever stay with a man through that kind of hard stuff?

Maybe he'd find out when he reported for work the next day.

Come nine o'clock Tuesday morning Alice was seated in a sound booth behind a huge microphone with Jerome Riddle by her side, a big, burly comfort as she made it through the opening remarks that had been scripted for her.

There had been plenty of promotion ahead of her arrival. A still shot had been lifted of Parker and her sharing a fist bump, and it had been put on the station's website and blown up to take temporary residence on the side of several buses tooling around town. How on earth that had been managed on such short notice and how much it had cost she couldn't begin to imagine.

"I'm here to learn about the world of sports," she said. "I hope you'll all help me." She smiled gratefully at Jerome. "And I've got Jerome Riddle, football star, with me today to help out when what you want to talk about goes over my head."

He leaned into his mike. "Glad to be here, Alice. And while we're here, Parker is over at Alice's bookstore, HEA Books in West Seattle, getting up close and personal with more of those books he's been reading on air. He might just find one or two he likes."

That would be the day. "So go in and say hi," Alice couldn't resist adding. Then returned to script. "Starting Saturday, Parker will be in Peoria, Arizona, where I understand he will be partying with many of you Mariner fans who are coming down for the beginning of spring training. And I believe spring training goes clear through March. Correct, Jerome?"

"Yes, it does," said Jerome.

"All you listeners know what spring training is for. Can some of you call in and enlighten me?" she asked. She'd already done her homework, and she knew exactly what spring training was for. But this was a gambit designed to get listeners involved.

It was working. The lines lit up.

"Cool that you're here," said someone named Gerald.

"I'm happy to be here," she lied. "What can you tell me about spring training?"

"It's to get players in shape mentally and physically for the season," Gerald explained. "And it builds team chemistry. You gotta be able to work together."

"Thanks, Gerald. That makes perfect sense. Are you going down for any of the exhibition games?"

"No. Wish I was. The wife insisted on spending the money replacing our carpet."

It didn't take a Sherlock Holmes to detect the bitterness in his voice. What would Parker do? Probably commiserate with him, tell him how selfish his wife was to demand new carpet. But Parker wasn't there.

"Well, that's too bad the budget wouldn't stretch to do both. What a great husband you are to give up a trip to a spring training game to improve your house."

There was a moment of silence on the line, followed by a reluctant, "Well . . ."

"I wonder if you might be able to negotiate a trip next year. Maybe your wife is like me and needs to learn about the game. I bet you're just the man to teach her."

"I do know a few things. Coached our son's Little League team when he was a kid."

"Well, there you have it," said Alice. "I hope you two can start a fund for that trip. Meanwhile, I bet you . . ." Was there a sports metaphor she could bring in here? "I bet you've hit a home run by supporting her on getting the carpet."

"Yeah, I did." She could hear the smile in his voice and see one on Jerome's face, and she, too, smiled. Home run.

Parker was listening to the show before heading out the door to the bookstore. He had to smile, hearing Alice's response to her first caller. Well done. Alice Willoughby was a smart one, and able to think fast on her feet.

So why had she wilted in their debate?

A fresh call came in, this one more hostile. "I don't know whose idea this was, but it was a lame one," said the caller. "This chick knows squat about sports and you guys have got her in here hosting a sports show."

"Hey now, how do you know that?" Uncle Jerome demanded. Go Unk.

"She said she's here to learn and that means she doesn't know squat. Did you ever play sports in high school, Alice? Run track? Girls' volleyball?"

"I'm afraid not," Alice said.

"So, you've done nothing, and you know nothing, but here you are. Hey, Alice, is Parker really even at your store or have you got him tied up in a basement somewhere?"

"Umm," said Alice.

Parker could envision her face turning red.

"You don't have an answer for that, do ya?" taunted the caller.

"Say something," Parker urged. She was shutting down, just like she had in their debate.

So that was the deal. Alice could hold her position until the bullying started. Then she lost her mental strength. But he hadn't bullied her during their debate. He'd just been pushing his point home.

Just like this caller. There was an unwelcome comparison.

Uncle Jerome stepped in and stopped the guy's tirade. "Okay, you got us. We have Parker stashed in Alice's basement. He's handcuffed to the radiator and is being forced to read romance novels. You found some good ones for him this time, didn't you, Alice?"

"I did," she said, recovering. "I could recommend one to you, John, if you're interested. Let's trade. You tell me a good sports movie to watch, and I'll tell you my favorite novel that features a football player."

No answer. "Looks like we lost John," said Jerome. "How about it, guys? Got a recommendation for a good sports movie Alice should watch?"

Next came Jay's voice. "Lots of calls coming in, Alice. Looks like you're going to be busy the next few nights."

She'd be busy with Parker. They had to talk about programming for the show. Maybe they needed to watch a movie, too. And if he hadn't been such a jerk to her maybe it would have been easier to apologize for listeners like the one she'd just had to deal with. Why couldn't men and women get it right?

He supposed he was about to be told.

Yep, he was. He arrived at the bookstore right as it opened to find his welcoming committee—Nola Willoughby and an older woman with steel-gray hair and steely eyes, the same one he'd encountered at his mother's book party. Yeah, this was going to be fun.

"Are you ready for your first day?" Nola asked, giving him a smile that should have accompanied an evil witch's cackle.

He refused to be intimidated. "Bring it on," he said.

"All right. Let's teach you how to work the cash register," she said.

The other woman said nothing, just glowered at him.

"Oh, by the way, this is Bettina. If I'm not around she'll be happy to answer any questions you might have."

More like happy to clobber him with a book. He nodded and followed Nola to where the cash register stood.

The little bell over the door tinkled, jangling his nerves, and in walked a plump woman holding a container of something edible.

"Hi, Georgia," called Nola.

"Thought I'd bring your volunteer some goodies," said the woman called Georgia.

"Are they poisoned?" he joked.

The woman laughed. "No. We're much more subtle here in Romance Land. We're going to kill you with kindness."

"Some of us are," muttered Bettina.

Yep, it was going to be a long day.

Another woman came in shortly after the cookie lady. She looked to be in her forties. "Had to stop by and get a picture for my blog," she said. She pulled a phone out of her purse and aimed it at Parker. "Say chocolate."

"Chocolate?" What happened to cheese?

She checked the picture, and her smile looked as evil as Nola Willoughby's. "Oh, that's a good one. I'll put it on Insta and label it *Clueless in Seattle*. So, what do you think you're going to learn in all this?" she asked Parker.

"Maybe that women aren't as manipulative and mean as I've been led to believe," he replied, determined to sound open-minded. "But I'm not holding my breath," he couldn't help adding.

"Oh, he's a cute one, isn't he?" the woman mocked. "Well,

girlies, good luck in your mission." She pointed to the container the woman named Georgia was holding. "There you are, being mean again, Georgia. Does Bill know you're being mean to other men besides him?"

"I left a plate of mean behind for him," said Georgia, straight-faced.

Great. Now they were mocking him.

Just like he'd mocked their books. Yeah, this was fun.

The women began to chat about some novel featuring an heiress and a cowboy, and Parker slipped away to a quiet corner of the store to call Jay and see how Alice was doing. It was a commercial break. He'd have a minute to talk.

"She's had a couple of callers out to get her," Jay said, "but for the most part, she's holding her own. Jerome's helping."

"Tell Mason to screen those calls better. Harlan will kill us if they crucify her," said Parker. And he'd hate himself. He didn't want to bring any more misery into Alice's life.

"Hey, I'm trying. A couple just sneaked by me."

"Tighten your defense," Parker snapped.

"They can't all be nice. It'll look rigged."

Parker gave a snort of disgust and ended the call.

Just in time to hear a woman ask, "So where's our famous woman hater?"

Oh, no. The world of media in Seattle was a small one, and he knew that voice. He peered around the bookshelf.

Sure enough, there stood Olivia Carson in all her perfect hair and makeup glory, dressed and prepped for an interview. Or a public shaming.

"He's around here somewhere," said Nola Willoughby. "Parker, where are you hiding?" she called.

He wished he could find a place to hide. He came out in the open. "I'm here. Busy working."

"So, Parker, got time for a chat?" purred Olivia. More like, *Got time for a public whipping?*

"Sure, Olivia. Bring it on," he said.

Two minutes later she had a microphone stuck in his face and was peppering him with questions. The strike had failed. (No time allowed to rebut that.) Had trading places with one of the bookstore owners been his idea?

His team thought it would be fun. (Yeah, fun.)

Was he finding the women he was meeting as demanding and unrealistic as he claimed women were?

Time would tell. (Hopefully, they wouldn't skin him alive.)

Did he think he'd end up changing his mind about romance novels?

Probably not. (He wasn't going to lie.) How did it feel to be surrounded by women?

More like hostiles, he thought, but he smiled and joked, "Just here to give them a chance to study a real-life man."

"That's bound to be interesting," Olivia joked back. "So, Parker Black, KWOW's favorite sports personality turned shock jock, is learning to be a good sport right here at HEA Books in West Seattle. Only time will tell if he masters it," she concluded.

She smiled for the camera and the women giggled and Parker wished he'd stayed behind the bookshelf. And it wasn't even noon yet.

It was going to be a long day.

It was, indeed, a long day. Parker was alternately lectured and scolded. And recommended books to read that would enlighten him. Two of them were by his mom. By the time Nola set him free—early, thank God—he felt like he'd been trampled by elephants. All he wanted to do was go home, shower and flop on the couch.

But he had a show to plan. And a woman to plan it with. And he felt like he needed to apologize for how she'd been treated on his show that morning by some of his listeners.

He called Jay, who he knew had Alice's contact information. "I need Alice's number. We've got to meet and talk about tomorrow's show."

"I've already prepped her so you can beg off if you want."

"No, we're supposed to meet." He needed to meet, needed to make sure she was okay, that no further damage had been done.

"You want me to be your wingman?" Jay offered.

The last thing he wanted was Jay around to see him choking on humble pie. "I can handle it."

"Okay," Jay said. "Sending it now. Let the games begin," he joked.

Parker didn't laugh.

CHAPTER 23

ALICE, IT'S PARKER."

Alice's caller ID had informed her she had an unknown caller. She half wished she didn't know him, wished her mother had never set these events in motion by accepting the challenge to that debate. Then Alice wouldn't be stuck doing a radio program, dodging verbal bullets like a duck in a shooting gallery.

She reminded herself that she'd survived her first day on air. John the angry listener had been a challenge, but after that the calls had gotten kinder, more patient, and she'd even enjoyed herself a little. The men had been happy to explain the basics of football and baseball to her. Two had offered to take her to a Mariners game that summer and one had offered to teach her how to play pickleball.

"You're already getting fans of your own," Jerome had told her.

His words had encouraged her. So had some of the callers. But their kind words weren't strong enough to push the angry ones out of her mind.

"I figured it would be you," she said to Parker. "Are you still at the store?" It was only five. He had an hour to go.

"Your mom let me out early for good behavior. Plus, I reminded her we still had to meet to plan for tomorrow's show. Speaking of the show, how did it go?"

"It was okay," she said.

"I heard your heckler," he said.

"John? I think he's a good example of why a lot of women would rather be alone with a good book than take a chance on a man."

"Ouch. Tell me how you really feel."

"I'm sorry," she said. "That wasn't very nice." But then neither was Parker when it came to sharing his opinions.

"You're right. You know, for someone who looks so sweet, you've got a hard edge to you."

"I do?" She never thought of herself as having a hard edge. She certainly didn't want to be hard-edged. That smacked of meanness. "I don't think I want a hard edge."

"Well, at least a backbone of steel," he amended.

That she liked.

"You ought to think about taking up boxing," he teased.

"Why would I want to deliberately offer myself to be beat up? I've never understood the lure of that."

"Hey, it's all about strategy and proving your strength."

And getting your brain knocked around and your body bruised. "Couldn't you prove your strength by working for Habitat for Humanity building houses?" she countered.

"You know, you're a good debater when the pressure's not on," he said.

She supposed that was a compliment. "I prefer being around people who don't like to argue. And, speaking of that, how was your first day at the bookstore?" He would have found plenty of women willing to verbally spar with him there.

"It's been a day. One woman brought me cookies; another hoped they were poisoned. I had two customers offer to buy me a book, and Bettina wants to stake me out in a desert where I can die of thirst and have buzzards pick my bones."

That made her giggle. "Bettina is very loyal."

"She's also very scary. Oh, yeah, and Olivia Carson from KOMO was on hand to do her best to make me look like a fool. So, I'd say the chicks won the first round today."

"Boxing metaphor," she said.

"We are duking it out," he said.

The thought made her a little sad. What would it be like to talk with Parker Black with no agenda. What would it be like to simply visit? Was he even capable of such a thing?

"We need to meet and talk about the program for tomorrow. How about dinner?" he suggested.

"Dinner," she repeated.

"Hey, I'm not proposing a march through a patch of poison ivy," he said, his voice light. More like a détente. "Come on, Alice, I promise I'll behave. And I'll pay."

Oh, no. "I don't want to be one of those women you've talked about who takes advantage of men. I can pay for my own dinner."

"One dinner is not taking advantage of me. Anyway, this is business."

"But fair is fair," she countered, "and I'm in business, too."

"Okay, fine," he said. "How about Anthony's Pier?"

The restaurant on Seattle's Elliot Bay waterfront. It would probably be pricey, but she'd use the company charge card. "Okay," she said.

"Six thirty?"

"Six thirty," she confirmed. "See you there."

"Good," he said.

Good for business, but not good for her emotional state. Parker Black both unnerved and attracted her, and she wished he did neither.

Why was he bothering to suggest dinner when they could simply meet at the bookstore again? Or talk on the phone. Dinner was for dates, and they weren't dating.

"Why did you want to meet for dinner. Really?" she pumped him once they were at the restaurant.

They were seated by a window where they could watch the ferries gliding back and forth between Seattle and Bainbridge Island or Bremerton. It was a setting for tourists, which they weren't.

Or lovers, which they'd never be. Although a tiny part of her half wished he was a different kind of man and they could be. How could a woman be out with a good-looking man and not let the thought pass through her mind? He'd shed his jacket to reveal a crisp white button-down shirt paired with his jeans. He looked elegantly casual.

Well, so did she. She'd ditched her baggy pants for leggings and boots and a cute tunic top. His appreciative look when he'd first seen her had boosted her confidence. Acting like a heroine, looking like a heroine. Becoming a heroine.

"Why not?" he countered. "We have to eat. And besides, I thought it wouldn't hurt for us to get to know each other better. Maybe we don't have to be adversaries."

A waiter appeared to fill their water glasses, followed by another who wanted to take drink orders. "White wine?" Parker guessed.

"Tonic water," said Alice. "The quinine in it is good for your nerve endings." And heaven knew hers were feeling frayed sitting across from hm.

"You are full of surprises," he said. "Jack Daniels, rocks," he told the waiter. Then, to Alice, "I'm surprised you didn't order a sidecar."

Starting the evening with an embarrassing memory. Was that some sort of strategy?

She frowned. "My sister suggested it. I thought it would be fun to try. I'm not a big drinker."

"Your sister doesn't sound like a very good influence," he observed.

He was referring to the doctored picture, of course. "You really did have it coming," Alice said.

"No, Jay had it coming," Parker corrected her. "He was the one who came up with the meme, not me. Remember? I don't know how many more times I'm going to have to keep telling people that."

Until they believe it? She cocked an eyebrow.

"I don't want to be at war with you, Alice. I don't want to be at war with anyone."

"For someone who doesn't want to be at war, you fire a lot of shots on your program," she said.

"That segment is popular."

"But you're a sports show."

She wasn't an adversarial type of person. What was she doing here, verbally sparring with this man? Their drinks arrived and she retreated into her glass of tonic water.

"I know. So I'm backing off."

"I heard about the book your ex wrote," she ventured.

He gave the ice cubes in his glass a thoughtful jiggle. "What I've been doing, it all started out as . . . I don't know. My own petty revenge, I guess. She was all over the internet, giving interviews, talking about her rotten ex-boyfriend who her bad guy was based on. She made sure she got as close to describing me as she could, making him the rotten monster who was a failed jock, who had a radio sports talk show. In Seattle. She stopped just short of saying, 'And his initials are P. B.' Sweet, huh?"

"It was a little vengeful."

"A little? It was war. Anyway, I showed the piece of crap

to Jay, and we came up with the bright idea of reading some of it on the show. None of the hockey stuff was right, so why not? Listeners loved it, so we read some more, made my point about romance novels. I ranted some, guys called in and ranted some, and next thing I knew I was doling out advice. As if I knew anything about women. As if I do now. As if I ever will," he added bitterly, and downed more of his drink.

"Why was she so mad at you?" Alice asked. "A woman doesn't go to all that trouble to get even for no reason."

"Oh, she had her reasons. I was the one who broke things off and she couldn't deal with it." He held up a hand. "I know what you're going to ask next. Why? I'll tell you. I got tired of her demands. I could never spend enough, do enough, be enough. She once told me I should read some romance novels. Then I'd know how to be a real man and would know what pleases a woman." He shook his head. "I thought I knew, but there was no pleasing her. And frankly, from what I've seen and heard there's no pleasing any woman."

"That's not fair," Alice said, forgetting to be nervous.

"Isn't it? Come on, Alice, you work in a bookstore. Can you honestly say that your customers don't want a man like the kind they read about in those books? They're all studs, they all know exactly what to say by the end of the book. Always have some grand gesture to make." Alice started to protest but he cut her off. "You forget I've read some excerpts on my show."

"Poorly written ones," she protested.

Their waiter appeared, interrupting the conversation. "Give us a couple more minutes," Parker said, and the waiter nodded and retreated. "Men can't do anything right anymore. I know there are cheaters and losers out there, I know there are guys still living in their mom's basement, but to hear women talk on social media we're all selfish and immature and controlling. Heck, I've even seen some men out there, joining in and dissing the rest of us. Maybe so they can get in good with all of you? I don't know. I heard one dude joke that marriage is a scam created by men. Really? So, I guess after we go down on one knee and open the ring box then we turn from Prince Charming back into King Rat."

"I don't know what to say to that," Alice admitted. It had been a long diatribe, and she had no idea where to begin.

"How about saying you'd like to live in the real world with a real man who doesn't always get everything right?"

"I haven't known enough real men." Oh, no. Had that just come out of her mouth? She tried to douse the fire on her face with more of her drink. It didn't work.

"What are you trying to tell me?"

"I've never been in love," she confessed. There, she'd said it. "I sell books, I live books, I talk about books. Mostly with women." Okay, now she sounded like a Fannie Failure. "I do know what a good man in real life looks like though. My father was one, and he and my mother were crazy about each other. They laughed together and dreamed together and supported each other. I'd come in the kitchen sometimes and catch them sharing a kiss while the potatoes were boiling over on the stove. It was sweet. He was sweet. Who wouldn't want something like that?"

"You won't find it in books," Parker said. It was not said gently.

"Maybe I won't ever find it in real life, either," said Alice.

"I haven't. And I've played this game twice."

And now he had more than one hurt stacked up inside his heart.

He didn't elaborate. Instead, he continued with his argument. "There are good men out there, men who want to get it right without being nagged and made to feel like less."

"I don't nag anyone," she protested.

"Then maybe you're one of the good ones."

"And how about you?" she asked. "Are you one of the good ones?"

"I'd like to think I am. Okay, not all the time. And, yeah, I started something that's blown up bigger than I thought it would. But I call it as I see it. And I can't be all wrong, not with the reactions I've been getting. I think I hit a nerve."

"You hit more than a nerve on me," she muttered, thinking of the awful meme. "And on our bookstore," she added. "Your strike was—"

"Again, not my idea. Jay thought it would be a great publicity stunt. Our program director made him take it down from the website, but some tool ran with it."

"That was my brother-in-law," she said with a sigh. "He's been your most loyal follower, which didn't do their marriage any good."

"Are you saying I wrecked your sister's marriage?"

"They both did their part," she said, "but you helped. Mark was the one who started the Facebook page for the strike."

"I figured that out," he said, and frowned.

"I know you know a lot about sports but is it possible you don't know as much as you think you do about women?" she suggested.

"Who does?" he retorted, and she heard the sourness in his voice.

"Maybe you'll know us better by the end of the week," she said.

He studied her a moment. "Maybe I'd like to get to know *you* better, Alice," he said softly, giving her the shivers. "Have you ever wondered if we might have been friends if we'd met under different circumstances. Earlier in life?"

"Would we have been the same people?"

"Good question. I'm not sure. I don't think I would have been. I fact, I know I wouldn't because I wasn't. In my twenties I was . . ." He shook his head.

"Happier?" she guessed, and he shrugged. "Are you fun when you're not . . ."

"Being obnoxious?" he supplied. "I think so."

Their waiter came and took their orders. Once he left, Alice returned to her line of questioning, wanting to know what that different, younger Parker Black had been like. He shared about his life growing up, about his mother and how his uncle had always been there for him.

"Which is more than I can say for my sperm donor, who left her when I was a baby," he added with a shake of his head. "I guess anyone looking for proof that men are rotten would hold him up as Exhibit A."

"But your uncle would be Exhibit A for the defense," Alice pointed out. Then sobered. "What would you be?"

Their salmon arrived. "Remains to be seen, I guess. Let's eat."

They did, and it felt as if a lot of debris had been swept aside, as if maybe they could move forward without tripping over it. As if maybe, they could be friends. He shared about his short-lived career as a pro ballplayer, and she told him how she got involved with the bookstore and about the weekly podcasts she did with her mother.

"I love how you smile when you talk about your life," he said. "I haven't done that in a while."

"Maybe it's time you started smiling," she said. "Or making a life you can smile about."

"You're not going to expect me to smile when I'm doing time in your bookstore, are you?" he teased.

"Maybe," she teased back.

"If I do, it will be through my tears," he cracked. "They're out to get me."

"Just deserts," she murmured.

He sat back in his seat. "Maybe you're right. Speaking of dessert, would you like some?"

"I think I've had enough," she said.

She'd definitely had enough of their personal détente. It felt strange leaving their past unpleasantness behind and talking like potential friends instead of enemies. And it made her nervous. Parker Black was a heartbreak waiting to happen, but her heart didn't seem to understand that. It wanted this dinner to be more, the beginning of something special.

The way he'd talked, maybe it could be.

He pulled out his phone. "Okay, then, we'd better talk about the show. I know Jay's met with you but I've got some suggestions for tomorrow as well. Let's go over them and then I'll text them to you."

Back to the show, yes. This was what they really were, two people thrown together and forced to make the best of it. This was a good reality check. For a moment there, she'd almost wandered into Fantasy Land. Now they were back where they belonged. No more personal sharing.

Which was just as well. Alice was already fighting off physical attraction to this man. She didn't need to start bonding with him emotionally. He was not a candidate for love. Too wounded. Too angry. Too different.

"How does that sound?" he said.

She jerked her attention back to the subject at hand. "That sounds good." Whatever that was.

"My uncle will be with you again," Parker said. "He's promised to come in for the next two days."

"It's really nice of him to help me out," she said.

"He's a nice guy. Most of us are if you give us a chance," said Parker.

Give Parker a chance? Alice didn't dare.

The waiter was back to see if they wanted dessert. "Are you sure?" Parker asked Alice.

She shook her head. "No. I should get going. I have a busy day tomorrow," she added with a little smile. "I need to get to bed."

Get to bed. Don't go there! He was the last man on earth Alice would want to go to bed with. She was holding out for a book boyfriend to come to life. Anyway, she was into books, he was into sports. They really had nothing in common.

Still, he found himself offering, "How about tomorrow you come over to my place? I think you need an education," he teased.

Her eyes got big as an owl's eyes. "An education?"

"On movies. I can show you a sports one." He'd picked up bits and snatches of the show on his phone and knew about the sports movie suggestions, and he liked the idea of showing one to Alice. "Maybe if you were to watch a couple you might see why I love what I do for a living. When I'm talking about sports," he clarified.

She cocked her head, considering. "I like movies."

"Well, there you go," he said. That settled it.

"All right. How about this? I'll watch some sports movies if you'll read a romance novel," she countered. He opened his mouth to remind her that he'd been reading romance novels on his show and that was what had gotten him in trouble in the first place, but before he could speak she added, "All the way through. Didn't you buy your mother's at the book signing?"

"Read my mom's book?" She might as well have suggested he stick his head in a bucket of mud and take a deep breath.

"You can skip any parts that make you uncomfortable," she said, "But honestly, there's nothing very racy in it. I would like to watch a sports movie," she added softly, her cheeks turning pink.

What the heck. It would make his mom happy if he read her book. It was past time.

"Okay," he said. He held out his hand. "Shake on it?"

She smiled and nodded and held out her hand. It was small. And felt soft. And she pulled away before he was ready to let go.

Their waiter arrived with the check.

"No," she said firmly as Parker reached for it. "Separate checks, please."

The waiter looked questioningly at Parker.

"You need to see that not every woman wants to take advantage of men." She smiled up at the waiter. "Right?"

"The lady is always right," he said.

Which made her laugh. "Not according to Parker Black," she teased as he left to separate the bill.

"You know, you've got a mouth on you," Parker said. And stupid him, right then he wanted to kiss it.

They paid their bills, and he walked her to where her car was parked.

"That was a nice dinner," she said.

"You think we've reached a truce?" he teased. "Tell me you at least believe me about the strike." A man shouldn't have to go before a female firing squad for something he didn't start.

"I do," she said.

Good.

"But I also believe you could have come out and done something to stop it."

Ouch. He could have called that hitting below the belt, but she wasn't. There was truth in what she'd said.

"I guess I could have. You gonna hold that against me forever?"

Why would it matter if she did? A few more days and they'd both go their separate ways and never see each other again. He frowned at the thought.

"It's a little hard to let go of," she admitted. "That and other things."

He didn't want to think of the other things.

"But people can change," she added softly.

"In books," he joked.

"Maybe in real life, too. Maybe in real life, just like in fiction, we all have a character arc."

"A character arc," he repeated.

"We all can learn from our mistakes and grow. Everyone deserves a chance to do that," she added. Then she unlocked the car door and prepared to get in.

"Good luck tomorrow. I hope my listeners learn a thing or two from you,' he said. Maybe he was. She smiled and he returned it. "My house tomorrow. Six thirty?"

"Six thirty," she agreed.

"I'll text you the address along with my show notes," he said.

She nodded, murmured a good-night, then got in her car and shut the door.

He stepped away, watched her back out of the parking spot and drive off. What was it about Alice Willoughby that insisted on creeping under his skin? Her looks, her determination, her spunk, for starters.

He went home, pulled out his mom's book and got busy reading.

And before he knew it, it was midnight, and he wanted to read just one more chapter. What was happening to him?

CHAPTER 24

BETTINA THE BOOK LADY wasn't any happier to see Parker the next day than she'd been the day before. She followed him to the back room, then pounced on him as soon as he'd shed his coat.

"Your fans are mean," she informed him. "Lina was listening yesterday and told me all about it. It wasn't very chivalrous of you to put poor Alice in the hot seat like that."

"This wasn't my idea," Parker said.

Bettina crossed her arms over her ample chest and glared at him. "I supposed that ugly meme wasn't your idea, either."

"It wasn't. I told Alice that. I've told everybody that. And, in case you forgot, it was one of your posse who called the station and took me up on my offer to debate," he added in exasperation.

The debate. He wanted to recall the words the minute they were out of his mouth. He'd just dug up an ugly corpse that should have stayed buried.

"We've all regretted it since," said a soft voice behind him, making him jump. He turned to see Nola Willoughby. "And I'm especially sorry my daughter feels the need to participate in keeping this battle of the sexes going, even if the store has been promised some free advertising."

"Look, I don't want to be here any more than your daughter wants to be at the station," Parker informed her.

"I understand," she said.

"But I enjoyed meeting with her last night." Now, why had he gone and shared that information? Bettina looked ready to beat him up, and Nola's smile didn't reach her eyes.

"Détente," he added.

The smile remained icy. "Let's all get to work," Nola said, then turned her back on him.

He was about as welcome in this pink box of books as the plague. He hoped things were going better for Alice.

"Hey, Alice, you said something earlier about Parker getting you to watch some sports movies. I got one for you," said a caller named Ed. "Watch *The Natural*. It's a classic. I bet Parker's got a copy. If he doesn't, you can stream it."

"Thanks, Ed. What's it about?" she asked.

"It's about baseball. And overcoming the tough stuff. Starting over and making it work."

Starting over and making it work. Why did that make her think of Parker and her?

She forced herself to stay in the moment. "It sounds interesting," she said.

"That movie is a classic," said Jay from where he sat behind the glass.

"Good suggestion, Ed," said Jerome, who was once again Alice's wingman. Ed went away and Jerome continued the discussion. "You know, there's something about sports movies. Actually, there's something about sports," he added.

"What is it? Tell me, everyone. I want to know," Alice said.

That lit up the lines. Every man had a theory. Sports tested a man's strength and endurance. Sports taught him how to be a team player. Sports were a metaphor for life—hard work and not giving up paid off.

"You all make it sound so noble," she said.

"There is a certain nobility to it," Jerome said. "We're all made different, and we're all given different talents. Whatever a person is gifted with, it would be a shame not to use it. There's another classic movie I love, *Chariots of Fire*. It was about the men who competed in the 1924 Olympics. One of them, Eric Liddell, was a runner. His sister didn't want him to go. He was going to be a missionary. What was the purpose of running a race, right?"

"Did he end up being a missionary?" Alice asked.

"He did. But he also ran. He reminded her that God had made him fast. 'When I run, I feel God's presence,' he said. I know how he felt. When I was on the football field it was like I was playing in a corner of heaven, showing off a little for God. Plus, sports are fun," he added with a wink. "Kind of like books, right?"

"You can learn a lot from books," Alice said.

"You can learn a lot from playing a sport, too," Jerome said. "You get Parker to show you *The Natural* and see if you don't get hooked. How about it, guys? Does she need to watch *The Natural*?"

Of course, this brought in more calls, all agreeing with Jerome.

"I definitely will watch it," she promised.

The next caller, a man named Cole, wanted to compliment her on being willing to learn about sports. "My girlfriend won't go to any games with me or even watch one on TV," he complained. "But she always wants me to watch her chick shows with her."

Oh, boy, here was a Parker acolyte. "I'm wondering if she

doesn't want to because she doesn't know anything about those sports, like me. Maybe you could play a video sports game with her."

"Alice, would you play a sports video game?" Cole wanted to know.

"I'd certainly try," she said. "Don't give up, Cole. Bribe your girlfriend with chocolate and tell her if she watches a game with you this spring HEA Books will reward her with a complimentary book."

"A football romance?" teased Jerome.

"Maybe," she joked. It was the perfect lead-in to read the ad copy she'd been allowed time for. "And, men, if you're losing at love and looking for a new playbook, come on into HEA Books in West Seattle. Our team of experts will be on hand to match you up with the perfect book. Real men read."

Jay gave her a thumbs-up and Jerome smiled his approval.

The rest of the program flew by. She got lost in more than one conversation Jerome had about several of the major league baseball coaches and the teams they were building, but she still enjoyed herself.

"Baseball sounds kind of fun," she said as they vacated the booth for the next radio talk show host.

"It is, once you know the strategy. Some women find it a little slow. My wife used to bring a book to read when I took her to games."

"That sounds like a good compromise," said Alice.

"It's always more fun to watch when you know the players. We went to all of Parker's Little League and high school games. Those she watched. He had what it took. It was too bad he blew out his shoulder. That ended his career. But he landed on his feet. Well, till his hormones took him down."

"At least you didn't say a woman," said Alice.

"She contributed, just like in that baseball movie we were talking about." Jerome shook his head. "He let it turn him sideways. All that stupid battle of the sexes stuff. It hides the fact that my nephew really is a good guy."

"Is he paying you to say things like that?" she teased.

Jerome chuckled. "Nope."

She might have seen glimpses of Parker's good guy side the night before. Or had that been wishful thinking? After all, what woman wouldn't want a gorgeous man to turn out to be a good guy?

"Get him to show you *The Natural* tonight," said Jerome.

"I will," she said. The words were barely out of her mouth when she caught a vision of herself cuddled up next to Parker on his couch.

There would be no cuddling, of course. He wasn't attracted to her. Once this gimmick of trading places was over that would be the end of seeing him. Which was just as well since they had nothing in common.

She'd done the post-show wrap-up with Jay, been complimented by Harlan the program director and was just getting into her car when Parker called. "We were listening in the store," he said. "You did great."

Why did she feel so pleased by his compliment? She decided she didn't want to know.

"How are you doing?" she asked.

"Bettina still wants to murder me and bury me under a pile of books. So far one customer has quizzed me on my love life, and another wanted to know when you're coming back. She needs a new book recommendation. Oh, yeah, and two guys came in half an hour ago to tell me they saw me on the news and felt sorry for me. They both bought books for their girlfriends. And I started reading my mom's latest."

"Are you enjoying it?"

"It's not bad. So, I'm reading a romance. That means tonight you have to watch a sports movie."

"*The Natural*," she said, the same time as him. "I guess you heard that part of the show."

"I did. It's a good place to start."

"You have it?"

"I have a whole collection of sports movies. Enough to keep you busy for a long time."

Watching sports movies with Parker Black, the idea sent a frisson racing across her chest. "What a coincidence. I have a whole collection of romance novels," she said. Good Lord, was she flirting? And why was she flirting with Parker Black?

"I bet you do. Got any without sappy dialogue?"

"I have all of your mom's."

"Okay, I'm not stepping into that bear trap," he said. "My uncle just walked in. See you tonight."

And then he was gone.

Uncle Jerome had come into the store, pretending to check on Parker, but Parker knew he'd come to check out Alice's mom. "How's your temp doing?" he asked her, giving Parker a teasing grin.

"He's adapting quite well," said Nola.

Jerome nodded. "Good. Looks like you'll be needing to show Alice a movie tonight," he said to Parker.

"That's the plan," Parker said. "By the way, I'm halfway through Mom's book. And yes, it's good," he added in grudging response to Nola's raised eyebrow.

"The boy can be taught," cracked Jerome. He turned to Nola. "Is it too late for you to grab some lunch? I'd love to fill you in on what a success your daughter is."

Way to suck up, Unk. But he wasn't lying. Alice was doing well.

"Go ahead. We can handle things here," he said to Nola. As if he was now a total bookstore pro.

The way she was smiling at his uncle, he knew she didn't really need any encouragement. He realized he was a little jealous. Uncle Jerome had no bad boy past to live down and the lady was more than willing to spend time with him. He wished he could say the same about himself. He was a regular love leper who had already struck out twice. What chance did he have of succeeding if he tried again with . . . anyone? Did he even deserve a chance?

Alice skipped into his mind and he couldn't help wondering what she would she think of him if they spent more time together.

A new woman entered the store. She was tall with legs that could have stretched from Seattle to San Francisco and long, wavy red hair. And the same big eyes as Alice, only hers were green. It was the woman he'd encountered at his mom's book signing.

Nola introduced her as "My daughter Scarlet."

The avenging sister. Parker didn't smile.

Which made them even because she didn't smile at him, either. "You are so lucky my husband came to his senses," she informed him. "Otherwise, I would have had to hire a hit man. I should have after the way you made a fool of my sister."

Here they went again. Jay owed Parker free beer for life for all the aggravation he'd caused with that stunt.

"For the millionth time, I wasn't the one who made that meme," he said irritably. "Guess you can't say the same about the picture of me with my mom. I really like being made to look like a boy toy."

A corner of her mouth lifted in a satisfied smirk. "You deserved it the way you bullied Alice."

"Yeah, well, my mom didn't. And to succeed at bullying the victim has to be weak," he added. "Your sister is anything but."

Scarlet responded to that with a snort of disgust.

"I thought you'd be working," Nola said in an effort to divert her daughter's attention.

"Lunch break. Mark and I have a counseling session," Scarlet said to her mother.

Mark. Ah, yes. "The guy who led the strike."

Scarlet pointed a finger at him. "No, *you* led the strike."

"I wasn't even there," Parker protested. Unless you counted him showing up to see it all unravel. "That was not my doing."

"We're putting that behind us," said Nola. "Did you need something?" she asked Scarlet.

Scarlet shrugged. "Just came in to say hi and get the next book for book club before I pick up Mark."

"Parker can help you," Nola said with a wicked smile. Then to Uncle Jerome, "I could use a lunch break. Let me get my coat."

"I could use a break, period," Parker grumbled.

"I'll be happy to oblige," Scarlet said.

"Maybe Bettina should help you," he suggested.

Bettina's voice soared over to them from behind one of the movable shelves. "I'm busy."

Parker ground his teeth. "What book are you looking for?"

"Hot to Handle." Her raised chin dared him to say anything about her reading choice.

"I'll put on my asbestos gloves and get it for you," he said. "Who's it by?"

"You could look it up in the computer but that's probably more than you can manage," she sniped.

Nola was back. "Be nice," she scolded as she pulled on her gloves. Then she waltzed out the door with Uncle Jerome, who had been enjoying the exchange way too much. Whatever happened to male solidarity?

Parker went to the computer and looked up the author's name, just to prove he could. Amanda Wilson. A nice normal name. He went to a shelf and fetched the book. The cover featured a headless male body, stacked, of course. The hands were ready to start unzipping the low-riding jeans. There would definitely be some heat leaking out of this book.

He returned with it and started to ring it up.

"Don't forget the fifteen percent family discount," she said.

"Family discount," he repeated, and finished the transaction.

"I don't need a bag," she said, and snatched the book. She gave him the same kind of smile her mother specialized in. "If you want to read it when I'm done let me know. You might learn something."

"Thanks for the offer," he said with a frown. "Have a good day. Good luck with the counseling." She'd need it.

She tossed her hair, then flounced out of the store.

Bettina came back into view. Naturally, now that his latest torture session had ended. "Scarlet's your number one fan," she joked.

"Haha."

Next in was his mom, offering to take him out for lunch.

"I shouldn't leave," he said. "Nola just went to lunch."

"I already ate. I can manage things here," Bettina offered.

Bettina being nice to him? What was that about? Was she sick?

"I get a break from my torture session?" he joked.

"You're messed up. You need to spend more time with your mother," Bettina informed him, and she wasn't joking.

"Thanks, Bettina," his mom said, giving the other woman a wink. "Come on, Parker. Harry's waiting."

Harry's Beach House was one of the hottest restaurants on Alki Beach, and he loved their clam chowder, so he didn't turn down the offer. Of course, she'd reserved a window seat so they could enjoy looking out at the water. Unlike Parker, she didn't have a water view from her condo on Queen Anne, but she liked the location, which was right near her other favorite bookstore, Queen Anne Book Company. The old building the condo was in had once been a high school and he had to admit, the condos in there were impressive. But nothing beat being on the beach, even when gray skies hugged the waterline.

As soon as they'd placed their orders she started pumping him on how his experience in the bookstore was going.

"Other than the fact they hate me?"

"Oh, I don't think they hate you. They just see you as a lost soul in need of saving," said his mom.

"More like a criminal in need of punishing."

"Has any of them made you read a romance novel yet?" Mom teased.

"No one's making me do anything. Well, no one but the station," he added with a frown. "I did make a deal with Alice though. She's going to watch a sports movie and I'm reading a romance."

"To diss on your show?"

"No, to read with an open mind. I'm halfway through your latest."

Mom had been about to take a drink of her water. She set the glass down. Probably afraid of choking.

"Don't worry. Like I said, I'm not going to read your book on air. It's actually good, and I'm enjoying it. Although I have skipped a couple of pages."

She laughed at that. "You know all that stuff anyway."

"I'll never understand why you decided to write romance novels. How is it that reading them didn't make you bitter? I mean, the old man left when I was just a baby. That's not exactly inspiring. You always talk about them giving you hope. Seems ironic considering the fact that he didn't leave you anything to hope for."

"But the books did. And writing about love and happiness, writing about a world I could control, well, that's helped keep the bitterness away."

His mom was always so positive. "It's hard to imagine you ever being bitter," he said.

Her reply to that observation was, "We all pay for the choices we make, and that includes not choosing wisely when it comes to a life partner. I messed up when I married the man who helped me make you," she continued. "I thought he was wonderful at first, but he kept his temper well hidden. He was abusive, and when he broke my arm your uncle stepped in. To this day, I'm not sure what Jerome said, but Gary moved out immediately. Maybe I should have, but I didn't ask for child support. I didn't want that man involved in your life, influencing you. I was happy when the divorce was final, and he disappeared. Your uncle gave you the best possible role model. Even when it came to love."

Parker gaped at her. "I'm just hearing all this now? You never said anything about the abuse. Just said that he was irresponsible and that you two fell out of love." It had always seemed like a flimsy reason to cut the guy out of both her life and her son's.

She looked out the window at the gray sky. Rain was starting to pockmark the window. "I didn't want you to think you might have that abusive gene in you. The only thing of his you inherited was his stubbornness. That can be a good thing."

"Yeah?"

"Oh, yes. Stubbornness and conviction are closely related. You just have to know the difference, when to give up the tug-of-war and let go of the rope." She raised both eyebrows, questioning whether he'd gotten the message.

"Anyone ever tell you you've got a way with words, Mom?" he teased.

"A few people," she said, and smiled at their approaching server.

After their food arrived the conversation moved from the philosophical to the concrete, with his mother talking about her various stops on her upcoming book tour, which would have her on the road for two weeks, and him sharing about his upcoming event at spring training.

Then they got back into dangerous territory with her asking how his agent was doing with selling his book. Mom hadn't been wild about the idea when Parker first told her, and she wasn't any happier when she learned he'd finished it. Instead of offering to show it to her agent she'd suggested he put it in the proverbial round file, claiming it wasn't worthy of him. First books never sold anyway. She was not going to be happy with his news.

"David sold the book, Mom. We've got a two-book deal."

She was quiet for a moment, digesting that information. He could tell it wasn't digesting easily.

"Well, looks like I was wrong," she said. "I suppose everything that's been going on has created a buzz. Buzz . . . bee . . . sting," she mused.

Suddenly his clam chowder wasn't sitting so well. "What's that supposed to mean?"

"I want you to be successful, Parker, but keep in mind, once something's in print, you can't call it back."

"I'm just trying to warn guys to look out," he insisted.

"Not every woman is out to use men," she reminded him.

"I know." They'd had this discussion more than once since he'd first told her about his book.

"Okay. I've said it before, but let me remind you, the choices you make now will travel into the future with you. You might, at some point, want to build a happy relationship. This could make it difficult to build," she warned. "But I've said enough," she promised.

"Good. Does that mean you'll come to my book launch?" he teased.

"I guess I'd better since you came to my signing. Finally," she added, also teasing.

He laughed. "You're the best, Mom. Why aren't there more women out there like you?"

"There are, as I'm sure you're going to discover," she said, and there came Alice, swimming into his mind.

Mom checked her Fitbit. "Looks like we've used up your lunch break. I'd better let you get back to the store."

Back to the pink prison. At least he had the evening with Alice to look forward to. She may have been a co-owner of that prison, but somehow, he was finding it harder to see her as an opponent. What would Alice think about his book?

He didn't want to know.

CHAPTER 25

GOOD HEAVENS, THOUGHT Alice as she took in Parker's fancy condo. Quartz countertops in the kitchen, a large living room complete with leather couch, armchairs and a coffee table sitting on a hardwood floor. He had a small dining area where a minimalist wood table and four chairs sat. An abstract painting of koi fish occupied the wall over the couch. Windows showing beach and water framed real-life art.

She walked over to a window and gazed out at the dark night waters. They were beautiful and mysterious. Under the sun on a summer day that view would feel like a vacation.

"If I had a view like this I'd never want to leave," she said.

"I spend my evenings out on that deck any time the weather's good," he said, coming to stand next to her.

She caught a whiff of his cologne and had to swallow down a mixture of nerves and desire. She may have never been in love, never really been kissed by an expert, but she'd read enough to know what was going on. She was falling for this man, her hormones wrapping a net around her heart.

She moved away, drifting to where a small barrister bookcase sat. It was filled. She bent to read the spines and saw what looked like business titles. No decorations on top of the case, simply a pile of books. She picked one up. It was, hardly surprising, one of his uncle's novels.

"I'm a fan," he said, then added, "See? I do read."

"I guess you do." She bent and read the spines again. "I've read *Atomic Habits*."

"Good book," he said. "What else have you read, Alice? Please don't intimidate me and say *War and Peace*."

Her cheeks flushed pink. "No. Have you?"

"Nope. I watched the miniseries. Does that count?" he added with a grin. The doorbell rang. "There's our pizza," he said, and went to open the door for the delivery person.

The aroma of pizza entered the room and her stomach rumbled. She much preferred smelling pizza over smelling Parker's spicy cologne.

He set the box on the coffee table. "What do you want to drink? I've got Coke, root beer and tonic water."

Tonic water. He'd remembered.

She smiled at him. "Coke."

"Coke," he said in surprise.

"I love tonic water, but pop just naturally goes with pizza."

"You are a woman after my own heart."

He fetched her a small bottle of Coke as well as one for himself and set them down along with paper plates and napkins, then moved to a console under the TV. He opened it and she saw it was filled with DVDs.

"I stream everything but my favorite movies. Gotta have those on DVD," he said. He pulled one out and put it in the player. "*The Natural*, by request." Then he picked up the remote control and joined her on the couch, seating himself at the opposite end. The polite thing to do, of course. The smart thing. There was nothing happening between them, nothing about to happen. She grabbed a piece of pizza and shoved a bite in her mouth.

The movie started and she was instantly pulled in by the music. All of life should have a soundtrack. What would be the soundtrack of hers?

As with her favorite books, she soon forgot about her own life and got pulled into the story as the movie progressed, horrified by the bad guys and rooting for Roy Hobbs, the hero who had stumbled and fallen and had one last chance to make his dreams come true.

And then came the ending, with Roy hitting his amazing home run, so far that it took out the lights at the far end of the stadium. Roy injured, starting to bleed. Was this where his dream ended? She held her breath as he ran the bases, then started tearing up as the triumphant music played and the shower of sparks fell.

The ending credits rolled, and Parker turned to her. "What did you think?" As if he couldn't tell.

She wiped a tear from a corner of her eye. "That was stirring. I loved the scene where his bat broke and he used the one he and little Bobby made. And the final run around the bases, even as he was bleeding . . ."

"That, in a nutshell, is sports. It doesn't matter if it's soccer, tennis, football or baseball. It's life. It's rising to a challenge and hoping you succeed. Alice, you may never know what it feels like to hit a baseball, but trust me, when you connect and that thing goes sailing it's one of the best highs in the world."

"One of the best?"

"Well, there are other highs. You read about them all the time," he said, and she blushed. "But that's why I love what I do for a living. I get to talk about something that makes life exciting. It's what I need to get back to," he muttered.

"I think you should. We all have our spot in the world where we belong, things in that world that make life exciting. Like books," she said. "We can't all play sports, but we can all read about people making their lives better."

He leaned forward. "Alice, be honest. Do the books you read help you make your life better?"

"They inspire me." She loved her books, loved falling into a story and cheering for the characters who often felt so real. But for all her reading, was she getting inspired to go out and find love? Reading gave her something to do at night. It was how she earned a living. Maybe it was also how she hid.

"Do they inspire you to get out there and do something?" he asked.

It was as if he'd read her mind. Instead of answering, she countered, "Does watching sports inspire men to get out there and do something?"

"You got me there. Maybe not. Maybe a lot of men just like remembering when they were in good enough shape to do something. Or maybe we like to hang out, watch a game and pound our chests. Kind of like how you like to get together and talk about what you read. Maybe for the average guy a game, or a movie like this is enough to make him forget about the bills and the fact that the house needs painting and the kids need braces. Maybe when you women read a romance novel you forget about the fact that you have to, I don't know, come home from work and make dinner or wash the kids' smelly socks."

"Why, Parker," she said in surprise. "You almost sound approving of romance novels."

He blinked. Then laughed. "Almost. I told you what got me started on my one-man crusade. It was that stupid book my ex wrote." He paused, frowned. "No, I've got to be honest. It was before the book. It was how screwed up our relationship was. And the one before it. I can't turn a woman's life into magic. I tried, but I'm not a cross between a navy SEAL and a . . . I don't know, werewolf. I'd hear Luna talking with her friends sometimes. They were always dissing their men who weren't enough. God only knows what she said about me. Oh, wait. God and I both know. I wasn't romantic enough. I didn't spend enough. I was . . ."

Hurt, thought Alice.

He shook his head and waved away whatever else was left on the list of his flaws. "I'm not the only one. Men aren't enough anymore. You know how that makes a man feel, when he's trying to be a good guy but nothing he does is good enough? Sorry," he muttered. "I didn't mean to puke my guts out."

"Not every woman reads a romance novel and expects her man to take down a bad guy or fight some evil force," Alice said. "Most of the women I know love their men. Not every woman expects her man to be an amazing lover, either." Well, maybe she was wrong about that.

"Yeah, right," he scoffed.

"I wouldn't," she said softly. "How could I when I'm . . ." Her words trailed off into a mist of embarrassment.

"What?" he prompted.

"I'm not exactly a romance heroine." Although lately she'd felt like she was coming closer, believing in herself more, doing things she never would have done. But so what? Where was the love?

She had a tiny dab of tomato sauce on the end of one finger. She reached for her napkin and wiped it off.

He moved closer, took that hand, and the contact gave her a jolt. "Don't talk like that. You are a heroine. You're smart and you stand up for what you believe in. Doesn't that sum up what a heroine is?"

"That was sweet. Thank you," she said.

"Hey, I'm not just being nice, although I guess that would be out of character."

He still had her hand in his and it felt so good. What would he say if she asked him to kiss her?

She decided she didn't want to know. "I'd better get home and get to bed," she said. Alone.

He let go of her hand. "That's right. You've got another early day tomorrow." He stood and she stood. "You're doing great, by the way."

"I'm learning a few things."

"So am I," he said. "By the way, your sister hates my guts."

"Well, you have had rather a strong influence over our lives," Alice said.

"That gate's swung both ways," he said. "I'll be glad when this week is over."

And they wouldn't have to see each other again. He was only being nice to her because he had to. She managed a smile. "Thanks for the pizza," she said, and moved to the door.

He walked with her, took her coat out of the coat closet and helped her into it. Handed her purse to her. "Tomorrow we need to go over what we want to say on Friday. How about another movie?"

"I'd like that," she said. "Do you want to come over to my house? I make a great meat loaf."

What was she thinking, inviting Parker over to her house for dinner? She was like someone in a TikTok reel, laying out bait. *Here fishy, fishy*. Pathetic. And Parker was no fish. He was a shark. But it was it too late to take back the invitation.

"Yeah? I love meat loaf."

"I also make a great chocolate cake," she said. Now she was bragging. Charlotte Brontë help her, she was out of her mind.

He grinned. "I like chocolate cake. Text me your address and tell me what time to be there."

He sounded like he really wanted to come over. He sounded like a different man than the snarky one on the radio. It was almost like he was two different men—Jekyll and Hyde, battling to see who would eventually dominate.

"I will," she said.

Back in her car, she realized she was smiling. Parker Black, the nice version, the wounded hero version, was coming over to her house. For dinner and a movie.

And to get ready for their show together on Friday. It was just business, she reminded herself. They'd both lightened up, but that meant nothing. This was only a publicity stunt coming to an end.

Parker hated to see Alice leave. Having her with him, watching her enjoy one of his favorite classic movies, eating pizza together. It had felt . . . comfortable. He hadn't had to be anything but himself and that had felt good. He'd meant what he said. She really was a heroine, one who deserved to be appreciated.

And kissed. He wished he'd kissed her. And if he'd had one more minute with her on the couch he would have.

"Listen to you," he scoffed, "talking like a character in a romance novel." Too bad they weren't. He could be assured of that happily-ever-after.

He went to bed and there was his mother's novel, sitting on his nightstand. He picked it up and started reading. And then couldn't stop until he'd gotten to the end. Of course, all the issues got resolved by the last page and he realized he was glad they did. No wonder these books were so addictive. They did leave a person feeling hopeful. His mother was right.

If only that kind of hope worked in real life. He turned

off his bedside light, shut his eyes and then spent the next two hours imagining different scenarios where he and Alice would have met and things would have turned out differently.

Things still could. They could put all this nonsense behind them. Get to know each other better. Watch more movies. Share pizza. Maybe even go to a ball game or two together. Go to a club and slow dance. He could win over her mom and her sister and Bettina the gargoyle.

Morning brought a reality check. Bettina still wasn't even remotely inclined to be won over, even when he arrived with lattes from Starbucks.

"I only drink decaf," she said.

Nola wasn't any easier. "Sorry, but I take mine with soy."

That left him to take his useless coffee drinks to the back room and dump them.

"But it was a nice offer," Nola called after him. "Maybe there's hope for you after all."

He was just beginning to smile when he heard Bettina say, "Don't count on it."

One of their first customers informed him that he was rude and mean and gave him a typewritten list of books he needed to read so he could transform from the beast he was into a prince. "Maybe," she'd added.

The next woman in, someone named Julia, wanted a historical novel set in World War II.

"You can learn a lot about history from a novel," Bettina said, smiling at her. "Even a romance novel," she added and sent Parker a look that dared him to contradict her.

He held up both hands. "Hey, I'm all for history."

"You need to work on living down yours," Bettina told him.

Yep, he was having fun now.

Next in was the pretty Lina, the woman who'd lit into him outside the bookstore. She was wearing jeans, boots and a leather jacket, her long, dark hair in a ponytail. Parker was in the process of ringing up Julia's purchase and Bettina was watching over his shoulder, hoping as usual that he'd screw up. As if he would at this point.

"I'm on a mission," Lina announced.

"What kind of mission?" Bettina asked.

"A mission to educate someone," she said, and looked at Parker.

Oh, no. What now?

"Will you ask Nola if I can steal Parker for a few hours?" Lina asked Bettina.

"You going to hold him for ransom? Nobody will pay," said Bettina. Such a funny lady.

"No, I want him to do a ride-along, to see what a day in the life of a demanding woman looks like."

Of course, throwing one of his tirades back in his face. Parker had a feeling he was going to smart in a whole new way for his many rants.

"I'll check," said Bettina, and practically skipped off to the back room where Nola had gone to catch up on some paperwork.

Parker put Julia's book and receipt in a pink bag and thanked her for coming in. "Enjoy your book."

"Oh, I will. And enjoy your ride-along," she teased.

"I will," he lied. Maybe Nola wouldn't let him leave. There was a first, wanting to stay in the pink prison with Bettina his jailor.

She was back with Nola in tow. "What do you have planned?" Nola asked Lina.

The proverbial twinkle in the eye? Check. A smirk? Check, check. Nola was all in.

"I just thought Parker should get a more realistic view of the life of a modern American woman. You know, one of us demanding ones who can't tell the difference between real life and a romance novel."

All three of them laughed. Like Shakespeare's witches. *Double, double, toil and trouble; Fire burn and cauldron bubble.* He was going to be the one in the cauldron.

"Can you spare him?" Lina asked, pretending she didn't know the answer.

"Oh, I think we can," said Nola.

"Great. Get your coat, big man, and let's go," Lina said.

"Fine. Sounds fun," he said, pulling out his best bravado.

He could hear them giggling as he went to the back room to fetch his coat. *It's your last day. You can survive anything.*

He returned with a big grin. "Okay, bring it on."

"Have fun," Nola called as he followed Lina out the door.

The Seattle sky was its usual gray and an icy drizzle tried to crawl under Parker's coat collar. *Drizzle, drizzle, cold and rain. Look what you started. Where was your brain?*

"So, first I have to run to the hardware store for Eduardo. He's working on a zipline in the backyard for the boys and he needs carabiners, whatever those are."

"A zipline, huh? Whose idea was that?" Parker was willing to bet Lina had come up with the bright idea and added it to a long honey-do list.

"His. We're saving up for a family vacation in two years. Costa Rica, Sky Trek. I promised him I'd zipline, too, and maybe this will help me get brave enough to do it."

So much for the honey-do list assumption. "You don't strike me as a woman who's afraid of anything," Parker said.

"I'm not afraid of bullies," she said with a cocky grin. "Get in."

Into the SUV Parker climbed. It smelled faintly of dog.

"Yes, we have a dog," she said as if reading his mind. "Her name is Alma. You'll get to meet her later."

Hopefully Alma was the friendly type. "What kind of dog is she?" Parker asked.

"She's a golden. Don't worry, she'll like you. She has no ability to discriminate between pendejos and nice guys."

He didn't bother to ask what pendejos meant. He got the idea.

They pulled into Junction Ace Hardware and he accompanied her in. She lost her hard edge and turned sweet the minute they were inside. Of course, one of the pros was happy to help her find what she needed.

"You know how to turn on the charm, don't you?" he taunted as they left the store.

"I know how to be nice," she said.

"You this nice to your husband?"

"Seriously? You gonna ask me tonterias like that?"

Again, he didn't bother to ask for a definition. "Guess not. What's next?"

"Grocery shopping. I have to bake cookies for the Cub Scout pack meeting tonight. And I need ground beef, lettuce, tomatoes and hamburger buns. Once I get home I have to put another load of laundry in, and I have a stack of clothes to fold. I need to make a reel for my followers. You can help with that."

"Fun," he muttered.

"And I have to clean the bathrooms," she continued.

"You make your man sit to pee?" Parker jibed.

She scowled at him. "What do you think?"

"I think you do."

"Well, you think wrong. Eduardo has perfect aim. And he puts the seat down when he's done, which I bet you've never done for a woman."

"Hey, I'm no caveman," Parker said.

"So you say."

Grocery shopping took an hour as Lina had to inspect every tomato, check out sale items and chat with a friend she'd run into. She introduced him as "Parker Black, the guy who hates women."

"I never said that," he protested.

The woman rolled her eyes. "I've heard of you."

"Don't believe everything you hear," he said.

"We're doing a ride-along. Parker's spending a day with a real woman," Lina said. "One who doesn't have unrealistic expectations," she added.

"When you're done with him, he can come follow my daughter around the office and then home to take care of the twins," the woman said.

"That's okay," Parker said. One ride-along was enough.

Once back at the house, it was time to help fold laundry, bake cookies, take the dog for a walk and help Lina film a reel where she dissected the latest novel she was reading. "Four jalapeños, everyone," she said with a wink. "Keep the Valentine fun going. I'm going to. And yes, I'm going to try out this new fragrance." She went on to tout some brand of perfume. "I have some sponsors who give me free merch," she explained when they were done. "And publishers send me free books to read and review. It keeps life interesting."

Parker suspected *she* kept life interesting.

Her cell phone rang and she answered with a chipper, "Eduardo, what do you want?" Whatever he wanted, by the way she giggled Parker suspected it was R rated. "Yeah, I got them. Guess who's here with me. I have Parker Black helping me out today. Anything you'd like to say to him?" She grinned and held the phone to Parker. Yeah, this would be fun.

"Don't mess with my woman," Eduardo said.

"Wouldn't dream of it," Parker assured him, and handed the phone back. He suspected nobody messed with Lina.

"I got to go drop Parker off and pick up the boys. See you later," she said, and ended the call with a smooch noise.

"Okay, time to go pick up the boys from school," she said. "Then I have to take them to basketball practice. Want to join us?"

"Uh, no." He'd seen enough and had enough.

She handed him a cookie. "You were a good sport."

And now you get a lollipop. He frowned, but he took the cookie. He'd already sampled one and they were good.

"Just because my friends and I like to read it doesn't mean we don't have our feet planted in the real world," she said as they walked out the door. "I don't expect Eduardo to buy me flowers every week—that's not in the budget—and I don't expect him to take me out for expensive dinners. I expect him to be my friend and respect me, and I do the same for him. That's love. Maybe someday you'll find it."

Maybe he would. A certain bookworm with brown eyes and freckles came to mind. Was the gate to love made of meat loaf, chocolate cake and sports movies?

CHAPTER 26

LINA HAD JUST dropped Parker back at the bookstore when Alice texted him with directions to her place. She lived in an ADU behind her mom's house. They worked together, they lived on the same lot. If Nola Willoughby didn't approve of Parker Alice probably never would, either.

"How was your ride-along?" Nola greeted him.

"Enlightening," he said. "We need more Linas in the world." And more Alices, too.

"There are more than you realize," said Nola. "The unhappy few you've encountered don't represent all of us. Maybe the same applies over on your side of the fence."

She was behind the checkout counter looking up something on her computer. He stopped and leaned an elbow on it. "As in I don't speak for all men?"

"You speak for all angry ones," Nola said.

"I speak *to* them."

"So we've heard. You know, Parker, we all have choices in life. We can either stir the pot or take it off the stove."

He had to smile at that. "Can't do both?"

"What do you think?"

"I think maybe I need to get out of the kitchen," he said.

"Maybe you do," she agreed. "I suspect a lot of what's been going on has gotten away from you a little."

"Maybe."

"Have you ever heard of Goethe's 'The Sorcerer's Apprentice'?"

He shook his head.

"It's a poem about a little boy who was supposed to fetch water for his master. He animated a broom to do his work for him, which seemed like a good idea at the time. But the broom got out of control and soon the boy had created a flood. In short, something that seemed like a good idea got out of hand."

Hit me over the head with a metaphor, why don't you. "So what happened?" Parker asked.

"The wizard came home and used his powers to clean up the mess."

"So maybe I need a wizard?" he joked.

"Maybe you are the wizard," she said.

Before he could stop them, the words galloped right out of his mouth. "I like your daughter." *A lot.*

Her hands stilled over the keyboard. She didn't look at him. "The big, bad wolf liked Grandma, too."

"And the beast liked Beauty," he countered. "How would you feel about me taking her out when this is all over?"

"You should be asking Alice how she'd feel."

"I'm going to, tonight. I'm going over for dinner."

Nola bit down on her lower lip and nodded. Took a deep breath. "Parker, you're a heartbreak looking for a place to land."

"Maybe I'm just a heart looking for a place to heal," he suggested.

"I don't care what the books say. My daughter's not a love hospital. You have to heal yourself."

"I'm working on it," he said as much for himself as her. "I guess you're not going to give me your seal of approval."

"I guess you're right. Not until I see a real transformation."

He nodded. "Fair enough. Like I said, I'm working on it."

"Meanwhile, don't work my daughter over."

He had no intention of doing that. He didn't want to hurt Alice the way he'd been hurt. He knew what that felt like. He just wanted to hang out, build a friendship.

Okay, maybe, down the road, he wanted more. He was human, after all. And maybe Alice wanted more. Maybe she wanted some romance IRL. Maybe she was tired of book boyfriends and wanted to see what a real man felt like. He knew he wanted to see what she felt like.

But maybe her mom was right, and he was a heartbreak waiting to happen. Their adventure was about to come to an end. He should leave it at that.

Then he walked into Alice's place, smelled the meat loaf, took in the ugly old brown couch with a colorful hand-knitted blanket thrown over the back and the vintage coffee table, the bookcase brimming with books, and the painting of flowers on one wall, and a warm feeling planted itself in his chest. The table looked vintage and so did the tablecloth over it. It was set for two and a little vase of dried flowers sat in the center. He felt like he'd walked onto a movie set.

Or into the pages of one of his mom's books.

Alice had dressed up her table but kept herself casual. She was in jeans and a top and wore a blue apron sporting a shelf of books. The caption beneath read *I Have No Shelf Control.*

She looked happy to see him. It was such a different expression from their first encounters. The warmth spread through his chest. This was what something good felt like.

He handed over the flowers he'd picked up at the grocery

store on his way over. It wasn't a very original hostess gift, but she was delighted.

"Thank you, that was sweet of you," she said.

"I can be sweet."

A black-and-white cat strolled into the room to greet him.

"That's Mr. Darcy," Alice said as the cat rubbed against Parker's leg.

"Mr. Darcy, huh?" he said, and bent to pet the cat.

"From *Pride and Prejudice*."

"I saw the movie." Luna had insisted he watch it with her. "I never could understand why what's-her-name wanted anything to do with the guy when he walked around with a stick up his butt all the time."

"People change, don't they?" Alice replied.

"Yeah, I guess they do," he said. Maybe there was hope for the Mr. Darcys of the world.

"And yes, he wasn't very nice in the beginning."

"Not much of a romance hero," Parker said.

"Not at first. But in the end, he proved his love, not by what he said, but by what he did."

"Actions speak louder than words, huh?" Of course, they did. Which meant Parker was in trouble.

"They do. Although both are nice, aren't they? Okay, everything's ready," she said. "What would you like to drink? I have milk, but I also bought some beer."

He spotted a chocolate cake on the little kitchen's counter. "Milk. It goes great with chocolate cake," he said. "And that cake looks awesome."

"I like to cook." She motioned to the table. "Go ahead, sit down."

"The blanket on the couch, did you make that?" he asked as he settled at the table.

"No, one of my grandmas did. It has a lot of sentimental value." She pulled a loaf pan out of the oven and began to slice up the meat loaf.

"That smells good," he said. Actually, it smelled amazing and made him feel like he was a kid again, getting ready to dig into his mother's meat loaf after coming home from baseball practice.

"It is," she said, the smile still in her voice. "And I baked potatoes and made a salad. Do you like salad?"

It felt like a leading question. What if he said no? Luna had always taken his food dislikes as a personal affront.

This was different. Alice wasn't Luna. Alice was . . . special.

"Potato salad, I like that," he said.

"I guess a lot of guys aren't into salad," she said. "Scarlet's husband won't eat it."

Scarlet's husband, Parker's big fan. He didn't want to talk about Mark. Or Scarlet.

"I'm willing to try some," he said.

She came to the table, carrying a platter of meat loaf slices with two baked potatoes sitting on the end. "Go ahead and start dishing up."

Next came sour cream, butter and bacons bits. And rolls. And then the salad. A bunch of lettuce with bits of tomato and avocado. And raisins? Okay, that was weird. But she'd also brought a bowl of croutons.

"Everyone loves croutons, right?" she said.

"Right," he agreed.

Once they started eating the first thing he sampled was the meat loaf. "This is awesome," he said, and she grinned.

"How did your day at the studio go?" he asked. As if they were a couple, each sharing how their day had gone. "I didn't get a chance to listen."

"It was good. Your uncle explained the different football

team positions to me and listeners all called in to convince me that I need to become a Seahawks fan."

"Think you ever will?"

She shook her head. "No. But I think I could get into baseball. I really enjoyed that movie last night. What are we going to watch tonight?"

"*Moneyball*. I love that movie."

She nodded. "We can stream it. Tell me about your day at the store."

"I was gone half the day."

"Wimping out?" she teased.

"Nope. I did a ride-along with Lina. She felt some of my theories needed to be debunked."

Alice smiled as she forked up a bite of salad. "Should we talk about that tomorrow? I bet it was interesting."

"Uh, no. I'm trying to put the whole thing out of my mind. She runs a circus."

"Eduardo has no complaints about their life. In fact, he's been known to buy books for her."

"Jalapeño ones?" A couple of days at the bookstore and he was becoming a book expert.

"Yep."

"Do you read jalapeño books?"

She blushed almost enough to match the tomatoes in her salad and gave a little one-shouldered shrug. "Sometimes."

"Yeah, those book boyfriends really come through," he teased. Then sobered. "But what about in real life, Alice? Who comes through for you?" He already knew the answer. A woman who thought she was nothing special had no one special. In Alice's case that felt wrong.

"I'm fine," she said, and picked up their empty plates. "Are you ready for cake?"

There was a dodge.

He let it go. "Sure."

The cake was better than anything he ever found in the grocery store bakery section. "This is stellar," he said.

"It's my mom's recipe."

"You're a good cook."

"It's a hobby of mine."

"What else do you do for fun, Alice?"

"Fun?" she repeated as if it were a foreign word.

"Yeah, fun."

"I have the bookstore and the book clubs. And I read."

"Reading is good. But what do you do?"

She pressed her lips together while she thought and he found himself wanting to kiss those lips.

"I go out for coffee. With my sister. We watch movies. I like to play Nintendo sometimes," she added. She sounded like a kid, fishing for the right answer for her teacher.

"You got a Nintendo?"

She shook her head. "Scarlet and Mark have one."

This was her big excitement. No going clubbing, no sports, no getting out in nature and hiking.

"How about outdoors? Do you like to hike?"

Her head dropped. "I haven't hiked since I was in Camp Fire. I don't know why," she added. "I liked being out in nature. I like going to the beach, bringing a blanket and a snack and . . ."

"A book," he finished with her.

"There's nothing wrong with that," she said, frowning.

"There's nothing wrong with getting in the water, either," he said. "Or going for a hike. Being active. Maybe going bowling," he ventured. Most people could handle that.

She laughed. "I have gone bowling. It's been a while. I threw mostly gutter balls. My boyfriend . . ."

"Wait. Boyfriend?"

The blush made another appearance. "It didn't last long. He found someone more glamorous."

"What do you mean by that?"

"She was French," Alice said as if that explained it all. She veered away from France with a perky, "How about that movie?"

"Okay, let's do it," he said. Wrong choice of words. Now he'd never be able to concentrate on the movie.

Moneyball was streaming, but not for free. He offered to pay, but she insisted on taking care of it.

"I'm hosting tonight, and this is a business expense," she said.

"Okay, fine," he said. There was no point fighting her on it. She was determined.

Once again, they sat on opposite ends of the couch, her hugging a sofa pillow, him wishing he was hugging her. He really was falling for this woman. He had to be insane. Everyone in her life wanted him out of it.

He sneaked some peeks her direction as the movie played, observing her reaction, noting how she leaned slightly forward, entranced. She was like a little kid, enjoying her first Disney movie.

"That was fascinating," she said afterward. "I loved how passionate Billy Beane was about finding a way to improve his team."

"He loved the game. All of us who ever played it do," said Parker. "Did you ever play softball?" he asked. "When you were a kid? At a picnic?"

She shook her head regretfully.

"Would you like to try sometime?" he asked. "We play every year when the station has its annual picnic."

"Oh, I couldn't hit a ball," she protested.

"Maybe you could if I took you to a batting cage and gave you some pointers."

"Maybe. I'm not very athletic, but I think I'd like to go to a game. I've learned a lot about it hosting your show."

"Want to share that tomorrow?" he asked.

"Sure."

"I'm glad you feel like you learned something," he said. Then had to spit it out. "I have, too."

"You have?" she prompted.

"I've gotten some things wrong. I've made a lot of sweeping generalizations."

And there were more to come. He thought of his book deal and the dinner he'd enjoyed suddenly sat like lead in his gut. "I wish I'd stuck to sports on the show." And not just on the show. He'd had enough of sitting on the opposite end of the couch. He closed the distance between them. "Alice, I'm sorry I was such a jerk when we first met. Sorry about the debate."

He was sorry about so much. Now it was too late. His mom was right. His angry man book was going to follow him down the road.

She hugged the pillow. "You were a better debater."

"But not a better person. I cut you off and never gave you a chance and I was an even bigger jerk in front of your store. I should never have gone along with that dumb stunt. I'm no hero. But I've got to say, I wish I was."

"You're not hopeless," she said, her smile teasing. "You did buy a book."

"Don't let me off that easy. Alice . . ."

He stalled out at her name. He needed to tell her about the book deal, but he couldn't get the words out. They were in a huddle at the back of his throat.

She was looking at him expectantly, still hugging her pillow.

"I told your mom I like you. She's not very happy about it. But it's true. In fact, I don't just like you, I admire you. I wish we'd met earlier."

Before everything had gone sideways.

"But then we wouldn't have had a very interesting story, would we?" she said. The sweet look she was giving him made him feel like a skunk.

"Alice, I need to tell you something."

Her expression changed. She suddenly looked supercharged. She tossed aside her pillow. "Don't tell me anything," she said as she hurled herself against him, wrapping her arms around his neck and mashing her lips into his. She hit him with enough force to send him backward, her on top of him. Whoa, what the heck?

He couldn't help himself. He ran his arms up her back and held on.

It had a been an impulsive move, but Alice didn't regret it. Parker wasn't the only one who'd been changed since they first met. She had, too. She didn't care if the books she read had the hero seducing the heroine. She didn't want to wait to be seduced. Or courted. Or anything. She'd been reading about romance long enough. It was time to reach out and grab it IRL. And grabbing Parker Black was the most satisfying thing she'd done in a long time. So what if she wasn't a great kisser? He didn't care, because here he was, kissing her back and her insides were turning to goo. And she was proud of it.

She ended the kiss, opened her eyes and studied his face, wondering what she'd see.

"Whoa, what was that?" he asked, smiling.

"That was me going for what I want," she said simply.

"Since when?"

"Never mind," she said. She had no intention of telling him she'd wanted him ever since she first checked out his pictures online, that she'd wanted him even when she actively disliked him. And that now, with him turning from a beast into a prince, she could finally give herself permission to do something about it, to break out of her shell and grab for her own happy ending. To start pulling love off the pages of books and planting it in her own life.

And if he didn't end up loving her back?

She'd take that chance. "Please. Kiss me again."

"Okay," he said, and did.

"You do that so well," she said with a happy sigh.

He traced her jawline with his finger. "Aww, you're just saying that 'cause it's true," he joked.

"I was never a very good kisser," she confessed. She hadn't exactly had a ton of practice.

"You have great potential," he murmured, and kissed her once more.

But then he sat them both back up. "Okay, we need to stop."

"Shouldn't it be me saying that?" she joked.

"Not this time. I want more of this," he said, fingering a lock of her hair. "But this isn't a novel. It's real life, and real life is messy. I have some stuff I need to figure out," he continued, not quite looking her in the eye. "Let's get through tomorrow first. Then we'll talk. Okay?"

"Okay," she said. But she didn't understand.

He left the couch, and she trailed him to the door, watched while he put his coat back on.

"I'll see you tomorrow morning," he said. Then he opened the door and was gone.

She'd hoped he'd kiss her good-night. Take her in his arms. Why did they have to get through tomorrow? Maybe he wanted to do things right, start them on the road to romance with dinner out once he was back from Arizona.

She touched her lips where his had been. No wonder so many fictional heroines did that. Anything to try and hang on to the blissful feeling. She'd been kissed by a pro.

A man who'd kissed heaven only knew how many women. A man who could have any woman he wanted.

But he wanted her. His arms wrapping around her proved that.

She texted her sister. Parker was here for dinner.

Her cell phone rang immediately. "Alice, what are you doing?"

"We had to get ready for the show tomorrow."

"Is that all you did?" Scarlet demanded.

"No. Oh, my gosh, Scarlet, it was amazing."

"Amazing? You didn't sleep with him, did you?" Scarlet demanded, her voice threaded with panic.

"No," Alice said, offended. "But he kissed me." After she'd gone after him. She decided not to share that detail. "Scarlet, he's like a real romance hero."

"He is not! Honestly, what are you thinking?"

"We're putting the past behind us," Alice said. "Really, we've had the most amazing two days."

"Two days! Do you think you're in Vegas or something? Stay away from that man. He's poison."

He sure didn't kiss like it. And he hadn't talked like it. He'd shared so much of himself.

"He's not genuine, Alice. You're nothing more than a publicity stunt."

"The stunt ends tomorrow," Alice said.

"And are you going out tomorrow?"

"I don't know." Would he have time before he had to fly to Peoria? "Maybe not tomorrow, but we will," said Alice.

"Did he say so?"

"Well, no."

"He wants you to be a good little bunny until after his show, then it will be, 'Bye, Alice, nice using you.' I know he's hot but he'll burn you."

"You're wrong. His whole attitude has changed. And now I'm sorry I said anything to you. I thought you'd be happy for me."

"I want to be happy for you."

"Then let me enjoy this. Scarlet, for the first time, I'm living a romance instead of reading one."

Scarlet groaned. "Oh, sis. Be careful."

"I'll be fine," Alice assured her.

She was done simply reading about romance. She was now writing her own. She called her mother. Mom would understand.

"Mom, I just had the most incredible night with Parker. I think something amazing is starting between us," she began. "He's not at all what we thought he was. Not anymore."

"That's what he says." Her mother's reaction wasn't as intense as Scarlet's had been, but it wasn't exactly enthusiastic.

"He means it," Alice insisted.

"Just take things slow," her mother advised.

"I'll be fine," Alice assured her.

Her whole life had been slow. Slower than a drugged tortoise. Alice was ready for speed, and she could hardly wait for morning to come, bringing her more time with Parker.

Crap. Crap, crap, crap. Parker was in such deep shit he was choking on it. Alice now thought he was Prince Charming. What was she going to think about him once he told her about the book? Would she understand? How would she feel about him out there promoting it?

Of course, she'd understand. It was cultural commentary, that was all. Okay, aggressive commentary. Passionate commentary. And some rude and insulting commentary. But he'd written it long before she and her band of romantics had come along to show him another side to relationships. She'd understand that. He was worrying for nothing. He'd tell her right after the show.

He had to. David had sent the deal announcement to *Publishers Weekly*, the big industry magazine. For all he knew, that magazine had already showed up at the store and was kicking around the back room, like a bomb waiting to go off.

If only he had time to take her to dinner, or at least lunch. But he had a plane to catch.

Okay, Plan B. He'd offer to fly her down to Arizona. Get her there in time for the big Saturday night bash. He and Jay had a suite. He'd stick Jay in a room with Arne and Butch and put her in the suite with him. He'd take her to games, introduce her to the players. She'd love it. They'd forget about the stupid book. And when it finally came out, they'd laugh about it. He'd promote it and it would all be a big joke. Everything would be okay.

He was in deep shit.

CHAPTER 27

NOLA DOUBTED SHE'D sleep a wink, not after the way Alice had gushed over the wonderful evening she and Parker had enjoyed. "I think something amazing is starting between us," she'd said.

If it had been any other man Nola would have been dancing for joy. But this man. Why him? Why had she opened the door by accepting that ridiculous debate challenge? More important, how could she get him out of their life before he hurt Alice?

But maybe he was done with his shock-jock behavior. Maybe he really was coming to care for Alice. Maybe this bad feeling Nola had was nothing more than imagination-induced worry.

She'd cautioned Alice to take things slow, but hearts tended to want to race.

"It'll be fine," Alice had said.

Her daughter was learning a whole new vocabulary of confidence. That was good to see. And she had been holding her own hosting his show. Nola was proud of how well she'd done. Her girl had spread her wings.

But Nola didn't want some fickle man shooting Alice

down just when she was starting to take flight. Still, she wasn't sure how she could stop him. He'd better have meant what he said to her in the bookstore.

She made herself some hot milk and took a melatonin and a hot shower. She was on her way to bed when Bettina's ring tone summoned her.

"You never read *PW* this week, did you?" Bettina said.

"As you know, I've been busy," said Nola.

"Well, I just did. And there's an announcement about a book deal for Parker Black."

Nola dropped onto the edge of the bed. "Read it to me."

Bettina read the announcement about the sweet deal Parker Black had gotten for his non-fiction book *Bye-Bye Babe*. "A snarky collection of commentary and advice for men on how to survive the latest culture wars between the sexes," she read.

"That man," Nola said in disgust. "Of course, to be fair, he wrote the book long before we met him."

"Looks like he made the deal since we met him. And he and Alice have been spending time together these last couple nights, haven't they? And wasn't he just buttering you up earlier today?"

Nola frowned. "Yes, he was."

"Did he tell you about this?"

'No."

"Did he tell Alice?"

"I'm sure he didn't." But Nola was going to. She ended the call with Bettina and called her daughter.

Alice didn't pick up. She'd probably already gone to bed.

Nola left a message. "Alice, don't rush into anything with this man. He hasn't changed at all. He's still woman bashing and has sold a book that will keep him happily continuing to do so. This is not someone you're going to want to become involved with, trust me. And trust your instincts." Alice hadn't liked the man from the get-go. She'd been right. Hopefully, she'd remember that. "And call me before you go to the station," Nola urged.

Alice hadn't needed to take a book to bed. Her head was filled with the conversation and kisses she'd enjoyed earlier. She and Parker had both grown—character arc!—and were on their way to a happy ending.

She slept beautifully and right before waking up dreamed that Parker proposed. In front of the Eiffel Tower. Present had been her mother and sister and Bettina. And her cat Mr. Darcy, who had been seated on a unicycle and could talk. It was a dream, after all.

She smiled her way into the shower, then to her closet to try and find something sexy to wear for her last day on air. There was nothing. She would have to do something about that. If she was going to be with a sophisticated, handsome man like Parker she needed to up her game. She'd get her sister to take her shopping. Once Scarlet got over thinking that Parker was the devil's long-lost son.

She picked out a pink sweater to go with her slacks and this time opted to wear the gold locket that had been her maternal grandmother's. It was old-fashioned but sweet. And wearing something of one of her grandmother's felt like the right thing to do. She decided she needed to honor both grandmas and dug out the pink pearl bracelet that had been her other grandma's. Neither one was around anymore, but if they had been they'd have been happy to see Alice finding true love. Especially Grandma Willoughby, who'd read her so many fairy tales when she was little.

"I got the prince, Grammy," she murmured.

She picked up her phone to see if perhaps Parker had texted her. There was no text from Parker. Only a voice message from her mother. The call she'd decided to ignore after their earlier conversation.

Her mother's words reached out and grabbed at her happiness. "He hasn't changed at all . . . This is not someone you're going to want to get involved with."

And here she was, getting involved. What was with the book her mother had mentioned? Why hadn't he told her? They'd had their share of confession time. Was this some sick form of revenge? Was he a male Miss Havisham, wreaking revenge on all women because one had wronged him? From the way he'd talked on his radio show and the way he'd behaved, it was certainly possible.

But he'd changed. Or at least was changing.

She felt like she was carrying a boulder in her chest as she finished getting ready to leave. She knew her mother was worried, but she couldn't bring herself to call back and hear more about how untrustworthy Parker was.

The boulder stayed in place all the way to the station, and she found it hard to give him a genuine smile when she joined him in the office he shared with Jay before heading into the actual soundproof studio. She walked in just in time to hear him saying to Jay, "I can't turn it down."

Turn down what? That book deal her mother had mentioned?

She said a tentative, "Hi," and Parker gave a guilty start.

"Alice, ready for your last day?" Jay greeted her.

"I think so," she said.

She wanted to ask for a minute to talk to Parker alone, but bold, new Alice had run away and the old Alice couldn't seem to get the words out.

There wasn't time, anyway. Jay had notes to go over with them and questions to ask. And advice to give out. "I like the whole game metaphor. Milk that for all it's worth."

Like Parker had been milking working in her bookstore.

Parker nodded. He smiled at Alice. "You ready to go on?"

She nodded and followed him into the sound booth. "Did you get your stuff sorted out?" she asked as they settled in.

"Not yet," he said and put on his over-ear headphones, signaling the end of all conversation.

She put on hers as well. The on-air light lit up and they were on, and Parker was sounding chipper, greeting his listeners, telling them he was glad to be back with them. "And Alice Willoughby is here one last time with us, guys, so it's your last chance to impart some sports wisdom to her." He turned and smiled at Alice. A phony on-air radio personality smile. "Alice, do you feel like you're becoming an expert on some sports now, enough to maybe write a sports romance and get it right?"

"I don't know. Do you think you've learned enough to write about women and get it right?" she countered, thinking of his book secret.

"I don't know if anybody ever knows enough about women to get it right," he said. "What do you think, Barker?"

"I'm flunking," Jay cracked.

"Let's hope the Mariners don't flunk this season. Right after the show I'm catching my plane to sunny Peoria to get the scoop for you guys. I know some of you have signed up for the big bash tomorrow night."

Leaving right after the show. There would be no time to talk. Maybe that was just as well. She wasn't sure what to say to him.

As Parker discussed stats and analyzed players, she tried to analyze him. He wasn't the duplicitous type. He said what he thought, wielding his words like a blunt instrument. It didn't make sense that he'd hide something that was such a big deal.

A nudge from him brought her thoughts back into the moment. "What?"

"What have you got to say to Eddie? Are you going to go to the games and root for the Mariners this year?"

"I'm hoping to," she said. "Of course, I haven't found anyone to take me yet. Know anybody really nice, Eddie?" she asked, and Parker frowned.

"Don't worry, guys, I'll educate her," he said.

"Maybe I'm already educated," she said, which made his eyebrows pull together.

A new call came in. "We've got Brittany from here in Seattle on the line," said Parker. "Brittany, what have you got to say?"

"I love how you sit there and pretend everything is just fine after all the harm you've done, Parker Black," she ranted.

"How have I harmed you, Brittany?" Parker asked.

"Your stupid Valentine strike. Do you know how much business I lost that day? And not just me. For some of us Valentine's Day is our Christmas. You had a good old time making fun of men buying things for their women, telling them to go on strike."

"Did you see me on the picket line?" he countered.

"No, because you're a coward. And, Alice, what are you doing being on a show with the man who tried to ruin your business? He's just using you for ratings."

"Hey, people change," Parker said as he got rid of Brittany. But he didn't deny the accusation. "Some of the women I met when I was hanging out at Alice's bookstore were fine, and they proved that there's lots of good ones out there. They don't all hate men."

"So, you've changed?" Alice asked.

"I'm rethinking some things," he said. "But don't worry, guys, I haven't turned in my man card yet."

Jay inserted himself into the conversation. "What do you think of that, Alice?"

"I think Parker's right. He's still the same man you all know and love," Alice said with a frown.

"There you have it," said Parker.

More calls came in, wanting to know what sports movies Alice had watched so far, and she shared about the two Parker had shown her. "I have a whole list to go through," she added. "I think I'll host a girls' night and we can have a double feature. "I'll start with *The Blind Side*," she added.

She'd been looking up popular sports movies and that one had looked good. The title about summed up her foolish infatuation with Parker. She'd been blind but now her eyes were opened.

"Or a date night," Parker suggested. Alice said nothing, so he rushed in to fill the dead air and began talking about the new sports movie set to come out in the summer.

She spent the last hour of the show wishing it was over. She longed to be back in the bookstore where her world was safe and well-ordered. Where the men she met in books behaved predictably, always doing what was right and proving their love.

At last Parker ended the torture. "That's it. Next week we'll be broadcasting from Peoria. Meanwhile, keep your head in the game."

The minute they were off the air, she removed her headphones and started for the door. "Have fun on your trip," she said over her shoulder. Politely.

"Alice, wait." He hurried after her and caught her arm. "We need to talk."

"No, we don't. I think I know what you needed to tell me. I heard about the book deal."

"Wait. How?"

"My mother told me."

He held out both hands, a supplicant looking for understanding. “Alice, you know how it is with books. I wrote that long before I met you.”

“And it will come out after . . . last night.” She opened the door and there stood Jay, all smiles, ready to congratulate them on a good show.

Parker shut the door and turned Alice to face him. “Okay, I still believe a lot of what I wrote. You can’t hold it against me that I think things need to change. It has nothing to do with us, with where I am now. *I’ve* changed.”

“You’re right, I can’t,” she said. “But I can hold it against you turning me, and HEA, and all our friends into nothing but a publicity stunt for your show. And I can hold it against you that you never told me about the book. How was I going to find out about it? Was I supposed to see the deal in *Publishers Weekly*? Are you going to go back in and add something to your book about my bookstore now?”

“It’s not like that,” he protested. If only he’d stopped there, but he didn’t. “And you got a lot of publicity out of this, too. Free advertising for your store here and on Jenny and Willis’s afternoon show for a whole month. She’s even starting a book club.”

As if Alice had done any of this for publicity. That hurt and she didn’t even know what she could say to explain why it did.

“I wish you all the best, Parker. With everything,” she said. “Now, please let go of my arm.”

He dropped his hand. “Alice, this is just a misunderstanding.”

Misunderstandings happened a lot in romance novels. The couple went through the whole book, fuming and fussing when all they’d needed was a conversation to clear things up. This wasn’t that. There had been plenty of conversations, but in the end, Parker wasn’t the romantic hero Alice was looking for. It was just that simple.

“I’m sorry, Parker, I think we’ll always see life too differently.”

She lowered her voice. "I'll never forget your kisses though. Good luck," she added. Then she opened the door, wished Jay good luck also, and hurried off down the hall.

Out of Parker Black's life. Where she didn't belong. Never had and never would.

She wanted to cry over how silly she'd been and how silly she wanted to keep being but commanded herself not to. This was one moment in her life, one quick brush with attraction, one taste of romance IRL. Now everything would go back to normal. No harm, no foul as Parker would probably say.

Who cared what Parker had to say?

"What was that all about?" Jay asked.

"She found out about the book."

"Hey, it's just a book," said Jay.

Not to Alice, it wasn't. "She hates my guts now."

"So, what else is new?"

"We were . . . connecting."

Jay's eyebrows shot up. "Alice connecting with you? You've got to be kidding."

"I'm not."

"There goes your image," Jay said with a mournful shake of the head.

"I don't care about my image."

"Well, you should. Come on, you know that wasn't gonna work out. Take an aspirin and get over it."

"I don't want to get over it," Parker snapped.

"Well, what are you gonna do? You can't unsell your book," Jay pointed out.

"I don't know. I don't want to talk about it," Parker said.

Jay shook his head and let out a long-suffering sigh. "Okay. Guess I'll call our Uber."

He let Parker stew all the way to the airport, keeping busy

on his phone, let him continue to stew as they crawled along through security, and as they went to their gate.

"Look on the bright side," he finally said as they found a couple of seats. "You sold your book, man. Our ratings are great. You're on top of the world."

Parker should have been happy. Only a month ago he would have been. Now look at him. He was on top of the world and miserable. All because of the way Alice had looked at him back at the studio, those pretty eyes filled with disappointment.

Parker revisited the moment she'd come after him on the couch. It had been so out of character, so cute. So awesome.

"I need chips," he announced.

"Get me some Doritos," said Jay, and began scrolling on his phone.

Parker marched over to Hudson News, frowning all the way. This was not how his life was supposed to be playing out. He was supposed to be happy. He was a success.

He was snagging two bags of chips when a twenty-something guy came up to him. "Parker Black, hey, I listen to you all the time. Me and my men are on our way to spring training. Missed our flight so we're gonna miss the game tonight. But we're coming to your bash tomorrow."

Parker donned his radio personality smile. "Good. Sucks missing the game, though, doesn't it?"

"Yeah. We thought you'd already be down there, doing your show."

"Kind of had to wrap some things up here," Parker said.

Had to sit next to Alice one last time. He'd envisioned it being the first of lots more times sitting side by side. At dinner with his mom and Uncle Jerome, at her mom's house at Christmas, on her couch, watching movies. He'd envisioned eventually moving on to doing more than sitting side by side.

"Oh, yeah, with that bookstore stuff," the guy guessed. "I

gotta say, Alice was kind of fun to listen to. I'm one of the guys who suggested a movie to her. Are you gonna show her *Field of Dreams*?"

"Maybe," Parker said. *Never.* He moved to the register. "See you down there."

He made his escape back to the gate, tossed Jay his chips, then pulled out his laptop, a shield to keep his chatty fans at bay and tune out his producer who'd gotten him into this mess.

No, that wasn't fair. Yeah, Jay had done a good job of stirring the pot, but it was Parker who'd filled it full of ugly to begin with, Parker who'd been a man on a mission, Parker who'd written a book. He didn't want to be on a mission to save men anymore. He wanted to save what he'd started with Alice.

There was the file for his book, waving at him from the screen. He opened it and began to read, determined to convince himself that it was good stuff. That he was good stuff.

It wasn't and he wasn't. It was mostly snarky ranting and anecdotes with a tiny seasoning of statistics thrown in for good measure. And lots of advice for the reader on how to live happily ever after without that troublesome chick in his life.

Some of his points were valid though. Modern men did struggle with depression, with identity and role confusion. Women made the perfect scapegoat. After all, it was them guys fought for, worked for, earned money for.

Women turned men inside out.

He frowned at his laptop screen. He was the king of sweeping generalizations, a man with no helpful solutions other than *if it ain't workin' ditch her.*

Well, Alice had beaten him to that. Luna all over again.

Except she wasn't Luna.

He left his seat and moved away to call his mom. "Did you listen to the show?"

"I did. You and Alice sounded good together. It's too bad about that one call," she said diplomatically.

"You mean too bad I let things get out of hand in the first place," he corrected.

"The strike was a bad idea."

"Jay's bad idea." More corrections.

"But inspired by you. The curse of having influence."

"More like blame," he said irritably.

"You'll get plenty of that once your book comes out."

"I don't want to look like a jerk."

Thankfully, she didn't say, "I'm sure you will." Instead, she said nothing, just waited for him to puke up more of his guts.

"I like the Willoughbys. I like Alice." *Like* was too lukewarm. He wanted Alice, wanted her in his life. "But now she's heard about the deal, and she's got people like that caller telling her she's just a publicity stunt. That's not how it is."

"Are you falling for this girl?"

"Yes. What should I do?"

"Undo what you've done?"

"Thanks, Mom," he said testily. "How am I supposed to do that? You're the romance writer. You should have all kinds of ideas. Pretend I'm one of your book heroes. How would you write me?"

"I'd write you doing some serious soul-searching," she said. "I'd have you letting go of all your justifications and maybe even some of your ambitions. Check your trajectory, Parker. Where are you headed? Is it where you want to be?"

With a published book.

And an empty life. "No."

"Lives and books have something important in common. They're both works in progress and if you don't like where your story is going you can always rewrite. Maybe you need to start rewriting. That's the best advice I can give you. Now,

I need to get back to work. I have to turn in this manuscript before I go on tour. I love you." And with that she was gone.

How was he supposed to rewrite anything at this point? He'd already sold the book.

His next call was to his uncle. He got right to the point. "Alice dumped me."

"I didn't know Alice had you to begin with," said Uncle Jerome.

"We were starting something."

"And now it's finished?"

"Yeah. She wants a hero."

His uncle laughed. "There aren't many of those around."

His levity was irritating. "It's not funny, Unk."

"No, it's not."

"I wish I hadn't sold the book. I started rereading it and I sound like a bitter loser." Like what he was. No, what he'd been. "But I'm stuck. I can't unsell it," Parker said.

"Talk to your agent and your new editor. Tell them you want to pivot in a new direction," his uncle said.

"I have no direction. I want out."

"Have you signed a contract?" Jerome asked.

"Not yet, but we've got a deal memo."

"A deal memo is not a contract. You can stop the deal. You've got a hard decision as there's a lot of money at stake."

"I've got a lot of everything at stake," Parker muttered.

"Love or money, that's the choice, I guess. I know love doesn't pay the bills. It can sure motivate you though."

"If I knew for sure things would work out," Parker began.

"You can't know for sure, any more than you knew for sure you'd sell that book. Everything in life is a gamble. I can't tell you what to do, but I can tell you there's always a way around a problem. Maybe you pull the book and write something different."

"If I pull it David will cut me loose."

"Then you'll find another agent. Write something halfway decent, maybe with more of a sports theme, and I'll introduce you to my agent."

Halfway decent. Ouch. But there was an interesting offer. One his uncle hadn't made when Parker had started on his current magnum opus.

"Look, I know you've got a message you want to get out there. But let's put all this in writing terms. What's your motivation, really? Are you out to help solve a problem or to even the score with your two exes? How much of your ego is involved?"

"Maybe there's some ego," Parker admitted. Okay, maybe a lot.

"Well, here's the bottom line. Sell the book and lose the girl. Lose the book and win the girl. It really is that simple, Parker. It's a big chunk of change. A lot to sacrifice. Can you afford to? And I'm not just talking about money."

"Good question," said Parker.

"Once you've figured out the answer, you'll know what to do."

And that had to be the end of the conversation. Parker's plane was loading. He walked on with his head spinning. What was his trajectory? What did he want for the rest of his life?

No. Who did he want for the rest of his life? The answer to that was easy.

Jay had plenty of work to do to get them organized for the week they'd be broadcasting from Peoria, which gave Parker time to read the entire manuscript, making notes as he went. There was some good stuff in there. But buried under a lot of angry man garbage. How was this really going to help men? It sure wouldn't help them fix their relationships.

KWOW had put them up at the Hilton Embassy Suites. Parker took in the two bedrooms and large living area with its sleeper sofa as he and Jay walked in and found it easy to envision Alice and him entertaining media pals and players in that room or settling on the couch. That wouldn't be happening now.

He ditched his luggage in one of the bedrooms, then slumped on the bed.

Jay found him there. "You don't have time to sit around. We got two parties to attend."

This was always the highlight of Parker's year—the games, the parties, the interaction, the nostalgia—better than Christmas. Except this year somebody had invited the Grinch.

Alice and Scarlet sat at Nola's dining room table, finishing off dessert while Mark sat in the living room, glued to ESPN's coverage of the first day of spring training.

"You were right to stop this before it went any farther," Nola said.

"Then how come I feel so bad?" Alice replied.

"I have no idea," Scarlet said, and Alice frowned at her. She shrugged and forked up another bite of her mother's chocolate mint pie.

"Because you hoped maybe things would work out. Of course, you're disappointed," Nola said reasonably.

"You should be relieved," Scarlet said.

"He's not the devil incarnate," Nola said. "But he's got baggage."

"Everyone has baggage," Alice argued.

"True, but he's not willing to put his down. If he'd done something to prove that he was, something on his own, not something the station made him do, that would be different," Nola said.

"A man who's not willing to change isn't worth hanging on to," Scarlet asserted.

They all looked to where Mark sat. Lucky for him he'd been willing to change.

"Well, so what if he wrote a book?" Alice argued. "Everyone has a right to his opinion."

"It's a book slamming women," Scarlet said in disgust. "*You're* a woman. Have some respect for yourself. He sure doesn't."

And there it was, the key to why she couldn't move forward with Parker Black. Love and respect went together. Parker's lack of respect for women showed in his words and actions. It would show up in their relationship at some point.

She sighed and took a sip of her tea. Why couldn't real life men be more like book boyfriends?

The whole night was a bust. So was the next day. Parker went through the motions, promoting his show, interviewing players, going to a game, his thoughts riding along.

Did women have unrealistic expectations when it came to men? Was it wrong to want to feel like they were living in a romance novel? Maybe everybody wanted to live a little above the mundane. Guys wanted adventure. Women wanted to be appreciated. Yes, Luna had been immature and demanded a lot but in her own selfish way, had she been onto something?

More important, was Alice onto something? She was sweet and kind and believed in love. That meant she'd have to give Parker a chance to explain himself. This was a bump in the road. They could get past it.

He found himself searching for a minute where he could slip away and call her. He finally found a few before his party. It was almost seven, but back in Seattle it was only edging toward six. The store would be closing soon but she'd still be there, recommending stories to women wanting some escape and maybe even some hope.

If he called her phone, it would go straight to voice mail.

He'd have to call the store and risk being stopped by either Bettina or Nola. The dragons at the gate.

To his surprise and relief, the voice answering the store phone was Alice's. "HEA Books, where we bring you happily-ever-after."

"I want one," he said.

He suffered through a moment of silence before she spoke. "Parker." All the warmth had leaked out of her voice.

"Alice, give me a chance here."

"I want to, Parker, really. But Mom and Bettina showed me your book deal announcement. How can we hang out when you're going to be promoting something like this? You pour yourself into a book. It's how you feel and what you think."

"But that's the point. What I think is changing. And that's because of you."

She didn't let him finish. "Your title says exactly how you think men should go about fixing their relationships. Parker, I know you were hurt."

"Writing this book is how I healed." Wait, that wasn't true. Any healing that had been taking place was thanks to her. He needed to tell her that. He started to, but it was too late. She was already talking.

"And what about publishing it? Who's that going to heal? I'm sure you're getting a great advance and I'm happy for your success, honest. It's just too bad that you're getting it this way. Anyway, I wish you all the best. I really do."

"Wait," he began.

She didn't. "I have to go now," she said, and ended the call. And what they'd started.

What now?

CHAPTER 28

"YOU WANT TO pass on interviewing Gabe Speier? Are you out of your mind?" Jay demanded.

Parker was beginning to feel like it.

Jay snapped his fingers in front of Parker's face. "Snap out of it. I worked my ass off getting this for you and you're not going to blow it just because you want to mope around and feel sorry for yourself. For getting a six-figure book deal," he added with a sneer.

"Okay, okay," Parker said, holding up a hand. "I'm going already."

"You bet you are. And after that it's the party with the MLB cheerleaders and ball girls. Oh, wait. Never mind. I don't want you showing up at that. You'll scare away every woman in the room."

"Fine by me. I've got stuff to do," Parker said.

Like think about how he was going to win Alice back.

He thought a lot but came up with nothing. Once back in the suite he flipped on the TV and streamed a movie. *Pride & Prejudice*. For research. Darcy was still a jerk.

Until the end. Alice's words came back to him, whispering, "He proved his love, not by what he said but by what he did."

Parker didn't know if he was in love yet, not all the way, but he was halfway in for sure, and he realized he wanted to be in all the way. Not the kind of love he'd fallen into before where it was drama and frustration. He wanted a love that involved giving on both sides. And respect.

Respect. He wasn't exactly earning Alice's. He wasn't so sure he respected himself at the moment.

Finally, come Thursday, Jay sat him down for a heart-to-heart talk. "Look, you have got to fix yourself. Or else quit telling listeners to keep their head in the game, 'cause yours sure isn't. And it shows."

"Sorry," Parker muttered. "I don't know what to do."

"Well, whaddya want to do?"

"I want to be with Alice."

"Then be with Alice."

"She doesn't want to be with me."

"So, do something to make her want to be with you. Call your mom and get some suggestions. She writes about this stuff for a living."

His mom hadn't been much help the last time they talked, but Parker needed a Hail Mary. He shut himself in his bedroom and called her.

"Mom, I'm desperate. I need your help. Give me some ideas on how I can get Alice to give me a chance."

"Parker, you have to prove you want to be with her," she said, her voice brimming with impatience. "It's just that simple. And, in your case, that hard. And whatever you do, you'd better make it public."

"This isn't helping," he complained. "I need specific suggestions."

"I could offer some, but it wouldn't be the same. You need to do this all on your own."

"Come on, Mom. I'm out of my depth here."

"You're a smart man. You'll figure something out," she said.

It was meant to assure him. It didn't.

It took him until the day before they flew home to come up with a new game plan, and it started with making a call to his agent.

"You're kidding, right?" was David's reply when Parker announced his intention to go a whole new direction with his book. He didn't sound happy.

Well, in a way Parker wasn't either. It was downright painful to watch all those dollars poised to fly away but there were more important things in life.

"No, I'm serious. I really do need to take a different angle on this book."

"Parker, the book you wrote is the one I sold. That's the one your new editor is excited about."

"I need to give him something different," Parker insisted.

"We have a deal." David's words were firm.

"But not a contract. Not yet," Parker said.

"You pull a stunt like this and you won't get a second chance, trust me."

So maybe Parker would never become a bestselling author. So what? He didn't need to be rich. What he needed was a rich life. He needed someone with a big heart and a soft voice and pretty eyes. He needed a second chance with Alice.

"I'll take that chance," Parker said.

"All right, if that's what you want, but you need to know I can't represent you after this," David said, his voice like steel. "Your behavior is completely unprofessional."

"People change their minds," Parker protested.

"It's too bad you changed yours. I'll make the call," David said.

"Thanks. Sorry, David."

"Good luck with your future projects," David said. Parker doubted he meant it.

That was life. You won some, you lost some.

But Parker didn't feel like he'd lost. In fact, for the first time in a long time he felt like a winner. He had no idea if he was going to win Alice's approval, but he'd at least found something he hadn't realized he'd lost—his self-respect.

He wanted more though. He wanted Alice, too. Alice was the Super Bowl ring, the Commissioner's Trophy, the World Cup. He hoped his plan would be enough to earn her giving him a chance.

Jay just shook his head when Parker shared his plan. "This is a bad idea, and none of your fans will be impressed."

"They've all met Alice. They like her."

"You're gonna look like a deluxe wimp burger."

"Or a guy determined to win," countered Parker.

"Hmm. There is that," Jay said thoughtfully.

"So, you going to help me out?"

Jay shrugged. "Sure. Why not? Parker's found a woman worth hitting a home run for. How's that sound?"

"Conceited."

Jay ignored him. "We can do a poll. Should Parker and Alice get together?"

"No poll," Parker said firmly. "I'm not trying to do this for ratings, and I don't want it to look that way." He could tell by Jay's fake innocent man expression that he wasn't going to listen. "I'm serious."

Jay heaved a sigh. "Okay, fine. When we get a break, I'll make a call and see if we can get you on the news."

"And I want Olivia Carson to cover it. She'll love this." She'd probably come, hoping to see him choke on humble pie.

His next call was to the woman who owned the flower shop down the street from the bookstore. Of course, she'd be thrilled to talk to him. If he was behind bars somewhere.

"Don't hang up," he said after saying his name.

"What do you want?" she demanded.

"I want to make up to you for the business you lost on Valentine's Day," he said. "First, I'd like a flower arrangement to be delivered to HEA Books when they open on Tuesday. Make it big and expensive. Then I want fifty long-stemmed roses you can give out the next day and send it to the store also. Can you make that happen?"

"I'll see what I can do," she said. Grudgingly.

"Also, I want a bouquet delivered to the home of Nola Willoughby. And Lina Flores." He rattled off the addresses he'd found.

"What do you want to say on the cards?" she asked, still all business.

Hmm. Good question. He'd almost need to write a mini book. But actions spoke louder than words. "Just say from Parker. With apologies," he added. "Oh, and do a separate arrangement for Alice. Whatever you think she'll like. Just make it impressive."

"How do you want me to sign that?" she asked.

"Sign it, hoping for a second chance," he said.

"You can hope," was the only response he got. "But flowers won't be enough."

No, they wouldn't. Still, they were a start. And while he was at it . . . "And I want to send flowers to Jenny Riddle."

"Same price range as the others?"

Why not? In fact, "No. Make this one bigger. Sign it, thanks for being my mom. And yeah, I wasn't hatched," he said before she could say anything.

He tried not to audibly gulp when she quoted a price. It would be worth every penny if it got him out of the big pile of shit he was in. He gave her his credit card information.

"If this doesn't win you points with Alice nothing will," said Jay.

It was Parker's best shot. He hoped it would work.

Spring training was in full swing in Peoria but come the auspicious second Monday in March it was game on in Seattle. Two owners and one employee as well as two customers gaped at Parker when he entered the store behind Jay, pushing a wheelbarrow.

"What on earth?" said Bettina.

"Hello, Parker," Nola said politely. But not warmly. "Your flowers just arrived."

The arrangement he'd sent to the store was perched right by the register. Alice was still holding hers, and it was so big Parker could hardly see her face.

"Thank you," Nola added. Still coldly polite. "How may we help you?"

"I need to buy enough books to fill this wheelbarrow," he said.

"Is this another stunt?" Bettina demanded, her upper lip curling.

"No. It's a public apology." Parker strode to where Alice stood, still quiet and staring at him. "Alice, I turned down the book deal."

She blinked. "You . . . ?"

He nodded. "I turned it down. That's not me anymore. I don't want to be that angry guy." He was aware of four females all paying rapt attention. He lowered his voice. "I'm hoping you can give me another chance."

"You turned down the book deal." She was shaking her head in disbelief.

"Parker, Olivia's gonna be here in half an hour," Jay prompted.

"Oh. Yeah."

"Olivia Carson?" Alice was looking even more mystified.

"It *is* another one of his stunts," Bettina said in disgust.

"It's not," Parker insisted. "I'm going to need a lot of books to fill that thing."

"What kind do you want?" Nola asked.

"Whatever you all recommend," he said. "You, too, ladies," he added, turning to the customers. "Help me out here."

"Oh, my gosh. This is like what they do on Instagram where the woman has ten minutes to get as many books as she wants," said the one customer.

"Let's go!" cried her friend, and all the women scattered around the store, pulling books from the shelves.

Except Alice. "I don't understand."

"I want to be like Mr. Darcy," Parker said simply. "The way he was at the end of the story. I could talk until I'm blue in the face and you probably wouldn't believe me. I'm hoping what I'm doing will speak louder."

She was looking at him like he was some sort of superhero. "Oh, Parker, this is . . ."

"Amazing?" he prompted, his voice teasing. Then he sobered. "Worth a second chance?"

She shook her head, a sure sign she still couldn't believe her eyes. "I don't know what to say."

The little bell over the door jingled and in came Lina. "You guys won't believe what just arrived at my house." She took in the flowers, the women pulling books from the shelves like game contestants. Her gaze drifted to where Parker stood with Alice, who was still half-hidden behind her enormous floral arrangement. "I guess you would. Parker, you're a real romance hero now."

"I'm working on it," he said as Bettina set an armload of books next to the register.

Nola was right behind her with some selections of her own.

"Clock's ticking," called Jay.

"For what?" Bettina demanded.

"You'll see," Parker told her. "Start ringing these up."

"This is going to cost you a fortune," Nola warned him.

"Not half as much as it was going to cost me if I lost Alice from my life." He turned to her. "Can we talk after this?"

"And then watch a sports movie?" she suggested, and he grinned as Nola kept tallying up his order and handing over books to go in the wheelbarrow.

His credit card bill was going to be through the roof. It would be the best money he'd ever spent.

The wheelbarrow was full by the time Olivia arrived with her crew. "Wait for my signal," Parker said to Jay and met her outside the bookstore.

"What are you up to now, Parker? This had better be good," she told him.

"Human interest story," he said.

She cocked an eyebrow. "You're human?"

"Just start filming," he said.

Her camera person got busy, and she began her spiel. "I'm here in front of a bookstore, which only a few weeks ago was the scene of a failed Valentine strike. And where, many of you know, KWOW's favorite sports shock jock and misogynist was doing time for bad behavior. Now he's back again, with a public announcement. What have you got to say, Parker?" she asked, tipping her mike to him."

"This is more like a public service announcement," Parker said. "You know guys, we've talked a lot on my show about sports."

"And other things," put in Olivia.

"And other things. And I still believe a man has to be strong." He knew it was all Olivia could do not to roll her eyes. "But he also has to be willing to see the other side of things sometimes and admit when he's wrong."

"Parker, are you admitting you're wrong?" she asked with a grin. Yep, Olivia was enjoying this moment.

"About a lot of things. I'm here today to publicly apologize to the owners of HEA Books for how much I've tipped their lives upside down these past few weeks. Especially Alice. She's been a good sport, and I hope she can forgive me for all the spitballs I've thrown at her."

Olivia took the mike away. "So, there you have it."

Parker pulled it back. "We're not done. I need to apologize to all the women out there for dissing what you like to read. Maybe it's okay to expect us men to be the good guys in your life."

"Parker, a lot of your fans will say you're turning in your man card," Olivia taunted.

"Hey, real men admit when they're off track." He thumped on the door, and on cue Bettina opened it with a flourish, enjoying her moment of fame. Behind her came Jay with the wheelbarrow. "I've bought a wheelbarrow full of books. Anyone who wants a free one, come on down to HEA Books tomorrow. Good while supplies last."

"Will you be here after your show to talk to readers?" Olivia asked.

Even heroes had their limits. And if they didn't, they should. "Can't make any promises," he said. "But enjoy a free book on me."

"So, Parker Black is a new convert to romance," Olivia finished. "Come on down to HEA Books in West Seattle, ladies, and get your free book."

"And then go down the street to Flowers L'Amour for a free rose on me," Parker added. In for a penny, in for a pound, as the saying went. Or a few hundred.

"Okay, what's the angle?" Olivia asked after they'd finished filming.

"I had a change of heart," he said with a shrug.

"Or you grew one. Anything to do with someone inside the store?"

"If it does you won't be the first to know," he said. "You got your story."

"Always interesting when you're involved, Parker. I hope you don't lose listeners over switching sides."

He hoped he didn't, too. But if he did, it was a small price to pay for winning Alice's respect. And for respecting himself a little more. Time to be better, not bitter.

"Seriously, what changed you?"

Jay, who'd been standing nearby, answered for him. "A four-letter word, Olivia. Love."

Love. Yeah, maybe it was. Otherwise, Parker was completely out of his mind.

He left Olivia and Jay and went back inside the bookstore. "Watch the news tonight, ladies," he said. Then, to Alice. "Want to come over to my place and watch it with me? Pizza and Coke?"

She beamed at him. "Pizza and Coke. And a movie."

Later, as they sat cuddled on his couch, watching him do his best not to look like a fool talking to Olivia, she hugged his arm. "Parker, this cost you a fortune."

"You're worth it, aren't you?" he responded.

She bit her lip and her gaze dropped. "It's a lot. And your book deal."

"I'll get another."

"Are you going to lose listeners over this?"

"You know, I don't think so. A lot of my listeners have become fans of Alice Willoughby. But if I do, I don't care."

"I don't want you to lose your job, your career."

"A man can lose things more important than that, like his self-respect. And the important people in his life. Alice, I want you in my life. I'd rather lose all of that than lose out on a chance of being with you. I hope this proves it. Am I a Mr. Darcy now?"

"Oh, my gosh, you're worth ten of him," she said. Then, she did it again. She surprised him, wrapped her arms around his neck and gave him an Alice lip smash.

The kiss could have gone on longer if not for the fact that he started laughing.

She looked at him, surprised and a little hurt. "What?"

"Oh, Alice, you amaze me," he said.

"Not half as much as you've amazed me," she said softly. "Parker, you're a real-life hero."

"Am I *your* hero?" he asked.

"Oh, yes," she said, and kissed him again.

Who'd have thought it? Parker Black, with his pirate good looks and bad-boy reputation, wanted her. "I can't believe you gave up so much," she said when he finally nestled her against his chest as they got ready to watch *Draft Day.*

"Don't make me more than I am. I needed to change my trajectory. And it was you who made me realize it. I can't promise to be perfect," he added.

"Even book boyfriends aren't perfect," she said with a smile.

And they weren't real, either. Parker was real. He'd probably always have strong opinions. And he'd want her to come to love sports the way he did. Baseball season would soon be in full swing.

"I hope you're going to take me to a Mariners game," she said.

He grinned. "I'm going to take you anyplace you want to go."

"The only place I want to go is to a happily-ever-after," she said. "But I think I'm already there," she added.

He smiled at her, a genuine, tender smile to match the look in his eyes. "Me, too," he said. "Alice, thanks for being my heroine. Thanks for bringing out the Mr. Darcy in me," he murmured. Then he threaded his fingers through her hair, looked at her lips like they were candy. "I think the movie can wait for a while. What do you think?"

"I think you're right," she said.

And the gates to happily-ever-after swung open wide.

EPILOGUE

Two Years Later, Living Happily Ever After

THERE WAS A big book signing event at HEA Books, the first of many stops for Parker Black and his uncle, Jerome Riddle. The men were talking about the book they'd written together. *The Playbook: How Men Can Win at Love*, had hit the *New York Times* bestseller list its first week, and half of West Seattle, both male and female, had crowded into the store to get a signed copy, leaving standing room only after Nola, Alice and Bettina hauled out as many chairs as they could get their hands on.

The launch party at spring training had been even more packed, with fans showing up to meet not only Parker and his famous uncle, but also Alice, who had officially joined the team, doing a once-a-week guest spot on the show, sharing her thoughts on everything from the best recipes for a Super Bowl party to her latest new favorite sports movie. And occasionally, she offered advice when men called in to talk about their problems with their women.

She smiled proudly as Parker and his uncle talked. Next

to her was her mother who now sported a simple gold band on her left hand, courtesy of an intimate destination wedding in Hawaii the year before. Scarlet and Mark were both present and Scarlet had already purchased a copy of the book as an early present for her husband. The best present would be arriving in about three weeks, and they had the nursery ready for their baby girl.

All the book club ladies were present, and as the men concluded their talk and everyone applauded, Alice could hear Bettina saying to Lina, "We really whipped him into shape, didn't we."

His mother, who was standing with them all, merely smiled.

"And now," Parker said into his microphone, "we have one more thing we need to do before we eat those cookies Georgia made for us." He signaled to someone at the back of the room and Alice turned to see that Brittany from Flowers L'Amour had arrived, carrying a bouquet of red roses mixed with maidenhair ferns and baby's breath. "Alice, would you come here, please?" he said, holding out his hand.

A murmur of voices followed her like a wave, making her face heat as she made her way to him.

He caught her hand. "I think most of you here know how Alice and I met. Like in one of those enemies-to-lovers romance novels. Lucky for me, we found our own détente."

And suddenly, there was Brittany, standing next to them, smiling and handing Alice the flowers. Her heart began to race and tears swam into her eyes.

"I read that roses symbolize love," he said to Alice. "I think this does, too, and I hope you'll accept it."

Then there he was, down on one knee, opening a ring box to show a diamond ring. The diamond was cut in the shape of a glittering heart. "You already have my heart, but would you like another one? Will you marry me?"

Everyone burst into applause, and her mother and sister and Bettina took pictures with their phones as Alice gasped in amazement.

Then she nodded, and laughed and cried, “Yes, yes!”

“And see?” she heard Bettina say. “This is why everyone should read romance novels.”

Yes, they should.

ACKNOWLEDGMENTS

THERE ARE ALWAYS so many people to thank when you're done with a book because even though this is a solitary occupation, in the end, a book is never written alone. Thank you to my lovely new editor, Emma Cole, not only for your insights but also for your kindness and patience. I so appreciate how you've helped me shape this story. Thank you, as always, to my incredible agent, Paige Wheeler, my advocate, advisor and friend. Still the best! I'd also like to thank my pal Suzanne Selfors, owner of Liberty Bay Books in Poulsbo, WA, for taking time to chat with me and let me peek into her life as a bookstore owner. (Which she does on top of writing amazing children's books and running a children's book festival. Yes, she is a superhero.) A big thank-you to the MIRA team, who continue to work so hard on my behalf, magically turning manuscript after manuscript into a book! And finally a big thank-you to readers like you, who make it possible for me to tell my stories.